Bratva Angel

Sabine Barclay

OLIVERHEBERBOOKS

0 9 8 7 6 5 4 3 2 1

Published by Oliver Heber Books

 Created with Vellum

Opposites attract isn't just for magnets. Here's to all the Eeyores who win a Little Miss Sunshine's heart.

Subscribe to Sabine's Newsletter

Subscribe to Sabine's bimonthly newsletter to receive exclusive insider perks.

Have you read *The Syndicate Wars*? This FREE origin story novella is available to all new subscribers to Sabine's monthly newsletter. Subscribe on her website.

The Ivankov Brotherhood

Bratva Darling

Bratva Sweetheart

Bratva Treasure

Bratva Beauty

Bratva Angel

Bratva Jewel (Coming 1.24.23)

Do you also enjoy steamy Historical Romance? Discover Sabine's books written as Celeste Barclay.

Chapter One

Aleks

"Wheeee!"

Someone's having fun. I wonder if the kid's riding his shopping cart.

"Whoa!"

As I turn the corner, I barely get my cart out of the way as one comes barreling down the store aisle. Who is she? She's riding on the back of the cart after pushing it and letting it glide.

"Auntie H, can we do it again? Please!"

Anti-h? What does that mean?

"I'm so sorry."

She doesn't sound sorry, and her little boy is giggling. This woman with the purple and pink hair and infectious smile is adorable as she rubs noses with her son. I bet Laura will be like that with Konstantin and Mila one day. Minus the wild hair.

"Don't worry about it. I should have used a turn signal."

Did I just try to make a joke? Her smile just got bigger, so maybe it worked.

"Are you a superhero?"

I look down at the little boy, who must be about five. Hardly, little one.

"No. I'm just a regular guy. Why? Do I look like Superman?"

"The Hulk! Arrrgh!"

"Cadence."

The pink and purple-haired woman hisses the boy's name. But if he's going to choose any superhero, that's probably the right one. Size and temper.

"It's all right. Why the Hulk?"

We're standing in the cereal aisle discussing why I remind this kid of a green giant who isn't jolly.

"Because you're big with big muscles like the Hulk. Why are you so big if you're not a superhero?"

Just like my three brothers and four cousins, I'm nearly six-foot-five, and I work out twice a day nearly every day.

"I played a lot of sports growing up, and I like to work out a lot now. I also eat all my fruits and vegetables."

"I don't like vegetables."

"That's not true. I watched you eat a bowl of carrots and ranch at lunch."

The woman grins at her son.

"I needed something to hold my ranch. Auntie H, don't tell Mommy how much ranch you let me have."

"Shh. It's our secret. I didn't expect it to come out of the bottle so fast."

Ah! Auntie H. I've lived in New York more than half my life, but I still miss some things in English. The little boy looks back at me after turning an earnest expression to his aunt.

"Will I get to be as big as you if I work out and eat my vegetables?"

"You might."

I'm watching this woman as much as I'm watching the kid, but I can tell she's looking at me even when my attention is on him. Does she think I'm some creeper talking to her nephew? Why am I nervous that I don't live up to her expectations? She expects nothing from me.

"Cadence, we should let this nice gentleman finish his shopping."

The little boy waves to me as I maneuver my cart around the pair.

"Bye, Hulk."

"Cadence."

She hisses his name again and shakes her head.

"Don't worry. Hulk won't smash."

I wink, and it's as much for her as it is Cadence.

"Thank you."

She mouths it, and I can think of plenty of things I'd like to do with those glossy lips to make her say thank you again. But the conversation is over, and I can't stand here and stare any longer. I would. But I can't.

We pass each other, but not before I offer her another wink. What am I doing? Am I flirting? I don't do that with women. I fuck. But I don't flirt, and I don't date. I glance back and notice she's watching me as she picks up a jug of milk. I flash her a smile. She takes a moment, but the infectious grin is back. I haven't gotten a woman's number in years, but I would get hers.

I recognize that voice. Twice in one day? I glance over; it's the woman from the grocery store. She's holding her nephew's hand this time as they walk toward me in the pharmacy. I watch her from my peripheral vision as she gets closer.

"Can I get the gummy ones?"

"May I. And yes, you may."

"Auntie H, you're not at school. You don't have to teach."

"But you can always learn."

She's a teacher? None of mine looked like that. Not that hair, not that face, and sure as shit not that body. Her tank top is even lower than it was in the grocery store. What I wouldn't give to lick between her tits. She's got the fucking Grand Canyon for cleavage. I can't see her ass because of that damn flannel she's wearing over her tank top and leggings, but the hint is enough to want to make me sin. The good kind, not the killing kind.

"There's the Hulk!"

I know she already spotted me. I know because she's staring at the bottle of prenatal vitamins I'm holding. Wonderful. She's probably thinking I was flirting with her and have a pregnant wife or girlfriend at home. I have my phone in my other hand, so I hit the contact and wait for it to ring.

"*Privet.*"

My youngest brother, Bogdan, answers in Russian, but I speak in English.

"Bogdan, what type of prenatal vitamins did you want me to get for Christina?"

I remember exactly what kind, but I can't stand here and try to deny I'm not getting them for my woman. I don't even have a woman. I would make Auntie H mine. At least mine in my bed. She comes to stand next to me, and I catch a whiff of her perfume. It's light and floral, but I swear I catch a waft of cinnamon. Then I realize it's the gum she's chewing. The desire to taste her is almost overwhelming.

"My sister used to take that brand."

The object of my desire points to the bottle in my hand. I nod as Bogdan says something, but I'm not paying attention.

"Thanks, Bogdan. I found it."

I don't wait for him to say anything more before I hang up.

"My sister-in-law tried another type, but I guess they made her feel sick. They're thinking about having a baby, so she wants to be on them before she gets pregnant."

Why am I sharing this? I share nothing about my private life with anyone who isn't my family. And they're usually already in the middle of it.

"I'm Aleksei, by the way. Aleks, most of the time."

That just fell out of my mouth, but now I'm offering her my hand to shake. Fuck, her skin is so smooth.

"I'm Heather."

"I'm Cadence."

I look down at the little boy and smile. He has dark hair and dark eyes, but he makes me think of Konstantin, Maks and Laura's son. Konstantin and his twin sister, Mila, are only six months old, but I can picture him like Cadence. Except with blue eyes. The Kutsenko brothers' blue eyes we got from our mother.

"Hi."

I offer to shake the little boy's hand, and he beams.

"Auntie H, can I get these?"

"I don't know."

She cocks an eyebrow, and Cadence huffs as he holds up a specific bottle of gummy vitamins. I can tell she's trying not to laugh.

"May I get these?"

"Yes, lovebug. Put them in the basket."

She's carrying a shopping basket that's overflowing with boxes of temporary hair color and bright colored makeup. I wonder what color she's going to choose next. She pulls off the pink and purple well. Usually, I'm not into bright colored hair. I'm too much of a fuddy-duddy. That's what my last girlfriend called me. And that was nearly eight years ago. She wasn't wrong once I knew what it meant.

"Which one are you picking next?"

I point to the boxes, and I can't believe I'm asking. But I can't help myself.

"Oh, these aren't for me. They're for my students. We're doing a modern spin on 'Hairspray.'"

My brow furrows. Isn't that something women use to keep their hair in place?

"You don't know the play?"

Heather sounds almost accusatory. But how should I know? I don't do theater, and if the people have bright colored hair, it definitely wasn't something I would have seen as a kid in late 1990s Moscow.

"I'm afraid not."

She stares at me for a moment, then that grin comes back.

"You should watch the movie at least."

"The cast has different colored hair?"

"That's what's modern about my production."

"And you've already been in it? Is that why yours is pink and purple?"

She laughs, and my cock twitches. When she shakes her head, her short hair sweeps her chin. An unexpected urge to tuck her hair behind her ears, so I can see her face better, washes over me. Her smile slips.

"No. I bet my students I could hold a note for fifteen seconds. I knew I couldn't. That's some Whitney Houston-Mariah Carey level skill. But it cheered them up. One of their cast members died in a car accident a couple weeks ago. Things have been really heavy."

I see the sadness in her dark hazel eyes. It feels so wrong

after how vibrant she's been. What can I do to bring that smile back?

"I would have gone for blue and orange."

She blinks several times before she laughs.

"Somehow, I can't picture you with that. You seem rather— serious. And I don't know that those shades would go together well."

I shrug one shoulder.

"If I were going to do it, I would go all out."

I would never—not in a million years—draw that much attention to myself. Never mind the reaction I would get from the other bratva members. The older ones are not exactly forward thinkers. I'd be a joke among the Irish, Italians, and Colombians. They'd think me weak, which means they'd think the rest of my family was too. That's not an option.

"There's a first time for everything."

Her eyes run over me, and I hope she can't see the hard on I have under my jeans. Thank fucking God I'm not wearing suit trousers like I usually am. There would be no hiding it. Her gaze darts back to my dick, so she must notice.

"Auntie H, can—may—we go now? I'm bored."

"Thank you for being patient while I talk to Mr. Aleksei. We'll get your coloring book, then we'll have lunch."

"Maybe we'll see Mr. Aleksei there too. It's funny we saw you here, too."

"It's a small world. It was nice meeting you, Heather. Have fun coloring, Cadence."

I have no reason to linger, so I head to the checkout. I'm about to get in my Land Rover when I hear a thunk. I'm ready to reach under the back of my coat and pull my gun. That's how loud it was. I spin around and spot Heather dashing after a bottle of Sprite rolling away from her. Cadence is standing with one hand on the car, looking at the broken reusable bag that lays sideways on the parking lot. I jog over and grab the runaway bottle and hand it back to her. Her hair's caught on her lips, and once more, the urge to tuck it behind her ear nearly overwhelms me.

"Here you go."

"Thanks."

She glances back at Cadence, and I can see her relief that he's where she left him.

"You're welcome."

I walk back to her car with her, and without a word, I gather the items strewn on the ground. She glances at me, not realizing what I'm doing as she straps Cadence into his car seat. I grab the other bags and place them in her open trunk.

"You didn't have to do that. Thank you."

"You're welcome." I shrug. "My mother would kill me if I ignored you."

"Chivalry?"

"She'd say good manners."

I hesitate for a moment, then I take the plunge.

"Would you go out with me?"

Fuck. I'm rusty at this.

"Yes."

I think she surprises herself with how quickly she answers. She reaches into her purse and unlocks her phone. She pulls up a blank contact, types something, then hands it to me.

Grocery store Aleksei

I enter my number and hand it back to her. She laughs. I try to see what she types, but she holds her phone toward her. My phone pings with a text with her number.

Damsel in distress Heather

"I don't think I'll forget who you are."

"I don't think I will either."

She types something, then shows me her phone again.

Knight in Shining Land Rover.

She put that in the notes.

I laugh. Hard. I can do it. I just don't do it often. She stares at me for a moment before she blushes. I wonder what she's thinking. She bites her top lip, and I want to pull it free. With my tongue.

"It's almost the holidays, so I bet things will get busy for you, Aleksei. Are you free tonight?"

"Yes."

It's my turn to answer without thinking.

"Do you putt-putt?"

"Mini golf? It's been a few years."

I can picture myself with the tiny mini golf clubs at my size. I'll look ridiculous...and I don't care.

"Would you be into that?"

I can think of something I'd like to be into. I nod as I answer.

"Sure. Do you want to do it earlier, while it's still light and not too cold?"

It's a mild December day, but the nights are fucking freezing. I hate the cold. It reminds me of being a kid in Moscow with a not-thick-enough coat and frozen runny nose.

"Is five too early?"

I wonder if that's so she can escape and have the night back if this bombs.

"That works."

She thinks for a moment before the grin that makes my cock hard comes back.

"Actually, there's a glow in the dark place in Garden City. We wouldn't have to worry about the cold. No need to—uh —rush."

That's promising.

"Would you have dinner with me too?"

Maybe I shouldn't push it.

"Dinner before at five? Then putt-putt?"

It's almost two now. I think it's a good sign that she wants to see me sooner rather than later.

"I'd like that." I glance at my car. "If you'd like, I can send a driver."

"A driver?"

Maybe I should test the water and see if this is going nowhere fast. If she's from Queens, she may already know my name.

"I'm Aleksei Kutsenko."

Her eyes widen, and I already know she's going to call this off. Fuck. But better she knows sooner rather than later.

"I was in Niko and Pasha's class."

My brother and cousin. Does she mean in high school? That wasn't the recognition I feared.

"Did you graduate with them? You'd be a year younger than me."

"I did. I didn't recognize you. I should have. You look exactly like them. But I haven't seen either of them, or you, in ten years."

I furrow my brow. She saw me? I guess since we went to school together. Then it comes back to me.

"You were in 'Once Upon a Mattress' with Niko."

"I was. I played Winnifred the Woebegone. I can't believe you remember that."

"It was Niko's only play. He—"

How the fuck do I explain he had the shit beaten out of him for it? Vladislav Lushak, our bratva leader before my older brother Maks, ridiculed and punished him for it. He used every homophobic slur we knew in English and Russian.

"He preferred being in the orchestra."

That's not untrue. He plays three instruments, and it didn't

10

make him a target for Vlad's torture. That was acceptably Russian.

"He was fantastic, even though he had a small part."

"You were terrific in the lead. Your voice…"

It may have been fourteen years ago, but I suddenly remember it all. She was hot back then, but not my type. She was the girlfriend type, and that wasn't an option. I was sixteen and already eyeballs deep in the bratva world.

"Thank you. It is a small world."

She studies me for a moment before smiling. I wonder if she believes the rumors from high school. That my brothers and I were in the Russian mafia. They were right, but we always denied them.

"I'll see you in a few hours, Aleks. I'll text my address. A driver—with you—would be nice."

She slips past me and heads to the driver's seat. Cadence waves to me before going back to his coloring book. I have a fucking date. What am I going to wear?

Chapter Two

Heather

I had such a fucking crush on Niko Kutsenko when we were in that play together. But it was Aleks who I really remember. I was practically infatuated with him for three years. How the hell did I not recognize him? He looks the same, except for all those muscles. He was a big guy and totally in shape back then. But now? Holy fucking hell. He's the hottest man I've ever seen. Now that I know who he is, I feel like that theater geek I was back in high school.

I couldn't believe he stopped to talk to Cadence and me. He seemed so sweet. Then I saw him looking at prenatal vitamins, and the disappointment was crushing. Hearing that they were for his sister-in-law was like a ray of sunshine, but I hardly thought I'd have a date with him in a half hour. I thought it meant I could lust after him without a guilty conscience. I almost swallowed my tongue when he asked me out. I wanted to ask if we could go right then and there.

I love my nephew, but I was so ready to drop him off at

home with my sister and brother-in-law. Fucking traffic. I barely made it home in time. I need to get my hair dry and get dressed. What am I going to wear? I guess jeans and some kind of top. I noticed he checked out my tits. Something that shows them off without being slutty.

How the hell does he have a driver? The Kutsenkos were not rich in high school. Just the opposite. There were rumors they ran street hustles and knocked off liquor stores. They were all nice guys, but all of them had a bad boy aura. I remember Aleks has an older brother and two older cousins. What were their names? Anton—he's a cousin. So was Sergei. Maksim. That was the older brother. Niko and Pavel—Pasha—they were my year. Pasha's Anton's brother. There were two more. Oh, Bogdan. The guy he was on the phone with. That's his youngest brother. Sergei had one too. What was his name? It'll come to me.

All right. Hair's done, makeup's done. I wonder how warm it's going to be in there. This sweater top should work. A good push-up bra and the v neck should get his attention without being over the top. Definitely flats for putt-putt.

Shit. He's here. Such a decisive knock. One last glance in the mirror.

"Hi."

I open the door, and he's even hotter than this afternoon. He's in jeans and a fitted sweater. Every muscle—even his fucking abs—are on display. Fuck you, bitches. He's my date tonight. Those jeans—I can't wait to see his ass.

"Hi. You look great."

That smile and that accent. I might need to run back to my room and change my panties. He hands me a bouquet I don't recognize, but they match the pink in my hair. His smile is kinda shy now. Does he think I won't like them?

"Thank you. These are so pretty. And they match my hair. Did you do that on purpose?"

I tease, hoping it'll make him a little less nervous. He seems unsure of himself. It doesn't fit with the Aleks I remember, or even the one from earlier. It's sweet.

"Maybe."

His smile is back, and I'm even wetter. I hurry to put them in water.

"Who's that?"

I glance over and see where he's pointing.

"That's Gloria, my guinea pig. I brought her home for the weekend. She's usually in my classroom."

He looks like he wants to get closer, but he also looks like he wouldn't dare invite himself in.

"Would you like to meet her?"

"My cousin's wife has a chinchilla, Pandora. She says they make wonderful pets because they're so low maintenance."

"So are guinea pigs. It's why I'm able to have her in my classroom. My students adore it. Usually, one of them will take her home over weekends, but this time, no one wanted to."

"If you teach theater, does that mean high school?"

"Yeah."

I take Gloria out of the cage and offer her to Aleks. He's hesitant, but then he's holding her. It might be the most adorable thing I've ever seen. He's so big; she's so tiny. And he's so gentle.

"The nose twitches. That's what Pasha says got him to like Pandora."

"Pasha? He's married?"

He watches me for a moment before he nods.

"So's Niko."

"That's nice."

14

He's still watching me, and I'm uncertain he likes what he sees.

"You had a crush on Niko, didn't you?"

Fuck. But that was twelve years ago.

"A little. Only while we were in the play. It was short-lived."

Because I thought you were the hottest one.

He grins.

"Don't let Pasha know. Everyone always says he's the pretty one. Niko won't let him live it down that a girl liked him better than Pasha."

"Aren't they both married?"

"Blissfully. But it doesn't mean they don't still tease each other. They're the closest of the cousins."

"Oh."

What the hell do I say now?

"Who are you closest to?"

He seems to withdraw. Was that too personal?

"My brothers. We're all equally close to one another. I suppose being a year apart naturally meant we would be. I was two when Bogdan was born, so I don't remember a time without all three of my brothers. Anton and Sergei say they can remember when their brothers were born. Anton was three and a half, and Sergei was barely four. I think they just know the stories so well that they think they remember."

He shrugs and makes it so damn sexy. I've put the flowers in water and Gloria back in her pen. There's no reason to linger at my place, which I made sure was extra tidy. A quick swirl of toilet bowl cleaner just in case. He holds the door open to my apartment, waits for me to enter the elevator first, holds the door open to my building, and waits for me to get into the town car first. Good manners or chivalry, I don't know. But it's hot.

"Would you like to eat first or play first?"

It takes me a heartbeat to realize he means putt-putt, not sex. Fucking shame.

"Dinner first still works for me. I admit I missed lunch. Cadence ate mine. The child has hollow legs."

"I'm thirty, and my mom still says that about me."

"Do you?"

I check out those fine legs in his jeans. I can imagine the muscle under that fabric. Did he just move his a little closer to mine?

"Yes. I eat the most out of the eight of us by far."

He grins, and I'm trying not to drool. There's a lull, and I get the sense that he doesn't know what to say. I get the feeling that he's rather reserved, which makes me want to curb my usual chattiness. I don't want to be too extra.

"How long have you been teaching?"

I appreciate that he asks about me rather than talking about his life. The last two guys I went out with never made it past a first date because they wouldn't shut the fuck up about their jobs, money, and expensive toys.

"Six years. I started halfway through my grad school program when I had my student teaching practicum. I've been at the same school ever since."

"Did you always want to be a teacher?"

"Hardly." I chuckle. "I thought I was destined for Broadway. But I had a couple bad experiences during college, and I decided that wasn't for me."

"Bad experiences?"

I look at the floor. Why did I bring this up? I'm unprepared for his gentle touch as he turns my head toward him. His voice is low, but there's steel in it.

"Did someone hurt you, Heather?"

Why do I feel like he'd defend my honor nine years later?

"Tried to. I got trapped against a dressing room table once, and another guy threatened me, and a third tried to blackmail me with a part. Fool me once, shame on you. Fool me twice, shame on me. Fool me three times, eff the peace signs."

"Isn't that a J Cole song from like a while ago?"

"I didn't think you'd know it, but yeah. It came out not long after this happened. It seems fitting."

He hasn't let go of me. Instead, he's cupping my jaw, and his thumb keeps brushing my cheekbone. It's comforting, even if it is pretty damn forward. I can't help it when my eyes drift closed, and I turn into his palm. But I get my shit together fast and lean away. I offer him an appreciative smile, but I'm a little embarrassed. He drops his hand, and now I regret it.

It doesn't take us long to agree on a restaurant that's near the mini golf place. He's a bit too serious to call it putt-putt. He's done it twice, and it looks like it tastes sour to him. It makes me laugh, and I point it out after the second time. He gives me one of those shrugs with that smile that makes me melt.

The man didn't lie about how much he could eat. But it's all healthy. He asks for double portions of his vegetables to go with his steak and salad. I feel bad ordering pasta with a side salad. I'm always conscious of cost and try to pick the least expensive item on the menu. I think he noticed because his look was speculative before he placed his order. We pick up the conversation where we left off. I wish we hadn't.

"What do you do?"

"My brothers and I are co-owners of a real estate development company and majority stakeholders in several other corporations, mostly pharmaceutical companies, venture capitalism, and a few others.

"Wow. Where'd you go to school?"

He withdraws again. He doesn't stop looking at me, but it's like a wall drops behind his eyes.

"I didn't. Maks and I went straight into the family business. We did some construction work when we were just out of high school and saved our money until we could do other things. Where did you go to school?"

"Barnard."

"That's where Niko's wife went to school, but she's a few years younger than us."

"Would she have been on campus when I was?"

I wonder if I'll ever get to meet her. It would give us something to talk about.

"No. Anastasia graduated six months ago."

"Wow. She's a lot younger than Niko."

"Yeah, but she's an old soul."

He sounds genuinely fond of his sister-in-law. It's pretty sweet.

"You said Bogdan is married. What about Maks?"

"He is. He was the first to get married about fifteen months ago."

"And Niko and Bogdan have gotten married since then?"

"Yeah, and Pasha. He got married about a month ago."

Damn! That's a lot of weddings. I can't even imagine the fortune that's been. But with his clothes, his watch, and the town car, construction apparently pays off.

"Doesn't Sergei have a brother, too? I can't remember his name."

"Misha. He's a couple months younger than Bogdan, but they were in the same class."

"I remember him, just not his name." My forehead wrinkles. "I remember everyone looked a lot alike, except Anton and Pasha looked nothing like Sergei and Misha. But you and your brothers are practically identical quadruplets and look like both sets of cousins. Is it still like that?"

"Yes. People still get my brothers and me confused. And

our similarities are usually the first things people comment on. Anton and Pasha are from my dad's side of the family. Sergei and Misha are from my mom's side."

"What do your parents do?"

There's that wall again. Aren't these normal date questions?

"My mom's a widow. She's a pharmacist."

Fuck. Now what do I say? Was it recent?

"I'm sorry for your loss."

"My dad died before we moved to America. It's been a long time."

He's dismissive, but I sense time hasn't healed this wound. It seems fresh, but that had to be nearly two decades ago.

"What do your parents do?"

He moves us back onto safer ground.

"My mom's a teacher too, and my dad's a cop."

Okay. Now he really has shutdown. Did he just sit back in his seat? So much for safer ground.

"What does your mom teach?"

"Biology and physics. I think you probably had her for one or the other."

"Mrs. Hampton? I had her for both."

"I look like her when my hair is my usual brown."

I just realized I never actually told him my last name. That's how fucking distracted I was earlier.

"I think I can see that. What about your dad? Is he NYPD?"

"Yeah. Staten Island."

Is that relief? Does my dad being a cop freak him out? We're not sixteen. My dad's not going to intimidate him.

"Do you have siblings?"

"Two sisters. I'm in the middle. One lives in Jersey, and the other in Connecticut. I have a much smaller family than you."

"There are a lot of us. There are nineteen now with my niece and nephew."

"How old are they?"

"Six-month-old twins. They're Maks's."

"He and his wife must have had honeymoon babies."

"Pretty much."

He seems way more at ease talking about his family again. Okay. Back on track.

"What do Niko and Bogdan do?"

"They work with Maks and me. They make up the other two in Kutsenko Partners."

"I can't imagine working with my sisters. I love them to pieces, but they'd drive me batty."

I caught myself before I said batshit, which is what I mean.

"It has its moments. Our cousins work with us too, and they own their own businesses separate from Kutsenko Partners."

"You must see each other a lot, then."

"Every day."

That fucking smile. Can I just drop my panties now?

The meal progresses with no more of those moments when he seems to retreat. We have a blast at mini golf. He's great. But I'm better. I can tell he's competitive, but he's a gracious loser. He takes me for ice cream afterwards, and we walk to a nearby park. We sit together as we eat it, despite it being flipping cold outside. The wind gusts as we walk to the car, which is at the corner. It must have followed us. He wraps his arm around me and turns me away from the icy blast. My face ends up against his chest. When he doesn't let go, I don't pull away. We only separate when we get in the car.

"Um, would you like to come up?"

He nods as he holds my building door open. Then it's the same as when we left. He waits for me to get on and off the elevator. I unlock my door, but he holds it open before he steps in. His eyes sweep over my apartment like they did when he arrived. It's quick but thorough. It's like he takes in every detail within seconds. I bet if I blindfolded him, he could describe my entire place.

I turn toward him once I hang up our coats. He cups my cheek like he did in the car on the way to the restaurant.

"I had a really nice time, Heather. I'd like to see you again."

For breakfast preferably.

"I'd like that too, Aleks."

He slides his arm around my waist, and I sway toward him. His icy-blue eyes mesmerize me even more than before. They're so much closer and piercing. They pin me to my spot. He's waiting for me. It takes me a moment to realize that. I'm already in his arms, but he won't kiss me unless he's sure that's what I want. I love his kind of chivalry. I part my lips and lift my chin. I can't stop thinking: what does he taste like?

Chapter Three

Aleks

Tonight's reminded me several times of why I don't date. Heather asked normal questions that a normal man could answer. I had to be evasive, and I know she noticed when I withdrew. But despite all that, I had the best night I've had in years. Now I'm standing here with her in my arms, and I'm waiting for a sign that she wants to kiss me as much as I want to kiss her.

Her lips part, and she's looking at mine. I'll take that as the signal I'm looking for. I press mine to hers softly. I'm not sure if she expects a peck, or if she'll let me devour her the way I want. When she opens her mouth to me, I waste no time. My tongue slides past her teeth, sweeping the inside of her mouth. I can taste the mint from her ice cream. The pressure is light, but she sucks on my tongue. I think I'm about to come.

My arm tightens around her until her hands start to slide around my waist from my chest. I snag her wrists, but keep my hold light, before easing them up to my neck. She runs her fingers through my hair and tries to press my head closer. I pull back my tongue and nip at her lower lip. She tries again to bring my head down, and again, I nip at her lip. This time a little harder. That moan. She didn't mean to make it, but it shoots straight to my cock.

She gives up trying to control the kiss, and that's when I swoop in and finally really taste her. My hands slide to her ass, and she arches her back, pressing her tits against my chest. I press her backward two steps until her back is against a wall. One arm remains around my neck, but her other hand clutches my sweater. I rock my hips against her pussy, and she shifts to welcome my thigh between hers. However, I make her wait, even though I was thinking the same thing. I squeeze her ass hard enough to bring her up onto her toes. Her kiss grows wild as she silently begs for more.

I can feel the heat from her cunt when I finally slide my thigh against it. I guide her to ride it. Her moans are so soft they're almost impossible to hear, but they're coming more often. I lift her away from my leg, and she makes her irritation known with a whimper. But I guide her legs around my waist, and she rocks against my cock. These fucking jeans are fucking painful. My cock is so hard, and there's not nearly enough room for it. I carry her to the sofa and sit with her straddling my lap. My hands on her hips guide her as she dry humps my cock.

When she has the rhythm I want, my hands slip underneath her sweater and up to her tits. She arches again, and her head falls back as I knead them beneath the fabric while kissing the tops. I swipe my tongue along her cleavage, and now it's my turn to make a noise. Holy fuck. I want to see her nipples, taste them.

"I've wanted to do that since the grocery store."

"Lick me?"

"Yeah. That and a few other things."

"Such as?"

"Suck yer tits, *malyshka.*"

Her brow furrows for a moment, but then she whips her sweater over her head. I pull her bra down and see the northern half of the promised land. Her dark areolas are wide around her puckered nipple. They're like a target, and my tongue is my arrow. I lick them before latching on like a starving baby. I love them and keep sucking until her nipple is tight enough for me to tug with my teeth. I pinch the other one at the same time, but I keep the pressure light until she tries to press my head to her again. I snag her wrists and press them against the small of her back.

"Oh, sir."

It's a breathy moan, but I look up. She seems to realize what she's said. She appears flustered.

"What do you want, *malyshka?* Vanilla or not?"

"Not."

I let go of her wrists and flip her onto her back as I come down over her. I have her arms above her head in one move.

"What do you want, Heather? Tell me, and I will give it to you. If you want me to stop, say so, and it's over immediately."

"I want you."

"Tell me exactly what you want, *malyshka.* Do you want me to finger fuck you? Eat you out? Fuck your pussy?"

"Yes."

I chuckle.

"All of it? Tonight?"

"Yes, sir. I—"

I've been rocking my cock against her pussy, but when she stops talking, I freeze.

"Is it too much, Heather? Do you want to stop?"

"No. Yes. I—Is this a one-night stand? I need to know

before this goes further. I—I'm all right with that. I just want to know—"

"You would not be all right with that, and neither would I. This is definitely not a one-night."

"How do you know I wouldn't be?"

"Because you're asking."

"And that's not what you want?"

I'm still holding her hands above her head, and she hasn't tried to move them.

"No. I don't do random hook-ups, Heather. I'm thirty. That hasn't been my thing in a decade."

"Do you have a girlfriend?"

I stare at her, genuinely insulted. But then I remind myself of what she probably thought I meant.

"No, I don't. I don't have a wife or an ex-wife. I've never been married, and I haven't had a girlfriend in more years than you'd believe. I'm not a monk, but I rarely date."

"You don't?"

"No. But I want to date you."

"Aleks, you sound very resolute."

"I am. I'm decisive in general. Tonight's been amazing. I'm obviously physically attracted to you. You're breathing temptation. But I had so much fun. I can't remember the last time I laughed this much."

She looks stunned. I suppose, by a normal person's standard, I barely laughed at all. Bogdan and Niko were the easygoing ones. Maks and I didn't have that luxury. Maks is less communicative than me, but I'm usually somber.

"I'm the serious one in the family."

She nods, and a smile pokes through her surprise.

"*Malyshka*, if you don't want this to go any further tonight, then I can go. Or we could watch a movie or talk."

"What do you want for breakfast, Aleks?"

I stare at her for a moment before I dive in for another kiss. I don't leave any doubt in her mind that I'm in control. The kiss is possessive, and she submits to it. I can feel it. It draws out until we're breathless. I pull back and yank my sweater over my head. She unfastens her bra and drops it to the floor. And I'm back to sucking her tits. They're magnificent. My hand rubs her pussy over her jeans, and she shifts restlessly beneath me.

"What do you want, *malyshka?*"

"You've called me that like five times? What does it mean?"

Do I admit it?

"Baby girl."

I guess so.

"Is that a common thing in Russian?"

I see her nervousness. She wants to know if I call every woman I fuck this.

"No. Only you, Heather. I've never called another woman that. I don't remember the last time I called a woman anything but her name."

She appears contemplative.

"What's wrong, baby girl?"

I finally tuck that hair behind her ear as I rest on one forearm, our chests pressing together. The feeling of our bodies against each other is so fucking hot.

"You know I like it kinky, and I called you sir. But I—I like that you have called no one else *malyshka.* I—I've never had a Dom or anything, but I have called other guys that. I wish—how do you say sir in Russian?"

A wave of affection washes over me, and I kiss her nose. It's sweet to me how she wishes to learn even one word in Russian, and her request sounds so heartfelt.

"That's a little difficult. After the Communist Revolution, those forms of address sort of went away. We don't exactly have a universal equivalent. The closest I can think of is *sudar'.*"

I listen to her whisper it as she repeats it a few times —*sOOdahr*. I can't help but smile. She's genuinely trying.

"Is that what you'd like me to call you?"

"*Malyshka*, I'll answer to just about anything you call me."

I kiss her nose again. Who am I? I'm never this gentle, and I'm only this affectionate to my niece and nephew. And they sleep more than anything else.

"I'm guessing comrade is a no-go."

I chuckle and shake my head.

"Not so sexy. You can stick with sir if you prefer. I don't mind."

It's her turn to disagree.

"I'd like to try *sudar'*. Is that all right with you?"

"Yes, *malyshka*. Thank you."

She lifts her chin but does nothing else to start our next round of kissing. But I'm not giving in. I shift back to kneel as I unfasten her jeans. She inches them down her legs, and I pull her thong down after them. She has a thin landing strip of dark hair, and I have to admit I prefer it to a full Brazilian. I don't know. I just feel a bit creepy when a pussy is completely bare. She's watching me for my reaction. I grab her jeans and thong and toss them behind me before I go in for the attack. She giggles at my eagerness, and I offer her the most wolfish expression I can muster.

I slide one, then two fingers into her as I blow cool air on her clit. My tongue flicks out and taps it as my fingers move within her. She's tight, but not so much that I fear hurting her when I put in a third finger or when I fuck her later. And fuck her, I will. Her body is an invitation to sin and debauchery.

I graze my teeth over her clit, and she moans. Her fingers dig into her leather sofa, and I know she's fighting not to press me closer. I tease her over and over, bringing her close and pulling away as I feel her tense.

"*Sudar'*, please may I come?"

"Not yet, *malyshka.*"

I lick my fingers clean before one hand squeezes her tit and the other pinches her free nipple. I suck hard on her clit until her body trembles.

"Come for me, baby girl."

Her moan fills the air as she shudders. She watches me through her orgasm, and I know she's fighting not to reach for me. I kiss my way up her belly and between her tits until I get to her neck. I kiss behind her ear before I whisper to her.

"Wrap your arms and legs around me, *malyshka.* Let me hold you too."

Her sigh seems to deflate her entire body. I slide my arms beneath her as I kiss her. I can tell she doesn't love tasting herself, but I'm ready to go back for a second serving.

"Is that enough for you, or do you want more?"

"More, *sudar'*. Please."

"Tell me what you want, *malyshka.* Do you want me inside you? Do you want to come on my cock?"

"Yes. I have condoms. They're in my room. Can we—"

I scoop her into my arms and carry her into the room she points to. I ease her onto the bed, and she reaches into the bedside table as I slip off my jeans and boxer briefs. I'm careful that they cover the gun I had holstered at my lower back. That is not something I want to explain. And those are definitely not the right size condoms. They're going to cut my fucking circulation off. She may as well put a cock ring on me.

"Oh!"

She looks at me, then down at the condom packet she has. She knows what I do. I dig out the condom I put in my wallet for tonight. I wasn't going to suggest sex, but I was going to be prepared. And I wasn't even a Boy Scout. I hand it to her as I climb onto the bed and kneel between her legs. I stroke myself as she rips open the wrapper and tosses it onto the bedside table. I grit my teeth as she slides the condom down my dick before she bends her legs and lifts her hips for me. I already know how wet she is. I thrust into her, and we both freeze. Holy fuck. This is fucking perfection.

"Aleks."

It's a light breath she exhales with my name. It makes my cock twitch, and she tightens her pussy around me. I need to taste her like I need my next breath. Our mouths fuse as I move. She meets each of my thrusts as she flexes her hips. I glance up and notice that she's grabbed her headboard to keep from grabbing me.

"What do you want, Heather?"

"Hard. Really rough, Aleks. Please."

Thank God. I'm barely restraining myself. I'll never lose complete control because I'm so much bigger than her. I'd hurt her, and that's the last thing I want. I find the idea of ever hurting her viscerally horrible. But I'm rough. I slam into her over and over as I pinch her nipple.

"Aleks, more...Please...*Sudar'*, I need..."

"What do you need, baby girl? Tell me, and I'll give it to you."

"Just more."

I wrap my hand around her throat and add pressure. Her expression relaxes as I tighten.

"Do you want breath play, *malyshka*?"

"Anything."

I roll us until she's riding me. I hold her hips and set the rhythm until she submits and lets me lead. Then I wrap my hand around her throat again. As I squeeze, I'm careful not to apply too much pressure. It's not true breath play. I'm uncertain if she's experienced with that, and I don't want to terrify her. But my other hand lands against her ass with a ringing slap.

"Yes!"

She tries to abandon the pace I set, but a hand on her hip controls it. Then I spank her harder for trying to disobey my silent command. I don't squeeze her throat any harder, but I do spank her four more times, each one harder than the last.

"Please, may I come?"

"Please what?"

Please, *sudar'*."

"How badly do you need it, *malyshka*?"

"I'll swallow your dick if you let me come now."

Fuck. I might come. She's not joking. I roll us again, my hand still on her throat. I'm hanging onto my control with a thread, but there's not a single gentle thing about how I move inside her.

"Come, baby girl. Squeeze my cum out of me as I fuck you. That's it. Fuck, *malyshka*. You feel so good. I shouldn't have made you wait. I'm too close. I'm not fucking coming until you do."

"I don't care if you do. I'm close. I want to make you come. I want to feel you and know I fucked you until you couldn't hold out."

I lower myself onto my forearms and bring my mouth to her ear as our hands clasp.

"Nobody has ever fucked me this well. It's a good thing tomorrow is Sunday because I'm not leaving your pussy alone till Monday morning."

"Promise?"

"Yes, *malyshka*. Come for me, baby girl. Come for—"

I catch myself before I say something that could completely shatter the mood. I don't know where that came from. But probably the same place as wanting to call her baby girl.

"I'm close, Daddy. I'm—Daddy!"

I watch her as her orgasm takes hold. Between her expression, her pussy clamping around me, and hearing her call me Daddy, I erupt. How did she know that's what I wanted to hear?

"Is that what you want me to be? You want your Daddy to fuck you, *malyshka?*"

She blinks several times as what she said, and what I just said, registers. Then her fingers are digging into the back of my hands as she nods vigorously. I enjoy the feeling of hers on mine as she arches into another orgasm. I slam into her two more times before I can't hold back any longer. My dick pulses inside this fucking condom as her thighs press against me, and she traps my hips between them. I have no desire to go anywhere, so I don't mind her holding me in place. Fuck. I didn't know I had that much cum.

As our gazes meet, I can see reality settling back to her. She realizes what she said, what I said, and the red in her cheeks isn't from her orgasm or exertion.

"I don't think you're a little, and I'm not a Daddy dom. But you are my *malyshka*, and I am your Daddy."

Chapter Four

Heather

That was the most mind-blowing sex I've ever had, and I'm so far from virginal that if I had a halo, it'd be around my ankles. I don't fuck every guy who looks my way, but I've had enough partners to know what I like and what I don't. That was so far past amazing. I don't even have a word for it. But I can't believe I called him Daddy. It just tumbled out of my mouth, and it surprised me. But not that much. Is that what he likes to be called?

"You're not a Daddy dom, but you're my Daddy. I don't understand."

"Are you a little, Heather?"

"No. I know what they are because I enjoy reading those types of romances, but I don't want to be one. I don't think I need to be one."

"And I'm not interested in age play or having a Daddy dom's little girl. I'm not a Dom period. But I do like to be the dominant one during sex, and I have a dominant personality, Heather. I know that probably sounds the same as being a Dom, but that's not the type of relationship I want with you."

"Relationship?"

"I told you, I don't do hook ups, and I haven't dated anyone in years. But I really enjoy your company, and this—this was—I don't know that I have the words in Russian or English. But even if we don't have sex again, I still want to see you."

"Oh, we're having sex again. You promised me until Monday morning."

I grin as I do a Kegel around his cock. He's not softened at all, and he thrusts into me again. Fuck.

"I need—"

"I know, *malyshka*. I'll make you come again."

He moves against me until I can't stop. He released by hands after he came. I grip his upper arms as I arch off the bed. Each orgasm gets better than the last. When I can open my eyes and focus again, he rolls us onto our side and draws my leg over his hip. He still hasn't pulled out.

"What do you want, Heather?"

"Even before the sex, this was the best date I've ever been on. I want to see you again too. Aleks, I'm not into DDLG either. I don't know where calling you Daddy came from. I'm—"

So embarrassed. But I can't even get that word out. I suddenly feel really awkward. His hand is stroking my ass, and it's super soothing. He offers me such a tender kiss I melt against him.

"I know you're not. But you told me from the start that you wanted it kinky. You called me sir. If you enjoyed our date before this, then I think you already know I have a dominant personality. I don't know why I want to call you baby girl every chance I get, but I do. Even before you made it obvious you'd submit, I got that feeling. Maybe you know that I'll—"

"What?"

"If I say what I'm thinking, then it'll sound like age play is what I want, but it's not. I don't want to freak you out by sounding too possessive or clingy."

"Just say it, Aleks. If it is, then I'll say so."

"Maybe you know I'll take care of you."

Why does that sound so good? Why do I just want to snuggle closer to him when he says that? I inch toward him until my body presses against his, and I can wrap an arm around his waist above my leg.

"Do you mean the way you hold open doors for me, pull out my chair, bring me flowers, wait until I take the first bite or sip?"

"Yes. Those things, but I also want to do things that'll make you happy. Your laugh and your smile make my day. My work is—challenging. It can be very—heavy. I don't get to laugh often, but you've made me forget all of that. Not just tonight but at the grocery store and pharmacy. Every time you smile, things feel lighter. I like it."

I brush the hair back from his forehead, unsure if he'll like me doing that. His eyes drift closed, and he sighs. There's still the intensity about him that's always there, but he isn't so brooding right now. It almost makes him seem vulnerable.

"Heather, I don't even know if that idea appeals to you. I don't want to make you feel like I think you can't do things on your own or that—"

"Shh, Daddy."

I press a finger to his lips before I give him a peck.

"I know what I can do for myself. But the idea of being taken care of sometimes isn't unappealing. It's like having someone offer to carry a heavy load, even if it's only for a little while."

"Not a little while, *malyshka*. I'm not saying I expect us to commit to forever, but I'm not interested in something casual. At least, not on my end."

"Aleks, I'm not sure you know how to do casual anything."

He grins, and I swear my pussy just sucked his cock back in.

"But what are you saying, Aleks? You said relationship before. Do you mean boyfriend and girlfriend already?"

"Does that idea freak you out?"

My immediate answer is no, but I make myself take a moment to think about it. I don't waver.

"Not at all. I waited to see if it would. But I feel like—" I push up onto one elbow. "You remind me of the Aleks I knew about in high school. But most of you is extremely different. And so am I. I admit, I had a massive crush on you for a long time. You didn't even know I was alive. I don't see any point in keeping that a secret that you'll inevitably discover. I don't want you to think I'm saying yes because I'm stuck on a fantasy from ten years ago. I speak English and Spanish and I don't have the words to explain why this feels so right. That having this conversation right now, after having sex on a first date, feels like the most normal thing we could do tonight."

"So you're all right with jumping straight into a monogamous relationship? One where we see each other regularly. One where we share things about ourselves and our lives like a regular couple that dates for a while before becoming exclusive."

"Yes. The idea of sitting next to you on the couch and watching a movie or getting ice cream again—preferably when it's warmer—sounds just as fantastic as the nice dinner you treated me to or the fun of putt-putt."

"And the whole Daddy-baby girl thing?"

"I think we understand each other. Hearing you call me that, especially in Russian, makes me feel special. I feel—spoiled and—" My brow furrows as I try to articulate how Aleks makes me feel. "—safe. I liked the way you shielded me from the wind. It was like you wanted to protect me from it."

"I did. That's what I mean about taking care of you. I don't feel like I need to tell you to wear a coat or explain why you should. You're an adult, and I know you get it. But if I can make you feel more comfortable, do little things to take care of you, then I hope you'll let me."

"It's chivalrous, but I suppose nowadays, it feels a bit like you taking care of me. I admit, I enjoy it. I've never had it before. I feel like I can rely on you. Can I?"

I suddenly feel a wave of nervousness. Am I setting myself up for the most colossal disappointment? He's not stringing me along, is he?

"Yes. I want you to know you always can, Heather. I'm not telling you this, so you'll fuck me again. I haven't talked this much about my feelings in—probably fifteen years. I used to talk to my mom about things when I liked a girl, and I didn't know what to do. But even that didn't last very long."

"I'm guessing you and your brothers don't sip lattes and talk about feelings."

"Uh, no. We don't sip vodka and do that either."

I giggle. Again. I laugh about plenty of things, but I don't giggle. Only with Aleks. He's probably one of the most serious people I've ever met, and yet life feels lighter around him. I must be certifiable to think this after one date. This is crazy. Even the shows with the people who get married the day they meet, or the ones who have three months to get to know their fiancé, don't talk like this. What is it about him?

"Heather, we can just see where things go. But you know

what I want, and I think I get what you want. We're on the same page about that."

"We are." I glance at the bedside table over his shoulder. "I think we need to see if Amazon Prime can get us some bigger condoms tonight."

His laugh is deep and rumbles in his chest. He kisses my forehead and strokes my back.

"Whatever you want, *malyshka*. I'd have more sex. But if you also just want to snuggle and fall asleep, I find myself more relaxed than I've been in ages."

He doesn't seem as tense as he did when he picked me up. His heat and the way he's running his hand over my back and ass are so soothing. Now that we've had this heart-to-heart, I suddenly feel super sleepy. I shimmy to pull down the covers, and he slips beneath them with me after he tosses the condom in the trash by my bed.

"Maybe we could take a nap, Daddy."

"I'd like that, *malyshka*."

I can feel myself dozing off when he moves. He pulls his arm free and reaches over the side of the bed to his pants and pulls out his phone.

"Amazon Prime has some delivering to do. I think my kinky *malyshka* might need me to get more than just bigger condoms."

"I think so, Daddy."

I yawn, and I'm not sure what I just agreed to. But I've never been so comfortable as when Aleks rolls onto his back, and I cuddle up to his side. How do I feel like we're an old married couple when we're technically still on our first date?

I come awake to the feel of someone kissing along my neck and over my shoulder. I'm trying so hard to open my eyes, but I'm still more asleep than awake. The feeling of a mouth on my tits, alternating sides, is making my pussy aches.

"Are you awake, *malyshka*?"

"Yes, Daddy."

Am I? I force my eyes open long enough to look over at Aleks. His hair is disheveled, and I can barely see him in the dark, but his icy-blue eyes seem to glow from the dim streetlights peeking through my blinds. I reach for him and tunnel my fingers through that deliciously tousled hair. He kisses along my belly until he shifts to settle between my legs.

"I need a midnight snack, baby girl."

My legs fall open as he licks me before sucking my clit. The sensations stir my mind even if my eyes still don't want to open. I'm aware, but in a haze. Is it a sleep haze or a lust haze? I'll take either.

"The kitchen is open."

All right. I must be more asleep than coherent. That was so fucking stupid. But he chuckles, and his stubble grazes the inside my thighs, making me shiver. He devours me like I'm a main course, not a snack.

"Aleks."

He doesn't answer my needy plea with words. He thrusts three fingers into me and works my pussy like a maestro playing his violin.

"Daddy, may I come?"

"Whenever you want, *malyshka*. This is purely for your pleasure."

Just like earlier this evening, my orgasm rips through me and steals my breath. My toes curl, and I clench the sheets as I moan. That only makes him redouble his efforts to draw out my ecstasy. It works. My orgasm just keeps going. But when it subsides, I'm clawing at his shoulders.

"I need you."

"We have no more condoms that will fit. I've never had sex without one, Heather. None have ever ripped. I tested six months ago, and that was the last time I was with someone."

I curl upward and look at him, my eyes finally open.

"It's been six months since you had sex."

He chuckles again.

"Why is that so shocking? When was the last time for you?"

"Because you're hot as fuck. And a month ago."

He lunges forward, and his kiss is possessive and demanding. I don't love tasting myself, but I love how he takes control.

"Because I'm not a teenager anymore, and I don't need to fuck to feel like a man. I can survive. At least, I could before I met you again. Who was he? A boyfriend?"

"An ex who I hooked up with after a friend's birthday party. We broke up two years ago. It was just sex, Daddy. Nothing more."

"What do you want?"

"You. We used a condom. I haven't tested in a while, but I was clean."

"Do you want me to fuck you without one? Birth control?"

"The shot. I want you, Daddy."

He surges into me and holds still. Fuck. I can feel the difference.

"Nothing has ever felt this good, Heather. I didn't expect— didn't know—I—"

I can't believe he's at a loss for words, but so am I. His kiss is hungry again as he thrusts over and over. He's rough, and I love it. My fingertips graze down his back until I can grip his ass. I feel the muscles flex over and over. They rippled under my fingers as I moved them from his shoulders to my final destination. The controlled power is incredible. Everything is incredible. I've been with guys who were in shape, but none compared to this perfect specimen of manhood.

"More."

"I don't want to hurt you, Heather."

"More. You won't. I like it rough. I like knowing you want me this much."

"I do. I want to be inside you and make you come until you can't see straight. You're mine. I won't share you with an ex or a fuck buddy or whoever."

"I know. That's what I want. Why is this so fucking good?"

"I don't know. But you're a drug that only took one hit to make me addicted."

I suppose that's rather romantic. We move together until I feel him tremble. He's holding back, and it's a struggle. He won't come until I do.

"What do you need, baby girl? How do you want me to fuck you?"

He's kneeling now and holding my hips up as he pounds into me. I open my arms again, and he entwines his fingers with mine and leans forward to bring my hands over my head. His public bone grinds against my clit, and I explode.

"This!"

He keeps going until my orgasm eases, then he pulls out and coats my belly and tits with his cum. As our eyes meet after watching, I know he's thinking the same thing I am. He's branded me, and I am his. I don't know how long we stare at the evidence of our lust. I hated the sensation of him pulling out with an equal ferocity to how much I love the feel of him entering me. He goes into my bathroom, and I hear the water run. He comes back with the hand towel, one end damp. He's so incredibly gentle as he cleans me, then dries my chest and belly. He drops a soft kiss on my lips before returning to the bathroom. I hear the water run again, and I can see him hanging up the towel.

When he crawls back into bed and pulls the covers over us, I roll toward him, my eyes drifting closed again.

"Thank you, Daddy."

"I can say the same, *malyshka*. Thank you."

He kisses my forehead, and I'm out. Morning comes way too soon.

Chapter Five

Aleks

What the fuck did I do?

I wake to the sound of my phone ringing. It's Maks. I glance down at Sleeping Beauty beside me. She's deeply asleep after our last round of sex an hour ago. Her body is warm and lax against me. The last thing I want to do is get up, but I pull myself free and reach for my phone, which I left on the bedside table after ordering a jumbo pack of condoms. What the fuck was I thinking?

"*Privet.*"

I greet my brother in Russian, and we continue in the language.

"Carmine, Luca, and Gabriele are back. I need you to come to the house."

"Now? It's three in the morning."

There's a pause, and I can guess what Maks is thinking.

"Are you with someone?"

"I don't want to get out of bed to talk about those fuckers."

"That didn't answer my question."

"I think it did."

"Aleksei."

"Maksim."

"The others are leaving their beds and their wives. Get your ass here now."

"Fine, old man."

Niko, Bogdan, and I have called our oldest brother that since we were kids. He's taken responsibility for us then for the Ivankov bratva, our branch, for nearly two decades. We've been in America for close to eighteen years. Ever since we arrived, he's been looking out for us, shielding us. Now he has thousands of people who depend upon him for their jobs, and plenty of them rely on him for their safety. If he says I need to come, then I need to.

"I'll be there soon."

"Thank you, little brother."

He's been calling the rest of us that as long as we've called him old man. I look down at Heather again. It's barely Sunday morning. This is not when I wanted to leave. But now that I'm awake, and I know I have to go, I'm second guessing what the fuck I thought I was doing last night.

A plan is always better than an impulse.

Vladislav Lushak drilled that into us. We had to repeat it for hours on end. The man was a sociopath. He enjoyed killing, and he enjoyed torturing. He did the latter to all of us and forced us to do the former. He sucked us into the bratva within months of our arrival, and we've never been able to leave it since.

I didn't have a plan when I asked Heather out. I had an impulse. I didn't have a plan when the date started. I had an impulse. I didn't have a plan when I talked to her about being my girlfriend. I sure as shit had a bunch of impulses, though. I don't date. I don't have girlfriends for the very reason I'm facing now.

I climb out of bed, careful not to disturb Heather. I slip on my clothes, my back turned while I check my gun. Nothing has changed, but force of habit. Always check it before holstering it. I turn back to face her as I ease it against my lower back. She'd freak and ask way too many questions I can't answer.

"*Malyshka,* wake up."

I shake her shoulder and kiss her forehead as I lean over the bed. I give her another couple shakes until her eyes flutter. I wish I was waking her for sex again. I'd woken with a raging hard on, having dreamed about fucking her in the ocean. I watched her sleep for a little while, thinking I would calm down. My need for her only became more urgent.

As I look at her sleepy expression and remember how being inside her felt, how natural sleeping beside her felt, I want to climb back into bed. But I can't. And that's why I don't date, don't do girlfriends. Bratva will always come first.

"Heather, I have to go. Something's come up at work. We have clients all over the world, so time zones don't matter."

"You're leaving?"

She glances at the clock.

"It's Sunday."

"I know, baby girl. But it's not the weekend everywhere in the world."

That's true, but this has nothing to do with the Arab world and everything to do with three bags of *Costa Nostra* ass.

"Is everything okay?"

She swipes the hair from her face as she sits up.

"I don't know. I'm so sorry I woke you, and I'm even more sorry that I have to leave."

I really am. This is *not* what I want to be doing. Fuck. I

should cancel the condom order. I don't want to end things at three in the morning. But I'm going to have to today. Fuck.

"Will you call me or text me later?"

"Yes."

Because I'm going to have to break up with you. That's not what I want to say or text, but I still can't believe how impulsive I was. She's not bratva. Her dad's a fucking cop. Dating her is a one-way ticket to death row, and not just for me. For my entire family. This is why I stopped letting my dick do my thinking when I was twenty. I'm fucking thirty. Fuck me.

"I hope everything is all right."

"It will be."

No, it won't. It sucks, and it's only going to get worse.

"Go back to sleep, *malyshka*."

"Bye, Daddy."

"Bye, baby girl."

I press a last kiss to her lips. I force myself not to make it into more. But it's almost worse because it's tender, and I feel things I shouldn't. Useless things.

I slip out of her apartment and down to the street. Stefan, one of our drivers, is already waiting for me. I don't have to tell him where to go.

Double fuck me. Maks is going to know I wasn't in Manhattan at my place because of how fast I get to his place in Queens. It's only a twenty-minute drive. I'm tired from only getting a few hours' sleep, and I'm disappointed that I had to leave. It's for the best, though. I have to keep reminding myself of that.

When I walk into Maks's office, Misha is the only one who isn't there. Bogdan, Niko, and Pasha now have homes in the same neighborhood as Maks. They bought them with their wives. Anton and Sergei arrived together and were probably here before Maks made the call. Sergei heads our intelligence gathering, and Anton is our chief enforcer. He strategizes all our illegal operations. They're the dynamic duo and have been since high school. Even though they're from opposite sides of my family, they've known each other their entire lives. They and Maks are only a few months apart in age.

I don't know what Maks, Anton, and Sergei have shared with the others, so I ask.

"How do you know they're back?"

Niko practically hisses.

"The fuckers sent a photo of themselves outside one of Salvatore's restaurants with the caption 'we're back.' Salvatore isn't answering his phone."

"Do you think it's legit? Is it an old photo?"

I wouldn't put it past them just to fuck with us and get us all amped up. They've been nothing but trouble for nearly a year. Salvatore needs to put his puppies back on their leashes. They're pissing on the carpet.

"Take a look. Zoom in on Carmine's phone."

I take Sergei's phone and slide my fingers apart. A New York Times article from yesterday. I'd say that means it's legit, but I'm still not convinced.

"Sergei, are you sure they didn't just drop the restaurant in as a background?"

"Yeah. I ran it, and there are no layers to separate. Even with this type of file, I can tell it's not blended."

Niko looks ready to lose his shit, and I can't blame him. These three fuckers targeted his wife, Anastasia—Ana—the worst. They badly injured her, and she needed surgery because of it. He's not content with just knowing about the photo. He grows more pissed with each word.

"Why the fuck are they back from their Tuscan vacation? A few months manual labor on a vineyard won't have taught them shit about staying away from our women and children. I want to know why the fuck Salvatore thinks it's safe for them to be back. If they're in range of a bullet, then they're my target."

"No, they aren't. Blow off your steam, Niko. But we can't touch them."

Niko glowers at Maks, but even he knows Maks is right. If these were mere peons in Salvatore Mancinelli's branch of the *Costa Nostra*, then Niko could off them. But Luca is Salvatore's heir and nephew, Carmine is also his nephew, and Gabriele's just been around for forever. He and Carmine are besties.

"I saw the pieces of shit."

We all turn toward the door as Misha enters. He and Sergei look so much like my mom that people often think they're her sons rather than my brothers and me. They share her blonde hair and blue eyes. My aunt, Svetlana, has red hair, and my uncle, Radomir, has light brown. They all got the blond hair and blue eyes from my *babushka*. My grandmother.

"Where?"

Niko's voice is still quiet because the twins and Laura are asleep, but it's a demand.

"They drove past Dolls, Dolls, Dolls."

Kutsenko Partners owns a slew of strip clubs and night-clubs, along with the more reputable real estate and venture capitalism endeavors. Misha and Pasha are heads of security at them. I'm often there to help, but I had the night off. It's why I was relieved Heather suggested we go out so soon. I was off tonight, but I haven't had any others off for at least two weeks. If these turds are causing trouble, I have no idea when I'll be off again. Misha and Pasha will rotate through the clubs, and so will Bogdan, since he runs them.

"Did they do anything? Say anything?"

Maks is barely reining in his temper as he asks. Our years of training to hide every emotion, every reaction are ingrained in us. But we read each other like open books. We survived too much together and are too much alike to keep anything secret for long. All the more reason I'm regretting my date.

That's not accurate. I don't regret my date or meeting Heather. I regret this fucked up life that's going to keep me from her. My brothers and Pasha may have figured out how to make their relationships work, but none of their fathers-in-law are fucking cops. What the fuck was I thinking?

"No. They just rolled by with their windows open. They were in Luca's G-Wagon. Gunmetal gray." Misha rolls his eyes. "Funeral black would be better."

"They just want to let us know they're back, and they think there isn't shit we can do."

I may say what we all know *they're* thinking, but I don't have to say what *we're* all thinking. They will pay. Maybe not with their life, but we don't forgive, and we never forget. Maks looks at Niko before he speaks.

"It was Ana they went after first, but they did plenty of shady shit to Pasha and Sumiko. I'll let you decide what happens, but be reasonable."

"Yeah, yeah, yeah. I don't need you to fucking tell me to be reasonable. I'm fucking amped now, but I know how this goes. A plan is always better than an impulse. I have a right to be pissed right now. I'm not suggesting or deciding anything until we hear from Salvatore."

Maks's phone buzzes on the desk, and we all look down at it.

Salvatore

"About fucking time."

Maks grumbles as he picks up his phone, but he's calm when he answers.

"Salvatore, your nephews stopped by. We didn't know their vacay was over. Did they have fun?"

"Shut up, Maksim."

"Not pleased to talk to me in the middle of the night? Imagine how displeased I was to hear, in the middle of the night, that they are back. Why?"

"That's my family business. You worry about your own."

"Your nephews made your business my business, Salvatore, when they went after my sister-in-law and my cousins."

"Cousins? It was only Pasha."

"Pasha's married. Sumiko is my cousin now. No women and children, Salvatore. Your nephews violated that sacrament twice. You sent them off for a little Tuscan holiday at a vineyard. That's not good enough."

"You saw the videos I sent. They hardly had fun."

"So what? You beat the shit out of them and so did some winery owner. Then what? They probably ate as many grapes as they picked. Wine and cheese aren't a hardship."

"You don't know what else went on there, Maks."

"Enlighten us. You're on speakerphone, by the way."

"Of course I am. Fucking hydra." Salvatore mutters to himself the first part. "I don't owe you any explanations. They were punished, and now it's over."

"Not by a long shot."

It's Niko who pipes in now. Maks glares at him. Niko just shrugs. I wouldn't be remorseful either. Maks scribbles something on a piece of paper and slides it to Niko. I can read it from where I stand.

We don't need him making a preemptive strike. Don't goad him.

"What do you want, Niko? A couple rounds in the ring with each of them?"

"Target practice."

Maks looks ready to strangle Niko, and even I think that went too far. I shake my head at my younger brother. Niko rolls his eyes, sighs again, and steps back from the desk. He leans against the wall with his arms crossed.

Pasha speaks up next.

"Niko and Ana aren't the only ones they crossed, Salvatore. They put Sumiko in the middle and could have gotten her killed if things had gone badly with Pablo."

Pasha's right about the last part. Luckily, he and Pablo were civil, but only for Sumiko's sake since she was still friends with her ex-boyfriend at the time. Otherwise, there's no way Pasha wouldn't have lashed out at the Colombian Cartel's heir. His anger's misguided, though, because it wasn't the Italians or the Colombians behind all of it.

"Let me talk to the grown up in the room. Maks?"

"What?"

"Griping at me isn't how you need to spend your energy. Your problems with the Irish are bigger than the ones with me."

"We have enough men to focus on both. Don't think I'm ignoring them just because we're talking about your assholes. Don't deflect."

"Look, the guys aren't out of the shit stew they made. I'm still dealing with it. But how is none of your business. They might have gone out tonight, but that taste of freedom is short-lived. You need to deal with Dillan and Finn."

Niko steps forward again.

"Salvatore, I won't stop Ana if she sees them. If she catches even a glimpse of them, hears a whisper from them, she will consider it a threat to her, the other women, and the twins. You know what we're willing to do because you've seen it. Let me assure you, my wife is capable of even more."

"Your wife scares the shit out of me, Niko. I'll take on all eight of you before I face her. I don't need Laura, Christina, and Sumiko staring me down, either."

Ana is beyond slim. She's 1990s waif supermodel thin. But

she proved to us the lengths she's willing to go to when she's protecting our family. She tapped into a darkness that my brothers, cousins, and I have but always hold at bay. I don't think she'll ever resort to that again, and Salvatore doesn't know the details, but he senses it. He won't cross her, and he won't let his mafiosos do it either. When he says he's scared of her, he isn't lying. But you would never guess she could do more than knock over a feather when you look at her. She's as easygoing as Niko normally is, and she makes all of us laugh. Even Maks and me.

He also knows the other women are highly intelligent, loyal, and resourceful. They're the type to wake you in your bed right before they slit your throat. None of them have a propensity to violence, and we men do our best to shield them from it. But family is everything to them, just like it is to us. I don't doubt they could discover the same beast in themselves that Ana found. Salvatore knows that.

Maks has had enough.

"Salvatore, you know we know we have to maintain a balance. The Devil we know is better than the one we don't. We don't need the Porellos trying to move in. They'll fuck things up worse than the Murphys. You know that, so you know your *piccoli cretini,* as you like to call them, will live. But that doesn't mean your little cretins will look so pretty anymore. Keep them the fuck away from us."

He hangs up and looks at each of us.

"He knows our hands are tied no matter what threats we make. But that doesn't mean we ease off. If there's even a hint of a strike against us, we move on their gambling rings, take out their loan sharks, and start fencing their goods. Fuck them with bells on. That'll just be the first round."

"Do we wait for Carmine to mastermind one of his brilliant schemes?"

I want to know how soon we're making our move. It isn't an if, it's a when.

"Sergei's checking with our informants. We'll see what we can learn. Preemptive is what I prefer."

Maks's plan is reasonable, and we all know it. He looks at Niko, who's calmer but not calm.

"Whatever happens, you and Anton strategize. Pasha and Misha lead."

Our cousins are *avotoritets*, or brigadiers, who lead these types of ops. They'll task the right men with whatever strategy Anton and Niko devise, and they'll oversee their completion. If it comes to a fight, they'll lead the attack. We all wear plenty of hats in this family. It depends on the day and the situation. But Vlad trained us to be paramilitary. The other syndicates might be violent and have a well-stocked arsenal, but the Soviets didn't train them. Our—mentors, teachers, mind fuckers, whatever the fuck they were—were all former KGB and most were bratva before they left Russia. Only the Germans and Chinese are as meticulous about planning as Russians. Half of Germany was Communist anyway, and China technically still is. The only good fucking thing to come out of that system. Our training keeps us alive and ensures we win. Surviving the childhood we had and our blood bind us. What we endured—that would break most men. It'll break the Italians.

Chapter Six

Heather

I woke up alone. I remember Aleks telling me something about work and having to leave. It was the middle of the night, and now the spot where he slept is cold. The sheets are rumpled, and there's a condom wrapper on my bedside table. The spent condom made it to the trash. That's all that's left of the most amazing night of my life. Dinner, mini golf, and ice cream were just as fantastic as the earth-shatteringly good sex. I really enjoy Aleks's company. And the things the man can do with his tongue. It should be framed and kept for posterity. He was kind when we weren't physical, but he was exactly the type of rough I like.

I can't believe I called him Daddy, though. I'm almost glad he isn't here because that is so humiliating. I have nothing against the Daddy Dom/Little Girl lifestyle, but it isn't me. Age play doesn't appeal. But he was right about why the term Daddy feels right. I don't for a moment believe he thinks I'm not an adult and capable of behaving like one. But he's protective and chivalrous. I feel safe with him, whether it's from the wind, runaway bottles of soda in a parking lot, or trusting him to be rough without hurting me.

When I was with him last night, all I had to concentrate on was what we were doing. I didn't even have to think about it. I could just enjoy it. I'm not an indecisive person, but it was nice to follow. I've had to lead in plenty of my past relationships, and I hated it. At the very least, I wished they had been equal partnerships. But I was always the one to make the plans. I was always the one to put more effort into sex. I was always the one who—fucking everything. It didn't mean the guys weren't into me. I just had to be the dominant one. All. The. Time.

Submitting to Aleks last night freed me from that. I felt like his equal when we picked what we wanted to do and where to eat. But here, at my place, I submitted. I want to do it again. But did he mean everything he said? He came out, guns blazing. I'm surprised it didn't freak me out. Any other man would have felt clingy and psycho. Aleks was possessive, but I liked it. It was the "I'll protect you and take care of you" kind. Not the "I'll never let you see your friends again because you're my property" kind.

It's one o'clock, and I came back to school to work on some props for the production this week. I don't really need to be here. But I can't lie and say I'm not disappointed that I'm not spending the day with Aleks. Sure, thirty-six hours of sex sounds like bliss if it's with Aleks, but even if we'd watched a movie or gone for a walk, I would have enjoyed it.

I'm sorry I had to leave so abruptly malyshka.

I wasn't sure if I was going to hear from him. I hoped I would. But I didn't want to appear desperate and text to ask what the fuck happened, or when am I seeing you again, or was I a good enough lay for you to come back?

> It's all right. Is everything ok at work?

> Yes. Some goods were returned to us and it caused a big headache. But nothing that can't be fixed.

> That's good.

What else do I say? Is this pause because he expects me to say more? Doesn't he have anything to say?

> I had a fantastic time last night.

But...

Another pause. Is it my turn, or is there more coming, and he's still typing?

> Me too

> What're you doing right now?

> I'm on campus. Opening night for Hairspray is tomorrow. I wanted to be sure all the props were ready.

> Did you make everything?

> Lol. Hardly. The art students made most of it. The cast did a lot too. I may sing and dance but that's as far as my fine arts go. I shouldn't be allowed to hold a paintbrush.

> If you're the director or producer, do I still say break a leg?

> Um...I guess maybe blow them away.

Now there really is a long pause. Did he have to do something else? Is the conversation over? He didn't actually wish me good luck. I'm about to put my phone down when another message comes in.

> You'll have to send me a video from the play. I know you won't be on stage. But I'm curious about the wild hair and spraying it in place.

> Lmao. It's not actually about the stuff that comes out of a bottle. It's about an overweight girl who gets a spot on a dance show in the 1960s. She suddenly becomes famous and she tries to use that to make the show more inclusive. That's the very short summary.

> I wouldn't have guessed that.

I scrunched my eyes closed, then open one to look at my phone. Am I making a huge mistake?

> Would you like to come to opening night tomorrow? I won't be able to sit with you b/c I'll be backstage. But if you'd like, I can have tickets for you.

Tickets. He'll bring someone because who wants to go to a play alone? And what grown ass man who looks like Aleks wants to go to a high school musical? He wouldn't bring a date, would he?

A ticket. And I'd like that.

> Doors open at 7:30. Play starts at 8. I'll have one at the Will Call window for you.

I look forward to it. Malyshka I wish I could see you today but I have too much work. I'm sorry.

> Me: Don't be. I have stuff to do anyway.

I'll see you tomorrow night.

> Ok. See you then.

What else is there to say now? I'm not even in the play, but he's coming. I need to wrap my head around that. It's so sweet. No other guy I've dated would do this. Most didn't want to go to my performances in high school or college. He's willing to sit through two hours because this is important to me. He's a keeper.

"Places, everyone."

It's so cliché, but I loved hearing that phrase when I used to perform. The excitement, the nerves, then the thrill of being on stage. I miss it, but not enough to ever consider Broadway again. I had promise, but I hated the lifestyle. Or rather three bad experiences were enough to scare me away. Maybe I should try community theater.

The curtain goes up, and my cast launches into the opening scene. It's a blur from there. They're so good I barely have to do anything, but that doesn't mean I can merely stand around and watch. There's always something to check, someone to encourage, something to remember. It's exhilarating, then it's exhausting. I plan these productions for just before winter break, so everyone has time to recover.

"Go out and take your bow."

The two hours flew by. My leads bow and wave to the audience before the ensemble joins them.

"And a special thank you to our favorite director and teacher, Ms. Hampton."

I watch my students gesture for me to take my bow. I walk out, trying to scan the audience. But the theater lights make it so difficult to see. I look toward the front, and there he is. He's beaming at me, and my heart races. I'm so tempted to wave.

"Thank you, everyone, for joining us for opening night. It means the world to us to see a full house. These performers have put in a little blood, tons of sweat, and thankfully only a couple tears to make this one of the best productions we've ever had. We're thrilled you could be here."

I accept the bouquet, then I can't help it. I wave. It's big enough to appear directed to the entire audience, but I'm looking at Aleks. It's a small gesture, but I see him wave back. I follow the cast offstage, and we all do what we have to at the end of the show to be ready for tomorrow night's showtime. It takes me nearly forty-five minutes before I can leave. I didn't think about that when I invited Aleks. He's probably left. He'd be bored out of his mind if he didn't.

I slip past the curtain to take a final look at the stage and the orchestra pit.

"That was fantastic, *malyshka*."

He stayed. He's still in his seat, and he doesn't look aggrieved or bored. I hurry to take the steps down, and he picks up an enormous bouquet of roses. It had to be a small fortune. He meets me at the end of the row, and I hesitate for a moment, but he doesn't. His arm wraps around my waist, and he pulls me against him. I feel him harden as he kisses me. It's no peck. Nothing appropriate for the workplace or a school. It's a damn good thing I know we're alone.

I clutch his shirt since I feel like I'm going to float away. His kiss is heady, demanding I accept his desire. I gladly do. We're each holding a bouquet. He puts his down on the seat next to him, then puts the one I'm holding next to it. He squeezes my ass mercilessly, and I want to jump his bones. It wouldn't be the first time I've had sex in a theater, but I would never at work.

"I want to strip you bare and taste you. Are you wet for me, *malyshka?*"

"Soaked, Daddy."

"Do you have plans?"

I shake my head. I hoped we would do something, but I wasn't counting on him actually showing up. He hands me the bouquet he brought and kisses my cheek. It's petal-soft compared to what we just shared.

"Will you let me take you to dinner?"

"I'd like that."

We went to high school in Queens, but I teach in Harlem. There are tons of great places to eat near here. We could walk to several, but it's fucking cold tonight. He helps me with my coat before taking both bouquets and wrapping his arm around my waist. We walk outside, and I find a town car waiting for us. The poor driver. Has he been here for three hours? The guy's standing next to the open back door. You would think the car would be freezing, but it's perfect when I climb in. I slide over to my seat, but Aleks is barely in the car with the door closed before he lifts me into his lap. He puts the flowers where I sat for only a moment.

I'm sitting sideways as he kisses me. One hand rests on my hip, holding me close—not that he needs to. The other roams my tits, belly, and legs. I wore a dress, so he slides his hand underneath. The feel of his bare hands on my stockinged leg is torturous. I sense he doesn't like it as much as I do. I think he assumes I'm wearing pantyhose. Wishful thinking that something like this might happen made me choose thigh highs. When his hand meets bare skin, his kiss becomes even more determined. With one hand underneath my dress and one on top, he guides me to straddle him. Then his fingers are working their magic.

"Is this what my *malyshka* needs?"

He thrusts three fingers into me without preamble. I can't stop my hips from moving. I shake my head.

"Does my baby girl need me to suck her pussy?"

That's so tempting, but I shake my head.

"Do you need me to fuck you?"

"Yes."

It's a begging moan. I told myself not to rush anything if I saw him tonight. That was before he was holding me, touching me. He opens the armrest compartment, and I see the box of jumbo condoms. When they didn't arrive yesterday, I knew he'd canceled them. I'll admit I nearly cried when I got into bed and knew they weren't coming. He peels off the shrink wrap, and I think he kept it on, so I would know that he had used none with someone else. He rips one off the length of gold packets.

"Can I taste you, Daddy?"

I never had the chance to give him head.

"No, baby girl. There's something too cliché about a woman kneeling and sucking off a guy in a town car."

"You could lie down."

"You could tempt the Devil. I won't last if I feel your mouth wrapped around my dick. Are you having second thoughts, Heather? We don't have to do this—any of this—if you don't want."

"I just asked to give you a blow job. I think you know what I want...But thank you for asking, for being sure."

I unfasten his pants and pull down his boxer briefs. I still can't believe what I get to play with. Saying he has a big dick is like saying the Empire State Building is big. Understatement of the century. I glance at the condom wrapper and know these are way better than what I had. I roll one down as he pushes my dress up to see my thigh highs. His fingers press against the bare skin. When the condom's in place, he guides me onto his cock. Fucking hell. I close my eyes and savor the feeling.

I feel him slide my coat off, then the zipper at the back of my dress opens.

"Naughty, *malyshka*. No bra."

The dress is snug enough to make a bra unnecessary. In fact, a bra would make my boobs obscene along the neckline. But that's not why I didn't wear one.

"For you, Daddy."

I hoped the thigh highs and no bra would be sexy to him. I thought I'd be standing when I got undressed, but the look in his eyes tells me he doesn't care where we are. It's entirely predatory, and my pussy clenches.

"Do you like the way I look at you, baby girl?"

"Very much."

"I like the way you look at my dick."

"I like the way it feels in my pussy."

"I like that too. Do you want vanilla, Heather?"

"No. Aleks, please. It aches. I need to move."

He places the flowers on the floor and shifts us, so I'm lying on the seat. He has one knee on the seat, and his other foot braces him on the floor.

"How rough do you want it?"

"Rough enough to hurt."

He shakes his head.

"I will never let it get to that point, Heather. I will never intentionally hurt you. I'm too much bigger than you. I will not risk going too far. I'll give you as rough as you want, but I draw the line at possibly harming you."

Did I just fall in love?

I never feared he'd take it too far. I know he'll always be careful with me. But that he explained means everything to me. He's not just careful; he cares. I cup his jaw and curl up to press the softest kiss I can to his lips before I lie back.

"I trust you, Daddy."

He's so reserved I often can't tell what he's thinking or feeling. But he lets me in now. I see how much those four words mean to him. He rocks into me, and I clutch his shirt again. He snags both of my wrists and draws my arms over my head. He presses my hands to hold on to the end of the seat before that hand pinches my nipple. Hard. Like all my muscles clench. He doesn't ease up, instead twisting. I think I might come.

His other arm is bracing him, fully extended, as he watches me. I look down and hate that my dress bunched too much for me to see him. He can tell, or maybe he can't see either. He releases my nipple and smooths out the material. He shifts so the arm holding him up rests by my ear and his fingers can entwine with mine. Then he really thrusts. He slams into me, his weight and force pressing me into the seat so that I can't move. He's truly fucking me. I'm taking the pounding he's giving me. If I didn't know better, I would think he's just trying to get himself off, uncaring whether I do. But that's not Aleks. It's the exact opposite. The only thing he wants is to get me off.

"This feels so good, *sudar'*. I'm close."

"Do not come unless I tell you, you can. I will spank you, *malyshka*, if you disobey me."

He pumps his dick harder, knowing he's going to push me over the edge. I push my feet against the seat and floor, doing my best to lift and tilt my hips. It's all it takes. I'm doing everything I can not to scream. My nails are pressing into the leather.

He pulls out, flips me onto my hands and knees, and rains down five spanks that make me kick my feet. Fuck they really sting. Then he's pulling my hips toward him, and I can feel his mouth around my clit. He sucks as his tongue works the sensitive bundle of nerves. I come again.

He surges into me, and he doesn't hold back. Or rather, he gets to that threshold of hurting me and doesn't push me beyond. His grip on my hips keeps me from moving on my own, but the force of his thrusts makes me rock on my arms and my tits swing. He turns us, so I'm kneeling and gripping the head rest while his legs bracket mine. Thank God for tinted windows, or the cars behind us would know what we're doing.

He slides his arm is around my waist as the other hand moves hair out of the way. He grazes his teeth along my neck, nipping where it meets my shoulder.

"You came twice without my permission, *malyshka*. I will edge you until you think the need to come might kill you."

"It already might, Daddy. I need to again. Please don't tell me no."

"Why shouldn't I? Who's in control, baby girl?"

"You. But I can't help it. I don't understand why my body responds to you like this. I don't understand why I need you so much. I—"

Waves of emotion crash over me, and suddenly, I'm scared I'm going to burst into tears. Aleks immediately pulls out of me and moves to sit with me straddling him again. He's inside me, but he pulls me to lean against him. He tucks my head against the crook of his neck and strokes my hair while his other hand guides me into a slower, gentler pace.

"Come, *malyshka*. I'll give you whatever you need."

"Just you."

His kiss is tender as he turns his head toward mine. His hand cradles my skull, but there's no pressure there. He's just holding it. My left hand cups his jaw as my other hand tries to slide around his waist, but he has his back pressed to the seat-back. I settle for resting it at his waist. My clit rubs against his pubic bone, and it sets off another orgasm. This time, I know he's coming too. Our kiss is a series of pecks.

"Baby, just rest. I'll hold you."

My eyes droop closed. He's still inside me, and I've never felt closer to a single human being. The moment he thought something was wrong, he changed how we had sex to give me what I needed. He went from rough to tender in an instant. Who is this hulking man? One moment I know he could smash me just like the superhero could. The next, he's gentle, like I'm made of porcelain or something.

"I'm sorry, Aleks."

"It's still Daddy. And there is nothing to be sorry about. I know I show little emotion, but it doesn't mean I don't feel them, *malyshka*."

I sigh. He understands. And saying he doesn't show much emotion is putting it mildly. Any time I can tell what he's feeling, it's because he lets me. I'm understanding that now. Does he think he's weak if he lets me see it? Or is he so shut off that he doesn't want to let me in?

No, that's not right. He is showing emotion, just not on his face. The way he treats me, the way he's holding me. I think he feels something beyond just lust. God, I pray he does. I sure as shit do.

Chapter Seven

Aleks

My mind is at war yet again. It's torn between what the fuck am I doing, and how can I hold on to Heather and never let go. The sex just keeps getting better. One moment it was the best fuck I've ever had, and the next, I think I might have made love for the first time in my life. I loved both. My need to meet her needs is unprecedented. I made sure I pleasured the women in my past, and I never got off until they did. But their emotions were never a consideration. Not beyond them being satisfied, at least.

Heather is entirely different. Part of why I never cared was because I never felt attuned to any other woman's feelings beyond lust and pleasure. It's like I feel Heather's emotions as my own. It's not like I used to be incapable, and now I suddenly can. It was disinterest, knowing that nothing could be permanent, and really just self-centeredness. The only thing that's the same with Heather is knowing it can't be permanent. And that's like a gunshot to the heart. It leaves a gaping hole.

Now guilt is settling in. I shouldn't be this tender and caring toward her when I know this will only end. Badly.

But as I gaze down at her, I want to hold her and never let go. I want to be worthy of her trust. It's so different from any other type anyone has given me. My brothers trust me to always be at their side, to always share the burden of our lifestyle and duty. My mother trusts me to always do my best to come home alive. My men trust me not to get them killed. I value all of that, but Heather's trust is more fragile. She trusts me not to break her heart. And that's what I'm going to do. And, in the process, I'm going to do the same thing to myself.

"*Malyshka*, we're here."

She leans back as the car pulls to a stop. She glances out the window as she scrambles to slip her dress over her shoulders.

"Shh. No one will open the door until I let them know we're ready, baby girl."

I zip her dress up, and she moves to the other seat and puts her coat on while I make myself presentable again. I wrap the condom in tissues and fasten my pants, feeling the gun at my lower back press harder against my spine as my pants tighten. It's why I couldn't let her slip her arm around my waist.

When I'm certain we're ready, I rap on the window. Once I'm standing, I reach in and help her out. I don't let go of her hand as she looks around.

"Are we in Queens?"

"Yes. I figured you might get tired and want to go home. I thought doing the drive back sooner rather than later would be easier for you."

She nods but won't meet my gaze as I look down at her. I stop and use my forefinger to guide her chin toward me. I raise my eyebrows, but I don't ask her to share her thoughts. Maybe she doesn't want to.

"You want to take me home right after dinner?"

"*Malyshka*, if you want to do something after we eat, we can. If you're tired and want to go home, then I'll take you there. If you want me to go, I will. If you want me to stay, I'll have you naked and in bed with me faster than you can say your own name."

I'm unprepared for how quickly she moves to hug me. I barely get her arms above my waist in time for her not to feel my gun. I get mine beneath hers, which brings hers up to my ribs. I'm not ready to explain why I carry one, and it will definitely ruin the night.

"Thank you, Daddy."

We go inside and slide into a booth that lets us sit close enough to hold hands over the table but still look at each other. Our food arrives, and my phone rings.

"Bogdan, I'm in the middle—"

"Someone shot at Maks and Laura."

"*Kakaya?*" What? I switch to Russian because whatever Bogdan says, I can't respond in English. Heather's watching me. She knows this isn't a casual conversation, even if I keep my tone light. My brother continues in Russian.

"They took the twins out to dinner. They'd just strapped them into their car seats, and they were about to climb into the third row when a bullet hit the glass beside Maks's shoulder. Another hit the tire next to Laura on the other side."

"Are they hurt? The twins?"

My heart is racing as I ask.

"No. They got inside and got the doors closed before more bullets hit the car. Fyodor was driving them. He's back to being Maks's regular driver as of yesterday. Niko feels better with Ilya, and Pasha wants Alexi. I have Stefan."

I knew my brothers and cousin made permanent assignments because they want to be sure they can trust whoever drives their wives to be the best security they can provide. The women don't go anywhere unless one of my brothers, or cousins, or I can go along.

"Who was with them? Sergei or Anton? Are they okay?"

"It was Sergei, and he was next to Laura. He helped her into the car and got in just before a bullet hit his window. It would have gone through the back of his skull."

"Where is everyone?"

"Mama's. They were closer to her."

They all live in the same neighborhood, just on different streets. If they went to our mom's instead of their own home, they were desperate to get off the street.

"I'm in Queens, but I can't get there right away. I'm on my way, though."

"What're you doing in Queens?"

My place is in Manhattan. Misha, Sergei, Anton, and I are the only ones left in that borough.

"Having dinner. I'll be there as soon as I can. Bye."

"Bye."

I put my phone back in my pocket. I watched Heather throughout the entire conversation. She grew more anxious the longer I talked.

"Was it work? Do you have to go again?"

She's trying to sound understanding.

"It's not work, but I need to go." I rake my hand through my hair. "Heather, my brothers and I, even our cousins, aren't the poor immigrants we used to be. We've done extremely well. There are people who think we shouldn't have, that we shouldn't own so many companies—especially the ones we've bought out—so there are threats sometimes. I don't know all the details, but something happened. I need to be with my family right now."

"Is everyone all right? We can get doggy bags. I can get an Uber or cab."

"We'll get the food to go, and you are not taking an Uber. I'll take you home. I just can't stay. I want to, Heather. But my family..."

"They come first."

"Right now, they do."

What am I implying? That maybe one day they won't. That a wife might become more important. She will, but she'll also be family, which means it'll always come first.

"I understand, Aleks. I'm bummed, but I'm not mad."

She squeezes my hand that she's still holding. I signal the waitress and ask for our food to be boxed. Five minutes later, we're in the car. Ten minutes later, I'm standing in her doorway.

"Thank you for coming to the show tonight. And thank you for sticking around."

"I enjoyed the show, but I came to see you. I wasn't leaving until I did."

She has the flowers in one arm, so I'm careful not to crush them as I pull her against me. I'm getting hard, and it's only going to frustrate me more that I have to leave. She sat beside me in the car with my arm around her. I knew I wouldn't let her go if she sat on my lap. I knew I'd fuck her, then dump her at her door. I didn't want that. I didn't want to fuck and dash.

"Thank you."

"I don't know what's going on yet. There's a chance I might be away for a few days, and I might not be able to get in touch. If that happens, I'm not ghosting you, Heather."

Away for a few days means the warehouse where we take care of those people we need gone. My phone will be off, so it's not a distraction and can't be tracked. The outside world ends when we enter the warehouse. Everything ceases to exist except for what we must do—the men we must become.

"I understand."

She couldn't, possibly.

Our kiss is brief and light when all I want to do is devour her, savor her since I don't know when—if—I'll get another. I need to stop doing this to her and to me. This has to end. I won't ghost her. Christina thought Bogdan did the first time he had to go the warehouse. It nearly ended their relationship. Grrr. That's exactly what I should do with Heather. End the relationship.

"Goodnight, *malyshka*."

"Goodnight, Daddy."

I need to jack off on the way to Maks and Laura's. What that one word does to me.

"Who?"

I only need the one word in Russian as I enter my mom's living room. Everyone rallied here. Christina and Sumiko don't speak Russian, so Maks answers in English.

"We don't know. They tinted the windows to the point of being illegal. They used rifles with sniper periscopes because not even eyes were visible. The vehicles didn't have plates either. Whoever this was didn't trust even stolen ones to hide their identity."

"Do you think it was the Irish or the Italians?"

I look at Maks first as I ask, then I look at the others in the room. It's Sergei who answers.

"It could be either. We have enough intel to know they're both in a position to strike. But we don't have enough info about tonight to know who. I'm working on it. I've already scanned the city camera footage, but there's nothing besides a car driving by. You can't even tell they fired any shots."

It's not a surprise that these fuckers used silencers, but

there's usually something that'll show gunshots. I'm certain Sergei watched the footage frame by frame.

"Laura, are you and the twins all right?"

I look at my sister-in-law, who's sitting next to Maks. My brother is holding both Konstantin and Mila. Laura has her arm wrapped around all three. Maks is rattled. He's an affectionate father, just like our dad was. But I'm surprised the babies aren't fussing from how tightly he's holding them. His biceps are straining his sleeves. Laura appears calmer than him. She's not. I'm sure of that. But she looks like it.

"Yeah. I'm shaken. They're in milk comas and happy to have their papa hold them."

If Laura and the twins are fine, and there's no actionable intel, I nearly don't see the point of why I had to leave Heather to be here. But family first. It's how we endured the torture Vlad inflicted upon us as he trained us. We were boys, and he made us into monsters. He would beat us if any of us made a mistake. If we didn't move fast enough, didn't answer fast enough, showed any reaction.

He manipulated Maks the most as the oldest, but Bogdan took the worst of the physical abuse because he was the youngest. Stuck in the middle, I'll never get over my guilt that I wasn't either of them. I got my fair share, but it wasn't the same as what they experienced. Vlad knew that about Niko and me. It was its own kind of torture.

Niko asks what we all want to know.

"What do we do?"

Is this just a waiting game to see how these unknown attackers will strike next? Or do we hit the Italians and the Irish?

I consider what Maks suggests.

"We fuck up Salvatore's building sites and steal from their money launderers. We break Dillan's dockside equipment and trash a couple warehouses. No deaths unless they're unavoidable. We're not carrying this too far, but we are sending a message."

As his second-in-command, it's my job to question him if I think something is unsound. Niko and Bogdan have that duty too, as the other members of the Elite Group, but my voice is meant to be the loudest. I don't dissent. Instead, I add to his suggestions.

"We don't just take the money. Whatever's in the Irish warehouses is ours. We hide it in Connecticut at our storage containers until we can sell it. We make an anonymous call about a fire tomorrow night after we break up that gambling ring Salvatore has going in Hell's Kitchen."

I look at Niko first and wait for his decision.

"Works for me."

Then Bogdan.

"I like it. Anton'll decide how to do it. We can go from there."

Maks nods and looks at our younger two cousins before giving his next instructions.

"Misha, you head the Italian ops. Pasha, you have the Irish."

As our *obshchak*, Anton is our best strategist and head enforcer. He's sometimes an *avotoritet*, but usually it's Misha and Pasha these days who are our brigadiers. We've all been *avotoritets*, but our roles have shifted over the years. They're our best drivers on ops because they're only a hair's breadth from reckless on the roads. They're also strong leaders with quick minds and the ability to assess and adjust course when needed. The rest of us may be senior to them in the hierarchy, but we all follow their orders when they're in charge.

Pasha's being smart when he divides us into his team and Misha's.

"Bogdan and Maks, you go with Misha to deal with the Italians. Aleks and Niko are with me."

Maks and Bogdan are too invested in a vendetta against the Irish. The same is true with Niko and Pasha with the Italians. It's better if they focus on the opposite group. I'm in no-man's-land. I loathe both for what they've done to our family, but my animosity isn't visceral like theirs.

"Sleep here. We start before dawn."

That's an edict from Maks that we won't argue. Even though none of us have lived with our mom in this house, we each have a bedroom. She's listened silently to the entire conversation, but now she's whispering with the wives. They know what to expect, but they all rely on my mom. She leans on them as much as they do her. It's been almost eighteen years since my dad died. Her broken heart will never heal, but she is an amazing mom to all of us. My brothers and I are grateful that the wives care about her as though she were their own mom.

I look over at Pasha, since I'm standing closest to him.

"Are your parents coming too?"

"Yeah. And Svetlana and Radomir will be here. They're all coming in a couple hours, just before we go."

Anton and Pasha's father was my father's brother. Uncle Grigori looks so much like my dad did that sometimes it hurts to see him. But he's loved us like extra sons, and so has Aunt Alina. She was my mom's best friend growing up. Aunt Svetlana is my mother's sister and Sergei and Misha's mom. She met Uncle Radomir through my dad and Uncle Grigori. My aunts and uncles fell in love within days of meeting each other. My parents fell in love when they were five, or so the story goes.

If we can, we never leave on missions without saying goodbye to our parents. As adults, my brothers, cousins, and I understand what my brothers and I didn't as children. This could be our last goodbye, so we never waste it. We couldn't imagine as kids that when we said goodbye to our dad before he left for the Second Chechen War, it was the last time we would.

Our grief isn't a constant companion anymore, but none of us—my cousins included—wants to make our parents relive losing my dad. None of us want to cause our mom that kind of pain. She'd survive it just like she did my dad's death because she has a family who needs her. But I don't know that she'd ever recover. I don't know that I would if I lost one of my brothers. It would be nearly as devastating to lose any of my cousins. We're as close as brothers, but there's something about sharing the exact same blood that makes the bond different.

I strip down to my boxer briefs and sit on the edge of the bed with my phone in my hands. I'm hunched over, looking at it. A plan is always better than an impulse. I recite that over and over, trying to convince myself. I'm so far from impulsive that most people would say I'm boring. But I'm struggling right now.

I left so abruptly that it's only polite to say goodnight to Heather and to apologize for leaving in a hurry.

> I'm sorry I couldn't stay. It's good that I'm with my family but I wish I could be with you. Was your dinner any good by the time you got to it?

I wait for what feels like an eternity, and nothing comes back. Is she pissed? I hope I didn't hurt her by running off twice. But that's my life. My family can rely on me for anything, but I'd be totally unreliable for her. I put the phone on the bedside table and climb under the covers. I'm suddenly exhausted, and my eyes drift closed.

My phone buzzes. If it was anyone in my family, they would just come to my room. I turn the screen on and tap the notification.

> Sorry. My phone was on silent from the play. I was brushing my teeth.

She sends the toothbrush and toothy grin emojis.

> No worries. Was the food any good by the time you got home?

> I zapped it for a couple minutes so it was. Yours?

I forgot about mine. I left it in the car. I hope Mikhail finds it before it makes the car stink.

> Saving it for later.

There's a pause for a minute before her next message comes in.

> Thanks again for coming tonight. It means a lot to me.

Fuck. It means a lot to me too. I want to tell her I'm proud of my *malyshka*. But I'm just digging myself in deeper. I should fucking end it. But the same impulse that made me text her says don't break it off. All three of my brothers and one of my cousins have wives. They're making it work.

But I won't risk Heather's life. They might be willing to do that with their women, but I'm not.

> It was a wonderful evening. Goodnight, Heather.

There. A little formality and distance. It doesn't match the tone of my other texts.

> Goodnight, Aleksei.

There's not been a damn good thing about this night since Bogdan called. The morning promises to be worse.

Chapter Eight

Heather

It's been twelve days since I got the goodnight text from Aleks. He said I shouldn't think he ghosted me, but what the fuck else am I supposed to think? These days, who goes nearly two weeks without being able to call or text someone?

Maybe it wouldn't be so bad, but half this time I've been on winter break with nothing to keep myself occupied. Gloria listens to me prattle, and she'll fall asleep in my lap during a movie, but it's not like she's offering any scintillating conversation or giving me orgasms that make my toes curl. Despite what most people would think about theater teachers, I have grading. But I finished that by the Monday break started. I worked over that first weekend, hoping it would free me to see Aleks this week. But alas...

"If you're not doing anything tonight, could you watch Cadence, so Mike and I can go out?"

I love my nephew, but he is hardly the distraction I want.

"Sure, Danielle. What time?"

"How about seven? I'll make sure he's had dinner and his bath. You can just hang out and eat the junk food you won't let yourself have at your place."

"That's better than getting paid."

"I know. I'll see you then. Thanks, sis."

That gives me enough time to shower and get to Connecticut. I'm washing cleanser from my eyes when my doorbell rings. Shit. I hurry to finish and grab my robe. I'm wrapping a towel around my hair as I walk to the door. Whoever it is rings the bell again.

"Coming!"

I check the peephole and practically yank the door off its hinges.

"I'll make you come."

That's my greeting from Aleks as he steps inside, kicks the door closed, and presses me against the wall. His kiss threatens to overwhelm me. He pulls the towel from my hair and pulls open my robe. His shirt buttons press into my tits as he grabs my ass. I'm fumbling with his belt, but I can't get it undone because he's pressed too close to me. I try to get his suit coat off, but he won't let go of me to slide it down his arms.

He drops to one knee, and his mouth is on my clit. He groans as his tongue flicks inside me. He's still holding onto my ass, and it's keeping me from sagging as my knees go weak. He hooks my right leg over his shoulder and redoubles his efforts.

"Daddy, please. I need to come."

"Not until I'm inside you. Your bed, now."

I hurry to follow his command. He tosses his suit coat on the bed. He's not wearing a tie. I see he has a condom in his hand, which he tosses to me as I watch him strip. His pants and boxer briefs come off in record time, then his shirt drops to the floor a second after his other clothes. He kicks off his shoes and socks.

Then he's on the bed, his fists supporting him as I roll the condom onto him. He thrusts into me.

"Fuck, *malyshka*. I didn't intend to walk in and ravage you, even if I had a hard on the entire way here. Then you said coming, and I couldn't hold back. I'm inside you now. Come as often as you can. I missed you so much."

"I missed you, *sudar'*." I glance at the clock. "But this has to be a quickie. I have to babysit Cadence tonight. I should leave in five minutes."

"How do you want it?"

I consider him for a moment. I want the passion and the roughness that makes me feel more desirable than any other woman in the world. But I've been sad. I have missed him, and it has scared me I turned him off.

"Vanilla, Daddy."

"If that's what you need."

I nod, and he lowers himself to his forearms. His kisses are languid and gentle. I still feel the passion, but I don't feel like he's going to consume me. His touch, as his hand roams over my ribs and breast, is soft. He draws my leg over his hip and holds my thigh as he thrusts. He's moving slowly, but he's in balls deep each time. My hands touch every part of him I can reach.

"I'm coming, Daddy."

"I know, baby. I feel you."

"I want to make you come too."

"You are." He growls. "Fuck. I can't last any longer, baby girl."

"Good. I want to know you want me that much."

"I want you more than I should. You're a drug, Heather. I'd sell my soul for another hit, another chance to be inside you."

"But drugs destroy. That's not what I want."

"Fine. A multivitamin. I know I'm better when I'm with you."

I can't help but laugh. My core contracts, and he thrusts hard before going still. He rests his forehead against mine. I cup his jaw.

"I have never been called a multivitamin before. That might be one of the weirdest and most romantic things I've ever heard."

I sigh as we kiss once more. Part of it is from satisfaction and post-coital bliss. But part of it is regret because I can't linger.

"How late do you think your sister will be out?"

"She and Mike'll probably be back by ten. Danielle isn't a night owl and never has been. Sleeping Beauty likes her rest. I can't blame her since she's home with Cadence all day. He's exhausting."

I consider what Danielle and Mike would say if Aleks came with me. It's not like I'm a teenager having my boyfriend over.

"Can I drop you off? Then—if you want—a driver could bring you into Manhattan. Or I—"

Aleks looks so uncertain, even nervous. He's worried now that our impromptu sex is over, I don't want to see him.

"Cadence goes to bed at eight. We'd have two hours to ourselves. Would you like to come with me?"

"Yeah. That would be nice."

"Okay. We have to get going."

He's back in his suit nearly as fast as I pick out jeans and a top. He watches me as I put on a bra and panties. He scowls at the thong. I laugh. It surprises me to see his Land Rover parked outside. I assumed he would be in a town car, especially since he said he'd send a driver to get me. Then again, he said he would drop me off.

He held the door open to the elevator and waited for me to get on first. Then he held the door open to my building and let me go ahead of him. Now he's holding the car door open.

Something tells me that someone ingrained these manners in his very soul. He's not trying to impress me or flatter me. How old-fashioned were his parents?

"Did you have a good time wherever you went?"

I try to keep my tone light. He glances at me before he answers. He just programmed my sister's address into his GPS.

"It was work. I got to spend time with my brothers, and even my cousins, but it wasn't a vacation. It got pretty monotonous."

"What were you doing?"

He seems to hesitate for a moment, but then he comes back with a solid answer.

"Negotiations sucked us in, and it got combative. It took some strategizing and patience, but it paid off. We gained what we wanted, but the cost was more than we planned. Before the negotiations started, we had to do some assessments and make a final determination on the valuation of the arrangement. Then we needed to ensure our valuation was accurate. So boring stuff, basically."

"Is that all real estate or venture capitalism stuff?"

I don't really understand what venture capitalism is. I think it's just investing in businesses that'll make you money.

"No. We handle a lot of international trade. We were dealing with some foreign adversaries."

We chat about how the rest of the week's performances went and what I've been doing since break started. He hears my hesitation as I tell him about my time off. He entwines his fingers with mine and brings my knuckles to his lips. He kisses them without taking his eyes off the road. We pull up to my sister's house in the burbs, and it's picture perfect with the solar powered lights along the brick path from the sidewalk to the door. There are potted flowers on the stoop. My brother-in-law's sports car is sitting in the driveway. I knock before I let myself in.

"Danielle? Mike?"

"Auntie H!"

Cadence comes skidding into the foyer from the kitchen in footie pajamas.

"Hulk!"

He skips me and crashes into Aleks's legs. Aleks squats down, so he's eye level with my nephew.

"Hey, little man. Have you been smashing those veggies?"

Cadence scowls, then gives his head a guilty shake.

"Are you still eating dinner?"

Cadence nods.

"Do you have vegetables to eat?"

He nods again.

"What do you have?"

"Beets and spinach."

Aleks tries not to grimace. Apparently, one of those is not a favorite.

"Those are good for you."

He doesn't look as convinced about the veggies as he did a moment ago.

"Do you want some, Hulk?"

"Cadence, it's Mr. Aleks not Hulk."

Aleks smiles at me, and my heart melts. It's boyish and relaxed. He looks younger than thirty when he grins like that.

"I'll still smash some beets and spinach with you, but only if you promise to eat yours."

"Fine. Mommy!"

Shit. I didn't tell Danielle that Aleks was coming with me. I haven't told her anything about Aleks, so she doesn't even know I went on a date with him or that he came to my play. I was too disappointed when I didn't hear from him. I didn't want any pity.

We follow Cadence into the kitchen, where Danielle and Mike are both standing at the island with a glass of wine.

"Hi." I turn back to Aleks. "Danielle, Mike, this is Aleks. Aleks, these are my sister and brother-in-law."

My relatives look perplexed. I can't blame them.

"Aleks and I met a few weeks ago and went out. But he's been away for work and just got back. He stopped by after we talked, Danielle."

"You're Aleks Kutsenko, right?"

I wasn't sure if my sister would recognize him.

"I was in Maks's class. I almost didn't recognize you."

"We all look a bit different."

Yeah. He went from being handsome in high school to the hottest fucking man on Earth as an adult. I watch as he sits down next to Cadence. He glances at the stove, and I can see where there's still some food left. I grab a plate and give him a healthy portion of the beets and the spinach before I grab a fork. He looks at the plate in front of him, and he looks like he might be ill.

"You take a bite for every two I take. Auntie Heather gave me a grown-up portion."

He doesn't sound thrilled, but he takes two bites of beets and one of spinach. Did he almost choke on the beets? Cadence watches him, but he eats along with Aleks. I'm pretty sure Aleks keeps holding his breath every time he takes a bite of beets. He loathes them. Aw. Poor sweet guy.

When they both finish, Cadence carries his plastic plate to the sink, and Aleks follows with his regular one. He listens to Cadence's instructions about rinsing and loading the dishwasher. Cadence goes over to Mike and reaches up. I was too intent upon watching Aleks and my nephew to notice how

Danielle and Mike were watching the pair. They're stunned. Danielle shakes her head in amazement.

"I can't believe you got him to eat all of that. He hates beets."

"Mr. Aleks told me I have to eat my vegetables to be big like he is. He's like the Incredible Hulk."

"But not green."

Aleks winks as he reminds Cadence.

"Auntie H, can we play with Thomas and Percy?"

He loves his toy trains. He might, possibly, have a college tuition's worth in his playroom.

"Of course."

"Okay. I'm gonna set them up."

Cadence wiggles down from Mike's hold and darts toward the stairs. Now that Cadence is gone, and the vegetable eating show is over, I notice Mike grows wary. Is he annoyed I brought someone—a guy—with me? Aleks is standing next to me again, so I turn to him.

"You didn't look like you enjoyed the beets."

He looks pained.

"I didn't. I'm not a fan."

"You looked like you were going to be ill."

I can't help but laugh as I point out what I saw.

"Beets are a popular food in Russian cuisine. When I was a kid, I thought they only grew in Russia. When we came to America, I thought I'd escaped. My mom made *borscht* the first night we were in our apartment. I cried. I was thirteen."

I lean against him. I notice his arm slides underneath mine, so my arm is around his ribs. He does that every time. I wonder why. I'm a lot shorter than him, so it's not the most comfortable.

"You were a good sport. Thank you."

His gaze is soft when he looks down at me. I think he would

kiss me if we were alone. I rest my head against his chest instead as I turn back to my family.

"What're you going to do?"

Mike's tone is a little rough when he answers.

"Just dinner. We should be back by nine-thirty."

I glance up at Aleks when I realize they're staring at each other. Aleks sounds more hospitable when he speaks.

"I hope you have a good time."

Danielle glances between the two men, then shoots me an "I-have-no-idea" look. They head out, and Aleks and I go to find Cadence. Aleks jumps in and starts building train tracks without hesitation. My phone pings. It's my brother-in-law.

> I want your Russian mafia boyfriend out of my house. Now.

I stare at my phone before I look at Aleks.

> He drove me.

I don't know what else to say. What's Mike talking about? Did Danielle tell him about the rumors from high school?

> I don't care. He leaves or I call the cops.

> You're overreacting.

> Call your dad. Ask him what he thinks about you dating a mobster.

> He is not a mobster.

> Then let's three-way call your dad.

"*Malyshka*, what's wrong?"

Aleks gets up and crosses the room to where I've practically backed myself into a corner. I don't know what to say. I don't want to lie, but I'm so embarrassed. I don't want him to go, but I can't leave too.

"*Malyshka*, what's wrong? Don't make me ask a third time."

The command in his voice distracts me long enough to push the limits and not answer.

"Baby girl, something is the matter. You're upset, and I can't help if I don't know what's wrong. You're purposely not answering my question. I will spank you, and it won't be for fun. What's wrong?"

I glance at Cadence, but he can't hear us as we whisper. I look up at Aleks and hand him my phone. He scans the texts.

> This is Aleks. I'll leave. I drove Heather, so I will send a town car for her. Just give her a thirty-minute heads up if you can.

"Aleks, no. You don't have to go."

"Yes, I do. This isn't my home. If your brother-in-law isn't comfortable with me here, then I'll go."

The phone pings.

> She's not getting in one of your cars. She doesn't take rides from the mafia. I don't trust that she'll get home. I'll drive her.

Aleks is still holding the phone, but I can see the screen. I take it back and respond.

> You don't get to decide Mike. Aleks agreed to leave. I'll take the town car. It's stupid to have you drive me all the way to Queens just for you to turn around and come back to CT.

> Call your dad or I will.

"Can you stay with Cadence? I'm going to call him. He'll put it on speaker. I want to hear what my sister has to say. This is nuts."

"No, *malyshka*. This isn't worth a battle with your family. I'll go. If he's that uncomfortable with you being in one of our town cars, then let him drive you home. We can see each other another night."

"No." I shake my head. "It's been nearly two weeks since I saw you. I missed you, Daddy. I—Take my keys and go to my place. Be there when I get home."

I nearly tell him I can't stand the idea of being alone another night. He considers what I say before he nods. He's reluctant, but he agrees. This fucking sucks.

He's leaving.

You should have called your dad.

My phone rings, and I can see it's a three-way call. It's Mike's and my dad's numbers on the screen. Fuck my life.

"Now what?"

I whisper, even though Cadence is completely entertained playing by himself. A true only child.

"Answer, *malyshka*. I can go now, or I can stay until you get off the phone."

"Stay." I blurt my answer before I answer the call. "Hi, Dad."

"Hi, honey. Mike said we need to talk to him about the guy you're dating."

"Mike had no business calling you, Dad. I'm dating Aleksei Kutsenko."

There's a long pause before anyone speaks. It's my dad who fills the void.

"You went to school with them, didn't you?"

"Yes. I was in Niko's class. He's the brother who's one year younger than Aleks. Danielle was in Maks's class. He's the oldest and a year older than Aleks."

"Have you been going out long?"

"A couple weeks. Dad, this is none of anyone's business. Aleks is about to leave. I need to say goodbye. I'm hanging up."

"Why's Aleks leaving?"

My dad honestly sounds confused. It's Mike who talks before I can.

"I want that thug out of my house and away from my kid."

My blood is boiling as I speak next.

"How do you even know anything about the Kutsenkos, Mike? Danielle, I know you can hear this. What did you tell Mike?"

"Nothing. Just what I remember about them from high school."

Danielle sounds really nervous. I almost feel bad for her. If anyone is really trapped in the middle, it's her. But I'm getting heated. Mike doesn't make it any better, as he keeps bitching.

"Heather, I work for RK Group. It's a company Kutsenko Partners merged with, then did a hostile takeover. The woman who negotiated a forty-billion-dollar deal for us then represented the Kutsenkos during the takeover. She married Maksim. They should disbar her."

I know Aleks can hear everything. I'm watching him, but he's showing no emotion. Not even when Mike mentions Aleks's family. If anything, he's even more shuttered than before. I wish Mike would shut the fuck up, but he doesn't.

"Everyone at RK knows they're Russian mafia. Only the senior partners wanted the merger, but no one wanted the acquisition. Laura fucking warned us it was coming, then she jumps fucking ship. She wasn't the attorney of record, but I know the bitch was behind it all."

I can't believe he's swearing in front of my dad. Even though Aleks's expression is completely neutral, I can feel the anger pulsating from him. But he remains quiet. He won't butt in. It's my dad who responds to Mike, which is good because I have nothing to say. I don't give a shit about Mike's job.

"I remember four nice young men who used to shovel snow in winter for free for the elderly in their neighborhood. I also remember they all worked year round to help support their family, since their mom is a widow. My guess is they're the same as they were back then, but probably just bigger. Mike, Heather is twenty-eight. She can date who she wants. If you don't want Aleks at your house, I'm certain he'll leave without a fuss. But don't come tattling to me again."

Is my jaw on the floor? I mean, I agree with my dad. But I can't believe he just told Mike not to tattle. This is not going to fucking blow over.

"Dad, I'm going to hang up. Aleks is ready to go. He waited to make sure I'm okay. Mike, I accept the ride home. Actually— you know what—no, I won't. I don't want to be stuck in the car with you for an hour. I'll take an Uber or Lyft."

Now Aleks reacts. He shakes his head. He doesn't look like he's backing down. I hold the phone away from my ear as he leans in to whisper.

"Either take the ride from Mike, or you Uber a block away and I pick you up, or my driver does. You are not Ubering for an hour. Pick. Do not argue with me, *malyshka*."

I don't understand why he's angry about this. I've taken plenty of ride services or cabs. I whisper back to him.

"I'll Uber to the McDonalds four blocks away. Then you drive me home."

He nods before he turns back to Cadence, who's now watching us and rubbing his eyes. I hear him say something about brushing teeth. Cadence skips down the hall to the bathroom. I follow with the phone back to my ear.

"Dad, I'm hanging up. Cadence needs to brush his teeth, and it's bedtime. Aleks is leaving. Bye."

I don't wait for anyone to respond. I hang up. I watch Cadence on the stepstool as he does a surprisingly thorough job.

"It's all right, *malyshka*. I'll wait for you, then I'll take you home. We'll talk then."

He gives me a kiss before I watch him from the landing. He looks back and waves before closing the front door behind him. I barely get Cadence tucked in before I hear the garage door open. Then the kitchen door slams. I'm pulling up the Uber app as I hurry downstairs. I've ordered the car by the time I get to the kitchen. I've saved our addresses, so it only takes me a minute. A car will be here in less than five.

"Cadence is in bed. I'm leaving. Danielle, I'll talk to you later."

"Where is he, Heather?"

"He left, Mike. You told him to go, so he did. He respects that Cadence is your son, and this is your home. He would have gone sooner if you hadn't been a dick and called Dad."

"Heather—"

"No, Danielle. This was completely out of line. If he doesn't want Aleks here, that's fine. I can understand and accept that. But it wasn't cool calling Dad like I'm some naughty kid who needs her parents called into the principal's office."

"You know the rumors from high school. What if they're true? He's dangerous."

I know this scares my sister, but I laugh.

"The man who forced himself to eat beets, so your son would eat his, is not a danger to me."

I don't convince her.

"Maybe not to you, but that doesn't mean he isn't dangerous. Heather, I'm worried too."

"The same rumors went around about Nadia's family, but that didn't stop you from being friends with her. She was a total bitch, but you wanted to be popular. Hearing her dad and brothers were mafia didn't stop you from hanging out at her house."

"I wasn't fucking her."

Danielle blurts out her response and shocks all three of us.

"But she went to prom with Maks. You double dated with them and shared the limo. A limo that no one had to chip in on but magically appeared. Maks made the arrangements, and you didn't question it."

"We were in high school then. We're adults now. Whatever he's into has to be way worse than any rumor from high school."

"You're making a lot of assumptions. Say what you claim is true. I still don't feel afraid to be with him. All three of his brothers are married, and Pasha is, too. Clearly, four women were willing to marry into the family."

Mike smirks before cutting in.

"They're probably mafia too."

"Mike, that would mean your firm hired a mobster for a lawyer. That means you have no leg to stand on. She got your company forty-billion, and even if Kutsenko Partners acquired RK Group, you still have a job. You could have been out on your ass. Don't look a gift horse in the mouth."

I give my sister a quick hug.

"My Uber is here. Goodnight."

"Heather—"

"Goodnight, Danielle. I love you. Night, Mike."

I'm not feeling even remotely loving toward my brother-in-law. He can go fuck himself. I don't look back as I leave the kitchen. I hurry out to the waiting car and am on edge until we get to the McDonald's parking lot. I spot Aleks's car. He's out of it before my Uber comes to a stop after I pointed where to drop me off.

"*Malyshka*, I didn't expect you so soon. Did they come back?"

"Yeah. Like five minutes after you left. I'd just tucked Cadence in and was leaving his room when I heard the garage door."

"I'm sorry this happened, baby girl. I know you didn't have dinner. Do you want to get something or go straight home?"

"I'm starving. Are you hungry?"

"After all those beets?" He grins. "I'll take just about anything to get that taste out of my mouth. I'm telling my mom tomorrow. I'm going to demand a pass from the next time anyone serves them. So gross."

"You're telling your mom you ate your vegetables?"

"Yes. She still insists I eat them. She says they're good for me. I think she likes to torment me for all the times I didn't listen as a kid."

"You're thirty."

"Yeah, well, I wasn't a good listener."

He opens my door for me, but I turn toward him before getting in. Our mouths meld, and I'm not sure who started the kiss. But it feels like the world is right again. All I want is to have dinner and go home with Aleks. I'll deal with my family later.

Chapter Nine

Aleks

I didn't plan to be away from Heather for nearly two weeks. My brothers and Pasha checked in with their wives twice. They all stayed at my mom's, and Anton and Sergei were with them most of the time. My mom has a full security detail like the ones at each of the Queens homes my family owns. I know it makes my brothers and cousin feel better, but they still hate being away from their wives. I hated being away from Heather. But she's not my wife. My family doesn't even know about her. I couldn't ask for anyone to check on her or tell them to take her to my mom's.

"Do you want to go back to Queens? Or we could go into Manhattan. It's not that late. You could come to my place."

"Manhattan. I'd like that."

I can tell she's still upset, so I don't press her to chat. It's fine because I'm lost in my own thoughts. We accomplished what we wanted to. We struck each morning for a week. We rained down chaos on the Irish and the Italians. For the first few days, we knew they thought they were attacking each other. Then they figured it out. But they can never get their shit together enough to get along and take us out. It meant we still had to split our resources and men, but we prevailed. Soviet precision. We leave no loose ends, and we only leave the tracks we want them to follow. If my family has to be mafia, I am glad we're bratva. We have the best training and lose the fewest men.

But we still lost a few. Guys I've trained, and guys who trained me. They weren't close friends, but we'd saved each other countless times. I couldn't save them this time. It weighs heavily on me—on all of us. Their deaths didn't go without retribution. We spent nearly a week at the warehouse. We ate and slept there when we weren't interrogating men who will never tell tales again.

A text flashes on my screen. I hit the hands free, and it reads it to me in Russian. '

> Misha: Where are you? I stopped by your place.

When my car asks me if I want to respond, I say yes. I don't think about the fact that my car speaks to me in Russian until Heather stares at me. I smile and shrug.

> Is it urgent? Are you free tonight? I need you at Belle Fleur. I'm with someone.

Misha will understand what I mean. I don't have to explain it via text, but I will have to explain it later. Explain it to seven pissed off guys. But I'm past thinking about calling it off with Heather. I can't.

> Yeah. I can be there.

45 mins

Misha sends me the thumbs up emoji.

"Everything all right?"

I take Heather's hand as she asks. I know she's curious, and I don't blame her.

"Yeah. It was my cousin. He stopped by my place, but I wasn't there. I told him I was out."

She nods, but she doesn't ask which cousin or whether I mentioned her. She didn't hear her name. She goes back to looking out the window, and I wonder if she's hurt. But she doesn't let go of my hand. She moves ours to rest on my leg, making it easier for me to drive, but it can't be the comfortable for her. My arms are longer, so I put her hand on her thigh and cover it with mine before entwining our fingers.

When she still says nothing, I float back into my own thoughts. We learned Salvatore is holding Luca's, Carmine's, and Gabriele's balls in a vise. Apparently, he was so pissed to learn they'd driven past our club that he locked himself in his office for an hour to calm down. Sergei's been tracking their bank accounts. Someone cleaned them out, and they deposited all the money as cash into Salvatore's accounts. The amounts match. An informant showed us photos of the three guys' cars, all booted in a garage. They have no rides. Or, at least, not expensive ones. From what we can tell, they're basically under house arrest.

"Is French okay, *malyshka?*"

"Sounds great. I'm not picky. I'm just happy to see you."

"Me too, baby girl. Tonight'll get better."

She squeezes my fingers curled around her palm and goes back to looking out the window. I need to make this night get better.

Dillan O'Rourke has proved to be the smartest of the D

name leaders. Donovan and Declan were fucking Muppets. Dillan pulled their strings. But when they thought they could lead on their own, they royally fucked up. It's how they both wound up dead. Dillan's harder to read. He's cunning and patient. Neither Donovan nor Declan were. Dillan's getting the Irish organized again, and the men rising into leadership roles are true threats to us. They're not just annoyances. Finn, Sean, Shane, Seamus, and Cormac are our ages. Dillan's the same age as Maks. It'll take them a while to recover from what we did the last two weeks, but we know to prepare for them to strike back sooner rather than later.

I let the valet park my car when we get to the restaurant. I look down the block and see the town car. Misha steps out of the building's shadow. I see his surprise because I have my arm around Heather, and she's leaning against me. Even from a distance, he must see my warning glare over her head. He holds up both hands in surrender.

There's a holiday display in the store window next to the restaurant. I guide us over, and we peer through the glass. I'm giving Misha time to sweep the place and find an unobtrusive position. When he doesn't rush back out, I figure it's clear. I lead Heather to the door.

"Is this all right, *malyshka?*"

"Yeah. I feel underdressed."

"You look beautiful."

"Thanks. But you're in a suit, and I'm in jeans. This is not a jeans sorta place."

"Do you want to go somewhere else?"

"No. We're here, and it's a fantastic restaurant."

It's a weeknight, so it's not as crowded. That's why I figured her more casual attire wouldn't matter. The place is near my penthouse. We could walk, but it's almost the holiday, and the weather has decided it's definitely winter. We might have a white Christmas.

I think she planned to sit in the chair with its back to the wall since it's farther, and she's walking ahead of me. I suspect she's the type to hand out everything to other people before herself. She won't take anything first.

I step around her and pull out the closer chair. She glances up at me, and I kiss her temple. I hope she didn't notice how I rushed to make sure I could sit with my back protected. It also means I can see everyone in the restaurant.

We've just ordered and handed our menus to the waiter when she glances to her right. I follow her gaze. I know she caught sight of Misha, who's discreetly standing near the hallway to the restrooms.

"Is that your cousin? Is that Misha?"

"Yes."

"It's a small world. Is he on a date too?"

"No. He's my bodyguard."

"What?"

If her head fell any farther forward, it would be in her water glass. After what Mike said tonight, the time has come to let her in at least a bit. I won't tell her everything, but I have to explain at least a little.

"Heather, Maks and I didn't go to college because we went into the family business. We were already doing very well for ourselves when Niko and Bogdan graduated a year apart from NYU. We are—very wealthy."

She nods but says nothing.

"Does that make you uncomfortable, *malyshka?*"

"No. I—I don't know. Should it? Why do you need a body-guard, though?"

"We're more than pro-athlete wealthy. We have competitors who don't enjoy earning less than we do. They'd gladly take what we have. You know that from me being MIA for nearly two weeks. I've told you there have been threats before, so we're careful. It's a precaution."

"Do you always have one? Was Misha there when we went mini golfing? Was he at the play?"

"No, he wasn't, and no, I don't. Most of the time, I run errands and go places on my own, and it's not a big deal. But I wanted to be sure you're safe."

"Me? What do I have to do with anything?"

"Heather, I'm cautious by nature. I'm not a conspiracy theorist or a pessimist, but I don't want to take any chances either. He's here in case anything were to happen. Misha knows his only priority is to make sure you're protected."

"Am I in danger going out with you, Aleks?"

This is freaking her out. But I take her hand, which is resting on the table next to her fork. Her palm is warm without being clammy. I draw hers toward mine.

"It's possible. Like I said, my family and I are very wealthy. We have competitors. We've had issues recently. But that doesn't mean I think something's going to happen. I just want to make sure you're protected."

"Thank you."

She's unsure what to make of all of that. If this freaks her out, then I can't tell her any more. At least not tonight. As the meal progresses, I notice her eyes jumping to where Misha still stands. It's not unheard of for people to have bodyguards in New York. Especially not in this part of Manhattan. If anyone's bothered to notice, it hasn't fazed them. I have to let go of her hand while we eat, but I'm holding it once more as we talk.

"Do you think Danielle and Mike will have more kids?"

I know my question surprises her. I know she assumed I wouldn't want to talk about them.

"*Malyshka*, they might not want me to date you, but they're still your family. They're important to you. I won't pretend like they're not."

"Thanks. But I'm too pissed to talk about them tonight."

"Are you mad at your dad, too?"

"No. He didn't know what Mike was going to talk about when he called. Maybe he did before they called me, but he didn't start this. And he said nothing bad about you."

But he could have. I caught the undertones because he must have known I could hear.

"I'm annoyed at Mike, but I'm hurt by Danielle. I know they were probably just talking on the way to dinner, then Mike got upset. But Danielle is being a hypocrite. She was close friends with Nadia. She double dated to prom with Maks and Nadia."

I freeze. Nadia is not someone we like to discuss in our family. The senior bratva pushed her on Maks when he became *pakhan*. My brothers and I were still too young to take our places in the Elite Group. Anton and Sergei were away at college and not yet the Two Spies, the heads of our Security Group and Support Group. The old Elite members claimed Nadia would make the perfect bratva wife. She was born in Russia, into a bratva family. But she couldn't be faithful to save her life. Maks never intended to marry her. He considered what they had a charade. He wasn't any more committed to her than she was to him. But it kept the old members quiet.

However, the bitch caused trouble when Maks and Laura were dating. It earned her a ticket back to Moscow. Anton and Sergei saw her to the airport, and Misha and Pasha happened to be there for a funeral. They ensured she made it back to her pissed off bratva boyfriend.

"We were kids then. Danielle has a son, and I was in their

home. You can't blame them if they aren't comfortable with someone there."

She takes a long look at me before she turns her attention to Misha. She stares at him for at least a minute before she returns her focus to me.

"Are you mafia?"

Chapter Ten

Heather

I grew up in Queens, near Brighton Beach at that. It's not like I hadn't heard the rumors about the bratva since I was a kid. I remember how people used to talk about the Kutsenkos. Aleks seems so refined and suave that it's hard to match him with the stereotype of a mobster. He doesn't seem skeazy or full of bravado. His dark hair, blue eyes, and build make him intimidating, but I've felt his gentleness. I've seen his kindness with my nephew.

I stare at Misha, really examining him. He's wearing a suit that looks custom tailored, just like the ones Aleks wears. The town cars from the other nights looked brand new and were immaculate inside and out. I peek down at Aleks's watch when I turn my focus back to him. It's definitely a Rolex. It probably costs more than a year's rent for me. He wasn't exaggerating about being rich.

But how did he get rich? How does he stay rich?

"Are you mafia?"

"Yes."

He doesn't hesitate to answer. He doesn't prevaricate or ignore my question. His unguarded moments are really just ones that he lets me see. There's vulnerability and anxiousness in his gaze.

"You won't deny it?"

"No. You grew up near my neighborhood, and we wound up at the same high school. You knew the rumors back then. You heard what Mike said tonight. Your dad hinted at knowing. Lying would be pointless. I don't want to do that when I don't have to."

"You'll have to lie to me?"

"By omission. I just admitted something that could end my life and that of every member of my family. There are things, Heather, that I will never tell you. Many, many things. Things from my past, and things that will happen in the future. It's not safe for you or others if I did. I will always be as truthful with you as I can. But if I don't answer something or don't tell you something, it's because it's not safe for you or someone else."

I think back to everything people used to say about Aleks and his family. They weren't the only ones people claimed were bratva. I said mafia, but I know what they're called. I know the Italians are *Cosa Nostra*, the Colombians are the Cartel, and the Irish are the mob. If I hadn't heard things at school, I would have heard it at home. My dad used to tell stories from work sometimes.

"Aleks, my dad's a cop. This cannot be a good idea."

"I know. I've thought about it a lot. Your dad didn't sound threatening, but for all I know right now, he could be filing a search order for every property my family owns."

"You don't think he is?"

"No. At least not until after he talks to you in private. He knows we're involved. If he's going to do anything, he's going to make sure you're far away from me. He'll do it to keep you safe and to protect your name. He won't want us linked in any records."

"I don't know what to say, Daddy."

I don't even realize what I call him until he takes my other hand and rubs his thumbs over the back of each of them.

"You still trust me."

It's a statement, not a question. And he's right. I nod.

"This is not a good place to dive into this. But we can talk at my place if you still want to go there. Or I can take you home."

"Aleks, stop. You're constantly offering me ways out. I appreciate it, but if I want to leave, I will tell you. I haven't because I don't want to."

I don't mean to snap at him, but this is overwhelming news.

"What do you want, Heather?"

I hate hearing him say my name. Not when I'm used to the terms of endearment already. It feels distant, but I did the same thing to him.

"Can we—I want to go to your place, Daddy."

I sound decisive because I want him to know I am.

"Come, *malyshka*. I have some stories to tell. Then there's a perfect little ass that needs turning red."

"What?"

"Did you think I forgot? I warned you about not answering me earlier. You didn't on purpose."

I stand, and Aleks helps me with my coat. When I turn to face him, I rest my hands on his chest to stop him from stepping away.

"Aleks, we already agreed this isn't a DDLG relationship. Is this domestic discipline?"

"I don't know. Maybe. I won't set up rules for anything but your safety and protection. I won't punish you for being an adult who can make her own decisions, even if I disagree with them. But if I tell you my expectations about your wellbeing, and you disregard them, then yes, I will spank you. You know now why I may have to be evasive sometimes, but I will always tell you whatever I can. If you hide things from me, if you don't treat me like a partner when that's how I see you, then yes, I will spank you. I will also spank you to hear you moan and make your pussy drip."

"When you talk like that, *sudar'*, it already is."

"Do you consent to what I just said?"

"Yes, Daddy."

"Then let's go home, *malyshka*."

Home. Not his place. But home.

I haven't even been once, but it sounds so incredible to think of ending the night somewhere that is ours. The prospect shouldn't excite me. I shouldn't even consider it since we've been on three dates now, and one got cut off. But I like the idea.

"Hi, Misha."

Aleks hands his cousin the valet ticket when he comes to stand with us. Misha looks like he's trying to remember where he knows me from. So Aleks hasn't told him about me.

"Misha, this is Heather Hampton. My girlfriend."

Misha's expression is as closed off as Aleks's usually is. But that has to surprise him. We talked about being all in the night he came home with me, but then he disappeared for nearly two weeks. My brother-in-law also just tried to get between us and ruin whatever this is. I guess Aleks still sees it that way. Good. So do I.

"Hampton? Are you Mrs. Hampton, the science teacher's daughter?"

"Yeah. I was a grade above you and Bogdan. I was the same class as Niko and Pasha."

"I didn't recognize you."

He's looking at my still pink and purple hair. He turns his

gaze to Aleks, who's staring at him, practically daring him to say something. I run my hand through my hair.

"My mom would have killed me if I showed up with hair like this in high school. Little did she know when I became a teacher, I would dye my hair and show up to school like this anyway."

"You're a teacher?"

Misha's looking at me while I talk, but he looks back at Aleks after he asks his question.

"Heather teaches theater. She just directed and produced 'Hairspray.' It was great."

"You went to a musical?"

Misha grins, and I can see how women would think he's gorgeous because he is. But he doesn't hold any appeal to me. I can tell he can be as brooding as Aleks, but the vibe just isn't there. I like Aleks's brooding, especially when I get to see the moments when he relaxes.

"It wasn't about hair products after all."

Misha stares at Aleks before he laughs.

"Did you just make a joke?"

"I do know how, cousin."

"But you don't."

Misha turns back to me, and I think I see approval in his gaze. At least, until Aleks elbows him.

"The car won't drive itself out of the garage. I don't want Heather to have to wait in the cold. Could you please get it?"

Misha nods, but his gaze is speculative as he looks at Aleks. It's not long before we're back in the Land Rover. Aleks gives me a tour of his place, ending with his bedroom. It's beyond luxurious, and enormous doesn't even begin to describe this penthouse. The furniture it top-end. There're original pieces of art all over the place. All of his electronics are top of the line, even his fucking dishwasher. I'm trying not to walk around with my jaw on the ground. We both know there's more to talk about, but it'll have to wait until morning.

"Strip, *malyshka*. Then come sit on my lap."

Aleks sits on the bench at the foot of his bed and watches as I peel off my clothes. I watch his dick tent his trousers. He likes what he sees, just like I enjoy watching him take off his clothes. When I'm naked, I sit on his lap, and he wraps his arms around me loosely. I guess we're talking now.

"Heather, I need you to know that you can tell me to stop at any time. You can tell me you want out at any time. It's why I keep trying to let you know you don't have to feel stuck with me. I meant what I said earlier. I am protective by nature, and I find I'm possessive of you. I've shared everything my entire life with three brothers and four cousins. I may as well have seven brothers. I have never been territorial or possessive of anything, but I am with you. I won't control what you do or what you think. That's not what I mean. I will do whatever I have to keep you safe, but I'll also do everything I can to make you happy. You're mine, *malyshka*. Mine to pleasure. Mine to protect. Mine to keep company. Mine to help. Mine to care about."

"Are you mine?"

"Completely. One hundred percent. I told you the other night that I'm in this for a relationship. Our sex is beyond belief, but that's not the only thing I want. You make me laugh. If you hadn't noticed, I tend to be rather serious. You make things lighter. You make me happy in a way no one else ever has. I haven't dated in nearly a decade, Heather. You know what I am now. You must get why casual relationships aren't wise. What I admitted tonight is something I have never admitted to another living soul who isn't bratva or in another syndicate. When you doubt if I trust you because there's something I can't tell you, remember that. You're the only one on so many levels."

"Thank you for explaining, Daddy. You make me happy too. And I trust you. I don't know why, but I have since the moment we ran into each other in the grocery store. Aleks, I knew the rumors, and I remembered them. I'm surprised you told me, but I'm not surprised by the truth. To be honest, with you being away, I had plenty of time to consider this. I'd already decided I wanted to stay with you, even if you are bratva. I don't know everything, obviously. And some things I think I know are probably wrong. But you're with a girl who grew up one neighborhood over from you. I know about all four syndicates."

"What about your dad being a cop? That could be what ends this. Heather, I cannot leave this life. I cannot leave my family. I'd be marked for sure if I tried to strike out alone. My family would never let me be unprotected, so it would make them targets, too. The other members wouldn't let me walk, either. Not because they care, but because I'd violate my oath. There is no leaving the bratva, no matter what I might want. I cannot pick you over this and live. If I did, it would be your death sentence, too."

"Can we deal with all of this tomorrow? I'm here because I want to be with you. I liked hearing you call me your girlfriend. I got the sense it's been a while since you've called any woman that because even though he hid it well, I could tell it shocked the shit out of Misha."

"It did. We can talk more tomorrow. For now, lie across my lap, *malyshka*. Hold my ankle or put your hands on the floor if you think you might reach back. If I slap your hands and hurt you, I will be monumentally pissed. Have you ever used a safe word?"

"No. But I know what they are. Mine is beets."

Aleks laughs, and it lightens our moods. He gives me a

playful, smacking kiss before he flips me onto my belly to smack my ass.

"Five on each side, *malyshka*."

"Yes, *sudar'*."

I'm unprepared for the sting of the first slap. It's harder than any he's given me. This really is a punishment. I try to steel myself for the next one, but it still hurts. He alternates sides, sometimes catching my horizontal crack. By the time he's done, I'm crying. It's partly from the pain, but it's mostly because I hate how I made him think I didn't trust him or that I would keep things from him. I hate how I made him ask me more than once when he was just trying to take care of me. I knew from the start I wanted that, and yet, when he had the chance to take care of me, I didn't accept it.

"It's done, angel."

He helps me up and guides me back onto his lap. He moves his legs apart so my ass can rest between them.

"I'm sorry, Daddy. You told me from the beginning that you want to be there for me, and I want you to. I got nervous about what Mike texted. Instead of trusting that you would understand or that we could work through it, I tried to hide it. That wasn't being all in like I said I wanted."

"I know you are. You know my expectations now. Think about what you expect from me. I don't want you to feel like it's all about what I want."

"Do I get to spank you if you don't meet my expectations?"

"I'll think about it, angel."

"Are you saying angel?"

It's his accent that makes me wonder because it sounds like the English word but a little off.

"It's the same word in both languages. It's just the pronunciation that's different."

He eases me off his lap before he gets undressed. I watch, enjoying every magnificent moment of it.

"Do you think Misha told anyone in your family about me?"

"I guarantee he did before we placed our order."

"Really? Is he a gossip?"

"It's not exactly gossiping because it's not speculation or malicious. But nothing remains a secret in my family for long. Each couple has their own private business that no one else is privy to, but we all know the general goings-on. *Malyshka*, there are nineteen of us. You make twenty. You don't just get me."

"I know, and you've already warned me about it. I'm all right with it as long as our most private stuff remains private."

I look at the bench where Aleks was just sitting and spanked me.

"I think my brothers and cousin have similar dynamics in their marriages to what we're developing. But that's the sort of thing none of us would ever ask and none of us would ever share."

"Good...If you never share, why do you think they're the same?"

"Because I may have never called another woman *malyshka*, but I've heard my relatives call their wives that. I know for a fact none of them ever used that word with another woman before they met their wives. I never thought I would, but you are my baby girl. It fits."

"I'm glad. How do you say daddy in Russian? Is it just papa?"

"*Papochka*."

"Can I call you that sometimes, too?"

"Any time."

He's naked and holding me in his arms. It feels completely

natural to share this affection. And it felt just as natural to submit to him. It was a relief to not feel alone in dealing with my family crap. I didn't have to worry about it, even though I was thinking about it. It reminded me I don't have to do this on my own anymore.

"Time for bed, *malyshka*. I know how wet you are. I could see it. Daddy took care of your punishment. Now it's time for Daddy to take care of your pleasure."

Chapter Eleven

Aleks

It's time to introduce Heather to my family. Just like I told her last night, I'm certain Misha's already told everyone. Maybe it's just as well they're forewarned. If anyone reacts the same way we did when we met Sumiko, I won't be as restrained as Pasha. Not that anyone disliked her or disapproved. It just shocked the shit out of us. He and I have been the two most resolute about not getting involved.

I spent the day with Heather, but I told her the truth: I have a family commitment tonight. I hope she can meet my family tomorrow. I'm in the car with Christina, leaving her and Bogdan's place in Queens. When we got back to my mom's after being gone for two weeks, they announced Christina's pregnant. The men in my family are doubly resolved that she goes nowhere without one of us. If my sisters-in-law or my cousin-in-law want to go anywhere, one of us goes with them.

Bogdan's at the warehouse again tonight to take care of the last couple guys we picked up. Misha went with him, so I volunteered to go with Christina while she has dinner with her family. We're headed to a restaurant close to her parents, which is about twenty minutes from Christina and Bogdan's place. On nights like this, I'm on duty. I sit in the front seat while Christina is in the back. The privacy glass is down, and we're chatting. By default, the glass is always up when a couple is in the back, or if the driver knows we're on a business call.

I'm only half paying attention to what Christina and Stefan are talking about. I'm thinking about Heather and how she's going out with friends tonight. She'd already made the plans when she thought I ghosted her. I need to talk to her about a safety detail. We've been out together three times. It was careless of me not to have assigned someone, but I'd wanted to keep my relationship private from seventeen sets of eyes. Only the twins won't have an opinion. I wanted to ease her into this life. Maybe I should have found out more about what she remembered growing up.

"Aleks, it's so nice to see you."

Christina's mom, Catriona, hugs me when we go inside the restaurant and greets me with her lilting Scottish accent. Her family is still by the door. Her parents know what we are because of her dad's job. Her brothers and their wives might have guessed after a car accident put Christina in the hospital for a week. But no one has said it aloud, and I'm certain her parents have avoided answering their inevitable questions.

"It's nice to see everyone, too. Liam."

I shake hands with her father, who's a burly Scottish Highlander, and nod to everyone else. I'm ready to take my place by the fire exit, but Catriona invites me to join them. Christina shoots her mom a look that she receives in return. I realize it would make the evening awkward and prompt those uncomfortable questions from her family now that they've seen me. If I don't have dinner with them, it'll be obvious I'm her bodyguard. Stefan takes his place near the back door. Liam and I sit with our backs to a wall and can see the entire restaurant. We're at opposite ends of the table, able to protect those between us.

Her family is excited about the baby, so the conversation is lively throughout the meal. Even though I'm the quietest at the table, I still enjoy myself. They're not quite as loud as my family, but there's also half the people. Christina is sitting to my left, and her brothers are to my right. My gaze sweeps the restaurant constantly, always aware of who's coming and going. I turn my attention to Christina's niece, who's the same age as Heather's nephew. She's sitting on Christina's other side, so I'm leaning forward to talk to her. The little girl looks just like Christina must have.

I sit up and movement catches my attention. I turn toward the door, and Heather is standing there. She's completely ashen. I'm out of my seat before I think about my duty to guard Christina. Heather spins on her heels and dashes toward the door. Her friends watch her, and two go after her. Three more wait inside.

"Heather!"

She hurries to the corner to hail a cab as I call out to her. Her friends keep asking her what's wrong.

"*Malyshka!*"

She looks at me with an expression of such betrayal that it almost stops me dead in my tracks. I run to catch her before a cab stops. My hands go around her upper arms, and I lead her toward the building.

"Heather, who is this? What happened?"

One of her friends is glaring at me as she tries to move between us, but I'm not letting go. I fear she might bolt again.

"I—I thought he was my boyfriend."

"I am."

"I am not dating a cheater. That isn't *your* family, Aleks. You're with your wife and her family. You have a daughter—"

"*Malyshka*, stop."

There's command in my voice even though my heart is breaking for her misperception.

"Let go, Aleks."

There's resolve to her response. Her friends try to intervene again, and I think the one who spoke a moment ago plans to push me out of the way.

"That's Christina. She's Bogdan's wife. I'm there like Misha was the other night."

"He didn't have dinner with us."

"I would have been pissed if he did. We were on a date. *Malyshka*, she's my sister-in-law, and the little girl is her niece. Her dad was sitting on the other side of me. I can guess how it appeared, and I'm sorry that you saw it and didn't know."

"You looked so—I thought—I—"

I pull her against me as I kiss the top of her head.

"I know, *malyshka*. It's all right."

"No. I thought you were gone for those two weeks because you were with your real family, with them. I shouldn't have jumped to conclusions. I feel like an idiot. I completely over-reacted."

"Angel, if it had been the opposite way around, I promise you would have seen a true overreaction." I lean forward to whisper in her ear. "You're mine, and no one would have doubted it."

"How can you call me an angel when I was clearly judgmental?"

"Because I've seen your kindness and generous spirit. I've seen how you watch over the people you care about. I know you uplift my spirit. You're my angel."

She nods her head that's still resting against my chest.

"Thank you, *sudar'*."

I know she wouldn't call me Daddy in front of her friends, so I accept the more formal address. But it's not what I want her to say. I don't want that dynamic right now. I want to comfort her in private. Tell her how I really feel. But I can't.

"*Malyshka*, I have to go back inside. Bogdan will kill me when he finds out how long I've been outside."

"Why?"

"Christina's pregnant. You know how protective I am. Bogdan used to be the same as me, but he's exponentially more now that they're expecting a baby."

"They're going to ask why you ran out of there. I've made such a fool of myself."

I lean back and tip her chin up. I press a soft kiss to her lips.

"It's fucked up on my part, but you getting upset tells me you're into me as much as I'm into you."

"All in."

She looks at her friends, who have given us space, but they're still hovering. We've been whispering, so I don't know how much they heard.

"Stephanie, Maxine, this is my boyfriend Aleks. Aleks, Stephanie and Maxine are teachers at my school."

I let go of Heather with my right arm to shake their hands.

"It's nice to meet you."

"I made an ass out of myself. Aleks is with his sister-in-law and her family. I assumed the worst."

Stephanie shoots me a questioning look.

"Why are you with her? Where's her husband?"

"My brother had to work late. They asked me to go with her in case she didn't feel well and wanted to go home. She's pregnant."

I gaze down at Heather and tuck a lock of purple hair behind her ear.

"Do you want to meet them?"

"I—"

She looks as panicked as she did a moment ago. I kiss her nose.

"Enjoy your dinner with your friends. I can have a car waiting for you, and you can come to my place instead of going home."

"I'd like that."

I lean to whisper in her ear again.

"We're supposed to be partners, and you assumed the worst of me. I will not punish you for this because I can see how much it hurt you. But don't make the same mistake twice, *malyshka*. When you get to my place tonight, be prepared. It will not be vanilla."

"Promise?"

There's excitement in her gaze, and her cheeks pinken. I'm certain she's wet for me. I'm like a fucking pylon for her.

"Yes, baby girl. Go have fun with your friends. I need to go back inside."

"Yes, Daddy."

Fuck me. I might need to take her to the restroom and fuck her before either of us makes it through dinner. Her friends are standing on one side, so they don't see when she reaches between up and cups my dick. That's all I need. To come in my trousers when I'm supposed to be guarding my sister-in-law.

"I will punish you for teasing."

"I know, Daddy."

I step back from her. Thank God for the cold air I now feel. It cools all of me. I walk back inside and to the table her other friends got. She makes a quick round of introduction. She's explaining what happened as I return to Christina's family. Christina looks up at me as I take my seat.

"Bogdan is going to pummel me when he finds out how

long I was away from the table. Maybe you could shave a few minutes off."

"Who's that? Is that the woman Misha was talking about?"

"Yes. That's Heather, my girlfriend. She saw me leaning over to talk to Therese, and you're sitting beside me. She feared the worst."

"Oh, no. She thought you had a family, and you were cheating with her."

"Yeah."

"She's lucky it wasn't the other way around. There wouldn't be a brick still standing."

"I told her something to that effect."

"The men in our family—they are predictable."

Christina laughs, and I breathe a little easier. She explains to her mom over Therese's head. Catriona says something brief to the people at her end of the table. The air lightens, and everyone goes back to their dinners. I can't stop glancing at Heather. I'm as concerned about her safety now as I am Christina's. What the fuck would I do if something happened? Liam and Stefan would protect Christina. I really don't have to ask myself. I would go to Heather. Nothing would stop me from getting to her.

"Baby girl, you teased me and left me hard, knowing I had to walk back into that restaurant."

I only have zip ties as my apartment, and I'm abso-fucking-lutely not using them on Heather. So I tied her to my bed with four of my ties and four belts. She's face down with a blindfold on. I haven't ordered any of the things I wish to share with her because I haven't had time, and our relationship has been so uncertain. At least on my part. Now I might buy out an entire store. Her bare ass is temptation enough to make me forget my own name.

I run my hands from her lower back up to her shoulders, massaging them and moving back down. I can feel her relaxing under my palms. The tension eases from her shoulders. It's there not just because she's restrained, and she's unsure what's going to happen. It's residual from the upset earlier tonight. When I feel her sigh, I draw back my hand and land it across both ass cheeks.

"Daddy!"

She screams her surprise. She tries to look back over her shoulder, but how she's positioned on her belly makes it difficult. I land another slap to both cheeks before alternating sides.

"What's your safe word, angel?"

"Beets."

The last two ring through the air before I squeeze her ass. She kicks her feet as best she can.

"You do not run from me, *malyshka*. This spanking wasn't about that. It was for teasing me and leaving me fucking uncomfortable. But I need you to understand the other part. If you do it again, I will spank you for that. These are my expectations. Can you live with them?"

"Yes, *sudar'*. I'm sorry."

"I know you are."

I stand at the foot of the bed and rest my body on the mattress. I hold her hips, careful where I put my hands, so I don't to apply any more pressure to her ass. I lick her cunt before sucking on her clit. Fuck. I love how she tastes. I love how she squirms. I love knowing I'm the man satisfying her. I already know I want to be the only man who does this ever again. When my family falls in love, we fall hard. We honed our intuitions to keep us alive. And it's that intuition that told me Heather is special. She wouldn't be here if I didn't know I want her with me permanently. I tried to convince myself that I shouldn't pursue her. I've accepted that my mind and my heart won't be at rest without her.

"Daddy, may I come?"

"No. Not until I'm inside you."

"Then can I suck you off before you fuck me?"

"Maybe later, baby girl. Right now, it's all about this divine little pussy."

I move off the bed and come back around the side. She's not prepared for when I slap it. I finger fuck her until she's writhing. Then I give her cunt four little taps before I slap it again and repeat the process three more times. She's panting by the time I'm done.

"Slow and hard, or fast and hard?"

I want to know her wishes as I slide the condom down my dick.

"Surprise me, *sudar'*."

I know she assumes I'll roll her onto her back or loosen the restraints so I can pull her onto her hands and knees. Instead, I climb onto the bed and stretch my body over hers. I press her into the mattress, but I'm always vigilant that I don't lower all of my weight onto her. I wrap my hands around her outstretched wrists before I thrust into her. I don't move.

"Fuck, Daddy. I didn't know this position could be so fucking arousing."

"Because you're restrained?"

"No. Because I have no control beneath you. And even though I can't move, I feel safe, like you're a shield."

"I will always protect you."

"I know. I love it."

I swallow. That's the first time either of us has used that word in any context about our relationship. I hope one day she says she loves me. I rock against her before withdrawing halfway and pressing back into her. I keep the pace slow, but I increase the force of each thrust until I'm slamming into her hard enough to make the bed shake.

"*Sudar'*, I need to come. Please...Please."

"Come, angel."

Her muscles tighten around me, and she trembles beneath me. But I'm not nearly done with her. I slide my left hand under her pelvis and work her clit. I know it must be sensitive by now, and she confirms it when she kicks her feet.

"Oh, fuck...Daddy...I'm..."

She doesn't need to tell me. I feel how her entire body goes taut. Her finger furl and unfurl as she tries to grab anything.

"Did you like that? Was it good?

"So damn good. I want to make you come, Daddy. What do I have to do to make it as good for you as it is for me?"

Love me. "You already are. Fuck, you're tight. I'm coming."

I caught myself before I spoke those two words aloud. But it's only a matter of time.

Chapter Twelve

Heather

I had a good time with my friends once I chilled out. When I walked in and noticed the crowded table, I was curious to see who was having such a good time. I thought I was going to vomit. My heart surely stopped. My ears were ringing. There sat Aleks beside a beautiful redheaded woman with a redheaded child next to her. He was chatting with the little girl and smiling. It was the same one he gives Cadence. My mind flashed to our time apart, and I immediately feared he'd been with his real family the entire time. That I was the side piece.

Now I feel horrible that I could imagine something dishonorable about Aleks. Nothing about him makes me think he would do something so deceitful and hurtful. I'm glad I went to his place afterward. We've spent the last two days together, and it's been blissful. We ran over to my place to grab some clothes, but otherwise, we've been in a world of our own. Amazon Prime brought Christmas a few days early. We've explored various positions, toys, ways to enjoy delayed gratification. It's been a sexfest, and I love it.

Today's Christmas Eve. We'll spend Christmas Day with our own families. Aleks invited me to dinner at his mom's tonight. I'm so fucking nervous. It's not just his immediate family. Apparently, all three of his sisters-in-law have their families coming. His cousin's wife's family flew in from California.

We're in the back of the town car on our way to Queens from Manhattan.

"*Malyshka*, come here. Sit on my lap."

I gladly let him lift me off my seat. I straddle him and draw my legs up. My arms tuck between our bodies. He strokes my hair and kisses my forehead.

"Why are you so anxious? You've met my brothers and cousins before."

"Ten years ago. A lot's changed since then."

I'm wearing a dress and no panties since we both know the thongs don't stay on, and I like him having easy access to my pussy. His thumb rubs my clit.

"Baby girl, do you want me to tell you more about my family? Would you feel better about that?"

I nod. I shift as I try to gain more pressure. My pussy aches from being empty. It's not just arousal. I miss the feel of our bodies joined. I think Aleks must feel the same way. He pulls his hand away and fishes out a condom from his pocket. I unfasten his pants, then he rolls it on. We both sigh as I lower myself onto his cock.

"Do you need to come, angel? Or do you just need me to hold you?"

"Hold me, Daddy. Tell me about your family. There is something I feel like I need to know because I'm scared I'll put my foot in it if I don't."

"What is it?"

"I know your dad died, but how? I don't want to say the wrong thing and hurt your mom."

"*Malyshka*, you're so sweet to consider that."

He tilts my head back and presses the softest kiss to my lips. When we pull apart, our gazes meet, and he's letting down his guard. He's letting me see into his heart. I cup his cheek and sweep my thumb over it. I realize in that moment that I want this to be permanent. I don't want any more questions of whether we are or aren't together. I want to wake up with him every morning and fall asleep next to him every night.

"The Second Chechen War lasted ten years, 1999 to 2009. Bogdan was born a year before it started. My dad was in the KGB before the Soviet Union fell. He tried really hard to stay out of the bratva, but once my parents married, they started threatening to take my mom if he didn't join. They took my aunt Alina when she was fifteen. My uncle Grigori, who was my dad's brother, and my dad rescued her. They nearly didn't find her in time. Aunt Alina and Uncle Grigori got married around the same time as my parents. They're Anton and Pasha's parents. My other aunt, Svetlana, who's my mom's sister, and my other uncle, Radomir, got married then, too. They're Sergei and Misha's parents."

I feel his deep inhale. He's working his way up to telling me what happened. He's stroking my hair and my back, and I think it's as much a comfort to him as it is to me.

"My dad, Uncle Grigori, and Uncle Radomir were KGB together. Then they became Podolskaya bratva in Moscow. This branch differs from a lot of other ones. They were para-military back then and still are to an extent these days. After the fall of the Soviet Union, the Russian Army wasn't in good shape. The Podolskaya sent men to Chechnya to fight on behalf of Russia. It was the same as being drafted. There was no choice. My dad and my uncles went back and forth several times until I was twelve. About halfway through the war, a landmine killed my father. He saved a friend's life and triggered the bomb in the process."

"Oh, my God, Aleks. I'm so sorry."

What is there to say? I lean back, and the shift in position sends a streak of arousal through my clit. It's the most inopportune and inappropriate moment to suddenly need to fuck.

"Uncle Radomir had just gone home because of an injury. Uncle Grigori was there. He saw what happened to his brother. He looks so much like my dad that if I picture it happening to my uncle, it's like I'm seeing it actually happen to my dad. I used to have nightmares about it. It would be so bad that I would spend the night with Anton and Pasha, so Uncle Grigori could be there when I woke up screaming. I don't know how many times I called him Papa in the dark."

I'm certain no one, not a living or dead soul outside Aleks's family, knows that.

"That was after we moved here. My uncle helped smuggle us to St. Petersburg when he came home from the war to tell us my dad was dead. Uncle Radomir had already gotten his family to New York. We left Russia and came to stay with Sergei, Misha, Uncle Radomir, and Aunt Svetlana. The Podolskaya found out within days that Uncle Grigori helped us escape. Without a father, they were going to take my brothers and me and make us recruits. They would have sold my mother into a whorehouse."

He tenses, and his hands stop for a moment before he exhales again.

"Uncle Grigori, Aunt Alina, Pasha, and Anton went into hiding, too. They followed us a couple weeks later. Everything my dad feared and wanted to prevent came true after he died. Or at least a lot of it. My uncles and my dad had already been working on getting us to the U.S. When we arrived with no father, we became easy targets for the Ivankov bratva. Uncle Grigori and Uncle Radomir did what they could, but if they'd done more, we would all be dead. They kept my cousins out about two years longer than my brothers and me."

"So you were twelve?"

"Thirteen by then. Maks was fourteen, Niko was twelve, and Bogdan was eleven."

"I—" I shake my head. "I can't imagine something like that. Eleven?"

"Yes. We all bear our visible and invisible scars. Maks took the worst of the mental and emotional abuse because he was the oldest and the previous *pakhan*, our leader, knew from the start that Maks should be his heir, not his sons. Bogdan took the worst of the physical abuse because he was the youngest and smallest. Vlad tortured Bogdan to make us cooperate. He would fuck with Niko and me because he knew how guilty we felt because we didn't have it as bad as Maks or Bogdan."

I'm trying to think of something to say that won't open old wounds but will let me get to know him more. My next question doesn't do the trick.

"You and your brothers are so close in age. Did your parents plan that?"

"Yes. It kept my mom from being sex trafficked."

All I can do is sit here and blink like an owl. I don't know what to say to that. Holy fuck.

"*Malyshka*, I don't know if you remember my mom. She's incredibly breathtaking. I'm not saying that because she's my mom. Aunt Svetlana is beautiful too, but my mom—she might well be one of the most beautiful women in the world. My parents had us because they wanted each of us. But they did it so close together because they knew the bratva wouldn't want a woman who was always pregnant or had delivered so many babies. It kept her with us. When my dad went to war, he made sure the men in our neighborhood understood what he was capable of to protect my mom. I don't know the details because my uncles refuse to tell any of us, but it was—violent."

He takes my hands and brings them to his chest. I'm back to not knowing what he's thinking. It's not that his expression is blank. It's inscrutable.

"*Malyshka*, I brought you into this world, told you my family's history, because I want you to be a permanent part of it. If I thought this was casual or would eventually end, you would know nothing of this. The threats my mom faced are more extreme than the ones you face being with me. But the threats exist. We've been out three times together, and I haven't assigned a safety detail to you yet. I should have. There are two things I want you to know now, and one of many things I need you to accept."

"You're scaring me now, Aleks."

"I don't mean to, angel. But this is important. I need you to know that if something ever happens to you, I will always come for you. Do *not ever, ever* doubt that. I will find you. Heather, there is nothing I won't do to protect you. In my world, that means some fucking dark and depraved shit. It's a side of me I never want you to see, but I will unleash it without a second thought if it protects you."

"Okay."

What the hell do I say to that?

"The thing I need you to accept is a security detail."

"That's what you think I need to accept? There was a shit ton from your past that I'm still trying to work my way through. And you just admitted that you'd torture and kill to protect me. I—"

"I know it's too much, *malyshka*. But this is my world. You know why I can't and won't leave. But if you want to, I will never force you to stay. None of that bullshit if I tell you, I'd have to kill you. But even if we broke up, I'd still want you to have a safety detail. At least for a little while."

"What does that mean?"

"You'd have a bodyguard like I was for Christina and Misha was for us. Their main responsibility will always be to put your safety first. Sergei usually guards Laura, and Anton is most often with Christina. Misha has been with Sumiko. Pasha and Misha are also usually the twins' guards."

"Wait. Aren't they only a few months old? They each have a bodyguard?"

"Yes."

What kind of fucked up family shit am I getting into? I don't know if I can do this. I start to climb off Aleks, and he lets me. But the moment only the tip of his cock is in me, I realize that's not what I want at all. I need to stay in his arms, connected to him. If I don't, I will feel like an autumn leaf being blown all over the place.

"Until three weeks ago, Misha and I were the most available to guard the women in our family. If I can't be with you, one of the men in my family will be. Most likely it'll be Misha because Sumiko doesn't go out as often as the other ladies. She recently became our in-house accountant and works from home alongside Pasha, who's also an accountant. We'll shift things around if both you and Sumiko need guards."

"What if all of us are going out?"

"Do you mean to the same place? Then all of us will guard you, but each man will have someone they're assigned to. Usually, it'll be husbands or boyfriends assigned to their women."

"Their women?"

"I know how antiquated that sounds, but it's the easiest way to explain. *Malyshka*, the other men in my family are just like me. They protect their wives the same way I will protect you."

"Who protects your mom?"

I want to swallow my tongue. His expression darkens, and he takes a moment to answer.

"Did you ever hear of Vladislav Lushak?"

"Yeah. Of course. He ran the bratva when we were teenagers. Is he—Was he the one who—"

"Yes. He's the one who forced us to join. He had brothers in Moscow who were Podolskaya bratva and threatened my mom. What my dad did to his brothers and what he trained us to do kept him away from her for nearly a decade. Once we all lived on our own, he thought he could pressure her. He pushed his way into her house one night, not knowing my brothers and I were over for dinner. We were in the backyard, but Maks had just walked in when he heard Mama scream. He was sworn in as the new *pakhan* the next morning. Vlad had already groomed him to take over."

"Maks—"

"Do not say it because I will not confirm or deny. But you know the answer."

"Have you—"

"Heather, do not ask questions you already know the answers to. They are ones I can't and won't answer. If you don't hear me answer, there is nothing for you to confess, nothing anyone can force out of you."

"That makes no sense to me. If people know I'm with you, they'll assume I know stuff. Why would they stop trying to force me to talk? Won't they assume I'm lying?"

He doesn't want to look at me when he answers this, so he looks out the window.

"There is a certain point when you know the person knows

nothing more. To keep trying is pointless unless it's purely to torture them."

"You know this because you've done it."

That wasn't a question.

"Vlad believed the best way to learn how to do something was to experience it yourself."

Aleks is now looking directly at me. The wall is up, and I'm back to not knowing what he's feeling. But I know how I'm feeling. I cup his jaw with both hands.

"Aleks, the shit you're telling me is fucking terrifying. But you are not terrifying. It hurts my heart to know how much you've suffered. It stirs an anger in me that will never have an outlet because the men who did this to you are dead or out of my reach. You are more considerate of my feelings and needs than any other person I have ever met. You're gentle when I need it, but even when we're rough, you are always hyper aware of not harming me. You never, ever will. I'm ashamed that I thought the worst of you at dinner the other night. Nothing about you could ever make me think you'd do something so dishonorable as to be unfaithful or to lie to me like that."

I pause for a moment as I try to gather my thoughts. I need my own deep breath before I go on.

"Aleks, the things you do—do you do them because it's expected? That they're the only way to survive and keep your people alive? Or is there even a small part of you that enjoys it? Needs it?"

"Always the former. I will always be the dominant one in a relationship. I crave control because it's what keeps me and the people around me alive. It's something that I spent more than half my life feeling like I didn't have. But I don't crave the power of hurting people. I don't crave knowing that I inflict pain. I will never be into the idea of a sex slave or certain types of Dom/sub relationships. What I do, I do because it's my responsibility. I don't live in a world where the phrase 'use your words' does shit."

My lips twitch. This is not a time to laugh, but I see a lightness come into Aleks's eyes when they do.

"Let me guess, that's a phrase you've used as a teacher with kids."

"Not so much high school students, but I have used it with Cadence about a bazillion times. It conjures a new image now."

"What of?"

I shake my head and grow serious.

"I shouldn't joke about any of this."

"Heather, part of what I enjoy most about being with you is that life doesn't feel as heavy when you're around. What do you see?"

"A scene out of one of those black and white private investigator movies. I can see you with someone tied to an old-fashioned metal desk chair. You have an iron pipe in your hand that you're hitting against your other palm. Whatever criminal or mafioso you have says you could solve everything if you just use your words. Or—oh, I just thought of another one. This one is better. You're at some diner, facing off against some mobsters, and everyone's guns are drawn. You say something like, 'if you could just use your words, maybe I wouldn't have to shoot you.'" I shake my head. "This is so not a laughing matter."

"It's all right, angel. We needed to make things a little lighter."

He says that, but something flickered in his gaze when I described the last scenario.

"Aleks, did something happen at a restaurant kinda like what I described?"

He takes a long moment to answer, and neither of us realizes that we're at his mom's house until we pull through the gates.

"There was a sit down a while ago with the other syndicate leaders. Someone targeted Maks and Pasha. Whoever it was, wasn't from one of the other mafias. It was a mercenary. There was a shootout. I hate telling you this, but I want you to make an educated choice about being with me."

"Aleks, I am with you. I told you the other day, no more questioning that. I mean it today. We're done with that. I'm spending Christmas Eve with your family. You've told me things you've told no one else. We are committed to each other. That's all there is to it."

Aleks nods before I move over to my seat. He slips off the pretty much unused condom, which he wraps in tissues, and gets his clothes back in order.

"Come on, *malyshka*. You're about to be center stage."

Chapter Thirteen

Aleks

I'm glad Heather and I talked. There's so much I can't tell her and never will. But there's nearly as much that she needs to understand. None of it seems to surprise her. I don't know if that's because it hasn't sunk in or if it's because she grew up hearing about the bratva. She knew it existed before I came back into her life. The one thing we haven't discussed, and still need to, is her father. I can't imagine anything about that will go well.

"Mama, this is Heather. Heather, this is my mom, Galina."

"It's very nice to meet you, Mrs. Kutsenko."

"Galina, and I remember you from when Niko was in that play with you. You were very good. Aleks says you teach theater now. He spoke very highly of your production that he saw."

Heather looks up at me, surprised that I told my mom about her. I have no reason to downplay my relationship with her now, but my mom was the only person I told before Misha saw us. I haven't asked, but I feel like she hasn't talked about me to her family beyond the uncomfortable call with her dad and Mike. She smiles at my mom as she accepts the compliments.

"Thank you. It was wonderful to have Aleks in the audience."

"Aleks."

I turn when Pasha calls me. I step away from my mom and Heather, and I find I'm nervous leaving her alone. But she's laughing, and she appears at ease.

"Misha said that's Heather Hampton. I remember her from high school. How'd you end up dating her?"

"Our grocery carts almost collided."

It's clear Pasha is waiting for me to say more. But I suddenly get nervous about sharing too much. I'm proud to call Heather my girlfriend, but I'm worrying about when my brothers and cousins remember her dad's a cop. I steer the conversation away from that.

"I'm sure the story will come up tonight. Right now, I need to introduce Heather to everyone. I don't want to abandon her and make Mama do that."

I don't wait to hear what Pasha has to say. Heather's moving into the living room with my mom, and I know when she spots the twins in their swings. They're awake and looking around. Their little arms and legs wiggle as people walk by. She kneels in front of them and shakes her hair as she makes funny faces at them. I can hear them giggling from across the room. She plays peek-a-boo with them, and it's hard to tell who finds her funnier. Konstantin keeps reaching for her, opening and closing his hands. Mila's legs kick like she's a frog.

"Fly's in the buttermilk. Shoo, fly, shoo. Fly's in the buttermilk. Shoo, fly, shoo. Fly's in the buttermilk. Shoo, fly, shoo. Skip to my Lou, my darlin'."

She has a beautiful voice, and she knows these hand gestures that have the twins' rapt attention.

"Skip, skip, skip to my Lou. Skip, skip, skip to my Lou. Skip, skip, skip to my Lou. Skip to my Lou, my darlin'."

Conversations are pausing as my family watches Heather sing to the twins. She looks completely natural and at ease, singing and performing. I can feel people glancing between her and me. But my attention is solely on her. Waves of affection pour over me, and I can't help but think about her singing to our children one day. That shakes me to my core. I swore I would never have children. I would not bring another generation of Kutsenkos into the world just to be swallowed by the bratva. Now I want to walk in the door and hear little voices call me Papa.

"Lost my partner, what'll I do? Lost my partner, what'll I do? Lost my partner, what'll I do? Skip to my Lou, my darlin'. Skip, skip, skip to my Lou. Skip, skip, skip to my Lou. Skip, skip, skip to my Lou. Skip to my Lou, my darlin'. I'll get another one prettier than you. I'll get another one prettier than you. I'll get another one prettier than you. Skip to my Lou, my darlin'."

"When's the wedding?"

I glance down at Laura, who's got her shit-eating grin in place.

"Do you think she could swing by and perform before naptime each day and wear them out a bit? She's fantastic."

"I'm nowhere near proposing yet. And—"

"Don't bother lying to me, Aleks. I give it a month."

Laura doesn't wait for me to respond. She goes over to Heather and introduces herself. Heather glances back at me, and I join them. Lord only knows what Laura is saying.

"It's nice to meet you, Laura. You have beautiful babies."

Laura chuckles and points toward Maks.

"They look just like him. Be sure to tell him how beautiful he is."

Heather's eyes widen before she joins Laura's laughter. Konstantin howls, clearly displeased that he and his sister are no longer the center of Heather's attention. I unfasten him and lift him from the swing. Heather watches me, and I see the moment she pictures a baby of our own. There's longing in her eyes as I bounce my nephew.

"I heard what you did to Uncle Niko the last time he held you. You'd better not be Mount Vesuvius while I hold you. You might not get to ride Uncle Niko's motorcycle when you get older, but I'll make you eat beets if you erupt on me."

I blow a raspberry on his neck, and he giggles and bounces. When I raise my head, I realize my entire family is looking at us. Because Konstantin looks so much like Maks, he could pass for my son. With Heather next to me, I think I'm shocking the shit out of my family.

"Mr. Konstantin, what did you to do to Uncle Niko? Was it explosive? You wouldn't dare to that to your favorite uncle. Not to Uncle Aleks. Not only will he make you eat your beets, he'll probably give you his helping, too." She chuckles as she looks up at me. "I don't think you'll be helping him eat his veggies if he poops on you."

"Probably not."

I can see Heather's fighting not to laugh about whatever she's thinking. She's pressed her lips between her teeth. I cock an eyebrow, and she shakes her head, making her pink and purple hair fly around her face. Konstantin snags a handful and tugs it toward his mouth. She's quick but gentle as she gets him to release it. It doesn't distract her from trying not to laugh.

"What's so funny, *malyshka?*"

"I was just thinking that purple looks way better on me than it would you."

135

My brow furrows because I don't follow.

"If you feed your nephew beets, and he blows out his diaper, you'll be wearing purple, too."

She gives up trying not to laugh. I look down at Konstantin and shake my head as I laugh with her. She turns to Laura.

"Have you started introducing fruits and vegetables yet?"

"Yeah. I'll be sure to put beet puree at the top of the rotation. Maybe we'll try them tomorrow."

Heather really laughs now.

"No lumps of coal for you. Just beets."

I pretend to scowl before I lean over to whisper to her.

"I'll show you just what a good boy I've been. If you're a good *malyshka* when you sit on your Santa Daddy's lap, he might give you a present that'll make you scream."

"Anything's better than beets."

She doesn't whisper her response, and I know people wonder what I said. She did that on purpose, and I can see the mischief in her eyes. When she waggles her eyebrows, I know she's baiting me. I hand Konstantin over to Laura when he rubs his eyes. I slide my arm around her waist, and my hand creeps to her ass since her back is to a wall. I squeeze and lean next to her ear again.

"I have a bedroom in this house, and there are nearly forty people here. No one will notice if we sneak away, but they might notice if you can't sit on a hot ass."

"Oh, Santa Daddy, you're such a tease."

She stands on her toes and gives me a smacking kiss. I tighten my hold around her waist and lift her off her feet. I can whisper without bending over.

"We'll see who's the tease when all I give you for Christmas is edging."

Then she does something I don't expect. She tickles me, and I nearly drop her. I didn't think she noticed the couple times I involuntarily responded when her hands ran over my ribs. I hadn't prepared myself those times not to react because I hadn't realized where she was going to put her hands.

"Daddy, will you spank me too? All I want for Christmas and all."

I'm about to answer when Bogdan saunters over. Oh, hell. What now?

"What miracle have you worked on my grumpy brother? You're Little Miss Sunshine, and he's—Eeyore."

"I'll make sure Aleks doesn't lose his tail anymore."

She pats the top of my hip, and her arm brushes against my gun. She looks up at me, and all the humor is gone. Bogdan looks between us, not understanding what happened.

"*Ona tol'ko chto uznala, chto u menya yest' pistolet. My seychas vernemsya.*" She just found out I carry a gun. We'll be right back.

Bogdan nods and steps out of the way. I say the first thing that comes to mind as an excuse.

"I'll show you the way to the bathroom."

"Aleks—"

"Not yet."

There's a half bath downstairs, but I steer her up to my room. I've only slept here a handful of times, but it still feels like my space. The moment I close the door, she spins around.

"That's why you never want my arm around your waist. Why are you wearing it with your family around? With the babies?"

"*Malyshka*, all the men have their guns with them. We might be at my mom's home, but we also have everyone who means the most to us under one roof. The guards on this property had to pass not just one person's consideration, but all four of us brothers. I trust them with my mom's life and anyone who visits. But when we're all together—and it's a holiday, so people know we're together—my brothers, cousins, uncles, and I are even more vigilant."

"You think someone would attack you on Christmas Eve in your mother's house?"

"It wouldn't be the first time a syndicate put a hit on an entire family."

"That's why you always take your pants and boxer briefs off first, then let your shirt drop on top of them. You don't step out of them because you know I'd see the gun before your shirt covers it." Her shoulders slump. "You've carried one every time we've been together, haven't you?"

"Yes. I told you tonight that I will do any and everything to protect you. The most basic and most obvious is to carry a weapon. I wish it were simple, and I didn't pose a threat to you, but being with me...You know the dangers now."

"Aleks..."

She collects her thoughts. I wonder what's going through her mind.

"Aleks, you know my dad's a cop. I've been around men who carry service guns all my life. I wouldn't have freaked because you have one. But thinking about that makes me worry about what my dad's going to say tomorrow. I—"

The vibrant woman from five minutes ago seems to wilt before me. I pull her into my arms, and she sags against me.

"Baby, shh. We'll face whatever happens together."

"No, we won't. I have to do it by myself tomorrow and on Christmas of all days. I haven't let myself think about it, but knowing you carry a gun and understanding why just reminds me of how impossible our relationship is because my dad's job is to arrest you, so the government can convict you. Oh, fuck. Aleks, does your family think I'm going to report everything back to my dad? Do they think—"

"*Malyshka,* slow down."

She's growing agitated as thoughts clearly bombard her. I scoop her into my arms and carry her to the bed. I sit and position her on my lap. She rests her head against my shoulder.

"I don't want to go to Christmas with my family."

I can barely hear her, and what she says shocks me.

"Heather, we will make this work. But I don't want to get between you and your relatives. You know family is everything to me. I don't want to ruin yours."

She pushes away from me.

"What happens if they refuse to accept you? If they make me pick, and I pick you?"

"I wouldn't let you pick me."

Her eyes fill with tears, and I realize how it must have sounded to her.

"I meant, I don't want you ever to be in a position where you have to choose. I don't want to be what ruins your relationship with your family. I won't be selfish and ask you to pick me over them, even if I want nothing more. Heather, it will never be a matter of me not wanting you or caring enough about you. It will always be about what I think is best for you."

"And if I disagree? What if I want to make that decision for myself?"

"You can, and you would. But picking me over your family isn't just something sad. It would put you in even more danger. If you pick me over your family, people will find out on the NYPD. They will target you as the daughter of a cop who chose the bratva over her family. They will target you for not bleeding blue alongside your dad."

"I don't know how he could accept this."

"Do you think he'd make a scene on Christmas?"

She shakes her head. I offer her a soft kiss, and she sighs as she relaxes back against me.

"Angel, after tomorrow is done, we'll talk to your parents together. Would that make you feel better?"

"No. That's just inviting them to tell me I should break up with you. I'd rather not deal with it at all."

"I know, baby girl. But we both know the conversation will happen. What do you need from me tonight to feel better?"

"Just hold me for a couple more minutes. I'll get my shit together. I don't want everyone talking about why we disappeared."

"*Malyshka*, you aren't the first woman entering this family who's needed a few minutes here and there to absorb what this means."

"What do you mean, entering this family?"

I hate how timid she sounds, and this is not how I want to make any declarations.

"Heather, you're here with me to celebrate Christmas. My family knows how important you are to me because you're here. Our future is together, *malyshka*. We will make it work as best we can. But I will never ask you to pick me over your family."

What I'm saying isn't reassuring her. But I don't know how else to put it.

"Aleks, thinking about this makes everything feel so beyond my control. I don't know what to do, and I don't know what to decide. But I'm going to have to. I thought I could have one night without this crap."

"And all I did was heap it on by bringing it all up in the car."

"I needed to know all of that. I want to be with you, but I'm scared. I wish..."

"What's your wish, *malyshka*? I'll give it to you if I can."

"If you like to be in control, then I wish you could make all this better. That you could just demand it work, and it would. I don't want to make these decisions, and that makes me feel like a coward."

"Stand up, *malyshka*...Pull your dress up...Lay across my lap."

I position her and run my hand over her bare ass. I dip my fingers between her legs and find she's wet. She always is, and it makes my cock twitch.

"I'm going to spank you, and it's just for pleasure. I'm in control, and all you have to think about is letting go. Just focus on this, not what else is going on around us. Can you do that, baby?"

"Yes, Daddy."

I feel her sigh just before my hand lands across her ass. I keep it light, but still enough to sting. I alternate sides before landing one across her horizontal crack. I give her ten total. They were light enough that her skin is only pink.

"How do you want to come, *malyshka*?"

"Soon."

"Not when. How? Do you want me to finger you? Eat you out? Or fuck you?"

"It feels wrong to have sex in your mom's house. Can I sit on your lap while you finger me?"

"Of course."

This is not how I envisioned the night at all. But I understand her, and I understand what she needs, and how our dynamic works. It may not be for everyone, but it is for us. She already feels calmer. Her body isn't so rigid and tense. I slide my fingers into her and work her pussy and clit until she turns her face into my chest to keep from screaming. She watches me lick my fingers clean before I kiss her.

"Thank you. I feel better. I just got really overwhelmed really fast. I'm ready to go back downstairs."

I help her onto her feet, and we rejoin our family. The men

pretend not to notice that we ever stepped away, and the women offer her understanding smiles. They envelop her into their fold until it's time for dinner. As we sit together, Heather tells the wives what she remembers about us from when we were in high school together. She's animated, and her smile takes my breath away. I'm happy watching her, listening to her laugh. I can see how she's won my family over without trying.

"How you got such a lighthearted woman to fall in love with you, is anyone's guess. Don't fuck it up."

Niko's standing next to me as we load the dishwasher. We can hear Heather singing while our mom plays the piano. I was right to call her an angel. She has the voice of one. It reminds me of Christmas Eve services when I was a kid. These carols are nothing like the Orthodox chants, but the quality of her voice is the same.

"I'll try my best not to. But she's not in love with me."

"Bull fucking shit."

Niko checks over his shoulder that our mom didn't hear him swearing. We both know she can't, but neither of us wants to be caught. Her threats of washing our mouths out with soap still echo in our heads as adults.

"I suppose you're going to tell me you aren't in love with her, either. You're in love with each other. You know that. I know that. Everyone in this house but Heather knows that. Fuck, even the twins probably know."

"I almost told her while we were upstairs talking."

"What happened with that? Bogdan just shook his head when Maks asked."

"She didn't know I carry a gun. She slipped her arm around my waist, and I wasn't thinking fast enough. It brushed against the handle."

"You've been dating for over a month, and she didn't know?"

"There were the two weeks where we didn't see each other. But yeah, she didn't know. I've been careful, so she wouldn't find out. I didn't want her to freak out until she understood a little more about this life."

"Do you really think she can accept it? Adapt to it?"

"Yeah. Our biggest fear is her family."

"About that. Sergei offered to run a background check on him, but Maks won't agree unless you do."

I guess it isn't a matter of time until they remembered Heather's dad is a cop.

"He's letting me decide? I'm surprised he didn't order one the moment Misha saw me with Heather the first time."

"Aleks, we trust you."

I dry my hands and look at my younger brother. I remember when I used to put his favorite stuffed monkey one shelf above what he could reach on a bookcase in our Moscow apartment. I was only barely taller than him since we're less than a year apart in age. I used to do it because I could. I remember him holding a bandage over my belly the first time I got stabbed. We're so close in age, none of us remember life without each other. We've trusted each other by necessity and by choice since we were children. But hearing my brother tell me he trusts me means everything to me.

"Thank you."

"Are you taking her home tonight and coming back here?"

"No. I have something else planned for tonight."

Chapter Fourteen

Heather

"I had an amazing time tonight, Daddy. Thank you for including me."

We just got back to Aleks's place, and we're in the elevator. I'm stuffed and happy. His family made me feel welcome the moment I walked through the door. I know people watched us, and I got the feeling we surprised them. I got self-conscious about how I look, and I wish I'd washed the color out of my hair before tonight. It's supposed to be out in one or two more washes. I was going to do that in the morning before I went to my family.

"Everyone was excited to meet you."

"Has it really been that long since you dated anyone?"

"Yeah."

I can't imagine how a man who looks like Aleks could go long periods without dating. What about loneliness? What about sex? He sure as shit has either had plenty of practice, or he's a fucking natural.

"*Malyshka*, I wasn't a complete monk. I've gone on more than one date with a woman, but I never let it get to where it was anything close to a relationship. It would get to the point where they said I was too emotionally closed off, and I would point out that we agreed from the beginning that it wouldn't get serious. But even that's been a while."

"So random hook ups?"

"No. A couple women accepted that and didn't mind seeing me every once in a while. And no, not late-night booty calls. What about you? When was your last boyfriend?"

I should have kept my mouth shut.

"I broke up with a guy a month and a half before we ran into each other."

I can tell he's trying not to react. He isn't really, except for not saying anything. I step around him, so we're looking at each other.

"Aleks, you are not a rebound. I was with him for a while, but it was over long before we officially broke up."

"What is a while?"

"Two years."

"That's more than just a while, *malyshka*."

"I really cared about him for a long part of that. But by the end, I stayed mostly because I didn't want to be lonely. After we broke up, I realized I was lonelier with him than without."

"Are you still friends with him?"

"Do you not want me to be?"

"Don't answer a question with a question, baby girl. And I honestly don't mind. I will never tell you who you can and can't be friends with. I'm just wondering if he's going to try to get back together with you."

I drop my gaze and swallow before I can look him in the eye again.

"He's been trying, Aleks. I nearly hooked up with him

when I thought you gave up on us. I was tempted because I was hurt and sad. But when I thought about what it would really be like to have sex with him again, I was miserable. He isn't you, and you're the only man I want. He's texted me a few times, but I've told him each time that I'm with someone, and it's serious."

"I doubt he believes that if you just broke up three months ago."

"He doesn't. But I don't care. It's none of his business. Aleks, you've already shown you're committed to me. I want this to be permanent. I want you to live with me."

The elevator pings, and the doors open. I look over my shoulder and realize we're on the rooftop, not Aleks's penthouse. The elevator opens directly into his place. He told me Niko and Maks preferred having a hallway and a door that separated them from the elevator in case someone tried to break in. He said he and Bogdan preferred not having one, since no one could lurk. They would know immediately. Now I think what he really meant was so no one could attack.

He doesn't respond to what I just said, and a pit opens in my belly. Instead, he takes my hand and leads me out of the elevator. We walk around the corner, and I'm floored. There's an enormous Christmas tree with multi-colored lights. It hasn't snowed, but it's cold enough that the fake snow hasn't melted. There's a snowman near the tree. There's even a present under the tree. I spot a table off to the side with some type of thermos thing on it.

"Daddy?"

"Come, *malyshka*."

He leads me to the tree and stops us in front of it. He wraps his arms around me as I continue to look around.

"What is this, Aleks?"

146

"I know we can't spend tomorrow together, so I wanted us to have our own Christmas."

"This is incredible. Thank you, Daddy. This—I can't believe. I love it."

Just like I love you. I want to say it so badly, but it seems too impetuous. It's not that I doubt my feelings, but I don't want him to think I'm just tossing the phrase around because it's too soon.

"Open your present, baby girl."

I let go of him and stoop to pick it up. I pull the wrapping paper off, and there's a little blue box. There is only one store that has a box like this, and every piece of jewelry from there is high end. I lift the lid to the Tiffany's box and move aside the tissue paper. There's a stunning gold knotted key-shaped pendant. It has a diamond in the center. I look up at Aleks, speechless.

"You just asked me to live with you. I was going to ask you the same thing, Heather. My elevator is biometric to my place and up here, so there's no real key to give you. And there's no real key to my heart, but you've already opened it. *Malyshka*, I love you."

"I love you, Daddy."

I go up on my toes and cup his jaw. I pull him toward me, and he lets me. It's my turn to give him a possessive kiss that practically devours him. We're breathless by the time I let go.

"Will you put it on me, please?"

Aleks lifts the necklace from the box, and I move my hair out of the way once I turn around. I look down at it resting against my chest. I can't help but run my fingers over the filigree. The diamond—I can't even imagine the value. It looks absolutely flawless.

"Thank you, Aleks. I've never received anything like this. Nothing with this type of sentimental value."

"You're welcome, Heather. I meant what I said. You have my heart, and I'd like us to have a home together. It doesn't have to be here. If you prefer your place, or if you want us to get a place together, we can."

The way he talks about getting a new place and the value of this necklace—which I can only guess is probably close to six figures—reminds me of just how wealthy my boyfriend is. Besides the nice watch and the tailored suits, nothing else about him screams wealth when you look at him. He's intimidating but not arrogant. He's suave, not flashy. He just told me things always ended with women because they said he was emotionally closed off. He tells me I've opened his heart. This means the absolute world to me.

"Since I work in Harlem, your place is more practical."

"But is that what you want, angel? If you want to stay in Queens, you can have a driver every day. If you want to drive yourself, then whoever is your guard would follow in their car. If there's a different borough you want to move to, we can do that."

"What about your work? Is there somewhere that's most convenient for you? Is that why you live in Manhattan?"

"You know I'm all over the place some days, but most days I work from home."

"Could we stay at your place and maybe look for something in Queens since your brothers and mom are there, and so is my family?"

"Our place, *malyshka*. And yes, we can stay here until we find something that's just right."

"I feel more like Cinderella than Goldilocks. You are my Prince Charming. I love you."

"I love you."

Aleks leads me to the table, and I realize the thermos must be filled with hot chocolate because there are marshmallows and whipped cream beside it. He pours me a mug and drops in way too many mini marshmallows. He makes a mountain out of the whipped cream. He puts far less of each in his own. He's truly spoiling me in every way. We go back to stand before the tree as we sip our drinks.

Once we're done, and we've exchanged several dozen more kisses, we go back down to his—our—place. I have his present hidden beneath the bed. I had to speak to the guys at the concierge desk and convince them not to tell Aleks when it arrived. I knew they would x-ray and open it, but they finally relented and kept it a secret.

"Here, Daddy."

I have a moment's trepidation that I missed the mark with the gift. We've talked a lot about musical theater since he knows I love it, and he's been curious since seeing the play. I discovered he has an amazing baritone after he started playing Broadway soundtracks. We've sung together as we made dinner.

"*Malyshka*, I love it."

I think he truly does. He's staring at the autographed playbill from the original cast of "Hairspray." It was nearly fucking impossible to find. I had to call in some favors from friends who are still in theater. But I wanted him to have something to remind him of me and the early part of our relationship. I suppose we're still in that, but it's all relative.

We spend the night sharing just how much we appreciate our gifts and one another. I'm exhausted by the time I drag myself out of bed. We get ready to spend the day with our families, and I'm dreading mine. I meet my new driver, Mikhail. I can tell Aleks doesn't love that I'm going somewhere without him or one of his relatives. But he knows that I'm going to my parents', then I'm coming back to his—our—place for the night.

"Merry Christmas, Daddy."

"Merry Christmas, *malyshka*."

He drops me off at my parents' house before heading to Laura and Maks's.

"Heather, let's talk."

Do we have to? My dad leads me into his office. The day has been wonderful. Way better than I expected. I don't want to ruin it by talking about Aleks. I know that's what's coming.

"Dad—"

"I won't report him to the feds or tell you to break up with him."

That takes me aback.

"Are you scared he'll do something to you if you do?"

"No."

"Are you going to blackmail him?"

"Heather."

My dad appears genuinely hurt because he knows I'm serious. But I need to know. No one has said anything so far, but Mike has been cold to me. Danielle looks uncomfortable, and my other sister, Mikayla, and her husband are pretending to be oblivious. None of the kids know anything. My mom has been doing her best to make everything seem normal despite the elephant in the room.

"Dad, you're a cop. You know who Aleks is. What am I supposed to think?"

"Better of me than that. Don't you think something would have happened already if it were going to?"

"I don't know. I'm with him all the time. Maybe there hasn't been a chance without implicating me."

"I can't believe—"

"Dad, I'm scared. Not of Aleks or being with him, but what could happen to him because of me."

"Sit down and let's just talk."

There's a couch in my dad's office, so we sit next to each other. I'm suddenly super uneasy, and I wish Aleks was with me. I haven't been this scared around my dad since I got caught lying to my third-grade teacher several times about not having gum in my mouth. Between breaking the rule and lying, my parents landed on me like a ton of bricks. I didn't chew a piece of gum again for at least two years.

"Mike's been haranguing me about Aleks because he's pissed that he's never going to get a promotion or the raises he'd been finagling for before the acquisition. I love him like a son, but he's really pushing my patience right now. He's the one who might make waves, not me. Heather, I've been on the force for thirty-five years. I've been a beat cop, a detective, a lieutenant, and a captain. I'm past when I can retire, and I'm ready to."

"Wait. Are you saying you would retire because I'm with Aleks?"

As the words come out of my mouth, waves of guilt and worry collide and threaten to drown me. I don't want my dad giving up his career for me.

"Yes. Honey, I'm ready to retire, anyway. This is a good reason to do it. I've already been setting up my retiree benefits and getting my paperwork in order. I'm going to file them. I knew you were serious about Aleks from how you talked about him on the phone. I know how he responded to the texts. He cares about you a great deal if he's taking this type of risk. He wouldn't if he didn't see his future with you."

"That's what he's told me. I believe him. We agreed to live together last night. We love each other. Do you think it's too soon?"

"It isn't on his part. I'm certain he has examined this every which way from Sunday. He had to because he's not just responsible for you as his girlfriend, but for everyone connected to him."

"He explained that too."

My dad's saying almost exactly what Aleks has. Maybe he does understand.

"What about you, honey? Do you feel it's too soon?"

"No. I mentioned it first. I didn't know he had a whole thing planned to ask me."

I touch the key pendant hanging around my neck. I never want to take it off. I dread asking the next question.

"What about everyone else?"

"Mom and I have talked about it, and we're on the same page. She's been wanting me to retire for a while, anyway. The call with you and Mike was on speakerphone. She heard everything. She's the one who told me I need to get the paperwork in immediately. Your sisters will want you to be happy, but they will never understand completely. It's best if you keep answers succinct. They'll get the hint."

"And Mike? What if he reports Aleks and his family to the feds?"

"That wouldn't be wise. I'm certain Aleks would never sanction anything happening to Mike, but he could make life very difficult. I don't think Aleks would get Mike fired because he knows that would hurt Danielle and Cadence. But that doesn't mean he couldn't get Mike assigned to the worst clients or delay Mike's raises. I don't know."

That would suck for Danielle and Cadence, though I don't feel bad for Mike. Instead, I feel way better about this conversation than I thought I would. I'm not freaked out after all. But I still want my dad's opinion.

"Do you think I should do this?"

"If he'll make you happy, then yes. I'm on one side of the law, and he's on the other. But he and I have shared many of the same risks. Your mom knew I was a cop when she met me. She had to come to terms with the danger I face, and she knew there were people who could target her for being a cop's wife. That's why I've always tried to work away from Queens. But Mom knew she wanted a life with me more than she feared the what ifs."

"That's how I feel already. Maybe I can accept this because I've always sorta known about the mafias. None of it shocks me. I'm just trying to figure out how I live with it and in it."

"I'll always do what I can to support you. If you're with Aleks, that means supporting him, too. It puts me in a tough position, but once I retire, I'm no longer sworn to uphold the law. What I don't see and don't know are things I can't feel compelled to report."

"I know this is jeopardizing a lot for you. Maybe Aleks and I should hold off until you retire."

"Honey, I'm submitting the papers before New Year's Day."

"That soon?"

"Yeah. Mom suggested it a while ago, and now it seems like the perfect time."

"Thanks, Dad."

"Just be careful. I might not work in Queens, but I live here and know about the Kutsenkos. I also know about the other families. Do not underestimate them."

"Do you think they'll go after me?"

"No. They have a rule amongst themselves. Women and children are off limits. They keep their business and their feuds among the men. Stay away from them, and they'll stay away from you. But don't think Aleks's life is any less dangerous than it is."

"Okay."

That makes me feel a lot better. I accepted Mikhail as my bodyguard today, and I know the poor guy is sitting outside the house in the town car. Shitty Christmas for him. But Aleks assured me it wasn't too bad since the Russian Orthodox Christmas is actually in a couple weeks. He'll celebrate with his family then.

Mikhail, or whoever guards me, is just a precaution, like Aleks said. If my dad doesn't think there's a reason to worry, then I won't. I know Aleks knows better than anyone outside the bratva, but the women and children thing makes sense. It fits with how Aleks and his male relatives treat the women in his family.

The rest of Christmas Day goes smoothly, and I'm excited to tell Aleks when I get home. I love thinking wherever we are together is home.

Winter break went too fast. Between Christmas and New Year's, we moved everything I wanted into our Manhattan penthouse, including Gloria, who'd fallen in love with Aleks while she was home with me. It still feels weird to say the penthouse is mine, too. We put some things in storage and got rid of others. I've been back at work for two days, and I wish I could reverse time and double my time off. But alas, I'm here with students expecting me to teach them.

"Hey, do you want to come to happy hour with us?"

Stephanie's sticking her head into my classroom during passing time.

"Sure. Straight after work? Like fourish?"

"That works."

"Cool. Where at?"

"McGinty's?"

"Love it."

"I didn't see your car in the parking lot this morning. Do you want to ride with me?"

That gives me a moment's pause. My car isn't there because Mikhail drove me. I suppose as long as I let him know where I'm going, I can ride with Stephanie. I guess he'll just follow.

"Sure. Thanks."

The last two periods of the day fly by, thankfully. Stephanie's parked on the opposite side of campus from where Mikhail dropped me off. I know he's parked on the street since he can't be in the school parking lots.

I slide into Stephanie's car and pull out my phone.

"So what's the deal with Aleks?"

I put my phone in my lap as I smile. I always seem to smile when I think about him.

"He's my boyfriend. I know you guys met in a weird way. I still feel badly that I freaked out. That's not how I wanted any of my friends to meet him. He's wonderful. We have a ton of fun together, and he gets me."

"He seems so—intense. Ryan was nothing like him."

"Thank God. Aleks is reserved. He doesn't mind that I'm more outgoing than he is, and I don't mind that he's quieter than me. I know he's really listening to me, and he's taken an interest in things that are important to me. He has a great voice, and he's learned show tunes just so we can sing them together while we make dinner."

"Sounds serious."

I steel myself for the judgement about to come.

"It is. I moved in with him last week."

"What?"

Stephanie glances at me as she merges into traffic. I'm

expecting her to say more, but she doesn't. I suppose that's a good thing.

"Yeah. He wasn't a complete stranger to me. I went to high school with him. He had my mom for two science classes. I was in a play with one of his brothers. We hadn't seen each other in years, but we knew each other."

"Were you friends back then?"

"No."

"So you knew *of* each other. You didn't actually *know* each other."

"We were acquaintances, and no, we never dated or slept together back then."

I glance down at my phone and realize I never told Mikhail where I was going. He probably thinks I'm still at school. I go to his contact and send him a text.

> Headed to happy hour with some friends at McGinty's. One of them is driving me. We'll probably be there a couple hours.

"What do your parents think of you moving in with someone so soon?"

"They seem to get it. I'm almost thirty, so it's not like I haven't been deciding for a while where I live. We're having dinner with my parents tomorrow night."

My phone vibrates, so I look down at it.

> Ms. Hampton please don't go inside until I get there.

> It's fine. I'll make sure you can see me once you're there.

I almost said he could just wait in the car. That seemed rude.

It would be better if I go inside first.

We're almost here. I'll keep an eye out for you.

Stephanie and I go inside, and we find our friends already at the bar. Even though we saw each other this morning, we still give each other quick hugs. I order my drink and look around. It's a crowded pub because it has some of the best deals and food around. I keep my eye on the door. It's Katie, our art teacher, who jumps straight in.

"Tell us about this boyfriend. Stephanie said he's hot as hell."

"He is. Like so hot, I still can't believe we're together."

I grin. It's true. The man's face and body are a work of art. Like something a Renaissance sculptor chiseled out of marble. The same perfection and about as hard.

Now it's Maggie's turn. Some kids call her the Creature Teacher because she's fucking strict. She also has some of the highest state test scores, and almost all her students score above the national average in Bio.

"What's he like?"

"He's sorta quiet a lot of the time. Really observant. But he has a killer sense of humor. Kinda unexpected. He and his brothers own a corporation together that deals with commercial real estate, venture capitalism, and I think they even own some pharmaceutical companies."

I notice the bartender listening, which takes my attention away from watching the door. He's trying to be subtle, but he's glanced at me a few times. He's cute, but I'm not interested. Katie's talking again, so I look at her.

"How'd you meet?"

"We knew each other in high school but not well. More

knew of each other. But we ran into each other at the grocery store while I was with Cadence. Like really ran into each other. I was messing around riding the cart and nearly crashed into him. Then we ran into each other at the pharmacy right afterward. He helped me catch a runaway bottle of soda when a grocery bag broke in the parking lot. We went out that night. We've been pretty inseparable ever since."

Loren leans forward to see past Katie and Maggie. It's almost hard to hear her, so I strain to listen. The bartender is still hanging around, and he's standing in front of Loren.

"I've heard of the Kutsenkos. My dad's company hired them to do some construction. He was telling me how rich they are. Like richer than God. That was like a year ago, but I remember. He said they might be Russian—"

"*Malyshka.*"

I spin so fast on my stool that I almost fall off. What's Aleks doing here? To anyone else, he might seem completely calm. But I can tell from his tone and his body language that he's pissed. Like super pissed.

"Kutsenko. Your girlfriend's pretty chatty. I never would have guessed you liked to sing Broadway stuff."

I look over my shoulder at the bartender, then back at Maks. The bartender doesn't cower, but he should if he were smart. How do they know each other?

"What can I say? God gifted me with more than one talent, O'Rourke."

O'Rourke? Fuck me. No wonder Aleks is pissed. Fuck me. Fuck me. Fuck me. There's something veiled about what he says.

"Drinks are on the house. Your girlfriend's still in the middle of hers. Unless you need to run off."

"Drink on your tab, Finn? Happily. Looks like that Johnny Walker Blue Label still needs opening."

This guy, Finn, looks pissed now. Aleks just asked for probably the most expensive alcohol in here.

"I thought you only drank vodka."

"Like water. If you're offering *drinks*, then the Beluga's always nice."

Oh, hell. I didn't notice that. It might not be as expensive as the Johnny Walker Blue Label, but I saw Aleks drinking with his family on Christmas Eve. Finn did say drinks—in the plural —Aleks is easily going to cost the bar a couple hundred bucks, and he'll walk out steady on his feet. His family jokes they've been drinking since they were eight. His mom and aunts, too. I can believe it.

Finn puts a shot in front of Aleks, who cocks an eyebrow as if to say "really." Finn pours another and puts it beside the first.

"I know I crashed your happy hour, *malyshka*. I hope you don't mind."

Aleks's hand rests heavily on my waist as I look up at him. I plaster a smile on my face because I don't want anyone to know how royally I screwed this one up.

"Aleks, you met Stephanie the other night. This is Loren, Maggie, and Katie."

I point to each of my friends, and he shakes their hand, including Stephanie's. My friends are staring at me. They know something's up between Aleks and Finn, but they don't know what.

"Small world. Did you come with anyone?"

Katie looks around since no one approached the bar with Aleks.

"Yeah. My friend Mikhail is at the table in the corner." Aleks looks down at me. "I know you're out with friends. I won't interrupt. I'll see you at home."

He presses a kiss to my lips and picks up his shots. I don't know what to do. Mikhail is a driver and bodyguard, not

Aleks's friend. At least, I don't think so. I don't want to make it awkward if I suggest we sit with them when now I know both of them are on duty watching me. But I also really want to be with Aleks. Fucking stage five clinger here, but now that he's nearby, I just want to be with him.

He must read my mind because he smiles at me, and I feel like maybe I haven't shat the bed as badly as I thought. He puts the glasses down and pulls out his wallet.

"Finn."

He hands the bartender his credit card. Before he jerks his chin toward the table where Mikhail's sitting.

"Put the ladies on my tab. Would you like to hang out here at the bar or join us at the table?"

He directs the questions to all my friends. I know they'd prefer a table. When we came in, there were none available. That makes me wonder how Mikhail managed to not only get one but get one of the biggest. Loren's the first to answer.

"That'd be great."

It means she won't have to lean across anyone. I can't blame her. Aleks picks up his glasses and mine. He points to the table, and my friends lead the way. Aleks is so close to my back, I'm surprised he hasn't stepped on my heels. He keeps his voice low as he leans toward my ear.

"We are having a talk about this. You ditched your guard and came to an Irish bar. You said you knew about the bratva. If that was true, you can imagine why coming to an Irish pub wasn't a good idea, especially without your guard."

"They wouldn't do—"

"Yes, they would. Finn O'Rourke is as senior as I am. His cousin runs the damn mob, Heather. We are not on good terms right now. This is the last place you should be, especially unprotected."

"I didn't know."

"I figured. We are going to talk about who's who in this world. Then I am going to paint your pretty little ass red for disobeying me."

"But—"

"We will deal with this at home. But you knew my expectations. And you knew what happens when you break them. Now let's play nice with your friends. I don't need them to think I'm an asshole."

"Yes, Daddy."

Fuck me yet again. This night already sucks.

Chapter Fifteen

Aleks

Why is shit going wrong at a build site? Christina heads our construction division, and she's incredible. She used to work for the city planner and has degrees in architecture and construction management. If something goes wrong with the city, then she can take care of it in half the time any of us could. But what's wrong now has to do with the fucking Irish.

This is just petty vandalism with some windows broken and graffiti, but we recognize the tags. It's not anyone high level. They wouldn't lower themselves to this, but it wouldn't surprise me if they sent someone to do this.

"How long's it going to take to get this cleaned up, and the windows replaced?"

I look at Christina, who looks like she's about to go ape shit on someone. It makes me wonder how Bogdan survives if they ever argue. My money would be on my sister-in-law, not my brother.

"At least a week. We're already delayed because of the

snow right after Christmas. The windows missing overnight let in dampness that's messing up materials stored inside. It's not just the glass that needs replacing. Some of the drywall does too. I'm not sure, but I think they stole some shit, too. I have to go through the inventory and look. Fucking waste of time. I had to send most of the guys home. They were pissed and understandably. I told them we'd pay a full day's wages today and a half-day's up to a full week. I just hope we get this back on track. It's going to cost us. If it were summer, it wouldn't be so bad."

"I know. Maks is going to call Dillan. They're pissed at us for being pissed at them."

This is payback for what we did right after I started dating Heather. But, as much of an inconvenience as this is, it barely puts a dent in our operations. They're still trying to recover from us. My phone vibrates in my pocket.

> Mikhail: Ms. Hampton left campus without me. She went to McGinty's with some friends. I'm on my way.

"Christina, I have to go. Heather's headed to a pub, and she doesn't know who owns it."

"Shit. Yeah. Go."

Once I know my *malyshka* is safe, I'm going to throttle her. I'm driving myself today, so I'm in my car and pulling away from the site before I even have my belt fastened. Blessedly, I find a parking spot right away. I spot her the moment I walk inside, but I look for Mikhail. He's at the end of the bar, watching her and her friends. I don't think Finn's spotted him. He's too busy listening to Heather and her friends. Fuck only knows what they've already said.

"How long's she been here?"

I stand next to Mikhail and whisper to him in Russian.

"About five minutes. I don't like how O'Rourke's hovering. One of her friends must have just said your name because he got even more interested in their conversation.

"Get that big table in the corner. I can't drag her out, so we're staying and watching."

I don't trust the fucker not to drug her or something. It wouldn't be the first time the Irish have done that to a woman in my family. I walk around to her.

"*Malyshka.*"

She freezes, then swings around to see me. My attention is only partly on her. I'm also watching Finn O'Rourke. The Irish have reorganized since we took out several of their top members and their last two leaders. Finn's risen through their ranks just like I have risen through the bratva's. As best we can tell, he's equivalent to me, Dillan's second-in-command. They're cousins through the old leader, Donovan. I don't get their family tree. The roots and branches cross too many times. I know the moment he hears me because he stares as I talk to Heather and the women.

He's dumb enough to offer me drinks on the house. Very well then. I can cost him a few hundred dollars in vodka and walk out looking like I've only been drinking water. I'll pay for the women's drinks, but he's going to swallow my tab for mine.

"Aleks, Heather said you're a venture capitalist. What is that exactly?"

I think that's Maggie asking me, but it could be Katie. I don't know. I know the questions are coming once we're at the table.

"Basically, my company looks for other companies that have the potential to make a lot of money. We invest in exchange for partial ownership. Depending on how much control we want will determine how many shares we get."

"Are they, like, all startups or something?"

I know this is Stephanie asking because I remember her from the restaurant the other night.

"Sometimes. Sometimes they're already established and have proven their worth, and we can see ways to elevate their value."

"Sounds like a lot of negotiating and reading contracts."

Stephanie doesn't look impressed. I couldn't care less. I want to get along with these women for Heather's sake, but I couldn't give a rat's ass if I impress them.

"That's about right."

The quietest one smiles at me, and she seems shy. Is it because of me, or is she always that way? I think she's Loren.

"Your company's done some construction for my dad's business. I remember him mentioning you guys. He said you're the only company he knows of who has a woman in charge. I think it impressed him."

"That's my sister-in-law Christina. She heads our entire construction division."

I'm ready for the attention to be off me.

"How was your day, angel?"

I keep my voice soft, but I know the other women heard me. I have my arm draped over the back of her chair. I know Finn can see me. I want him to. At this point, there is no pretending I'm not with Heather, so now it's a matter of making sure he and his shitbag family know I'm serious about her.

"It was good. The kids are a bit bummed that my hair is back to normal. They're trying to find ways to get me to color it again."

It's a rich honey brown. I never would have guessed when we met in the store. The last of the color washed out before I dropped her off at her parents. Mikhail stayed there, and another driver met us to take me to Laura and Maks's. It brings the green out in her dark hazel eyes. I love the color, but I find I kinda miss the wilder colors.

"I told you, I think blue and orange are the way to go."

"Aleks, I am not dying my hair blue and orange. I'll look like a Knicks jersey."

I laugh, and the women look at me. Heather playfully scowls at me.

"Aleks thinks I should dye my hair blue and orange, and I think I'll look like a Knicks jersey."

Maggie grins, and I already know she's going to side with me.

"I don't know. It could work. You like basketball a lot."

"Not the point. You're not helping." She turns to me. "I'll dye it like that if you'll dye yours pink and purple."

"Deal."

I stick out my hand to shake. She stares at me for a moment, entirely uncertain if I'm serious. It's wash out. I might take three showers a day for a few days, but I'd do it. She shakes her head.

"I like your dark hair the way it is."

"Don't think I could pull it off?"

"I think you could pull off anything, but that doesn't mean I don't want to see you the way I'm used to."

I lean over to whisper in her ear.

"Do you think I'm sexy? Do you want my body?"

"Yes."

She's quick to turn her head and kiss my cheek. We spend the next hour hanging out with her friends. I think I've won them over, and they won't give her a hard time. But I'm still not pleased that Finn saw her and knows she's my girlfriend. I've only had Mikhail with her for the past two days because she went straight to work and straight home. Now I need Misha with her all the time. It sucks because it means my cousin will spend his days in the car with Mikhail, looking at a building. There's no other option, though.

I stick to my word when we get home.

"*Malyshka*. Go in our room, strip, and stand by the bed. I'll be there in a moment."

I pull out my phone as she walks away. I know she's nervous. She should be.

> I need to add you to Heather's detail. She went to McGinty's tonight not knowing. Finn was there. He knows we're together.

> Misha: Didn't Mikhail tell her not to go?

> She went with a woman she works with. She didn't tell Mikhail until after they left campus.

> Doesn't she get it?

> I haven't told her enough about the others. She didn't know it was an O'Rourke bar or why it was dangerous. I'm about to explain now.

> Fine. What time do I need to be at your place in the morning?

> Seven.

> Got it.

I blow out a long breath and head toward our room. I see her toes wiggle as she waits for me. She's definitely nervous. I toss my suit coat on the end of the bed and loosen my tie before unbuttoning the top of my shirt. She's watching my every move. I undo my tie and leave it draped around my neck. I prowl

167

toward her, and I can tell she's tempted to take a step back. I tunnel my hand into her hair and fist it, tugging her head back.

"*Malyshka*, I know you weren't aware of who owned that bar. And I know I still need to teach you who's who. But you left without Mikhail. You went inside a building without letting him check first. You sat with your back to the door. You put yourself and your friends in danger."

"I'm sorry, Daddy. I recognized the name O'Rourke as soon as you said it. I know who they are. I just didn't know they owned that bar. I wouldn't have gone if I'd known."

"But you would have left campus without Mikhail. It's fine if you wanted to ride with your friend. It's not fine that you left without telling anyone. *Malyshka*, unless it's something like today, where you went into the lion's den, I won't tell you where you can and can't go. But I will insist that you have a safety detail."

"But Finn knows who I am now. Shouldn't that protect me?"

"It should. But it could also make you a target. Not everyone is still playing by the old rule that women and children are off limits."

"My dad told me about that."

That's something to consider at a later time.

"I'm going to fuck your ass tonight, *malyshka*. But I'm going to edge you first. Lean over the bed."

I go to the dresser drawer where we put all the toys we bought. We haven't had anal yet, but we've talked about it. She said she's done it a few times and didn't mind. I doubt whoever fucked her that way made sure she enjoyed it as much as he did. I gather what I need and return to the bed. I put it all on the table, knowing she can't see everything. I slide the blindfold over her eyes before using my tie to bind her wrists at the small of her back.

I nudge her feet apart and flip open the bottle of lube. I hold a medium sized butt plug and pour the liquid over it. Some of it drips between her ass cheeks. When I'm certain the plug is coated, I pour more lube onto her ass, making sure it hits my target.

"*Malyshka*, what's your safe word?"

"Beets, *sudar'*."

"I'm going to put a plug in you to get you ready for me. If this is more than uncomfortable, then you tell me immediately. Do not take it thinking it's what I want. I want to pleasure and punish you. You know how I feel about harming you. Do you understand?"

"Yes, *sudar'*. I promise."

I toy with her as I ease the tip of the plug in and out and twist before pressing it in. I watch her breathing, her face, how her body moves. I'll stop the instant I think I'm hurting her. Once it's in all the way, I reach for the next—implement. It's hardly going to feel like a toy. The riding crop lands on her left ass cheek, and she squeals. I land it in the same spot three more times before moving to the other side and doing the same thing. Then I adjust my hold and flick it up to land on the bottom of her ass cheeks.

I snag a large vibrator and turn it on its medium setting. I tickle it across her clit until she squirms. I'm not that gentle when I thrust it into her.

"Daddy."

It's a strangled sound, and I know she's fighting not to come.

"Do not come, *malyshka*."

"But—"

"Do not come. You know I'm already going to edge you. Do you want me to stop and not let you come at all?"

"No!"

It's a plaintive wail. She shakes her head.

With the vibrator still going, I switch to a flogger. I trail the ends along her back, between her ass cheeks, and over her pussy. I drag it back up and then down again. I add a little more force than with the crop as I land it across her ass. It covers a much wider area than the riding crop. It creates different sensations before the same burn sets in. She stomps her feet, and I can tell she's crying. I massage her shoulders in between each strike. When her breathing becomes shallow, I pull out the vibrator and put down the flogger. I give her a second to catch her breath while I strip off the rest of my clothes.

I know her ass burns, so I'm careful not to press too hard against it as I lean over her. But I press my chest to her back, remembering how much she likes it when I'm on top like this. I wrap my hand around her throat. It's not breath play, but it is controlling.

"I don't think you understand how much you scared me, baby girl. Mikhail texted me to say you left without him and told me where you went. I couldn't get there fast enough."

"I'm sorry, Daddy."

"I know you are, baby."

"Can I make it up to you? Can I suck—"

"*Malyshka*, you do not have to do sexual favors to make things up to me. If you wish to give me a blow job, then it's because you enjoy it, or you think I'll enjoy it. I might have you suck me off when we're together like this. But you do not have to do it to earn forgiveness."

I know enough to know that is a way some Doms resolve things and how their subs make amends. That's fine for them, but it's not what I want. I don't want her ever to worry that my love is contingent upon her servicing me. It's unconditional.

I untie her wrists and guide her onto the bed, positioning

her on her back. I retie them and fasten them to the headboard. I lengthen a spreader and connect it to her ankles. I dump a pair of Ben Wa balls into my hand from a little velvet sachet and ease them inside her. She tries to lift her hips, but I press them back down. I slide two, then three fingers into her, swirling the balls within her. I know each time I hit her g spot because her abs contract. My lips inch along the inside of her thighs, nipping and kissing. I graze my teeth over her pussy lips before latching onto her clit. Each time I feel her body tense, I draw away. I keep her on edge for as long as I think she can bear it.

I can tell she wants to beg, but she's not letting herself. Her teeth are making grooves into her lip, and I keep prying it loose. I brought the lube and the plug's box with me when I walked around to the foot of the bed. I draw the plug out as I cover my dick with the liquid. I drop the toy into the box and lift her legs into the air as I climb onto the bed and unfasten her ankles before I position myself between her thighs and drape her legs over my shoulder. I lean forward until I can kiss her. One hand goes back to her throat as the other stretches to grab the small vibrator I forgot to pick up.

"What's your word, *malyshka?*"

"Beets, *papochka.*"

She says it perfectly. She must have been practicing and feels comfortable now. It makes my heart swell.

"If it goes from uncomfortable to real pain, tell me. If this hurts, we stop. I will not be upset. It isn't disappointment or a failure."

"I know, *papochka.* You would feel horrible, and I don't want that. You know I like all of this. I want you to like it too. I don't want to ruin this and make you worry about us being together this way."

"Baby girl, nothing will ever be ruined when it comes to us

being intimate. If it changes as we need it to, then fine. But if we can't do one thing, we find another."

"I know. I just like this kind of intimacy with you. It's so special to me."

"Me too, *malyshka*."

I ease my cock past the tight ring and slowly rock forward until I'm balls deep. It's so fucking tight it's almost painful for me.

"Daddy, say something. Do something. Does it not feel good? You're making me nervous."

I whip the blindfold from her eyes and yank the tie free. I move her legs to wrap around my waist before I draw her arms around my neck and kiss her. I hate hearing even a moment of doubt in her voice. I want her to know how much I love her, desire her. I feel vulnerable that I haven't taken care of her well enough if she's asking for the reassurance. I worry I'm failing her as a partner and a lover.

"I think you like it after all, don't you, Daddy?"

"Very much, baby. You're so fucking tight I was trying not to come. Here. Put this against your clit however you want. Come when you're ready."

She turns on the small vibrator that's about the length of her palm. Her nails dig into my shoulder when she puts it against her clit. I rock, drawing her hips up and down, moving the Ben Wa balls within her. She's breathless when she talks.

"I'm really close."

"Me too. Come."

Her head tilts back as she shudders. She's quick to meet my gaze, and nothing has ever felt so intimate as this moment right now. I give in to my body's demands and come.

We lie together for a minute before she goes for a moment of privacy in the bathroom, and I put away what doesn't need cleaning. Then I slip into the bathroom to freshen up too.

When we climb into bed, she strokes me back to life. With silent agreement, she straddles me and lowers herself onto my cock without a condom. She got her birth control shot the day before New Year's Eve. Our movements are slow until we get off together. She curls against me, and we're asleep before my body withdraws. Would that we could fall asleep together like that every night. If only reality were so accommodating.

Chapter Sixteen

Heather

"*Malyshka*, everything will go well. I'm here, and we'll do this together."

We just pulled into my parents' driveway to have dinner with them. I'm so nervous I think I might vomit. Only a few guys have met my parents, and the stakes were never this high before. I let us into the house, and I can hear by parents in the kitchen.

"Mom? Dad? We're here."

Aleks gives my hand a quick squeeze before letting go. He helps me out of my coat before hanging them on the coatrack. I lead the way into the kitchen as my parents turn toward us. My heart is racing, and I'm feeling lightheaded from the anxiety. Aleks's hand rests on the small of my back, and I feel like I can breathe again. He knows I'm panicking.

"Hello, Mr. and Mrs. Hampton. Thank you for having me over for dinner."

Aleks hands my mom a small box of chocolates. I didn't even know he had them until we got out of the car.

"Thank you, Aleks. This is very thoughtful."

"You're welcome."

He shakes hands with my mom and dad. I get the sense that he was taught to never arrive at someone's home without a hostess gift. Who would have thought a mobster would have impeccable manners?

"How was your day, honey?"

My dad sounds totally normal. I can do this. He isn't glaring at Aleks or riddling him with questions.

"It was nice. I'm starting to get things in order for the spring play. The kids voted before winter break and chose *Our Town*. It's the one I least want to do, but I told them they could pick."

I look up at Aleks as he speaks.

"Why don't you want to do it?"

"Because I've been in at least five productions of it. I would be glad to never hear a line from it again. It's a great play, don't get me wrong. I'm just over it."

"Will you give this a modern spin too? I still say blue and orange would look good on you."

My parents watch us as Aleks grins, and he looks purely mischievous. It makes me wonder if this is what he looked like as a little boy in Moscow. My mom brings me back to the present.

"Blue and orange?"

"Yeah. Aleks thinks that now the pink and purple are gone, blue and orange should be my next choice. I said I would look like a Knicks jersey."

"You could pull it off."

My dad's comment leaves me speechless. My straightlaced father wasn't thrilled at the prospect that I would show up at Christmas with wildly colored hair.

"That's because you like the Knicks, Dad."

"Would you like a drink, Aleks?"

My mom points to a bottle of wine, then the beer my dad's holding. He watches as I grab a Sprite from the fridge.

"A Sprite, please."

I know Aleks drinks both, even if he prefers vodka. He purposely picked something benign. I hand him the one I just took and get myself another. My mom passes us each a glass. I put my can down next to the glass and reach for the ice bucket, which I place between Aleks and me. He takes my glass, fills it with three ice cubes—I can't believe he's paid enough attention to know that's how many I always get myself—then opens the can and fills my glass. He skips the ice for himself and pours his can of soda into his glass. My parents merely observe us while I observe Aleks, so I notice his cheeks darken slightly when he realizes how intently my parents watch us.

"Dinner's almost ready. The roast cooked a little faster than I expected."

My mom turns toward the dining room, but Aleks and I both head to the sink. Force of habit. He flips on the water, gives me a pump of soap, then squeezes one into his own hand. I finish first, so I hand him the towel when I'm done. He puts it back as though he's always lived here. Again, my parents watch us. I feel like a zoo animal.

Dinner progresses much more smoothly than I expected. Aleks keeps up a lively conversation, telling my parents what it's like to have three brothers. He makes them laugh when he shares stories about the trouble he, his brothers, and his cousins got into. Apparently, Svetlana called Sergei and Misha *lisichka*. She says they were—are—little foxes because she knew they were in the thick of the trouble, but she could never catch them.

By the time my mom offers us coffee or tea, my cheeks hurt from laughing. My parents and I shared stories about my childhood, but none were as funny as the mischief eight little boys could find together. Even the teasing and good-natured rivalry he says they have now is nothing like my relationships with my sisters. We're super close, but not like these guys.

"Thank you for a wonderful meal, Mr. and Mrs. Hampton."

"Aleks, it's John and Maureen. I think being so formal is a little pointless. Maureen and I look forward to more meals together."

I can tell my dad is sincere, but there's still an elephant in the room, and it's blowing its trunk now that the evening is almost done. Aleks glances down at me, and his gaze is so reassuring that I'm unprepared for his next comment.

"Heather doesn't know where it is, and she never will. She'll always have a security detail, and one of my brothers or cousins will be with her when I'm not."

Where what is? My mom looks as confused as I do, but my dad nods before he looks at me. He clearly understands what Aleks means.

"If you can't get to Aleks or his family, come here and wait for me."

"I don't understand. Dad? Aleks? What are you talking about?"

"If something happens, Heather, your dad means he'll know what to do. He accepts me."

I looked at Aleks when he spoke, but now I look back at my dad. His smile tells me everything. He does accept Aleks, and so does my mom.

"Aleks, a dead man could see how much you love Heather. Maureen and I thought you might both be more infatuated than anything else. We thought it might take a while to really grow into love. We live a few miles from Brighton Beach. This neighborhood might not be Little Russia, but it's next door.

People know your family for more than the obvious. It's said your aunts and uncles are the types of couples romantic movies are made about. I know what happened to your dad, Aleks. I'm sorry your mom had that time stolen from her, but people talk about more than just her beauty. They talk about how deep your parents' connection was because she still looks like a woman in love and who is loved. I've heard about your brothers and Pasha. Apparently, they're the same with their wives. Your family has had too much misery during your lifetime. But most of your family has been blessed to find their soulmate. I think you're among them. Maureen and I can tell you're Heather's."

"Dad, Mom, you're really all right with this?"

My mom reaches across the table to take my hand. She squeezes it and runs her thumb over the back of it. Aleks's hand is on the back of my neck. Between the two of them, I've never felt more secure. There's not a hint of my earlier panic.

"Yes, Heather. Is it what we expected? No. Will it be hard? Yes. Does it scare us? Yes. Will we try to get between you two? Never. Your dad and I grew up in Queens. Between spending our lives here and your dad being a police officer, we know plenty. We aren't naïve about this, and we don't believe everything we hear. We know Aleks will protect you and love you. That's what matters to us."

"We love you, honey, and we want you to be happy. It's obvious that's with Aleks."

My dad reaches across the table and shakes Aleks's hand. I'm pretty sure they didn't just accept our relationship. I'm pretty sure they just welcomed Aleks into the family.

We've shared the penthouse for two weeks, but Aleks was gone for two days. All he would tell was there's a place they go—a warehouse—to take care of things that he will never tell me about. I'm pretty sure it's the place Aleks vaguely mentioned to my dad at dinner. It freaked me out a little, and he could tell. He relented and explained a little more. When they're there, they're in control. Apparently, it's in Queens, but he didn't give any hints beyond that. I felt like I was pledging my life when I swore never to look for it or talk about it. I thought that went without saying, but I know he felt better after I assured him I would never break that promise.

I've had a double shadow since the night at McGinty's. I know Mikhail and Misha are there, but they're unobtrusive. I've started driving to work again since I like the time alone to think about the day to come. I know I'm practically alone when I'm sitting on the opposite side of the privacy glass from them, but it doesn't feel the same.

"Hey, Mags. I left my lunch on the counter this morning. I'm headed across the street to the deli. Do you want anything?"

Our classrooms are next door to each other, so we usually have lunch together.

"No, but thanks."

The lunch period is pretty early at just before eleven, so I know the deli won't be crowded with the lunch rush. I'm careful as I pick my way along the sidewalk and cross the street. There's slush and ice, and I don't care to end up on my ass.

"The Italian on wheat, please. No oil or vinegar and light olives."

"Ms. Hampton."

I know it's Misha before I turn around. His disapproval is clear. I knew they parked their car out front, so I knew they'd see me as I came in here. It's a practically empty deli. How the hell can this be a danger?

"Would you and Mikhail like lunch? I left mine at home."

"No, thank you. We would have gotten that for you."

"It's not a bother. Thanks though."

Misha watches the guy behind the counter as he comes to stand next to me. He keeps his voice low.

"It is a bother, and I believe Aleks explained that already."

"There's no one in here."

"You didn't know that before you came in."

"And you can see the place from your car, Misha. If you'd thought there was someone dangerous lurking in here, you would have already done something because they're so close to the school."

"True. But you're missing the point, Ms. Hampton."

"I live with Aleks. Don't you think you could call me Heather?"

Misha's expression tells me that isn't happening, especially not now.

"Aleks won't be pleased about this, and no, I can't keep this from him. And neither can nor will Mikhail. Aleks assigned us because he's serious about your safety. He told all of us he's explained this to you."

"I know, and I get it. But I didn't think this would be a big deal since you could see me and this place."

I walk to the end of the counter to pay, but Misha hands the guy money and puts his change in the tip jar. We say nothing as we leave. I should have known he would escort me back to the school's door.

"Thank you for lunch. You didn't have to do that."

Misha takes a long blink as he puffs an exhale and shakes his head slightly. I'm pretty sure he just rolled his eyes under his eyelids. I just keep annoying him. It's clear he thinks I don't get it. I thought I did. But I don't have time to hash this out if I'm going to eat before next period. I head back inside. My phone pings, and I already know who it'll be. Misha must have texted Aleks as he walked back to the car.

How's lunch?

I didn't take you for passive aggressive.

I didn't take you for foolish. We've talked about this several times.

I ran across the street. They could see me. If there was someone skulking around they would have done something about it already. It was fine.

It doesn't matter that it was only across the street. The point is you let one of the men enter ahead of you to be absolutely certain. You let them know if you're leaving a place. You don't have to ask permission. But you have to let them do their job.

I think you're all overreacting.

And I think I want to keep the woman I love alive. This is serious Heather. This is twice you've done this. The first time I gave you a pass because you didn't know.

You did not give me a pass. My ass remembers otherwise.

That wasn't the kind of pass I meant. If you can't live with this then there is nothing left.

What the fuck does that mean?

> It means I'm not going to risk your life to be with me. If you won't accept this lifestyle then we aren't together.

I sit there and stare at the phone. He's threatening to break up with me over a fucking walk across the street for a fucking sandwich.

Then I pull my head out of my ass. He gave me an abridged version, but I know about what happened to Laura, Christina, and Ana. And they had their security details with them. The one time Christina didn't and drove herself, she was in a car accident that could have killed her.

> Fine.

> That's it?

> Yeah. I need to eat or I won't have time. I'm sorry. It was thoughtless but it's still new to me. I should have considered what's happened to your sisters-in-law. I guess it didn't seem as big a deal as what was going on with them. I don't want this to end, Aleks. Please.

> I know malyshka. I'm just glad you're all right. I love you.

> I love you too.

Did I really ruin what we have over a fucking sandwich? I feel a lot different about the damn thing than I did a minute ago.

> Enjoy your sandwich. I can think of something way more delicious to eat. I'm thinking about having it for dinner.

> Dadddeeee!

I'll see you at home.

He sends me the kissy face emoji. I send it back to him. Maybe things are okay. I don't think it was an empty threat, but maybe this is repairable.

> See ya.

I run my hand through my hair before I head into Maggie's classroom. I have about twenty minutes left before the bell.

"What'd you get?"

"The same as always. The Italian."

"You never forget your lunch. You only go across the street if you plan it."

I feel the heat in my cheeks as I look down to unwrap my food.

"Ah. Running late this morning."

"A little. Shh."

She laughs, and I join her.

"Do you and Aleks want to have dinner with Pete and me tonight? I know it's last minute."

"I can text him and see."

I guess Aleks's dinner plans are changing. I might not be the main course anymore.

"How about six at Donavelli's?"

Italian. I wonder if we can do that. I don't know who owns it.

"Let me check."

> Maggie invited us to dinner with her and her husband. Six at Donavelli's. Is that somewhere we can go?

I wait, but there isn't a response.

"He must be busy. I'll let you know when I hear back from him."

We chat until the bell rings, then it's advanced choral and intro to theatrical production before the day is over.

> Sorry. I didn't see this come through. That sounds nice. Are you coming home first or going straight from work?

> I think I'll stay and get some lesson planning done. It makes no sense to go home then double halfway back.

> Ok. I'll meet you there.

> I'll behave. I promise.

He sends me the kissy emoji again. He is not a man I would have ever guessed would use emojis period, let alone the kissing one. It always makes me smile. I doubt he uses emojis in most of his other texts.

Like usual, the afternoon flies by. My morning classes sometimes drag, but the ones after lunch are always too busy. Once the dismissal bell rings, I cross campus to get from the auditorium, where my two classes are, back to my classroom. It's colder than it was a couple hours ago. I have my hat and scarf on, and I'm keeping my head down against the wind. I don't see the man to my left until I walk into him.

"Sorry."

I glance up and don't recognize the guy. My eyes sweep over him, but he doesn't have a district lanyard or guest sticker. He shouldn't be on campus without either, even after dismissal. Why is he here?

"Are you looking for somewhere?"

"Just headed to the gym for practice."

Nope.

"Could I see your ID, please?"

"I left it in the car."

"Then you should head to the office for a guest sticker and to check in. You know you have to have the ID to be on campus."

"It's not that big a deal. I'm late. Have a good day."

I step in front of him.

"No. If you don't have your ID, then you need to sign in. If you coach here, you know that's the deal."

We have coaches who aren't teachers here. Some are parents. Some are teachers from other schools. Some are community members. But campus security is strict.

"You're making a big deal out of nothing. Have a good day."

I don't push it any further. I let him walk past, but I look around for any of our campus security guards. I spot one and run to him.

"Tony!" I wave to him. "Hey. There's a guy who said he's headed to the gym. He claims he left his district ID in the car. He refused to go to the office and sign in."

"Don't worry, Ms. Hampton. I'll track him down."

"Thanks. I'm sure it's nothing, but I didn't like how he refused to go to the office."

"I appreciate you letting me know."

I get back to my classroom, and I'm fishing around my bag for the only hair tie I'm certain I have. I have an office back-stage, but I usually have to carry stuff back and forth, so I always have this bag with me. The damn thing must be all the way at the bottom. I check all the pockets, and I run my hand along the bottom of the main part.

What the fuck is this?

I pull out a small metal disc. It's like a lithium battery, but I don't think it is. I have no idea how it got in there. I dump out everything on my desk. Nothing else suspicious falls out, and I find my hair tie. I wiped out the bag this morning because hand sanitizer leaked. I know this thing wasn't in there. My bag was on my left shoulder—the side the man bumped into.

I grab my stuff and shove it back into the bag. I'm pulling my coat on as I hurry out of my classroom. I'm running by the time I burst through the door. I spot the town car immediately. Mikhail has to move it a few times a day, so it isn't too obvious. Misha and Mikhail are out of the car and running to meet me before I'm halfway across the parking lot.

"What happened?"

Misha's hand is at his back, and so is Mikhail's. I realize they're both ready to pull their gun. I hold up the disc.

"What is this?"

Misha takes it from me and crushes it under his foot.

"A tracker. Where did you find it?"

"In my bag. I just bumped into a guy I didn't recognize. He didn't have a school ID or visitor badge. I stopped him, but he refused to check in with the office. He said he was going to the gym for practice. I sent campus security after him."

"Did you see his face?"

"Not really. He had a hat and scarf and sunglasses on."

Mikhail is standing behind me now, and Misha is in front. Fuck. Mikhail's seriously guarding my back.

"Are you ready to go?"

"Yes. I was supposed to stay late and work. Aleks is meeting me for dinner with one of my friends and her husband."

"Aleks is in a meeting in the Upper West Side. I'm taking you there."

"What about my car?"

"Mikhail can drive it."

"But—"

"Heather, someone tried to track you."

Misha's tone leaves no room for argument. I give Mikhail my keys, and I walk between them until I'm in the back of the town car. Once we pull away from the curb, Misha lowers the divider.

"It's better if I call Aleks and tell him. When we get there, he may not look like he's reacting to this. He may seem really calm."

"I know, Misha. He won't let me know what he's thinking or feeling unless he wants me to."

"Knowing that doesn't mean it won't feel like he doesn't care enough. All he cares about is you being safe."

"Do you have any idea who this could be?"

"No."

That doesn't make me feel better. Misha raises the privacy glass, and I know he's calling Aleks. All I can do it sit back and wait to get to wherever Aleks is.

Chapter Seventeen

Aleks

Misha: Otvet' na moy zvonok.

Answer my call.

I glance down at my phone when the message comes in. I'm with my brothers and Laura in an investment meeting. There's a company that's been courting us since they announced their intention to go public. Maks has been schmoozing these guys for months at every private event they attend together. We're going to invest, but we'll pull our money right before it goes public. It'll devalue the company. Then we buy a majority stake after we bankrupt them. Our financial backing will drive the value back up, and we will own another profitable corporation at a fraction of what it would have cost us in an acquisition.

I lean over to Bogdan before my phone even rings.

"*Eto Misha.*" It's Misha.

I'm outside the conference room when my phone buzzes.

"*Privet.*"

"*Ya yedu s Khizer. Neskol'ko minut nazad ona stolknulas' s kakim-to parnem v kampuse, a potom nashla v svoyey sumke treker. Ona ne znayet, kto eto byl.*" I'm on my way with Heather. She bumped into some guy on campus a few minutes ago, then found a tracker in her bag. She doesn't know who it was.

"*S ney vse v poryadke?*" Is she all right?

"*Da.*" Yes.

"*Kak daleko vy nakhodites?*" How far away are you?

"*Okolo desyati minut.*" About ten minutes.

"*Mikhail s toboy?*" Is Mikhail with you?

"*Nyet. U nego mashina Khizer. On budet iskat' drugogo sledopyta. On znayet, chto delat', yesli naydet yego.*" No. He has Heather's car. He'll search for another tracker. He'll know what to do if he finds one.

He'll drive Heather's car somewhere like a grocery store parking lot, then wait to see who shows up. They may not approach the car, but they'll drive around it a few times. Then they might go inside wherever Mikhail winds up. He'll watch the doors. If someone comes out with nothing, he'll have a good guess who it is.

And who it is could be just about anyone. It could be someone Dillan or Finn sent. It could be someone Enrique sent from the Cartel. It could even be Salvatore's guy. But Salvatore's the least likely, since Ana still scares him enough to stay away from the women.

Fuck. It could be Robert Simms. The man is a mercenary we've hired in the past. But someone put a hit on Pasha and paid him to do it. It got personal when Simms's son was there, and Pasha convinced him to leave. The man was a ghost until a few months ago. Now we know way too much about him.

I slip back into the conference room and pull a sheet of paper from my notepad. I scribble a note in Cyrillic that I pass to Bogdan, who will pass it until it makes it to Maks. I know

Laura can read it too since she reads, writes, and speaks fluent Russian.

I need to leave. Someone put a tracker on Heather. Misha's bringing her. Come to my place when this is done.

I don't wait. I slip out of the conference room again and leave Maks to explain my disappearance. I'm waiting in the lobby when I spot the town car at the end of the block. I'm at the curb before it pulls up. I practically yank the door from its hinges before I slide in. Heather tries to move over, but I slam the door closed and pull her onto my lap.

"I'm all right, Daddy."

I won't believe her until I run my hands over her and kiss her. I fist her hair and hold her head in place, but the kiss is tender. I want to feel in control again, but I want to take care of my *malyshka* just as much. Her hand is on my chest, and she must feel my heart racing because she pulls my head to rest against her chest instead of the other way around.

"Shh, Daddy. I'm all right. I found it a couple minutes after the guy must have dropped it in there. I'd gone straight to my classroom and was searching for a hair tie before I even sat down. I found it and immediately went to Misha and Mikhail. Misha crushed it. Then they walked me to the car. We left right away, and Mikhail is taking care of my car."

"You did the right thing, *malyshka*."

"I'm so, so sorry about earlier. I feel like—I feel like shit. I didn't take your warning nearly serious enough. I blew it off if I'm being honest. I thought you were overreacting and being overprotective. Now this happened. The exact shit you've been trying to protect me against. How the fuck did I not remember what happened with Ana and the others?"

"I can understand why running across the street doesn't seem as dangerous as what they went through. Even with the tracker in your bag, it's not likely anything would have happened at the deli. Whoever this is knows you have a detail. That's why they wanted to use the tracker. They want a chance when you're alone or somewhere crowded."

"To do what?"

"I don't know."

She curls up against me, and now she rests her head against my chest.

"Baby, I'm here, and it's going to be okay. I'm taking us home, though. My brothers will be there soon. So will Misha, Pasha, Anton, and Sergei. You're safe, but it's not over."

"I'm suddenly so tired."

"You can rest at home. I don't know how long this is going to take, and I don't feel comfortable with you going out without me tonight. Do you mind rescheduling with your friend?"

"I don't want to go anywhere but home."

She hesitates. I can tell there's something more that she wants to say. I don't want to push her to share all her thoughts. But I want to be sure she knows she can ask me or tell me anything.

"*Malyshka?*"

"Will you stay with me until I fall asleep?"

"Of course. Whatever you need."

"Just you."

Why can't one of us have an easy relationship?

No one has. Not my parents. Not my aunts and uncles. Not my brothers. And not my cousins. It's hard not to be bitter and resentful of life. Vlad ripped our hope away and made us

191

monsters instead. He gave us a life sentence without the possibility of parole.

Heather is the opposite of everything that's been in my world since I was born. I cling to her easygoing nature, but rather than uplift me, I'm scared I'm going to drag her into the bowels of hell with me.

She leans away from me.

"You're even tenser than when you got in the car, Aleks. Are you afraid I'm going to leave because of this? Do you have doubts we should be together?"

I nod. I can't get the words out. She shifts to straddle me, so we can more easily look eye-to-eye.

"Aleks, I am not going anywhere. This was a shit way to convince me I need my detail. I wish it hadn't happened, but it did. I trust you're taking care of it, and I trust you to take care of me. My dad made a good point when I talked to him on Christmas. He reminded me that even though you and he are on different sides of the law, the danger you face is similar. He was already a cop when he met my mom. She accepted the danger because she loves him more than she fears his death. It doesn't mean she doesn't get scared, but she wants the life they've built more than she wants to go without. I feel the same way."

I breathe a sigh of relief. I didn't press for too many details about that conversation. I figured she'd tell me what she wanted me to know. We're home, and two of my guys come out to escort us inside. Misha must have called. One walks in front of Heather and the other behind. I'm on her right, and Misha is on her left. They stay with us until we step off the elevator. I turn to my cousin.

"I'll be out in a few minutes."

I follow Heather into our bedroom, where she dumps her stuff. She usually puts it away in the spare bedroom we converted into an office for her. She strips down to her bra and panties and climbs into bed. She looks back at me and pats my spot. I strip too, climbing in beside her in just my boxer briefs. She snuggles close to me, and I hold her.

She thinks I'm a far better singer than I do, but I sing the same lullaby my mom did whenever we were sick or couldn't sleep. The only time it didn't work was when I had nightmares about my dad dying. It was only time and seeing Uncle Grigori and pretending he was my dad in the dark that made them go away.

It's not long before Heather is asleep, so I ease out of bed. I grab a pair of jeans and a t-shirt before I go out to the living room. I already know my family is there.

"Is she all right?"

I didn't expect Laura to come, but she was at the meeting. I doubt Maks wanted to send her home without him, since they're here to deal with a threat.

"Yeah. She's asleep."

"Good. Can I use your office to get some work done? Ana's with the twins, but she can email some documents."

"Sure."

We head to the dining room table, which seats eight for a reason. Once Laura's in the room with the door closed, we talk. We default to Russian, which I'm glad of. Laura could understand if she wanted to listen, but Heather can't. If she comes out of the bedroom while we're talking, she won't learn what we're planning.

"Do you think it was Finn or one of his guys?"

Bogdan launches straight in, and I'm glad. I need this conversation to organize my thoughts because they're going a mile a minute in every direction.

"Maybe. Heather said the guy had on a hat, sunglasses, and a scarf. She couldn't get a good look at his face. She didn't mention any type of accent. I think she would have if there'd been one."

Maks's expression tells me he's going to say what I already know but don't like.

"It wouldn't be wise to strike until we know who. We can plan for everyone, but we don't act on it yet."

I nod as I let him know I accept that.

"I didn't think we would do otherwise. We've already fucked with the Irish's warehouses at the docks. We've stolen equipment or broken it beyond repair at Salvatore's sites. But that was retaliation against what they did to Pasha. Do you think Salvatore or Enrique has broken their word and are targeting Heather? Is Dillan still waging his vendetta?"

Enrique's brother lives next door to Laura's parents. She grew up best friends with the younger son. Their families were so close Enrique had her initial and her sister's tattooed on his arm along with a P for Pablo, and a J for Juan. Each letter is at the tip of a cross. Things soured a while ago, but he's sworn not to hurt any of the women, for Laura's sake.

Maks glances at the office door before he answers.

"It could still be Carmine. The fucker's proven he isn't the toady most of us assumed. He's pulling Luca's strings instead of the other way around. I don't think he wants to be the don once Salvatore is gone. But I think he wants to be the brains behind the organization. I think he's still trying to prove himself and make himself indispensable to Luca. Gabriele's just the muscle."

Niko crosses his arms. He can barely control his temper whenever we talk about the *Cosa Nostra*. He would never reveal it to anyone outside us. But I think he'd hurl something against the wall if we were at his place, and something was within reach.

"Maks, if this is them, then we're done worrying about the

balance of power. They nearly got Stasia killed or sold her to God only knows where. They planned to have Simms give Pasha to them. I'm done fucking around. Let them find out."

Niko's the only one who calls his wife Stasia. Everyone else shortens Anastasia to Ana. Only Bogdan calls Christina Tina. She doesn't shorten her name for anyone else.

Pasha leans forward with his elbows on the table.

"Salvatore won't give a shit if Gabriele goes. He's a worthless target unless we want to kill him for the sake of him being out of the way. We can't take Luca, and I get that. He's Salvatore's heir. But Carmine can take a bullet between the eyes. He's never going to stop being trouble."

Bogdan shakes his head.

"That'll mean all-out war. Salvatore will have no choice, even if he's grateful the turd is gone. Lorenzo, Matteo, and Marco are flying under the radar right now. Maybe we fuck with them."

Niko sighs before he speaks, and I know he's relented. He'll accept the alternative.

"That isn't a bad idea. Salvatore's been keeping them out of sight ever since Carmine and Luca started this bullshit. If we can't deal with Luca, then we can fuck with his little brothers and their friend."

There's nothing little about Lorenzo or Marco. They're a couple inches shorter than us, but just as big. Matteo is Marco's best friend. He's not as broad shouldered as us. He's more barrel chested. They're related through their mothers.

I turn to Sergei as I consider one possibility.

"Lorenzo's their accountant. Can you get into their accounts and let Pasha move some money around? Pasha, could you make it look like when we thought Gabriele was trying to launder his own money? Just on a big enough scale to trigger an audit. Make it look like Lorenzo's embezzling from the family."

"Yeah. I can do that. I just need Pasha to tell me what to look for and what to do. Misha's due a vacation. I think the Caymans are nice this time of year. We all know Marco's a fucking miser. He's got a healthy bank account. I can move his money to offshore accounts. I'll stagger them by an hour or two intervals at different banks. Then Misha clears them out in cash. Anton can make a passport and other identification under Marco's name."

Anton nods. He's one of the best forgers I've ever met, and I've met a shockingly large number of them. He'll have the counterfeit passport printed in a few hours, so it'll be ready if and when Misha needs it.

"If Misha travels, that means I need Anton or Sergei to guard Heather."

Bogdan grimaces before he looks at Anton.

"Christina isn't feeling so great these days. She's going to be working from home most mornings. She's hovering over the toilet until close to noon. If she's going anywhere, it'll be with me to the clubs. She can work in my offices and rest when she needs to. We won't need you for right now, Anton."

Maks glances toward the office where his wife's working.

"With the twins, Laura's not going out that much either. If she's going to any meetings, I'm with her, anyway. As long as two people can come with us when we take them to the park, then we'll be fine. Sergei, you can help guard Heather."

I don't want to inconvenience anyone or keep Laura and Christina from leaving their homes. But right now, the most imminent threat is to Heather. So far, we've only strategized for one enemy.

"What about Dillan?"

Pasha snorts.

"He's still pissed that we figured out what they were up to.

I'm certain he's still trying to work something out with Simms. I don't know what, but he won't have suddenly stopped wanting me dead. Especially not now that his thoroughbred ended up in Hong Kong with the head of the Wo Shing Wo. We have those photos Sergei took of Cormac and Seamus bribing the aldermen. We leak those to the honorable elected officials, but make it look like the Irish are extorting them for more money to keep quiet. We collect whatever they're going to pay, then send the photos to the DOJ. Time in Rikers until Dillan can bribe their way out will do them some good. Let them be somebody's bitch."

RICO, or the Racketeer Influenced Corrupt Organizations Act, means the DOJ will have to investigate. It'll let us see if Dillan has the resources needed to bribe their way out of the city's main jail. Being on an island between Queens and the Bronx means no one's coming or going without being approved or well hidden. The East River isn't exactly somewhere a person dives into in the middle of January.

Maks considers Pasha's suggestion before he responds.

"Sergei, see about getting something on Shane and Sean, too. If they go down for anything, it'll punish Finn. Cormac and Seamus are closer to Dillan. This'll give us leverage with both of them. Pasha, you met Simms's son and heard him on the phone with his uncle in Hong Kong. Could this be the Wo Shing Wo reaching across the ocean and continent? Could something have happened to the man-child, and now we're paying for it?"

"No. I think it would be Simms before it would be Winghung. If Simms wants revenge for his son leaving, then he would direct it at me. It would be a personal vendetta. I don't think Heather would matter enough to him. It would be me or Sumiko before anyone else."

Maks looks at me, and I know what he's going to say.

"When the time comes, it's your decision whether we do some or all."

Maks is our leader, and he will let no one go into an op ahead of him. But he knows how each of us has felt when someone's threatened our woman. He gave Niko, Bogdan, and Pasha the final say on how we dealt with those foolish enough to come after Ana, Christina, and Sumiko. He's giving me that right now. But we haven't considered everything yet.

"Thanks. We planned for the Italians and Irish, and we ruled out the Triad. What about Enrique and Pablo? They came to warn us before the shit hit the fan. I know Laura wants nothing to do with them, and neither does Sumiko. But Pablo still cares about both of them, and Enrique cares about Laura. Do you think they're the ones? Or do you think their hands are clean?"

Maks glances toward my office and lowers his voice.

"If it's Pablo or Enrique, Laura will bury them in lawsuits that are frivolous but costly and time-consuming. She'll make sure the DEA camps out on their doorstep, and they'll be vying for space next to the ATF. She won't pull a trigger, but she will destroy them. She's warned Enrique that if the Cartel crosses us one more time, it will mean war. I knew from the day we met her that she's tenacious and brilliant. But I did not know she's my level protective of this family."

A cloud passes over Niko's face, and he speaks at barely more than a whisper.

"All our women are like that."

None of us will ever forget the sight that greeted us when we found Ana in Greece. There was so much blood, and none of it was hers. I think Niko still has nightmares, even though he said Ana's have stopped.

I clap my hand on his shoulder since we're sitting next to each other and give it a quick squeeze. I feel like we have a plan in place, and I'm ready to check on Heather. I'm sure Maks wants to check on Laura. But Sergei glances at Maks before he looks at me.

"Is this about Heather's dad?"

I authorized Sergei running a background check on him. I don't think I'm going to like what I hear. Dinner with her parents made me think things were going to be all right.

"Yes. The initial search came up clean. John Hampton's a thirty-five-year veteran. He's had precincts in Brooklyn and Staten Island, but he was in Queens for more than twenty years. His precinct was in Brighton Beach. That made me do some more digging. His training officer was Larry Moynihan."

"Shit. I remember him."

I know exactly who the guy was. My younger brothers were still in elementary school, but Maks and I were in middle school. Vlad introduced us. This guy was the dirtiest cop I've ever met. He could have rolled around in shit and gotten up cleaner.

"Guess who's grandfather he is."

I stare at Sergei for a moment before glancing back at my bedroom door.

"Her mom's dad?"

"Yeah."

One of Sergei's earliest hacking jobs was getting money into an account for Moynihan. He was away at a wrestling camp the summer after freshman year of high school, and Vlad made him come home for a weekend to deal with it. It was more of a test for Sergei than anything else. Moynihan took bribes from the highest bidder, and that was Vlad. He'd already been on the bratva payroll for at least two decades. He had no direct ties to the mob, but he was an active member in the Irish community. He passed along what he heard from friends and other Irish American cops. He sold us one too many secrets, and Donovan O'Rourke put a bullet through the back of his heart. If Heather knew any of this, I'm sure she would have told me. And she would never have stepped foot in an O'Rourke owned pub.

"What else do I need to know about my girlfriend's family? If Moynihan was Hampton's training officer, how dirty is Hampton?"

"Not that bad. At least not nowadays. But he was on our payroll for three years. It coincides with when he became Moynihan's rookie through the time he dated Heather's mom and ended two years after they married. When Moynihan died, Hampton was already partnered with someone else and was already working in Brooklyn. I asked my dad and Grigori if they remembered him, and they vaguely do. Said he was a good guy stuck with a fucked-up partner who became his fucked-up father-in-law."

Bogdan doesn't look like he's buying any of it.

"How good a guy could he be if he was taking bribes from us?"

"Good enough that he never spent a penny until he paid for all three daughters to go to college. It took a shit ton of time to go back to the early digital records, but I found the accounts he opened and the deposits he made. He withdrew nothing from any of them until he started making tuition payments."

I lean back in my chair in disbelief.

"We paid for my future wife's and my future sisters-in-law's educations."

"Future wife?"

Niko elbows me. My jab back was a little harder than his nudges. I'm not in the mood. There isn't a person sitting at this table who doesn't know I plan to marry Heather.

Chapter Eighteen

Heather

I told Maggie I was coming down with something to get out of dinner, then I called in sick for a week. It wasn't even Aleks's suggestion. I wasn't actually sick, but I felt ill all the time. Bad enough that I took two pregnancy tests, which came back negative. I concluded it was anxiety that had my stomach in knots and made me so tired.

It's been three weeks since I found the tracker. Aleks hasn't disappeared at all, so I don't think he's been to that place. He's been attentive without smothering me. When he told me about the warehouse, he explained they never leave in the clothes they wore there. They always change. He didn't explicitly say why they do, but he wanted me to understand, so I never feared he was cheating or something. That didn't cross my mind until he said it, but I'm glad he did.

I've packed my lunch every day for the past two weeks, making sure I never forgot it. I try to time my walks across campus, so I'm near groups of students or with another teacher.

I pack my stuff just before the bell rings, so I leave the auditorium with the kids. I'm not driving myself anymore, and Misha escorts me to and from the door. I go nowhere without a guard in front of me and one behind me. It surprises me that I don't feel like a captive. Now that I really get the gravity of the situation, I've accepted the detail with as much grace as I can. I even sneaked them freshly baked cookies one morning. Aleks went to work out with the guys, so I made them and smuggled them into the car. Misha and Mikhail devoured them. Aleks would say I don't need to reward them for doing their job. I want to say thank you.

Aleks and I have been out to dinner a few times, and we went to the movies twice. Both times we got there really early, so Anton and Sergei could sweep the theater before we went inside. We got seats in the top row, and Aleks paid to keep the other seats empty. It must have cost a pretty penny to buy twelve tickets to an evening showing. But I know he wanted to make sure no one could get close to us, and we had a clear path from our seats. It also meant Aleks didn't have his back to anyone.

He's doing everything he can to make the rest of our lives as normal as possible. The lingering threat is ever present in my mind, but I'm not terrified. I'm wary. I'm accepting my new normal is living with constant danger.

"*Malyshka*, are you nearly ready?"

"Yes, Daddy. I can't believe we're going to Fashion Week."

Even though Christina doesn't wear flashy clothes or much makeup, she has a flair for fashion and enjoys it. Bogdan got tickets and invited Aleks and me to come along. He's trying to cheer her up since she's been so miserable with morning sickness that starts at three a.m. and lasts until noon.

"You look gorgeous, baby girl."

"Thanks, Daddy. I can't get over this gown you picked."

It's a deep ruby with a sheer back adorned with diamond sequins. He surprised me with it. Then he had a seamstress come to the penthouse to do a custom fitting. I have evening gloves, which I know are rather passé, but I don't think so. They made something of a comeback a couple years ago. I'm wearing my key pendant. Aleks offered to get me something else, afraid it would appear too sophomoric. Nothing about the diamond in the center makes this thing cheesy.

"It's almost as beautiful as you."

Now that sounds cheesy, but I know Aleks is sincere. I can hear it, and I can see it in his expression. He helps me into my coat before we set off. He and Bogdan arranged for the limos, so neither Christina nor I have to worry about crushing our gowns. It's not a long drive, and we're soon on the red carpet. We exchange hugs before we take our places in line.

Christina has her arm linked around Bogdan's, and I'm standing the same way. She looks back over her shoulder.

"I'm a little apprehensive about going to another gala. The last one I attended was disastrous. But I'm still excited. Even the event at the mayor's mansion wasn't such a big deal as this."

I nod and grin.

"I've never been to anything so exclusive. I'm trying not to stare as I recognize people I thought I'd only ever see on T.V."

Once we're inside and mingling, I realize how important the Kutsenko brothers are because one person after another greets us. Some clearly come to curry favors, others to say thank you. A few are snide, and my guess is they lost a substantial amount of money, and the Kutsenkos profited from it.

"Who's that? The woman is stunning."

I point to a dark-haired woman who must be about ten years our senior. Her hair is perfectly coiffed, and she must have had the gown stitched around her. It's a beyond perfect fit. It's unbelievable.

Aleks turns to look, but I notice it's the man with her who he watches. He doesn't look at me as he answers.

"That's Sylvia Mancinelli. Her husband, Salvatore, is sitting to her right."

"As in the don and his wife?"

"Yes."

Bogdan and Christina turn to see, and I can tell neither man is pleased. Christina appears wary, and I'm now silently observing. I don't know how these public encounters work, and it only gets way more uncomfortable when we realize our seats for the runway show are directly across from them. Sylvia smiles at us, but it looks forced. Aleks and Bogdan nod to Salvatore, which he acknowledges with his own nod. Then we spend most of the night pretending not to know each other.

We keep our distance, but Aleks points out three men our age. They're clearly bodyguards like Anton, Sergei, Misha, and Pasha are tonight. Each of Aleks's cousins is stationed by a door.

"The taller one is Lorenzo Mancinelli, and the one with the lightest hair is Matteo. They're Salvatore's nephews, his younger brother's sons. The guy with the black hair is Marco. His mother and Matteo and Lorenzo's mother are best friends and cousins somehow. Marco and Matteo have been best friends since the cradle. I think they might share a birthday. I don't remember. If not, they're super close."

"Are they really important? Are they like you, Bogdan, and Niko?"

"Close. Salvatore and Sylvia have two daughters, but they're really young. About five and eight. Salvatore is like fifteen years older than his wife. Luca is Lorenzo and Marco's older brother."

"He was involved in what happened to Ana and Sumiko."

I remember Luca's name from what Aleks shared. He

showed me some photos, so I would recognize them if I ever saw them. He pointed to Lorenzo, Marco, and Matteo, but they didn't make the same impression on me. They do now.

"Yes. Do you remember me showing you Carmine's photo? He's Salvatore's nephew, through his youngest sister. She had what they've always called an indiscretion when she was nineteen. She wound up married to Carmine's father because of it, and Carmine arrived seven months later."

"They forced her to marry the guy because she got pregnant?"

That seems so archaic, but I guess it's not entirely shocking.

"Yes. Salvatore and Sylvia have an arranged marriage. She'd barely been in America a month before she married Salvatore. They met when she arrived from Sicily. They fell in love, and I know he relies on her more than most dons would. Do not let her aloof manner fool you. She is as ruthless at Salvatore. She was born into the *Cosa Nostra*, and it's all she's ever known."

This is quite an education, and it's sorta overwhelming. Christina is seated on my other side and taps my arm.

"I've been to a couple events and seen Sylvia. She's very pleasant to other women, but never trust her. Never tell her anything you don't want Salvatore to know. She's like us. She will tell him everything she knows. We think no one knows I'm pregnant yet, and we're trying to keep it that way. Our family has a private physician who's been monitoring my bloodwork. I'm going to have to see an OBGYN within the next week or two, and I admit I'm nervous about the digital records. People found out about Laura's pregnancy that way. Please do not tell anyone."

"I won't. I figured you weren't talking about it since you're still in your first trimester."

"That too."

I watch the three men Aleks told me about. They have a different shade of sun kissed skin from the Kutsenkos, and they all have dark eyes compared to the Kutsenko ice-blue. But beyond that, their build, their walk, their mannerisms are so similar they could all be family. I can guess what Aleks, and his brothers and cousins are capable of, and I assume these three guys are the same. Aleks must read my mind.

"*Malyshka*, they can be charming, but they're like us in many ways."

"Many ways? What does that mean?"

Aleks looks like he wishes he could suck back those words.

"We had some additional training."

Oh, fuck. That is ominous. Does that mean my boyfriend and his family are even more ruthless and violent? Or are they just better organized? I don't want to know.

The fashion show is spectacular. I wouldn't buy a single item if I could afford it because none are my taste. But it's the experience. After the show, we find our table.

"Aleks, could one of the guys escort me to the restroom, please?"

He signals Misha, who's standing to our right. He walks slightly in front of me as we leave the ballroom. He knocks before opening the door. One stall door is shut, but we can see a pair of stilettos and slim ankles. He nods, and I step in. I hurry as I try to maneuver the train to my gown. I hear the other toilet flush, then the water running. When I step out of the stall, I recognize Sylvia. Up close, I can see a couple lines around her eyes, and one between her brows. Besides those, she's flawless.

I walk to the sink, and I'm the first to acknowledge our encounter.

"Hello, Mrs. Mancinelli."

Is that how I'm supposed to address her? I don't know if using her first name without being introduced is appropriate. I remember what Christina said, so I err on the side of formal and respectful.

"Hello, and it's Sylvia. You are Aleks's date."

Her Italian accent is still strong and only makes her more intriguing. But I catch it's a statement, not a question. I don't know if I can admit he's my boyfriend.

"Yes. It's nice to meet you."

"And you."

She finishes washing her hands and dries them, but she doesn't walk out. I control my nervousness, not wanting to give anything away.

"If you are anything like the women who married into the Kutsenko family, then you are highly intelligent and fiercely loyal. I am the same with my family. I will do what I must to protect my family and will sleep like a baby that night. I know you will tell me nothing I can tell Salvatore, and I will tell you nothing you would tell Aleks. But I hope we can be friendly when we run into each other at these events. It makes people less suspicious. Curious and skeptical, but not suspicious. It's safer for all of us if we don't look like syndicates ready to kill each other, bystanders be damned."

"That makes sense."

What else am I supposed to say? Clearly, she assumes I know who and what the Kutsenkos and Mancincellis are.

"I think you are more than Aleks's date because it's clear you love each other. But I won't pry. I've never had the opportunity to speak to the other women. I would tell them the same thing I'm about to say to you, and I know you will not only tell them, but you will tell the men. Salvatore knows where I stand on this. He doesn't disagree, and even if he did, he knows he will not sway me. The issues are between the men. I cannot protect you against my family, but if anyone else threatens you, and you can't get to the Kutsenkos, come to me. My sister died five years ago because someone followed her. She knew she was going to die. She knew no one would give her shelter. She was four months pregnant."

I'm stunned. She is not someone I would imagine as an ally, and I won't trust her until Aleks tells me I can. I'm heartbroken for her family—assuming she's being honest. But there is some reassurance there. That someone else understands this world, and that I'm not alone if I can't get to my family.

Wow. I guess I consider the Kutsenkos my family. Aleks and I aren't married. We're not even engaged. But I know that's where we're headed. He's made it clear he's only waiting, so I can be sure I can live with all of this.

"Thank you. I will keep that in mind."

"There's one other thing. Salvatore doesn't even know about this yet because I received a text as I walked in here. I'm going to tell him as soon as I get to the table. Aleks needs to look out for your brother-in-law. He's in bed with someone dangerous, and I don't mean metaphorically. And it's not your sister."

"Which brother-in-law?"

"Mike. It's someone he was with before he married your sister. I have no proof they're still sleeping together, but they meet once a week. There are multiple calls each week, too."

"He's been with my sister since college."

Mike's having some sort of affair? I'll fucking murder the bastard. I will find my own fucking warehouse and do unspeakable things to him if he's touched another woman since he started dating my sister.

Sylvia shrugs.

"What man meets with a woman every week who isn't his shrink or his pastor?"

"Why do you know this?"

"I had a hunch based on something I overheard in a restroom like this. This woman would gladly see all the

Kutsenkos fall to punish Aleks. That's bad for business. The Ivankov bratva needs the Kutsenkos in charge. Any other family would disrupt the tentative balance we have."

"Who is this woman?"

"Shannon McGinnis. She used to be Shannon O'Rourke."

Sylvia says nothing more, leaving me staring at her in the mirror as she walks out. I see Misha in the reflection when the door opens. I take a deep breath and steel myself to go back out there. I want to demand Misha tell me who Shannon McGinnis née O'Rourke is.

"Everything all right?"

"I don't know."

I'm not saying anything else until I talk to Aleks. Misha stays by my side until we get to the table. Aleks looks at me and smiles, but it falls immediately. He stands and slides his hand into mine. I see the other couples wondering what's going on. A man other than my boyfriend walks into the ballroom with me and walks me to my seat. Now my boyfriend is guiding me out of the ballroom. He looks around the lobby until he finds a quiet place. I see Misha and Pasha, but they don't approach.

"Who's Shannon O'Rourke?"

Aleks blinks at me for a moment before he wraps his arms around my waist and kisses my forehead.

"She isn't a woman I was ever involved with, *malyshka*. Her older brother, Patrick, and I got into a fight he picked when he went after Bogdan. He's the first guy I—" He gives me a pointed look. "Her two younger brothers came after me a week later. They shot me and left me for dead—at least tried to. They didn't leave the alleyway, but I did. A few years later, someone assaulted her sister, Megan, in Brighton Beach. The woman who found her called us because she found out Megan was an O'Rourke. I was the only one available, so I took her home. She swore up and down I never hurt her. Her uncle Liam ran the mob back then. He believed her, but Shannon didn't. When she went away to college, I heard nothing about her again. As far as I know, she doesn't have much to do with her family anymore. Why?"

"Because she has something to do with Mike. I just had the most—the strangest conversation with Sylvia Mancinelli in the restroom. She didn't threaten me or anything. Just the opposite. She said she hasn't had a chance to tell any of the other women this, but she knows I'll tell them and you. She said she can't protect us against her family, but if another syndicate ever comes after us and we can't get to our family, then we go to her. She said Salvatore knows and can't stop her. I didn't know whether to believer her. She said her sister was pregnant and died because someone followed her, and she knew she had nowhere to go."

"She did. Her name was Sophia. A rival family captured her guards in a crowd. She figured out she was being followed and called her father, but they lived across the island. She knew who was following her. She could have reached two other families before being caught, but she knew they wouldn't care that she was a woman and pregnant. She tried to hide, but they found her. They raped her and killed her."

I feel sick imagining what that woman's last moments must have been. Her terror for her life and her baby's.

"His nephews have broken the sacrament, but Salvatore still believes women and children are untouchable. He knows if he commits that cardinal sin, none of the women in his family are safe. He's fortunate no one in the Ivankov bratva would dare go after them like any other family would have after what his nephews have done. Trust no one but Sylvia about this. If anyone says they're acting on behalf of Salvatore, assume it's a lie."

I nod. Tears come to my eyes as I brace myself for the other half of the story.

"Sylvia said Mike was sleeping with Shannon in college. He started dating Danielle freshman year. They were on again-off again, but Sylvia said they see each other once a week and talk multiple times. I can only assume he's having an affair with her. Sylvia didn't tell me what you did, but she said Shannon would happily see the demise of the entire Kutsenko family. Especially you."

"She believes I took everything from her family. If she's involved with Mike, and Kutsenko Partners bought the corporation he works for, then they both have reason to wish us ill."

"I don't want to know, but I need to know if Mike is cheating on Danielle."

"I know, *malyshka*. Sergei can start investigating tonight. Do you want to go home?"

I shake my head.

"I sure as fuck won't let Mike ruin this night in case he is a cheater. He's not fucking up anything else for my family. There's nothing I can do until Sergei finds out the truth. I would never go to Danielle with just speculation. I don't even want to go to her if it turns out to be true."

"I'll do whatever you need, Heather."

"I know. I love you for it."

With a sigh, we head back inside. Aleks gives what must be an abbreviated explanation in Russian to Bogdan, who promises to explain to Christina in the car. Sergei rides with us back to Aleks's and my place. He sits across from me as I tell him everything. He's sympathetic as he promises to uncover anything he can. Even if it's good news, I know I want Aleks with me when I find out.

Chapter Nineteen

Aleks

Heather is asleep beside me, but I'm nowhere near sleepy. A loop of memories has my mind in a steel trap. I remember walking home from a friend's house when I was fourteen. I was nearly home when I heard someone running toward me. As I rounded the corner, Bogdan slammed into me. His face was bleeding, and his clothes were torn. I looked up and recognized Patrick O'Rourke, a complete asshole. Bogdan was twelve and half a foot shorter than Patrick, who was sixteen. Pathetic fucker picked a fight with Bogdan because he thought he was an easy target.

Patrick looked like shit. He was bleeding as badly as Bogdan, so I knew my little brother defended himself before getting away. I pushed Bogdan behind me and pulled my knife. Patrick already had his gun drawn as he ran after my brother. He squeezed the trigger, and the bullet grazed my thigh. He aimed higher and was ready to shoot me in the arm. I hurled my knife, and it landed in his shoulder, making him drop the gun.

I remember telling Bogdan to go home. We'd only been in America for a year, and I was still so angry about my dad's death and about Vlad sucking us in. He hadn't yet trained us to control our rage, at least anywhere but in front of him. Everything that boiled beneath the surface came out. I beat Patrick until he was unrecognizable. Then I put a bullet through his heart.

A week later, on a Sunday after they'd been to Catholic Mass, and we'd been to our Russian Orthodox one, they found me coming home from the store. They backed me into the same alleyway where I shot Patrick. Donny and Mickey thought they'd do to me what I did to Patrick and pulverize me. Except the shitheads shot me first. They thought they killed me and decided not to beat me. Neither wanted to get close enough to check, so they assumed I was dead. I wasn't. I hadn't carried the gun to church, but I had put it in my waistband before I went to pick up onions, tomatoes, and fucking beets. I remember because I thought I would die and the last thing I saw was a beet. Fucking poetic justice.

But I pulled my gun and shot them each in the back of the head before I passed out. Maks, Anton, and Sergei found us. It couldn't have been very long because I hadn't bled out. It was a gunshot to my ribs. A little more to the left, and it would have killed me. Our family doctor, Boris, removed it and stitched me up. The man is a mountain with bushy hair all over his head. He was a Russian Army doctor, then a KGB doctor, and finally a Podolskaya one. He's been treating us since we were all babies. I'm surprised he didn't deliver any of us.

Vlad struck back hard once he found out the Irish had already attacked Bogdan. He thought I started it. It was Bogdan who confessed he'd been goofing off with a friend and not aware of his surroundings. He got a beating for it, but Vlad defended us against Liam. You would never know we were the teacher's pet from how Vlad abused us, but we were. Liam O'Rourke lost a hundred grand in drugs for his nephews' stunts. His son Donovan was in the hospital for two weeks with a collapsed lung. It was bad. But that was when the Irish understood fucking with a Kutsenko would cost them. It was one thing to go after bratva businesses. But to go after us personally? Liam shut that shit down.

"Daddy?"

"Yes, *malyshka*."

"You need sleep too."

Her head is on my chest, but her hand slides down to wrap around my cock. She strokes me to life, and I pinch her nipple.

"You're supposed to be asleep, angel."

"A good rough fuck will either put you straight to sleep or give you the energy to start the day."

"I think you're trying to distract me from my thoughts."

"Maybe, Daddy. Is it working?"

"Yes."

I roll her onto her back and slide my fingers into her pussy. What a fucking glorious place to be. Warm and silky, and oh so inviting. She opens her legs to me, and I slide down the bed.

"I'm supposed to be fucking you, Daddy. Not the other way around."

"And if this is what I want, *malyshka*? What if I crave a midnight snack? Who decides, baby girl?"

"You, *sudar'*."

"Don't come unless I give you permission. I'll spank your ass raw if you do."

I lick the length of her pussy before I thrust my tongue into her. I swipe it up and flick her clit before I thrust three fingers into her.

"More, *sudar'*. Please."

"Do you want my cock? Is that what you're asking for?"

"That or you could fucking fist me. Whatever you want. Just more."

She's too tight right now to do that, but I don't dislike the idea. I slide a fourth finger in, but I don't press any deeper than I already am. She writhes on the bed, pulling the sheets into her grasp and fisting them.

"Let me hear you, *malyshka*."

Her moans fill the room as she arches toward me. I listen to them, and my balls ache. She started this to distract me, but I know how upset she was by the time we got home. I consoled her on the dining room table before we even made it to the bed, but it resolved nothing. She needs this as much as I do. I can tell from her moans that she's getting close, but she's fighting the urge. When it becomes more frustrated than aroused, I blow cool air across her pussy.

"Come, baby girl."

"Thank you, *sudar'*."

Her body trembles as her abs contract. She sighs as the euphoria ebbs. Her cheeks are flushed and sweat beads along her forehead and temple. She's so fucking beautiful. I climb off the bed and open the dresser draw where we keep our collection of toys and kinky shit. I've spent more time online than I probably should, but we share an interest in bondage. It took me a while to realize it because I couldn't envision doing anything more than cuffing her to the bed. It seemed far too close to what I do as part of my—day job. But when we talked, and I researched, I realized this was something I wanted with Heather. I want that kind of trust between us.

We chose a few types of rope to experiment with, and this is the first time we're using any. I grab the silky one because I want to be certain I get this right before risking using a rope that might cut into her skin. I unwind part of it.

"Come here, *malyshka*."

"Yes, *sudar'*."

"I need you to talk to me as we do this. If it's too tight or doesn't feel right—"

"Daddy, I know. I won't let you harm me. If anything gets numb or tingles, I'll tell you immediately."

The warnings echo in my head. Don't put knots behind knees or tie under the armpits. To stay away from knots on the inner wrists and inner thighs. To watch where I place the knots to avoid nerve damage. That last one nearly freaked me out enough to refuse. But the video tutorials—of which there are far more than I imagined—helped put me at ease.

The one thing I will absolutely avoid is binding only her wrists. I've tied too many together with rope, and I don't want that part of my life crossing into our intimacy. When we discussed what we wanted to try, I mentioned I wouldn't do it. She understood without me having to explain. She simply kissed my cheek, then we moved on.

"We're going to try the cross-chest box tie, *malyshka*."

"Yes, *sudar'*."

"That excites you, doesn't it? You want to put those pretty tits on display."

She nods, and I pinch her nipple. At her sharp inhale, I twist and tug. I kiss her, nipping at her lower lip. She's crossed her wrists at her lower back, and I know she wants to wrap her arms around me.

"Cross your arms behind your back and grasp your forearms, baby girl."

I walk around her and slap her ass. I love watching the flesh move. But I make myself focus. I already know how to create single column wrists cuffs. I'm only doing this because it's one step in the larger harness. I'm also keeping them behind her back, not lifting her arms over her head. That would be way too reminiscent.

I run the tail up to her left shoulder, then pass it across her upper chest before sliding it under the opposite arm. I pass the tail through the cuff and bring it up and over her right shoulder. It goes across her chest and under her opposite arm before I wrap it beneath her tits, binding her arms to her ribs. It's snug, but I'm careful not to tug her arms too far back or to make it difficult for her to breathe.

"Are you all right, *malyshka?*"

"Yes, *sudar'*."

"This is just to test out how we like it. I'm looking forward to much more intricate harnesses."

"Me too. Can we try the diamond chest harness next?"

I can picture her with the rope wrapped around her tits, making them stick out further. Fuck. My dick needs some attention. I stroke myself, and I see the flash of annoyance in her gaze. There are plenty of times when she likes to watch me, making her more eager. Tonight is not one of those times.

"Are you frustrated that you have no control and can't reach out for me?"

"Yes, *sudar'*."

"This isn't the first time I've restrained you. How is this different?"

"I don't know. Maybe because my hands are behind me, and I can't even try to reach out to you. Maybe because my arms are completely pinned to me. I know I accepted giving up control, but I'm realizing exactly what that means."

"Is it too much, Heather?"

"Don't call me that when we're like this. Please. I know you want me to know you're serious about me being okay. But I hate it. It feels too distant. Too shut off."

"All right, *malyshka*. I'll remember that. I'm sorry."

"Thank you, *sudar'*."

Her tone was decisive, and I realize she's not exaggerating how much she dislikes feeling any emotional distance between us. I feel the same. Saying her name felt off.

I walk back to the drawer to remove the Wartenburg pinwheel and a velvet covered paddle before I stand behind her. I run the pinwheel down her neck and along her shoulder before I land the first swat on her ass. It's enough to make her go onto her toes and take a step forward. Too much. I bend over and drop a kiss on each ass cheek.

I step back in front of her and draw the pinwheel down her chest, lifting it over the rope before bringing it to her right nipple. Her areolas are wide, and her nipple's a tight dart. She's looking over my shoulder as I tease her with the prickling sensation. I flip the pinwheel back to face me as I close my palm around the handle. I tuck my index and middle fingers into her pussy, and she's drenched. Just like she wasn't ready for the swat on her ass, she's surprised when I bring the paddle down on her tit. I do it three times before drawing my hand from her pussy and running the pinwheel over her nipple. I run it around her areola, watching it contract. My fingers go back into her pussy just before the paddle lands twice more. I'm cautious and keep the swats light. I don't know how she's going to react with them tied. She's liked me paddling her tits in the past, but this is new.

I repeat everything I do on her left side. But this time, I run the pinwheel over her belly and over her clit before I finger and paddle her. Her head falls back as she fights to stand still. I bring her to the precipice over and over, but I don't let her jump.

"Do you still want to jack me off, *malyshka*?"

"No. I want to suck you off."

"On your knees."

She obeys immediately, her mouth open and eyes down. I brush the tip of my cock against her lips before sliding it along her tongue. I hold the pinwheel and paddle in one hand while the other presses her head forward. There's very little pressure, only enough for her to remember I'm in control. I'm fucking her throat; she's not sucking me off. There's a nuance rather than semantics. Fuck, does it feel good.

When the need to come gets too strong, I pull back and leave the pinwheel and paddle on the dresser. I help her onto the bed, her feet hanging off the end as she kneels. I guide her down to rest on her shoulders.

"If your neck hurts, tell me, *malyshka*. I'm going to fuck you hard. I want to feel your pussy squeeze the cum out of me."

"May I come, *sudar'*?"

"Yes, baby girl. Whenever you need to."

I grasp the rope that runs across the center of her back. We abandoned condoms after the first time I went without. I thrust into her, and she cries out as I pull back on the rope and push my hips forward. She does a Kegel, and I'm tempted to just leave my dick inside as she clamps around it. But we both need to fuck. I plow her over and over. When I hit her g spot, she screams. The rest of the time she pants and moans. Her fingers curl and flex around her forearms.

"Daddy!"

She cries out as my fingers circle her clit. She thrusts her hips back at me, and I let her take part rather than just take my dick. I'm standing between her feet when I ease her back onto just her knees.

"Lean back against me, baby. I have you."

"I know, Daddy."

Her eyes are closed as her head rests on my shoulder, her face toward mine. She presses soft kisses that don't match the force I'm using to fuck her. She's still moving with me, but her kisses are affectionate. I alternate sides as I massage her tits, my other hand working her clit. When she comes a third time, I don't hold back.

"Take my cum. Who does your pussy belong to?"

"You, *sudar'*."

"That's right. I'm going to fill you with my cum because it's mine, and I can."

I blow my load into her pussy with a roar. We tumble forward, but I'm careful to catch her before she lands beneath me. I kiss her shoulder and the crook of her neck over and over before I pull out. She rolls over and arches her back to me, her tits too swollen and pink to ignore. I latch on and suck like a starving baby. I find something soothing about it after the passion we shared. I reach beneath her and untie her as I continue to lick her nipple before sucking again. I alternate sides as her fingers dig into my shoulders. I know the sensation must be intense as the blood freely flows in her arms and chest.

"That's intense, Daddy. Keep sucking, please. It eases some of the tingling."

"Is it too painful?"

"We're doing this again, Daddy. I want that diamond harness. It's just a lot of sensations at once."

She offers her tits to me as I make a meal of them. When I feel her sigh, and her body relax, I lift her into my arms and carry her to the head of the bed. We lie on our sides with her leg over my hip. I rub her arms and back.

"Daddy, I love you. I love the man you are. I love the woman I can be with you. I love what we share. I can't imagine doing something like that with anyone else. It would have felt too awkward, too embarrassing. I've never trusted anyone else to try that. I never worry with you."

"I love you, *malyshka*. Bringing you pleasure brings me pleasure. I never imagined that could be so true. I don't know how to explain the control I crave because it feels like it shouldn't equal how much I want to take care of you. But they do. I can't separate the two."

"I don't want you to. You're not 'Sleeping with the Enemy' controlling. I remember that scene with Julia Roberts where she has to make sure she lined all the cans up exactly right, and the towels had to hang perfectly. You would notice because you notice everything. But I've never worried about you punishing me for not being perfect or not doing something perfectly."

She pushes up onto her elbow.

"Aleks, I'm not scared of you. I know I can tell you if something is too much. Even if I know you can't or won't change, I know I can still share whatever I need or want. I wish I knew how to stop you from obsessing over not harming me. Even if you did—shh, I'm not saying you ever would—but if it happened, I know it would never be intentional. I know you'd feel guilty and not forgive yourself. But I can tell you now, there wouldn't be anything to forgive. I trust you without a single reservation."

She lies back down and kisses me. It's so incredibly tender and loving. I feel so completely accepted and loved for all my faults and my strengths. I'm marrying this woman before the end of the month. I want to make the commitment, and I want her to know how much I want it. I won't issue an edict of a two-day-turned-three-day engagement like Maks gave Laura. But it will be soon. I will fuck up anyone who thinks to fuck with that.

Chapter Twenty

Heather

Aleks told me Sergei's spent all day searching any and everything he can find on Mike. He came over before dinner to talk about it. Aleks said he won't keep anything from Maks and the others, but he wants me to hear it first. And he wants us to have some privacy in case whatever it is upsets me. I suspect it's not what, but when it upsets me. From Sergei's grim expression as we move to the living room, I won't like it.

"They're not having sex."

Sergei doesn't beat around the bush.

"How do you know? Like Sylvia said, what man sees a woman who isn't his shrink or his pastor every week and isn't having sex?"

"It probably was sexual when they started in college. From what I can tell from hacked photo cloud accounts and the oldest social media posts, they dated a couple times while he and Danielle weren't together. They coincide with the times Danielle wanted a break."

Sergei appears to brace himself, and he looks markedly uncomfortable.

"Ms. Hampton—"

"Could everyone who's related to Aleks please stop calling me that?"

Aleks grins.

"Everyone is related to me in some way, Heather. Second cousins. Cousins once or twice removed. That sort of thing.

"Okay. They can call me that if they aren't your brother or first cousin. It's ridiculous. I know it's respectful, but it makes me feel like I'm not—"

I snap my mouth shut. I'm about to make a humongous fool of myself.

"What does it make you feel like, *malyshka?*"

My eyes widen, and they dart to Sergei. He doesn't seem to notice.

"Can I tell you that later and just say for now that I don't like it?"

"Of course. Sergei, let the others know."

"Thank you. What is Shannon to Mike, if not his mistress?"

"His Domme."

My head falls forward, and I blink at least ten times in like two seconds. I swallow before I speak.

"Like pleather and Lycra with stiletto boots? Like whips and licking her boots?"

"Actually, exactly like that. Mike isn't Shannon's only client."

"Wait—client? He pays her for this?"

"Yes. She's a legitimate licensed therapist. Apparently, it's called Kink Therapy. They do breathing exercises, set goals or intentions, and they talk through things even as she dominates him. No sex though."

"Is he naked? Is she? Even if they're not having full blown

sex, are they doing sexual stuff? Is he fucking cheating on my sister?"

"Yes, he's naked. And sometimes she is. They are doing sexual stuff without having full blown sex. And no, he's not cheating on Danielle. They go together most weeks. Heather—"

Now Sergei looks really uneasy. He wants me to know, too. I think he wants to be sure I understand he takes no pleasure in divulging this to me.

"Heather, Danielle has a Dom, and it is sexual. It's Shannon's husband. He's a licensed therapist too. It's like couples' therapy led by a couple."

"How—how—do you know all of this in one day?"

"Digital records. It wasn't hard to figure out that Shannon's a therapist. It made me wonder if Mike is a patient. Once I discovered he is, I just hacked those files. I skimmed most of it except for the parts where our family came up."

Our. His and Aleks's. Not mine. Mine's too fucking fucked up.

"Nothing gives me the impression Mike knows Shannon's family ties. I listened to the session audio recordings. He's telling her things as his therapist, not bitching like to a friend. She's using it, though. I found emails, and she calls Dillan as soon as Mike leaves."

I rest my elbow on my knee and rub my fingers over my forehead. Aleks's hand rests on my thigh as we sit on the sofa together. Sergei is across from us in an armchair with his laptop open.

"Danielle's having sex with another man?"

Fuck. I thought my sex life was kinky. My sister's practically a fucking swinger.

"Yeah. Apparently, Mike likes to watch. That's how it started. He was having trouble performing and asked Danielle to try this. That's when they started seeing Shannon and her husband. At the heart of it, Danielle and Mike are both submissive, and they both crave someone dominant. Mike is dominant in business, but not in his personal life. He likes Shannon to issue him orders. He likes the degrading ones. Danielle likes Steven—that's his name—to do the same, but sexually."

"I thought you said you skimmed it. Sounds like you learned a lot from glancing at it."

"I skimmed the written reports. There wasn't a way to skim the audio and be sure I missed nothing. I'm sorry, Heather. I know this is really uncomfortable for you, but I'm glad to tell you he isn't having an affair."

"And Mike doesn't consider my sister having sex with another guy an affair because he watches."

I cover my face with my hands as I lean into them. Aleks wraps his arm around my hips, and I lean toward him. I can see Danielle being into kinky shit. I knew she liked guys who were dominant in bed. I assumed Mike was. But this—this is a lot to take in. I wipe my left hand over my left eye a few times before I sit up.

"If it can, this goes to my grave. I don't want either of them to know any of us learned this. I know you have to tell Maks what's going on, but please try not say as much about my sister as you did."

"I wish it were that simple, Heather. I really do. Mike's revealed a lot to Shannon, but Danielle's told things to Steven that Mike told her. Stuff Mike didn't tell Shannon. Steven and Shannon are manipulating Danielle and Mike to get information about Mike's company doing business with our family. Steven plants seeds by suggesting ways to have more open communication with Mike. Then he asks how it went."

Aleks lifts me into his lap, and I don't care what Sergei sees or hears. These people my sister and brother-in-law trust with the most private parts of their lives as individuals and as a couple are manipulating them. I lean against Aleks and concentrate on listening to his steady heartbeat. I let him talk to Sergei.

"How much could Mike have to say at this point? The acquisition already went through."

"He knows Kutsenko Partners is basically using it as a shell corp. He almost lost his job when RK Group downsized after the merger. Despite getting the big payday, the board wanted to trim the fat. They had passed Mike over for promotion a couple times. He scored a couple big clients in time to keep his job. But it was close enough that he looked for other jobs. No one called him for an interview. Once he knew his job was secure, he was content. Then the acquisition happened, and he almost lost his job again. He scrambled again and kept it. But that's when shit got personal for him. He's been digging, trying to find anything that'll stick. He hasn't, which pisses him off more. He's told Shannon his entire paper trail and search history. He couldn't find shit, but the O'Rourkes have the same tools as I do. Finn just isn't as good at hacking as I am." Sergei shrugs with a grin. "If only he'd gotten into an Ivy League like me."

I frown.

"I went to UPenn and studied computer science with Anton. Finn went to Rutgers. Good school. Just not as good as mine."

"You and Anton went to school together? That must have been nice."

Neither Aleks's nor Sergei's expression changes. Aleks's doesn't move. But somehow the air's changed.

"It was. I took to hacking while Anton prefers programming. We work well together. Anyway, Shannon must have been feeding everything to her cousins. The last few session recordings have been Mike getting angry that you and Aleks are dating. He's pissed because he wishes he could provide more for Danielle. His manhood is linked to it, and he feels emasculated, especially knowing how wealthy you'll become."

I look up at Aleks, who glares at Sergei, who rolls his eyes.

"It's no national secret."

Aleks says something in Russian that makes Sergei laugh. Looking at Aleks's face, he did not mean it to be funny. Sergei stands up, so Aleks and I do, too. He hugs me.

"I'm sorry I was the bearer of bad news. I promise I'll keep my report to Maks and the others as discreet as I can."

"The others? What?"

I turn a horrified expression to Aleks. Do all eight of them have to know this about my family?

"*Malyshka*, Sergei has to tell Maks because he's our *pakhan*. I would know, even if I wasn't your boyfriend. Niko, Bogdan, and I are Maks's most trusted advisors. If we have to act on any of this, it's Anton who'll plan it. Misha and Pasha will lead it."

"Act on it? Lead? You make it sound like a battle plan."

Neither Aleks nor Sergei disabuse me of the notion. All I can do is nod.

"Sergei, you and Anton are equals of some sort, right?"

Sergei's gaze flickers to Aleks's before he nods. Why couldn't he answer without looking at Aleks? What are they hiding?

"If you both went to college for the same thing, how did you end up with only you gathering intel?"

Sergei looks at Aleks, and neither says anything. I look up at Aleks, and the wall is up.

"I'm sorry, Aleks. I shouldn't have asked. That's getting too nosey."

"Much of the bratva is split into two groups. Support and Security. Sergei is our *sovietnik*. He's the head of the Support Group and chief intelligence officer. Anton is the head of the

Security Group and the *obshchak*. Anton is an excellent strategist. He analyzes the information Sergei gives him and goes from there."

I'm surprised Aleks is telling me this, especially in front of Sergei. Even if he hasn't kept what I know a secret, I didn't expect them to ever have an open conversation about this.

"You two are kinda like Tony Stark and Iron Man. Two sides of the same coin."

Sergei laughs, but Aleks only nods. What did I say that makes Aleks so uncomfortable? I just meant that they're practically the same person. They're so in tune with one another that they could practically be the same person.

Oh, shit. My eyes widen. I look up at Aleks, and he spins me toward him. His hands are on my upper arms as he leans to meet my gaze. There's an intensity to it, and I catch a glimmer of what men must see before they die for crossing Aleks's family. I shake my head and try to take a step back.

"Aleks, you're going to freak her out. I trust her. With the shit I know about her family, I think she can understand why she can never talk about it."

"Aleks, you're scaring me."

He lets go immediately, and he's horrified. I take a step forward, and he pulls me against him.

"I'm sorry, *malyshka*."

"I know. It's all right. I know you won't hurt me, but I don't understand why you're upset. I know not to tell anyone about Sergei and Anton. You're Russian, and I'm not stupid."

"I never thought you were, baby girl. But I don't know if you truly understand how dangerous this is for my cousins."

He must be upset because I don't think he intended anyone to hear him call me baby girl in English, even if he says it in Russian. I look over at Sergei.

"You've been kind and patient with me. I know I irritate

your brother. But I would never do anything to endanger you or anyone else in your family."

"Our family."

I look up at Aleks as he corrects me. My mouth forms an O, and heat flares in Aleks's eyes. When Sergei speaks, it tears my attention from how Aleks is looking at my mouth.

"You don't irritate Misha. He worries about you. We all do because we know what you mean to Aleks, and because we like you. How the hell you get him to laugh is beyond any of us. We thought that mode broke years ago."

"What do you mean? Aleks laughs all the time."

"No, I don't. At least, I didn't before we started dating. I'm the dour one. Maks is the uncommunicative one. Bogdan's the easygoing one. And Niko is—who the fuck knows? Some people say he's as easygoing as Bogdan. Others think he's arrogant. Ana thinks he's God's gift to a tired world. She'd say he's the deep one."

That's a revelation.

"What about you, Sergei? What about the other cousins?"

"I'm the meathead."

I laugh so hard I snort.

"I like it that way. No one knows what's coming. Anton is the observer. Pasha is the pretty one. And my brother is—who the fuck knows with him, either? The jokester, maybe. He thinks he's funny. The jury's still out."

I love listening to them describe their family. I don't know everyone well yet, but their assessments seem spot on.

"I heard Bogdan call you Little Miss Sunshine and Aleks Eeyore. That was so fucking spot on."

"*Zatknis' mudak.*"

I look up at Aleks, then over at Sergei.

"What does that mean?"

Sergei chuckles and smirks at Aleks.

"He told me to shut up, asshole."

"That's no way to talk about family, Aleks."

I tickle his ribs, and he wiggles.

"Holy fuck! You're still ticklish? I'm telling *everyone*."

Sergei practically has tears falling from his eyes, he's laughing so hard.

"Don't forget what happened the last time you told my brothers."

"Yeah, you got grounded for two weeks for punching me."

"It was worth it. Now Pasha's the pretty one."

I stand aghast.

"You hit Sergei?"

Aleks shakes his head.

"No. I punched him in the boxing ring. He was bigger than me and thought he didn't need to wear headgear."

"And you knew you weren't supposed to be throwing punches that hard. That's why you got in trouble."

"It's not my fault you're so slow."

I doubt there's anything slow about any of them. They're in better shape than most pro athletes, and I know Sergei and Anton go running all the time. I know they all warm up with an hour on the treadmill when they go to the gym in the morning.

"Yeah, well, Anton defended my honor, and you got grounded. That was worth it, too."

"Wait. How long ago was this?"

"I was thirteen, and Sergei was fourteen. We'd only been here a few months. I was scared Vlad would find out about that weakness."

Sergei gets serious quickly.

"I never would have let that happen, Aleks."

"I know that now. I didn't back then."

Sergei glances at his watch.

"I need to get going. Anton and I are going with Pasha and Sumiko. They're having a late dinner with her friends."

I step forward and hug Sergei again.

"Thank you for everything. I know this is so fucked up. But I appreciate how considerate you were when you told me. I trust you to do what's best with that info."

"I'll be discreet, Heather. I promise."

I beam at him, letting him know how much more I prefer that to Ms. Hampton. Once Sergei's on the elevator, I turn back to Aleks.

"I know I didn't take the whole having a bodyguard at all times seriously enough. But I've seen the news. I will never tell anyone what I figured out. Do the other women know?"

"Yes. At least, I think so. I think they all figured it out, too."

"Have they been together long?"

Aleks nods before taking my hand as we walk to our bedroom. We're going out on a date. They assigned Misha, and a guy named Stefan to us tonight, but Aleks said they'll follow in their own cars. Aleks is driving us.

"They were best friends when we were all kids. They're close with their own brothers like I am with mine. There's something about sharing parents or the same DNA. I don't know. It's just different. They were in love by the time we were all teenagers. They didn't tell any of us at first. But everyone sorta guessed. It was my uncles who finally brought it up."

"Really?"

"Yeah. It was one of the earliest missions I went on with Maks, Anton, and Sergei. In the past, Anton and Sergei partnered with their dads, and Maks partnered with a guy named Igor. He was a good mentor, but once I started going on the missions, he didn't join us anymore. We were all at Uncle Grigori and Aunt Alina's getting ready. My mom and Aunt Svetlana were there too, to say goodbye. Uncle Grigori and

Uncle Radomir said they would partner with me and Maks. They were so casual as they explained it. They just said they knew Anton and Sergei would protect each other better than anyone else. That's what you do when you love someone. None of us knew what to do or say. Our moms obviously already knew because they just gave us hugs and kisses and told us not to get hurt because none of them had time to nurse us better. My brothers and their brothers were with us to help the six of us get ready and to say goodbye, too."

"I can only imagine how that shocked all of you."

"Yeah. My uncles were KGB and bratva. That scared Anton and Sergei enough to tell none of us. Our parents figured it out, and like I said, the rest of us had pretty much guessed."

"Life's extra unfair for them. My guess is they can never live together."

"They talk about living together when they're old men and people could see how two best friends would when everyone believes they need roommates to keep from being lonely."

"That's not for a few more decades!"

"They've already been together nearly two. They have a partnership that makes them unstoppable at work and unconditionally committed in their private life. I don't know two people who work better together than them. They make it work. They're usually the ones who accompany anyone who's traveling. It makes it a little easier to justify sharing rooms and stuff like that."

"Will Anton and everyone else be okay with me knowing?"

"Yes. You're family, *malyshka*."

We changed as we talked. Aleks rests his hands on my waist as we look at each other in the elevator.

"Baby girl, you know what the next step is. If and when you want that, I'll ask."

"I think you can say those four words before the elevator stops."

Aleks laughs, and his eyes crinkle. He kisses me instead.

"Know without a doubt, I'm marrying you, baby girl. But I'm not proposing in an elevator."

"That would make a memorable story for the family."

We step off the elevator and into the underground parking garage.

"Nope. Not how it's happening. Who gets to decide?"

"Nope. Not how it's happening. We get to decide. And I don't need some flowery proposal."

Aleks opens the car door for me but freezes. His head whips around before he drags me away and shoves me into a run. I don't understand what's happening until scorching heat blazes against my back, and the loudest noise I've ever heard deafens me. Aleks wraps his arms around, and it's like we're in slow motion as we fall to the ground. He does what he can to absorb the impact before he rolls onto my back and shields me as another explosion goes off.

I hear tires squealing as the smell of burning rubber and oil fills the air. I try to twist under Aleks, but he doesn't move.

"Aleks?... Aleks?... Aleks!"

I struggle out from under his dead weight. The back of his coat is shredded, and I can see debris embedded in his back. I put my fingers to his throat and feel a pulse. It's way stronger than I expected. My gaze sweeps the parking garage. There's a car coming, but I can't see it yet. I scramble to my feet as I shake him again. Beyond breathing, he does nothing. I slide my arms under his and drag him toward the elevator. It's like a mouse dragging an elephant. I know he's only ten pounds shy of double my weight. I let go and run to hit the button for the elevator before going back to drag him the last few feet.

Fuck. Hurry. Where the fuck is the elevator? Fuck.

The car I heard is coming up the ramp to our level. It was parked below. My guess is so they could drive straight out without having to turn around. I don't recognize it as it comes into sight. The elevator doors open as a guy in a black bala-clava leans out the window with a gun pointed at me. I drag Aleks the last few feet and cover his back with my body as I reach for the door close button, then the closest floor button I can reach. I hear bullets hit the metal as the elevator rises. I hit the stop button as soon as I'm certain they couldn't pry open the doors and get to us. I fumble for my phone as I roll off Aleks.

"Maks!"

"Heath—"

"Someone blew up Aleks's car. We're stopped in the eleva-tor. He's breathing. Help!"

"Slow down. Where are you?"

"Our building."

"Can you take the elevator to your place?"

"What if someone's waiting for us?"

"Heather, there will be. It'll be our men. No one is getting into your place without being watched on camera."

It's not until later that it registers that someone has seen us fucking in the elevator if no one can get in without being watched.

"Misha and Stefan are already outside. They'll come up too. Have you ever shot a gun?"

"Yeah. My dad taught me."

"Okay. When you get to the penthouse, take Aleks's gun. Men will already be in there through the fire escape. I've already sent a text. You'll know them. Misha and Stefan will come up in the elevator after you. If you see anyone you don't recognize, shoot to kill. Do you understand?"

"But what if they're—"

"Heather, I don't give a shit if you kill one of my men. I will give a shit if my brother or you die. Fucking shoot to kill."

"All right."

I don't think he really means that he wouldn't care, but I get it. I look down at all the blood that's pouring out of Aleks's wounds. There's so much.

"M-M-Maks." I sob. "Aleks has to go to a hospital. This is not something your doctor can fix. He's bleeding so much. He —" I swallow. "Call an ambulance or I will. I don't give a shit about the not going to the hospital at all costs. I'm taking him."

I find my backbone as the elevator doors open. I pull Aleks's gun and sweep my eyes around the living room. I recognize the five men running toward me, so I lower the gun.

"It's already on its way, Heather. I'm with Bogdan and Niko. Their phones have been ringing with our men reporting the bombing. They heard it and saw it on the security monitors. They saw you. Are you hurt?"

I take a moment to assess myself.

"I don't think so. He pulled me away from the car and then shielded me."

"All right. I'll find out more later. Misha and Stefan will be there in a minute."

The men are already helping me off the floor and carrying Aleks into the penthouse.

"Maks, what do I say at the hospital? How do I explain this?"

"You don't. You're his distraught wife. Let Misha do all the talking. Do you understand?"

"Yes."

"Heather, I am trusting you to make medical decisions for him until we can all get there. You ride in the ambulance with him. Put his gun in your purse or somewhere you can easily reach. Keep your hand on it the entire ambulance ride. Misha and Stefan will be in cars in front of and behind the ambulance. If the ambulance stops anywhere but the hospital, you shoot anyone who opens those doors. Shoot first, ask questions later. Do you understand?"

"Yes."

I do, but there's so much information bombarding me I'm struggling to keep up. I turn around and raise the gun when the elevator pings again. Thank fucking God. It's Misha and some guy that kinda resembles Anton's side of the family.

"Misha's here."

"I know. I'm going to hang up with you. You do everything Misha and Stefan tell you. You can trust Stefan, but only as long as Misha can see and hear you."

"But he's—"

"You heard me. Do you understand me?"

"Yes, Maks. Hurry."

The call ends as Misha and Stefan run toward us. I didn't even realize the other men lifted Aleks onto the dining room table. He's lying on his belly with blood pooling on the granite and the floor. How is he alive? Is he?

Misha steps toward me, but I shove him out of the way. I try to find a pulse again, but I can't. I slide my fingers around but find nothing. Misha tries to pull me away, and I lash out.

"Heather, he's still bleeding. He's alive."

"What?"

I spin toward Misha.

"Heather, blood stops flowing when the heart stops. Gravity sucks it toward the internal organs. It wouldn't still be flowing up and out of his back. He's alive. Do you hear that? The ambulance is almost here."

"How will they get up here?"

"I'm going down to meet them and bring them up."

"But Maks said—" I snap my mouth shut and lean forward

to whisper. "He said not to trust anyone but you and Stefan, and only if I can see and hear you."

"I know, but with the biometrics, someone has to. You need to stay where there are guards. I don't want you to speak at all. Pretend you don't speak English if you have to. You'll ride in the ambulance with Aleks. They'll be busy and not asking you questions. I'll tell them all they need to know."

I nod, and then Misha's gone.

Chapter Twenty-One

Aleks

I knew immediately that something was wrong. When I opened Heather's door, the interior lights didn't come on. Each of our vehicles has a mounted vehicle bomb detection system. The lights not shining immediately are one indicator. It could have been nothing, but that I just woke up in the hospital proves it wasn't.

"Aleks?"

Heather leans forward, and my vision focuses more as I look at her. She's holding my hand, but my arm feels incredibly heavy. I'm mostly on my left side, with pillows behind me. I try to take a deep breath and discover there's a tube down my throat. I squeeze her hand, and she kisses my forehead.

"Mrs. Kutsenko, we'll take the tube out now that he's awake."

Mrs. Kutsenko? I don't see my mom, my aunt, or my sisters-in-law. She means Heather. Did I forget getting married? I glance down at her hands. No. There's no ring. Didn't my family come? Did she say that so she could decide what happens?

"Shh, Aleks. Everything is going to be all right. Everyone is on their way back."

Back? How long have I been here? They wouldn't leave if this happened today. My gaze shifts to the woman I heard speak. She's in a lab coat, not scrubs. I didn't just come out of surgery. Heather tries to step aside, but I won't release her hand.

"I have to move out of the way."

She pries her hand free, and I watch as a man takes her place. The woman in the lab coat and the man in scrubs move things around before they withdraw the tube. It makes me gag, and my throat burns. The doctor stays beside me, but the man —an RN from his ID—hurries to move out of Heather's place. I need her back. I need to touch her. I need to see her.

"Talk to me, *malyshka*."

My throat is on fire. My voice barely comes out and is little more than a rasp. I don't know if she can understand me.

"I will, but Dr. Morgenstern is going to explain everything."

"Can I walk?"

I direct my question to Heather, but the doctor answers.

"Yes."

"Will we have children?"

I watch Heather's eyes nearly pop out of her head and her face flush. I'm more concerned with whether we can practice making those babies, but I have the good graces to not ask if I can fuck my wife. God, how I want to hear Heather called Mrs. Kutsenko again.

"Yes. Mr. Kutsenko, we expect you to make a full recovery. We were concerned about brain trauma and took preemptive steps to minimize any long-term damage. All of your neurological tests came back clear. The wounds on your back and legs are healing well. There will be scars, but no infection set in. They're doing better than expected, actually. You have a healthy constitution. Hold off on your hobby for a while. I've never met another blacksmith."

I show none of my surprise, but I'm fucking shocked. Who the hell came up with that explanation? I suppose metal working might explain how chunks of a fucking car were likely imbedded in my skin. I wonder what the hell Heather told the EMTs when they showed up. There was clearly no forge that blew up in my building's garage.

"Mr. Kutsenko, I'm Lev Sidorov's daughter. Like I said, I've never met a blacksmith before."

"Yana?"

"Yes."

The doctor's father used to be part of the Elite Group when we first arrived. He was the one who told Vlad about our arrival. He was the one who ruined our lives.

"I know what my father did. I can't undo any of it. But I could save your life, so I did."

Heather's obviously confused. I tug her arm, and she leans forward, so I can talk softly without straining my throat further.

"Her father recognized Uncle Radomir at Mass and told Vlad about us. He was an Elite Group member and the reason we're all in the bratva."

She cups my cheek and nods. She kisses just above her hand.

"Mr. Kutsenko—"

"Aleksei."

It seems pointless to be formal considering how history connects our families, but neither are we friends.

"You bruised most of your ribs. You have lacerations and abrasions that will take a few weeks to heal. The stitches will all dissolve. In the meantime, avoid lying on your back as best you can. I mentioned the neurological tests came back with flying colors. We'll discharge you in a couple days, assuming nothing changes. I'll let you have time with your wife."

"Thank you."

Heather smiles at the doctor, but I can see it's strained. I guess it's a combination of exhaustion, ongoing worry, and uncertainty how to react to what I told her. I loathe seeing her this distressed.

"*Malyshka*, are you all right? Were you hurt? Did they check you out too? Do you—"

"*Papochka*, you saved me. Nothing more than a few bruises."

"A few? One is too many."

"Shh. Before you plot revenge, please just get better."

"Call me that again, *malyshka*."

"*Papochka*."

She's only said it once since the day she first learned it. I didn't realize how much I enjoy hearing it until she says it now.

"Put the bed rail down."

She looks around and finds the button. Once it's dropped, I grimace but make more space between me and the edge.

"Lie down with me, baby girl."

"No. I don't want to bump into your ribs or tug on any tubes."

"*Malyshka*."

She shakes her head and bites her bottom lip. Well, I know now that I can still father children. Fuck, she's hot when she's bashful. I know if I wait, she'll give in. She does. It's not because I commanded her. It's because she needs the contact as much as I do. She's careful as she eases onto the bed. I lift the covers so she can get closer. The moment we're touching, we both sigh. There are deep shadows beneath her eyes.

"Baby, how long have we been here?"

She's not covered in blood, wearing the clothes she wore to our canceled date. Canceled. Ha.

"Four days."

"I was unconscious that long?"

"They kept you that way because they feared possible Traumatic Brain Injury. Debris hit you, but there were no visible wounds to your head."

"Did any hit you?"

"No. You completely sheltered me from it."

"And I didn't hurt you when I knocked you down?"

"Just the few bruises."

"Where?"

I need to know. I'm afraid to see, but it's like a compulsion. She glances at the door before she pushes down the waistband of her yoga pants and pulls up her sweater. A bruise covers the entire front of her ribs and down to her hip. I can see my fingerprints. I think I'm going to be ill.

"Breathe, Daddy. It's sore, but it doesn't hurt. I don't mind them because they mean I'm alive."

I brush the back of my fingers over her ribs, careful not to put any pressure on them. Whoever did this—whoever caused me to bruise my baby girl—is going to die the most torturous death I can conceive. I have no chance to say more because the door opens, and I know immediately my family is here. Heather tries to get up, but my expression tells her not to move. She's embarrassed, but for once I don't care. I need her. She whispers to me.

"I'm not going anywhere, but your mom needs to hug you. I can't keep her from you. I won't."

I nod. That's reasonable. Thank goodness one of us is being so. She gets up as my mom hurries around the privacy curtain. I reach for her, and I see her relief. I hate knowing she feared I was dead or would die. Guilt and fear have motivated my brothers and me since the beginning. We never want our mom to grieve for us like she still does for our dad.

"Mama."

"*Pchelka.*" Little bee. She's called all of us that since we were born. "*Ya lyublyu tebya i tvoikh brat'yev bol'she vsego na svete. Net nichego luchshe, chem obnyat' tebya pryamo v etu minutu. Ya tebya lyublyu. Ya tebya lyublyu. Ya tebya lyublyu.*" I love you and your brothers more than anything. Nothing is better than hugging you right this minute. I love you. I love you. I love you.

"*Ya tozhe lyublyu tebya, mama. Tvoi ob"yatiya delayut vse luchshe, kak kogda ya sidela u tebya na kolenyakh, i ty pel mne.*" I love you too, Mama. Your hugs make everything better, just like when I used to sit on your lap, and you sang to me.

"*Ty nikogda ne budesh' slishkom bol'shim ili slishkom starym dlya ob"yatiy so svoyey mamoy.*" You're never too big or too old for a cuddle with your mom.

She kisses my forehead, and my eyes flutter closed for a moment. I know Ana is interpreting for Heather. I don't fear my relatives hearing me. All of us have had similar conversations with our parents. I'm hardly the first or only of us to get injured. I draw a different sort of strength from my mom's embrace than I do from Heather's. They both feel vital right now.

She moves out of the way, and each of my brothers hugs me. None of us deal well when one of us is hurt or sick. Salvatore calls us a hydra. We are. We are one beast with four bodies. If two minds are better than one, then four are brilliant. We are undeterrable, and whoever did this should count themselves dead. I want my pound of flesh for someone endangering Heather. My family will want the rest to punish them for my injuries, to remind everyone else there is never just one of us. There is only ever all of us.

Nineteen people somehow got into this hospital room with me. They're all here. My mom, my brothers, my sisters-in-law, my aunts, my uncles, my cousins, and my cousin-in-law. Laura looks a little uneasy, but even my niece and nephew are here. She holds the twins, one on each hip. Misha and Anton stand near the door. Niko and Bogdan are by the windows. Maks, my uncles, and Sergei shield the women's backs.

I have one burning question.

"Who?"

Sergei's blue eyes, which match mine, are like shards of ice in a Siberian lake. It's determination bred from an instinct to survive, nurtured by a desire for control, and honed with experience at revenge.

"We don't know yet."

My throat is dry, and I reach for the water on the tray. Heather helps me, propping up my head after guiding the straw to my mouth. I feel helpless, but the underlying healthy male loves the view of her cleavage as she tends to me. It's a fucking good thing I'm on my side with the blankets around me, or my family would know I'm the most inappropriate fucker around. Not the time. Not the time. Not the time.

I sound much better when I speak.

"No one's claimed nearly killing the *pakhan's* brother? We're still dealing with this bullshit." I glance at my mom and wince. "Sorry. I miss the days when people took pride in their work and bragged. It made dealing with them way more efficient. Have you ruled anyone out?"

Sergei gives me the rundown.

"No. No one's in New York though. Salvatore and all of his family, nephews included, are in Palermo. There's something going on within the *Cosa Nostra*. My guess is a wedding.

They're not here to have done this personally, but it could be some of their men or mercenaries. Dillan and his cousins are in Boston for a funeral. Pablo and Enrique are in Colombia fu— dealing with their new competition. The Irish and Colombians are the same situation as with the Italians. Could still be any of them."

Heather glances at Sergei before she looks at me again.

"Could it be Shannon?"

Before I can say anything, Maks blurts out what everyone is thinking.

"What the hell does Shannon O'Rourke have to do with this?"

It mortifies Heather. It didn't take a guess to know who Heather meant.

"Uncle Radomir, Uncle Grigori, please take my mom and the others outside. My brothers and cousins stay." I glance at Heather before talking to everyone again. "If the husbands and sons wish to tell their wives and parents once you leave, fine. But this conversation is not happening with twenty people."

Everyone appears surprised. Usually, anything discussed among the men are matters that are safest not repeated to the women. But this is my soon-to-be extended family, which means my blood family must know. Once everyone is gone, I tug Heather's hand and use my other one to pat the bed. She perches on the end. I grasp her waist and pull her closer. She gasps.

"Stop. You'll hurt yourself. Use your words."

There's humor in her tone as she reminds me of that conversation we had when we first started dating. I laugh and let go. She moves closer. Everyone stares at us. As usual. She made what's going to be a shitty conversation a little more comfortable, even if only for a moment. I squeeze her hand, but she shakes her head. Reality sets back in, and she has to force the words out.

"Sergei, can you explain, please? I can't."

My cousin basically tells the rest of my family the same things he told us. He glosses over Danielle's sexual activities. I know Anton and Sergei have never been with anyone but each other. I'm aware of what Niko and Bogdan got up to in college, but I also know none of my brothers or Pasha would agree to having sex with someone other than his wife. Their wives would probably castrate them if they suggested a wife have sex with anyone other than her husband. But I suspect all of us lean toward the kinky side. Our shared trauma has made us alike in almost every way, so it wouldn't surprise me if we have similar proclivities. They won't judge Danielle and Mike about their Dom/sub dynamics, but none of us would be on board with the voyeurism or sharing.

Heather relaxes after Sergei finishes talking, but she's watching me. I don't think she can look at anyone else yet. I don't blame her. Between her sister's private life and the connection to the Irish mob, she feels completely out of place.

"Watch out, *malyshka*. I'm going to sit up."

I adjust the bed and myself, so I'm more upright without pressing against my back. I draw her into my arms, and it takes a moment, but she sags against me. Heather sounds so despondent.

"I'm so, so sorry."

Maks speaks before I can.

"Heather, this isn't a personal reflection on you at all. It isn't even one on Danielle or Mike. He may resent us, but he's not knowingly setting us up."

She nods before she looks at Sergei.

"Do you really believe neither of them knows what Shannon and Steven are doing?"

Sergei sounds resolute as he answers.

"I'm certain. Neither Mike nor Danielle would have reason to believe someone would hack their patient files. They aren't withholding anything, and unless they're conspiring on their phone calls to lie during their sessions, there's no evidence that Mike and Danielle are colluding with Shannon and Steven. I am tapping their calls from now on, though. I have to be certain."

"Should I talk to Danielle about this? How do I warn her without having to give away how I know?"

Maks was rarely sympathetic before meeting Laura, but now that he's more communicative than he once was, he can be. He offers Heather a kind smile before answering.

"Not unless you really feel you have to. I understand why you want to protect your sister from being manipulated. But it's useful to us if they continue as they are. If Shannon and Steven believe something's changed Danielle and Mike's trust in them, then we won't learn anything else. I also don't want to endanger your sister and brother-in-law if Shannon gets suspicious."

"So we just let them keep talking? I—"

Heather stands up and looks at me. There's such anguish in her gaze that my heart breaks. She also looks like she's going to bolt.

"Everyone out."

I startle her, but my brothers and cousins don't need telling twice. They'll wait in the hallway with the rest of my family.

"What's wrong, *malyshka?*"

"I don't want to talk about it."

"You look like you want to leave."

"You're in a hospital bed after nearly being blown up. I'm not leaving."

"That doesn't mean you don't want to. Do you need some space? Do you want to go for a walk?"

"Who would have to follow me? Who's stuck with that job this time?"

I know this same conversation has happened four times in the last year and a half. It's been necessary each time. It's important our women understand they are our world. They are everything that is right and good in a universe of darkness.

"*Malyshka*, no one is stuck guarding you. There are only seven other people in this world who I trust implicitly with your safety. They all just left this room. I wish I could always be the one with you, but we know I can't. It wouldn't be good for us if I were. But I will never be completely at ease when I'm not. The only peace of mind I can get is knowing you're with my brothers or cousins. No one else is good enough to protect the person who means the most to me. I know I can count on them to do whatever they have to, sacrifice whatever they have to, to keep you alive and safe. We know this about each other. None of us take for granted the trust and faith we have in each other. They get what it means for me to let you walk away and go with someone else. When my brothers and cousin entrust their wives to my protection, it reaffirms our loyalty and love for each other. It's an honor. It's no small thing, baby girl."

She takes a shuddering sigh, and I can tell she accepts my explanation, even if her mind still isn't at ease.

"What do you need? Space? Companionable silence? To talk? I will do whatever you want, baby girl."

"Aleks, if I say nothing to Danielle, it's because I chose your family over mine. Or rather, I chose one side of my family over the other. It feels disloyal to them. It feels like I'm turning my back on them to help you."

I suspected that was the problem. Our situations will never be the same. There is no option to consider ever choosing her family over mine. To do so not only endangers the people I'm related to, but it endangers every member of our community who relies on us. But I get it. I can imagine being in her shoes.

"Heather, I promised from the beginning that I wouldn't keep things from you if I didn't have to. I wish I could keep all of this from you, but if we make a life together, then there's no avoiding it."

She doesn't do anything. She just stands and looks at me. For someone who craves control, this situation makes me want to crawl out of my skin.

"I don't know what Shannon is capable of. I haven't seen her in more than ten years. I still know nothing about her husband. I don't know if he's doing this to support her or if he has ties to the mob, too. I don't know what they would do to Mike and Danielle if they discover we know, and they think Mike and Danielle are in on it. It's safest for your sister and brother-in-law to stay blind until we understand Shannon's purpose. If she's anything like the men in her family, she's brutal. Maybe she isn't. But if she turns your family over to hers, they will die and not before they're tortured. You're not picking my family over yours. Right now, you're keeping your family alive."

I know from her body language that she's still considering leaving. What the hell am I supposed to do?

"Aleks, is dating you making it worse for Mike and Danielle? Would Steve and Shannon tire of them and stop manipulating them if we weren't together?"

"I don't think so. This started before we became a couple. Mike was already angry and searching for ways to hurt our business. This might have amped it up, but I don't think it would be different if we weren't together."

"Are you saying that because you think I'm going to break up with you?"

"No. But I fear that anyway."

She doesn't rush to reassure me. That hurts. What she says next just twists the knife.

"I guess it wouldn't matter if we weren't together. We already have been. Mike will always resent that."

"Is that why you'd stay with me? Because it wouldn't matter, so you might as well settle?"

"What? No. I'm staying because I love you, and the thought of being apart from you makes me feel like the entire world is falling apart and nothing would ever be right again. I meant, Mike is going to stay angry, regardless. He doesn't get to ruin us. What about Cadence? Is he in danger? Do I need to tell them because he might be in the middle? Should I tell my dad if I don't tell them?"

That makes me think for a moment. The last thing I want is for her dad to get involved in anything between the bratva and the mob. But he has the training and experience to protect Cadence if something ever went wrong.

"Let me think about that, *malyshka*. I can see the benefits of doing it. I just need to decide whether they outweigh the dangers."

"So we're just in a holding pattern for right now."

"Yes. It sucks, and I get that. But until we know more, you're not choosing us over them. You're not acting impulsively. A plan is always better than an impulse."

"That sounds like a mantra or something."

"It is. Vlad drilled it into us. We had to repeat it for hours and hours."

She stares at me for a protracted moment, unsure what to say. Then her gaze shifts to the door.

"Should we have everyone come back in? I hate telling them to leave, so we can talk in private. It feels rude. Especially since your mom has been out there so long. She must be going nuts wanting to see you. I feel horrible."

"Are you all right with waiting to tell Danielle and Mike?"

"I'll get there. I get why it's better. It just feels—I feel guilty knowing this, and they don't."

"Do you understand no one is stuck guarding you? Laura and the others have all felt that way, and their husbands have all explained what I did."

"Yes. I get it, even if I still feel badly about that too."

"You're adjusting, *malyshka*. If it's too much—"

"Don't, Daddy. It's a lot, but it's not too much. I'm not going anywhere unless you send me away."

"I can't think of a worse fate than you leaving."

"I feel the same."

"Do you feel better for at least talking?"

"Much. A lot still feels unresolved, but better."

"I love you, *malyshka*."

"I love you, *papochka*."

We finally kiss. A real one. It's like neither of us realized we hadn't until we start. It's like a feast after a famine. It threatens to make us forget the rest of the world exists. But my IV monitor beeping brings us back to reality. Heather has my family come back in, and a nurse follows. She gives us a reproving stare for so many people being in here. At least, she does until she meets my mom's gaze. She's suddenly all smiles. Tiger moms have nothing on a Russian bear mom.

Chapter Twenty-Two

Heather

Aleks is home, and a much better patient here than in the hospital. He insisted upon getting out of bed and going for a walk after his family left. He waited until his mom was gone because I think he would have given into her—obeyed her—but he wouldn't give in to me. I know he was in pain, but he completed every exercise they gave him. Once he did, he insisted he was well enough to leave. We were back at the penthouse within eighteen hours. He's been moving slower than usual for the last two days, but he's not trying to be Superman anymore.

"*Malyshka*, you can go back to work. I don't need you home with me anymore."

I know I can, but I don't want to. It's not that I think he needs my help. He's proven that he doesn't. But I'm scared to let him out of my sight for longer than it takes for either of us to go to the bathroom. I don't necessarily think something's going to happen. I just feel panicky at the idea of being away from him. I don't fear for myself. It's entirely about him. I guess I get why he only wants his brothers or cousins with me.

"Will you promise to have one of the guys with you?"

"I don't need a babysitter."

"You believe I need a bodyguard and insist I have one. It's your car that blew up, and you're the one who was in the hospital. Right now, frankly, I don't give a fuck what you want. I need you alive."

I've been patient. I've bitten my tongue. I've agreed when I didn't want to. Apparently, this was my line in the sand. I'm not stepping over it.

"*Malyshka*, I don't want to be a burden. And you have a career and responsibilities."

I know that's how he feels, and he's right. But I can't reconcile them. I walk over to him since I was in the kitchen, and he's in the living room. I'm careful as I wrap my arms around his waist. It's actually strange not to feel a gun holstered there.

"Daddy, I can't yet. You aren't a burden, and no responsibility feels more important than being with you. I don't want to smother you. I don't have to be up your ass."

"I wouldn't mind being up yours."

"Dadddeee."

It's good to hear his sense of humor. It's good to see his boyish grin. It soothes my battered soul.

"Heather, you love teaching. I know you have a spring performance you're gearing up for. Your students need you more than I do. I want you with me all the time. I never want you out of my reach. But what I want—what you want—doesn't match what should and needs to happen."

"I know. You knew something was wrong. You got us away in time. I can't stop thinking about how I didn't know. I couldn't have saved us. I'm struggling with how out of control that feels. It feels like no one has control right now—or rather, the wrong people have it. We don't even know who this is. I feel like no decision I make will be the right one. Whether it's about going back to work or staying home with you. Whether it's about Danielle knowing or not knowing. All of it."

"Come with me."

He leads me into our room, and I can guess what's coming next. I'm desperate for it, but guilt claws at me. He shouldn't be doing this yet. What if he pulls something? What if it tires him? What if —

"*Malyshka*, stop thinking about all the what ifs. We both need this. I feel the same way you do. You need to let go of not having control and let me make some decisions for you. I need to feel like I can take care of you and give you what you need. Take off your clothes."

Tears well in my eyes. It's not because I don't want to do this or because I think he's ordering me around. Just the opposite. It's a relief. The lifting of this burden is so intense, it's a physical change in me. It's like it lets the flood gates open after too much pressure has built against the dam. I nod and practically rip my jeans and long sleeve t-shirt off. I unhook my bra and let it drop to the floor.

"What are those, baby girl?"

"Panties."

"Why do you have them on? You assumed I wouldn't know. Or if I did, you assumed I would do nothing about it." He fists my hair and holds me in place. "Or maybe you knew how I would react, and you're baiting me."

"That one, Daddy. It scared me to ask in case you weren't up to it but felt obligated."

"Nothing about being with you is ever an obligation, Heather."

"I really don't like hearing you say my name when we're

like this. But I get you want me to understand how serious you are."

"I do. *Malyshka*, we will always find ways to take care of each other, give each other what we need. It might not be the same or what we're used to, but I don't doubt you'll always support me. I will always support you."

"I know, Daddy. I'm just really struggling with how much I worry about you. I'm terrified. I need this right now. I need the outside world to go away. I need some normalcy. But I won't let what I need come before what's best for you."

"I know, baby. But who decides?"

I sigh. When we're in moments like this, when this is our dynamic, hearing those three words is everything.

"You do, *sudar'*."

Saying those three words is everything.

His kiss is fierce. We've shared passionate ones since he woke, but this is meant to tame me. To let me know he has control, and he will keep it. I have not a single problem with that. His fist in my hair has tightened until my scalp tingles. My pussy aches with how badly I need the cock pressing against it. His free hand grabs my ass and squeezes so hard there will probably be marks. I want to see them. The first spank comes, and it drives my hips against his dick even harder. He reaches behind me as we continue kissing. He fishes around for something, and he must find it because I hear the drawer slam shut.

"This is too much. Put me down."

He ignores my complaints as he hoists me in the air, and my legs go around his waist. It's the paddle that lands across my ass. Four rapid slaps. He walks us to the bed and sits. His mouth trails along my jaw, down and back up my neck, and behind my ear.

"I am going to spank you. Then I am going to fuck you. You

will take all of it. You will take my cum when I fill that sweet little cunt. I've missed it. I missed filling you with *my* cum.

"I love knowing my pussy is the only one in the world that gets your cum. My pussy is yours because your cock is mine."

"It is, *malyshka*. All of me is yours. Everything I have. Everything I am. It's only for you."

"Is it wrong that some of how I feel is so superficial? I can't help that I love knowing a man as hot as you wants me and no one else. Is it wrong that there's, like, a sense of accomplishment to it?"

"No. But do you judge some of your worth by the fact that you think I'm attractive?"

"I don't have to think it, Daddy. Anyone who's breathing knows it. And yes, I admit I do."

"Do you feel like our—" he shakes his head and shrugs "—measure of attractiveness isn't the same?"

"Yes."

"*Malyshka*, you are the most beautiful woman in the world."

"To you maybe. That's not how other people see me. But the rest of the world can't not know you're sex personified."

He puts the paddle on the bed beside him so he can rest both hands on my ass. There's no pressure beyond their own weight. I can tell any type of roleplaying is suspended right now. I didn't think I needed this conversation. But he gets me, and it's such a relief not to hold this in. I enjoy knowing I can confide in him.

"Heather, are you scared that one day I'm going to realize I could do better and leave you for someone you think is more attractive?"

I note his word choice. Could do better not can do better. You think not I think. That difference means the world to me.

"Sometimes. I know you would never cheat. It's not in your

nature, and your family would never allow it. I don't worry about that. I worry that you'll get fed up with me being less serious than you and find me childish or something. I worry that I'm only good enough for now. You've given me absolutely no reason to feel this way. Just the opposite. It's completely irrational that I do."

"Are these new insecurities?"

"No. But how hot you are and how intensely you love makes them flair up. The thought that you could stop loving me and start loving someone else the same way is suffocating. What if I can't adapt to this life the way I need to, or you want me to? What if I become too much effort or too inconvenient? Nearly losing you brought all of this rushing to the surface. Like I said, I know it's completely irrational and completely my fucked-uppedness. Not you."

"You and I are perfect together because we're more alike than people can see on the surface. What if my looks aren't enough? What if you get fed up with me being so controlling? What if you get fed up with all the limitations you're going to face? What if you don't want to live with the danger? What if you meet someone who makes life so much easier than being with me? What if I am too closed off, and you get tired of not knowing what I'm thinking or feeling? What if I'm just not good enough?"

My eyes burn, and the gorge in my throat threatens to choke me. This man who appears utterly in control of every-thing, who appears like he doesn't even know what fear is, has his own insecurities. He masks them because they trained him not to show his emotions. I have to remember that he's still human. He feels everything, even if I don't know it. I brush hair from his forehead.

"*Papochka*, I understand why you worry about those things. But being with you just is. There's no realm of possibility where we aren't together. I can't picture not being with you. Like, my mind *cannot* conjure that image. Not being with you just isn't something that can happen. Just like the sun can't rise in the west and set in the east. Just like Earth can't suddenly be at the end of our solar system. It's just impossible."

"Then you understand how I feel about you. Heather, you're my soulmate. I've always believed they exist because I can remember my parents together. I see it with my aunts and uncles. I just never thought I would find mine. I didn't think fate had that in store for me."

"I didn't believe in them because I never thought I would find one. It was easier to think that than to accept everyone else could have a love like that and I wouldn't. Now I know differently. You are my soulmate, Aleks. The spaces in me that were empty are now full."

He lets go of me, and I stand. He helps me over his lap, and I steel myself for the paddle hitting my ass. When it does, my body relaxes. It hurts like fuck. But it puts me at ease. I focus on the sensations. I focus on the man I love, loving me.

"*Malyshka,* come whenever you need to."

I know this was supposedly to punish me for wearing the thong, but we both know it's for our pleasure. He slides his fingers into my pussy every few spankings. Every time he does, I come. When the pain gets too intense with the sixth spank, one that lands across my horizontal crack, I grab his ankle, and it grounds me.

When he's done, and my ass is apple red and burns like I sat on the stove, I help him undress. He sits on the bed, and I straddle him like I did while we talked. But his cock and my pussy are where they belong. Joined. We enjoy just being one for several minutes before we grow restless. He flips me onto my back as he stands at the side of the bed. He pulls my arms over my head as our fingers weave together. He's back to being

Superman. No one who just went through what he did should be able to exert himself like this.

"You're such a good baby girl. Fuck. Your cunt is so tight... That's it...Take my cock...Fuck. You make me want to come too soon...You like it rough, don't you?...You need your pussy full of Daddy's cum."

I moan through it all, knowing he loves it when I do. I nod my head whenever he asks a question. It is rough, but this isn't being fucked. Not with the emotion that shines in our eyes as our gazes lock. This is one of our many ways of making love.

But a thought flashes through my mind that threatens to steal the joy of connecting with him like this. He can endure this because they tortured him to where he can ignore any and all pain and push through. He's like this because a fucked up dead man destroyed part of him.

He senses the shift in me. I'm not meeting his thrusts with the same force as before. He slows, and our movements become tender as we continue to gaze at each other. I love the different types of sex we have. Sometimes we need a good fuck, but moments like this, we need to make love.

Why can't the world be as easy as it is to be here in this moment?

This morning was intense. I'm glad Aleks and I talked. It was a reminder that everything in our life is heavy. But I wouldn't end this. I couldn't.

What I can do is go back to work tomorrow. I'm updating my lessons plans to account for a week with a substitute. I know the woman, and she's fantastic. I trust her to actually teach, but her background isn't in theater. There are just some things I had to drop and give her other things instead.

I'm in my office when I hear voices and recognize Maks, Niko, and Bogdan. I wait, but none of the cousins speak. My guess is there are only the four of them out there. They're speaking in Russian, so I assume it's something they don't want me to know. I stick to what I'm doing, even though I'm curious. They're talking for at least an hour before anything's said in English.

"Heather, can you come out here?"

I smile to the guys before I stand next to Aleks. Whatever he's about to say, I won't like.

"I'm going to be gone for a few days. I'd like you to stay with my mom."

I fight the urge to argue, to refuse to let him go. I fight the urge to demand an explanation. All I do is nod. He wraps his arm around my waist, and mine goes around his. I lean against him as he kisses my forehead. I love how much taller he is than me. I love these little signs of affection.

"If I'm going to be gone more than three days, I will get a message to you. I hate asking this because I just told you to go back to work, but I need you to take a few more personal days. I trust the security we have at my mom's place, but no one will be available to guard you."

I only have one more personal day, which includes sick leave. If I'm out longer than that, then I dip into my pay. This doesn't count as something I can apply for Family Medical Leave. We're barely two months into the semester, and the kids are counting on me, so they can have their spring play. They deserve to have me there, but they also deserve consistency and continuity. I don't think I'm going to provide that for them, possibly ever again. Laura is a lawyer who can work anywhere since she's the Kutsenko Partners' in-house council. Ana is her paralegal. Christina heads their construction division and works from anywhere, too. The same for Sumiko, who's their legal operations' accountant. I can't do that. What am I going to be? Konstantin and Mila's governess? Home tutor?

I can't keep the teaching position I have now and be in and out unexpectedly. I doubt there are too many online theater teacher positions. Do I take a leave of absence for the entire rest of the semester and go without pay? Do I quit and definitely have no income? It's not like Aleks needs me to chip in on the water bill. And it's not like I need it in case we break up. But I want to continue to contribute.

"Heather?"

"Sorry. We can talk about it later, but I'm going to make it more permanent than calling in sick for a few more days."

Aleks watches me, and I know he wants to talk about it immediately, but his brothers are standing with us.

"Can you hold off until I'm home?"

"Yes. Be careful. I love you."

"I love you too.

We kiss, then we let go of each other. It's like all this situation sucked the warmth and oxygen out of the room. He already has a duffle bag packed that's sitting near the elevator door. I try to tell myself it's just a work trip, but that's a load of bullshit.

"Aleks, wait. You've shown me photos of guys in the mob, Cartel, and *Cosa Nostra*. Is there anyone I need to watch out for who you didn't show me photos of?"

"Only one. He usually goes by the name Robert Simms. He's about six feet tall, thinning blond hair, brown eyes. We had some trouble with him a few months ago. He cannot get onto my mom's property, and you will not leave. No one who isn't approved by my brothers and me will come and go. My aunts and uncles are the only exception, and my mom will still go to work. I just need you to stay there."

"Your mom will still go to work? Why do you trust her

safety to people outside your family? What about your aunts? How do they go anywhere?"

"My uncles are pretty much retired from the bratva. They guard their wives. They have their own systems for when my aunts are at work. My mom doesn't go anywhere without four men who grew up with her and my dad. They've known her for more than fifty years. My dad trusted them to watch us when he had to be away."

That makes sense. There really is no one available who he'd trust. And, honestly, I don't want to go anywhere without him or his brothers or cousins.

"Pack a bag for three or four days, *malyshka*. If you forget anything, order it. I don't want you coming back here or going to any stores unless my mom's guards or my uncles go with you. Even then, I would rather you not. It takes them away from guarding my mom and aunts."

"I'll stay put. Give me a couple minutes. I'll be right back."

I rush into our room and pull out a small suitcase. I drop a week's worth of clothes in there. I look at my underwear drawer and grab a week's worth of panties. I don't mind going commando, but it still feels stranger to be pantiless than not. I'm back in the living room in five minutes. The ride to Queens feels like an eternity.

"*Malyshka*, when I get back, we're finding a house near our family. It's time we make our forever home."

Chapter Twenty-Three

Aleks

"Dillan and Salvatore might think they have brass balls teaming up and hitting us while they're out of town. Like they're fucking unstoppable or shit. They ran away like little bitches and got their henchman to do shit they're scared to without us catching their family."

Pasha's driving the second SUV as he talks. Misha's in the lead, along with Maks, Anton, Sergei, Alexi, and Stefan. I'm in the car with Bogdan, Niko, Ilya, and Mikhail. We're on a call with the other car, so everyone can hear the conversation. Maks's voice comes through the speaker.

"Strength in numbers won't do shit for them. By doing this while they're away, they've left themselves completely vulnerable. They only annoyed us by stealing that gun shipment. And it's merely an inconvenience that they stole those semis. That's not what we use to run our product, anyway. They're a distraction that works since they went after them and got nothing. No pot and no coke."

I lean forward between the two front captains' chairs as I look at the GPS on the screen. It's pitch black out at two a.m. We're headed to the docks the Irish control. Again. We need to watch out that we aren't becoming too predictable, or they will lay traps for us. Taking out the Dubliner a few months ago definitely shocked them. It was the pub that made them the most money. A "gas leak"—yes, air quotes and all—was blamed for the explosion. That was Uncle Grigori's expertise with improvised explosive devices. About the only useful knowledge that came out of his time in Chechnya.

We waited until it got this late, not just for the cover of darkness but because my uncle had some building to do. The wives gathered at my mom's, including my aunts. When Laura was a few weeks away from delivering, my mom ordered two cribs, two highchairs, two swings, two of everything, and a slew of toys. Anything Laura could need is there. Now that Christina is pregnant, nothing will go to waste. We went to Uncle Grigori and Aunt Alina's to help him. It took a few hours since we have nearly two dozen. It's a good thing Misha and Pasha still have Bear Imports, which began as an agricultural import and export business. No one questions the amount of fertilizer that comes in and out of their warehouses.

"Misha, I'm going dark. Don't fucking brake suddenly."

Pasha flicks off the headlights, and Misha does the same. Our SUVs don't just have reenforced features. They're as quiet as hybrids, even with enormous engines under the hood. They should sound like a tiger roaring, but they barely even purr. All of our personal vehicles have silent locking systems that don't even flash the headlights. These veritable tanks are the same, and they have infrared sensors, so we have three-hundred-and-sixty-degree visibility when we go dark like this.

All Pasha gets is a grunt in response. We're wearing night vision goggles, so we flip those down. Anton and Sergei hop out of their SUV when we get to the docks. Sergei cuts the wires to the gate, and Anton pushes it back. I'm certain Sergei already jammed the camera feeds. They pull their doors closed with the least amount of sound they can before we all roll into the shipping yard.

We waste no time. Misha and Pasha lead each team, Maks at Misha's side. I'm next to Pasha as Maks's second-in-command. The rest of the men pair up. We move like wraiths, our dark clothes barely casting a shadow as we move along the shipping containers. Anton and Sergei take their share of the IEDs to one ship, Pasha and I go to the second. Ilya and Stefan head to the third. The rest of the men keep watch as the six of us board Irish mob ships. Silencers allow us to take out the scant crew on each boat before we get to the engine rooms, then the holds. We all know better than to toss them and dash, but we don't lollygag either.

The moment we're off the boats, we all grab bolt cutters from the crate Niko carried out of our SUV. We move around the containers, breaking locks and taking anything worth stealing before dousing the contents with gasoline. The Irish are paying Enrique for the privilege of docking and avoiding customs inspections. That means some goods here are Cartel. We're careful what we toss gasoline onto. Right now, we have no reason to target Enrique. But this sends a message to everyone, the Cartel included. Come after us, and we will obliterate you. We might not kill you, but we will kill your business.

Bogdan grins as we regroup at the cars, the containers already ablaze

"It'll take Dillan months to recover from the damage."

This isn't even retaliation for the car bombing. We still don't know who's responsible for it. This is for tipping off the ATF agents to impound the stolen semis. This is for stealing guns and selling them to our rivals in Texas. They're on both sides of the border right now.

We're in the SUVs and through the gates before Anton detonates the IEDs. They work on the same premise as the one planted on my car. There's a remote to set them off rather than a trip wire or someone turning on an engine. We had our own forensics team look at the scene to determine the cause. It wasn't cheap to pay off the cops or firefighters who responded to the scene to downplay what happened. But it's not a coincidence where our Manhattan condos are. They're all in precincts loyal to us—or at least loyal to being paid by syndicates.

The explosions rattle the car, and we all look back at the fireballs licking the night sky. Phase one of tonight complete. Now to move onto what will keep us away from our family. We hit the underground gambling ring Salvatore's been running. We know tonight's family and friends rather than outside members. We're not worried about targeting the wrong people. Friends of Salvatore's aren't friends of ours.

We trade our night visions goggles for balaclavas. I hand out the rifles in the car, just like someone is doing in the other one. The men in my car head to the back of the building, while Misha's team goes around front. No one moves until we hear Misha's voice in our earpieces.

"*Seychas!*" Now!

It's hand and arm signals only as we sweep inside and make our way to the natural foods store's basement. A granola crunching, tree hugging front that fools most people. As we pour into the open underground space, pairs break off again. Anyone quick enough to pull a gun gets a bullet through the chest, throat, or head. Those pulling knives get a bullet in the kneecap. Everyone else either surrenders, or we make sure the bullet grazes them. That usually keeps people from running.

We move with precision. Anyone outside looking in would think we're some type of law enforcement or military unit. We aren't, but we move like one. That's what happens when former KGB and Russian soldiers turned bratva take charge of your formative years. We are paramilitary to our core.

We know who we're looking for. When we find them, we no longer need the rest of them. They kneel as commanded, then they don't speak another word. We have three other SUVs waiting near the back alley that we parked before heading to the docks. Stefan, Ilya, and Mikhail bring them around to the back door. With hoods on and zip ties around their wrists, we load our temporary guests into the cars. They'll leave in a few hours or a few days, depending on how soon they accept their fate. They'll leave as ash or ooze.

Maks orders the men dragged from the vehicles once we're at the warehouse.

"String 'em up."

We replace their zip ties with rope that's looped over a meat hook. Men are already here, so those of us who just arrived turn around and head back out. It's time for the third wave.

The city's Department of Sanitation controls personal garbage collection, but it doesn't have a monopoly on commercial trash hauling. We head to Salvatore's largest company and its garage in the south Bronx. It happens to be attached to a junkyard and landfill. Just like we did with the shipping yard, we move systematically from garbage truck to garbage truck, planting the explosives. Then we move to the landfill. We're careful where we place the bombs. There are some parts we won't touch. We don't want to release those types of toxins into the air because there are neighborhoods in the vicinity. We also wire the car crushers and other heavy equipment.

I hear Maks over our earpieces as we get a block away.

"*Podsveti eto.*" Light it up.

Immediately, the roar of the explosions is deafening. There are more buildings in the area, reverberating the sound. The open space at the docks didn't intensify the noise like the nearby structures do. We don't stick around to admire our work. Three out of four tasks are done.

Pasha's driving the lead SUV now. I glance back over my shoulder at Misha's vehicle as Pasha hits the call button on the car.

"Sergei, we still headed to Sunnyside? We don't have much time before the sun's up."

We started in Queens with the docks and the gambling ring, then we headed to the south Bronx for the trash collectors —carters as they're known around here—and now back to Queens.

"Yeah. There's an Iron Order meeting."

The Iron Order Motorcycle Club isn't strictly speaking an outlaw group like other motorcycle clubs because most members are prior military and current law enforcement. They don't get on well with the Hell's Angels, so my guess is Sergei learned about this from one of his Angels informants. If it's in Sunnyside, then it'll most likely be Irish American cops. And where we find them, we'll find some of Dillan's little bitches.

Niko's sarcasm oozes from every word.

"That wasn't hard. Twenty odd fucking bikes in an Irish pub's parking lot. Why not fly a fucking flag? We're three blocks away, and I can see all of them."

We stop when we're a block away and watch. Bogdan taps me on the arm and points.

"Is that Shannon?"

I squint as I look through the front window as a blonde leaves the pub with a man. The woman's hair is braided and wrapped with a leather thong. She's got on a biker club jacket, black jeans, and black boots. The guy she's with has a matching jacket and blue jeans. He's slim but moves like an athlete. His dark hair is short, and he's wearing glasses. But it's impossible to make out more than that from this distance. I'm not even certain about the glasses.

"Yeah. Sergei, is that Steven?"

It's a moment before an answer comes across the speaker.

"That's him."

A plan is better than an impulse.

I repeat that to myself three times as we watch more people leave. It's almost five-thirty, so last call has come and gone. The bar should have been closed an hour ago, but when every patron pouring out of it looks like a current or former cop, the laws don't matter.

I hear Anton's voice next.

"Maks, do you want to pick up Steven now? It means leaving Shannon."

"No. Let them go. They're about to pull away. Once they're gone, we go for the rest."

We picked up extra men at the warehouse because we didn't know how many members would be here, and it's a guarantee they're all armed better than most of the men at the gambling den. We listen as Steven revs his bike, and Shannon climbs on the back. He waves over his head before his heel lifts the kickstand. Then they're off. The moment they're out of sight, we pull forward. Half the bikers are drunk off their asses as they stumble toward the parking lot. Excellent. We're doing a community service and keeping a bunch of drunk fucks off the streets.

Our balaclavas are back in place as we jump out of the SUVs. Anyone in the third rows goes out the trunk. Everyone else has their doors open before we fully stop. The drivers will stay close to the vehicles, ready to leave as soon as everyone is back inside.

Anton, Sergei, and Niko take out the cameras on the building and the ones the city owns. Once we know we're not being recorded, we herd the members to the center of the parking lot. Four of our men shoot out the front tires of all the bikes.

We're in our Kevlar bulletproof vests and helmets. We take some fire, but we're prepared and protected. The bikers not so much. Fortunately, there are only a few women outside. We won't take them, and we won't hurt them either. They don't need to know that. Alexi and Bogdan maneuver them to a back corner of the parking lot. I notice them stomping on the women's phones that the women toss behind themselves. I hear them order the women to sit facing the wall. The ground'll be freezing, but it keeps them out of the way, and will slow any who think to charge us. We're not worried about shielding them from the gore. They married cops or veterans, and they joined a motorcycle club. If they didn't know what they signed up for, they do now.

Niko issues a command to our new prisoners. He hides his accent remarkably well. I guess his time on stage all those years ago still serves him well.

"Pull up your shirts and drop your phones."

The men look around, but with guns pointing at them from all directions, they comply. The ones with a shamrock over their hearts get yanked from the group. Ilya, Stefan, and Sergei nail the remaining guys in the temple with their rifle butts. They crush the phones like Bogdan and Alexi did. Hoods go over all of them, even the ones knocked out on the ground and the women. The men with the O'Rourke mark get their hands zip tied behind them before they're dragged to the SUVs.

"Go."

It's Misha's command in our earpieces. We won't speak Russian amongst ourselves. No need to give our identities away immediately. The SUVs don't have tags, so we're not worried about that. We've taken out the cameras, disabled the bikes, cut off their communication, and blindfolded them. We do the whole thing in five minutes.

"Who are you?"

There are four men huddled in the back of our SUV. There's one in the center seat of the second and third rows. All of us except Pasha have our handguns drawn, ready to shoot if one breathes in the wrong direction.

No one answers.

"Why us?"

The same man, one in the trunk, asks both questions. We don't give answers. They do. And not until we're at the warehouse, and we're completely in control. I pull back the safety on my gun, and the sound echoes in the car. Our prisoners are silent the rest of the way to Flushing, which is about twenty minutes. Like the first time we arrived at the warehouse, Maks gives the order.

"Get them strung up looking at the *paisans*. Let's see how good they are as countrymen now."

Maks taunts both the Italians and the Irish with his Italian slang. We'll soon see if the Italians are as loyal to Italy—or rather Sicily—as they love to claim. Will they dime each other out?

We're quick to get them immobilized. They all dangle with their toes barely touching the floor. We strip prisoners before they go onto the hooks, so most are shivering and a few trembling. We'll make these bitches cry. Once they're all secure, we whip off the hoods. The confusion is fun to watch until the Irish spot the Italian map on the forearms, and the Italians spot the shamrock on the chests. We searched the wallets of our second group of captives, and as we suspected, they're all cops.

Maks taunts them as he picks up a led pipe. He saunters between the two rows and appears to swing the weapon carelessly. Without warning, he lashes out, striking an Italian, then an Irish American, before he keeps moving.

"Since Dillan and Salvatore are such good friends, we thought we'd have a party and invite everyone over. We have a ton of fun and games planned for you. Who wants to go first at whack-a-mole?"

He lands the pipe against another Italian's ribs. I cross my arms and laugh before I take a turn taunting them.

"Maybe you should explain the rules. I guess they don't play this game with their friends."

Maks appears thoughtful as he nods and continues walking back up the row.

"I whack whoever I want until someone talks. If I don't like what I hear, I take out your kneecaps. If I still don't like what I hear, I'll crush your nuts. Pretty simple, and now you know."

Maks stops in front of the skinniest Italian. He'd only swung with one hand as he walked by the others. This time, he turns toward the guy and wraps both hands around the pipe. He takes a position like it's a baseball bat and brings it up to his right shoulder. The man opens his mouth but says nothing fast enough for Maks's liking. My brother slams the pipe into the guy's left side. The sound of his ribs breaking is horrible, and it fills the otherwise quiet warehouse.

Maks spins around and does the same thing to the cop standing in front of him.

"Oink, oink, motherfucker."

Niko calls out, and for a moment I can hear his parrot, Sammy, saying the same thing. And Bogdan was supposedly the one who taught the bird to swear. Thinking about Sammy reminds me of the menagerie that showed up at my mom's house. Laura has her mastiff, Sebastian. Christina brought Bogdan's cat, Cleo. Sumiko has a chinchilla named Pandora. And Heather took Gloria. I have never met a more food-oriented animal than that guinea pig. Heather's trained it to play hide and seek and go through mazes to find treats. It can snuffle them out like a pig looking for truffles.

I snap my attention back to what's happening in front of me. Too many days and nights spent here have desensitized me to the violence. My mind wanders despite the cries of pain and the blood. I need to focus.

Bogdan steps forward with the pliers. By default, it's his tool of choice. It doesn't take a remarkable amount of strength to use them to snap off toes and fingers. It's more about pressure and leverage. Since Bogdan was the smallest when Vlad conscripted us, the pliers were the easiest tool for my little brother. He's stuck with it because he got good at applying just enough pressure to terrify people before actually cutting off the digit. That said, he won't hesitate to amputate anything.

He snaps them open and shut before pointing them to a cop's toes. When the guy next to the cop looks down, Bogdan swings them up and catches the second guy's nose. He pinches and twists until there's a crack. Bogdan tsks.

"So much for a fucking brotherhood on either side. No one over here bleeds blue after all. You're willing to let each other suffer. Tell us what we want to know, and this is over right now."

A few look ready to crack on the Irish American side. Withstanding torture isn't a long lesson at the police academy. The O'Rourkes must be getting soft training their recruits. They must assume badges will protect these fuckers. Nope. Not so much.

Maks walks back to stand beside me, and we watch as

Misha and Pasha gather bamboo shoots, handing some to Anton, Sergei, and Niko. Misha explains as though he's telling a story.

"These bamboo shoots are an excellent tool for interrogation. Slipping them under nails creates excruciating pain. Most people will last through one or two. Some even make it through an entire hand or foot. But I'm yet to meet anyone who makes it to ten digits without pissing themselves or telling us their entire life story."

Maks and I work the cranks, hoisting our brother's and cousins' chosen targets higher. They pry the shoots under toenails, and howls of pain blend with pathetic sobs. I place my hands on my hips as I walk forward.

"You do all get how this ends, right? None of you are leaving alive. So, at this point, talk. If you do, then we put a bullet between your eyes, and it's all done. If you don't, then we do one thing after another to entertain ourselves until you bleed to death. What's the longest that's taken before? Three weeks?" I look at Maks, who dramatically shrugs. "I think a Cartel guy lasted twenty-five days. I'd say he had some balls, but my baby brother snapped those off with those pliers around day four."

Bogdan holds them up and snaps them open and closed a few more times. He moves onto another cop and catches the guy's nipple. He squeezes until the skin rips, and he's almost taken it off the guy's chest.

"What do you want to know?"

The nearly nippleless guy pants his question, and he looks like he's fighting the urge to piss himself. Not so tough without his badge and gun. I walk over to Bogdan and the whimpering cop.

"Did Dillan order the car bomb?"

The man's brow furrows, and the confusion is real.

"What car bomb?"

"The one that nearly killed me and my girlfriend."

I'm focused on the guy in front of me, but everyone knows who they're assigned to watch by their position on the hooks. Ilya, Stefan, Mikhail, and Alexi have their lookout spots for their assigned prisoners. If someone blinks too soon or holds his breath a second too long, he'll be the next target. I turn when I hear Sergei's voice. He's standing in front of a *Cosa Nostra* guy.

"You look surprised to hear that. Are you so low on the food chain that we can just kill you now? If you know nothing, then you're just taking up space. *Pakhan*, you're closest. Could you turn on the meat grinder?"

"Wait! No!"

The Italian in front of Sergei shakes his head vehemently.

"It wasn't us. Salvatore called the morning after so pissed he couldn't pick which language to use. Every sentence was a mixture of Italian and English. He demanded to know if one of us took it into our own hands to set the bomb. He wanted to know if someone else in the *familia* ordered the hit. None of us knew what he was talking about until he told us someone tried to blow Aleksei up. We shut everything down until tonight. When you didn't retaliate right away, we thought maybe you were waiting for the don to return. We thought it was safe to open again."

Sergei laughs in the guy's face.

"We know."

All right. That rules out the Italians. The anger on the other men's faces speaks volumes. Vlad trained us to see what isn't there, to understand what people think and feel that doesn't show in their expression. There is no sign of relief that this guy is lying to protect the *Cosa Nostra*. There's no surprise at what he's saying. None look like they're praying for him to shut up. Their faces might look blank, but their eyes aren't dead. That's where the anger lies. They did nothing, and yet because they are here, they will die tonight. Unlike bratva men, their eyes are still windows to their souls. In situations like this, the bratva have none.

Each bundle of bamboo shoots had a wire around it, not to bind them together but to hide its length. Anton wraps his around a cop's throat and stretches his arms out to the side. The guy flails and kicks.

"I sp-ick."

Anton loosens his hold, and the guy splutters.

"Dillan didn't call me, but I heard the conversation. Dillan is paying one cop you pay way better. The guy was on the scene. Apparently, he called Dillan the moment he got in his cruiser. He was too eager and didn't wait to find out if Aleksei survived. Woke Dillan up, but Dillan didn't mind. He made the call I heard immediately after getting the news. He was excited. He thought someone showed initiative. The person who got the call and I didn't know what he was talking about. We asked around. No one knows. When Aleksei left the hospital, Dillan called back. I don't speak Gaelic, so I didn't get half the shit he said. But my guess is it was the same sorta stuff the don must have said in Italian. He's not convinced it wasn't one of us, but instead of being proud, he's going ape shit. He knew it was only a matter of time before you hit us again. He would have come back already, but the wake was four days long. They just had the funeral."

Four days? Someone thinks highly of the dead fucker. How many people needed to see the corpse? One or two nights is customary.

Maks puts his hands on his hips, and his stance matches mine as he walks forward.

"Decisions, decisions. If anyone wishes to step forward, now is the time to do it. Tell us something useful, and it's a bullet between the eyes the moment you're done. Don't tell us anything, and it's a slower death in the acid. What shall it be?"

Misha and Pasha grabbed respirators before they turned on the massive extractor fans, then they pried the lid off the industrial hydrochloric acid vat. When Maks speaks, nearly two dozen heads swing in that direction before they look at each other. Panic sets in. It's obvious no one has anything to say, but they're all hoping someone else will confess. Maks sighs dramatically.

"What a pity."

With a nod, Anton and Sergei use the cranks to lower the men until their feet are on the ground. All of us work to get the rope binding their wrists off the hooks. We force the two lines to walk to the massive barrel. We grab respirators too. I know I don't want to go near those fumes without one. The vat stands nearly ten feet tall and has several thousand gallons of liquid in there. There is a double set of steps leading to the top. Each line takes a set.

It's hard to understand me when I speak, but I think they got it.

"In you hop."

The two men on the top steps shake their heads and turn as if they think they can get back down. Ilya, Stefan, Alexi, and Mikhail are back in their places near the office and exits, holding their rifles toward our prisoners. They slung them around their backs when they helped us earlier. The rest of us have our pistols out. The men accept that they can't flee. They're facing Pasha and Misha when they step onto the rim, and two shots ring out simultaneously. Bullets go into each skull before the bodies tumble forward. My brothers and cousins and I aren't new. We're standing well outside the splash zone. But the bodies hitting the liquid sends up a spray that rains down on the others.

We keep the acid at a steady one-hundred-sixty degrees Fahrenheit, so the temperature alone burns. Never mind the type of acid.

Misha waves his gun toward the vat as he speaks.

"Get on with it, and we give you mercy. You're dead before you hit the surface. Fuck around and keep us waiting, and we'll let you wait to die in the tank. Fuck around and find out."

That clearly appeals to no one. Our prisoners are done being dead men walking, and my cousins snap the lid back into place within three minutes. I checked my watch.

Once we're in the office, we talk freely.

"If it wasn't the Irish or the Italians who came after Heather and me, and we really don't have a reason to think it's the Cartel, then who's left? Did Robert Simms do this because of his vendetta against Pasha? Has it spread to all of us? Or is one of the other syndicates responsible, and none of these lowlings know their boss hired a mercenary?"

Pasha appears grim when he answers.

"It could be any of those. Simms has been involved since the beginning, but it became personal with me. It surprises me that he isn't still coming after me, but maybe he wants to keep me alive and miserable by taking away someone I love."

He shrugs. None of us know the answer. Sergei glances out of the office window toward the vat.

"Remember how one of them said Dillan got excited and thought someone took some initiative? What if he hired Simms, and it excited him because his guy pulled off the bombing before Simms got around to taking the hit on Aleks? It would save him money, and he could claim the kill as their own rather than having to admit he needed a mercenary to do his dirty work. I really don't think it's Salvatore. The only guy he has who knows anything about explosives is Matteo. That guy is way too loyal to Salvatore and stands nothing to gain by defying him. Salvatore knows planting any type of car bomb endangers the women. He wouldn't do that. If he condones violence against women, then his become fair game. We know the Irish have no such compunctions. But now that Declan's gone, they don't have anyone who knows explosives. They had that guy when we were kids who was IRA before coming to America. He only taught Declan because no one else wanted a Northern Irish guy around. That knowledge probably died with Declan, so I think that's why they hired it out. If it was the Irish, then it was Simms who did it for them."

Sergei's reasoning makes sense. I could see that. Plus Simms could have dropped the tracker in Heather's bag because he's working on his own and doesn't have or doesn't want to hire people to follow her. Simms, working for someone or for himself, is looking way more likely than the other options.

Maks makes a call. There's plenty of going back and forth before we hear what we want.

"You have my word, *amigo*."

None of us are Enrique Diaz's friend, and we'll take any pledge he makes at face value. For now, we'll accept what the Colombian Cartel's *jefe* says. Word already reached him about the car bomb and about our strikes tonight.

"Diaz, we are not partners. Just so we are clear. But with Salvatore and Dillan as probable culprits and working together to fuck up at least some of our shit, you know you'll be next. If you're saying you'll stand beside us, you better be ready for me to call in that promise."

Maks would rather go to the grave than rely on another syndicate for anything, and we feel the same. But Enrique's still trying to make things up to Laura, which means playing nice with us.

"As long as you stay away from my goods, like you did at the docks, we have no problem. We all know what Juan did, but he's gone now. That bomb wouldn't have just killed Aleks. They targeted his woman too. I'm done with these *mamahuevos.*" Cocksuckers.

That's one I haven't heard in a while, but I learned it in high school.

"Maks, I may not be married, but I have sisters and nieces. This *pura mentira* needs to stop."

He's right; this bullshit needs to stop. Maks and Enrique exchange a few more words, but the call ends. My older brother looks at me.

"We've resolved nothing when it comes to Shannon and Steven. Maybe Dillan wasn't the one to order the hit, and he really didn't know about it. Could she have a way to contact Simms? Would she even know who he is?"

"Those are good questions. I don't know. I mean, as far as we all thought, she wasn't in touch with her family much. Shows how much we knew. I suppose we keep her on the list of suspects. Not much more we can do tonight."

"It might be a good idea if you and Heather went away for a while."

"I was already planning that before the bombing. Now it seems like an even better idea."

We strip off our clothes, which will go in a barrel and burn outside the back of the warehouse. I wait for my turn in for a shower. I'm standing next to Maks and ask what everyone is thinking. I don't envy him hearing the same question over and over.

"Now what?"

Chapter Twenty-Four

Heather

"They're on their way."

I turn toward Laura as she comes into Galina's kitchen. She was feeding the twins, who must have gone back to sleep because she enters alone. The rest of us are helping make breakfast or staying out of the way. The women appear relieved, but I'm uncertain what to make of it since Aleks told me he'd be gone for a few days.

Galina wraps her arm around my shoulders, and I sigh. Her hugs are nearly as good as my mom's. Her experience and wisdom kept me from falling apart last night. This isn't the first time Aleks has been gone, but it was the first time it was serious enough that I couldn't stay at our place.

"It's a good thing, *pchelka*. It means they got what they needed sooner than they expected. It doesn't mean something went wrong, and they had to give up. They're not returning with bad news."

I'm not convinced, but I nod. Laura walks over and squeezes my hand.

"Galina's right. Maks didn't tell me anything, but I know from his voice. Even if he tried to hide it, if something went wrong, I would know."

I prepare myself for what I assume will feel like the longest wait ever, but the men pour into the house five minutes later. Wives greet husbands, then sons greet parents. I'm not a wife yet, so I hang back and let Galina hug Aleks. It's good that he does, so she isn't the only one left watching. It must be hard enough for her knowing her husband will never walk through the door. Add being a mom waiting for all her sons to return, it must be excruciating even if she masks her feelings.

"*Malyshka*, that was kind what you did for my mom. But I never want to wait to hold you again."

Aleks whispers in my ear before his lips lock with mine. If I weren't so engrossed with welcoming him back, I would be self-conscious about how obscene it must be. It is not a kiss that should be shared in public. I peek at the other couples and discover they're just as bad as we are. When we finally pull apart, I rest my head against his chest. Bogdan stands with his hand on Christina's belly. I hear Maks ask about the twins.

When the guys' parents mumble about needing their coffee and finishing making breakfast, it's each guy's signal to scoop his woman into his arms. Only Misha is single, so he rolls his eyes and mutters about more food for him. Sergei and Anton head up the stairs behind the rest of us. Each of Galina's sons has a bedroom, and I discovered there are rooms for the cousins and her in-laws.

No one says a word, but it's like a finely choreographed dance as the men lift and carry their wives—or, in my case, girl-friend—before entering their rooms, the doors closing at the same time. Aleks and I tear at each other's clothes before he backs me against a wall. He pulls my arms over my head, grasping my wrists with one hand. His other hand rests at the base of my throat.

"I will come home to you, *malyshka*, and when I do, nothing and no one will stop me from touching you, tasting you. It was kind of you to make sure we didn't leave out my mom. I love your generous heart and your respect for my family. But believe me, my mom understands. I remember when my dad used to come home. They were as bad—if not worse—than any of us. My grandparents used to shield our eyes when we were really little. It was probably worse as we got older because we understood what was happening when they sent us outside to play."

"I didn't want your mom to be the only person without someone to greet. I didn't want it to remind her that your dad won't come home. Aleks, don't doubt that I want nothing more than to hold you and feel the proof that you're okay. But I won't make your mom wait. I love you with everything I am and have, but she gave birth to you. I can't imagine what she, Alina, and Svetlana go through when all of you leave. I can't imagine watching all my children leave, knowing one or all of them might never come back. I'm in here with you. I'll go to bed with you tonight, and I'll wake up with you tomorrow. I'll do that over and over. I can wait five minutes for your mom to have the reassurance that her children are safe. I won't back down on this, Aleks."

His kiss steals my breath. I wasn't ready for it. I thought he would argue with me, but instead, he's spinning me around. Then his hands are on my hips as he impales me. He pins me against the wall as one hand goes back to my throat, and the other fists my hair. He whispers in my right ear as I try to look back at him.

"I love you so fucking much, Heather. There is no one

better for me than you. Everything about you makes my heart so full it might burst. You're a good person, and I'm so proud to know I'm yours."

"You're mine?"

"God, yes. All of me."

There's a vulnerability in his voice. Despite how things might appear as he fucks me from behind, he's admitting I have the power to hurt him. These moments when he fully lets me in are priceless to me. It sparks a deeply protective part of me.

"Daddy, I need to hold you."

He doesn't hesitate and pulls out before spinning me back to face him. He lifts me, and my legs wrap around him as he thrusts back into me. I smatter kisses over his face before I press his cheek to my chest and stroke his hair. My kisses and tender touches don't match what's happening with the lower halves of our bodies. I'm riding him, and he's getting rougher each time he surges into me. My gentleness is feeding our need for each other.

He carries me to the bed, and I cling to him as he climbs on and eases me back onto the pillows. Our movements slow as our hands roam over each other. His thrusts are deep, with a little extra force at the end. As much as he loves hearing me moan, he knows I love hearing him grunt.

"Daddy, is this too much? You were in the hospital a couple days ago. I don't know if you got hurt tonight."

"*Malyshka*, I belong inside you. Not just because nothing feels better than having sex with you, but because I'm only ever completely at peace when we join our bodies. It's the only time when duty, fear, and bitterness don't drive every thought, every breath. It's purely love."

"I would keep you inside me for the rest of our lives and shelter you from everything. Daddy, you might have to do horrible things, but you are a good man. I don't think you see yourself that way. Even when you have to be that way, you're still doing it because of all your honorable qualities. I love you for that. You are the least selfish person I know. Everything you do, you do for other people. Your family, the bratva, your community, me. If I can give you respite from that, then I want nothing more than to hold you every minute of every day."

"*Malyshka*, I'm taking you away somewhere, anywhere. Just the two of us."

He grimaces and shakes his head before kissing the tip of my nose. For a moment, my worry spikes, thinking he's in pain.

"Not exactly just the two of us. We have to take security, baby girl. But the vacation is for the two of us. The men will be ghosts most of the time, but they have to be there."

"I understand. I—Daddy—Fuck...Just like that...I can't think straight—when—fuck—yes. May I come, Daddy?"

I can't formulate a full thought as my body races toward an orgasm. We were having a wonderfully sentimental conversation while making love. But I need to come.

"Yes, *malyshka*. Over and over, whenever you can. I want to feel your pussy squeezing me. I want to leave my cum in you. One day, baby girl. One day."

I cup his jaw, and my kiss is ferocious. It's unrelenting until we're panting. My body tightens as I arch my back. He sucks my tit, and I contract all my muscles. He grunts louder as he slams into me hard enough to bring pain with the pleasure, which only heightens the pleasure as I come. He shudders as he spills in me. We cling to each other, our perspiring bodies exhausted.

"One day, you and I are going to make a baby with that cum inside me, aren't we, Daddy?"

"Yes, *malyshka*. I was serious about us finding a forever home."

He hasn't proposed, but he said he would. Does he plan to

do it while we're on vacation? Or is that something further down the road, after a baby?

We roll onto our sides, and he sweeps back the hair that's now grown below my shoulders. His hand slides down my back to rest on my ass while my hand rests on his trim waist.

"Where would you like to go, baby girl? It can be anywhere in the world as soon as you're packed."

"Don't we need to book plane tickets and find a place to stay?"

"*Malyshka*, Kutsenko Partners owns a private jet. My brothers and I are equal owners and can use it as we like, when we like. As for finding a place to stay, we have the means to be financially convincing to accommodate us."

We have the means... Is that including me? Or does he mean he and his brothers?

"Angel, I can tell what you're thinking. We means you and me. We're already living together. My hope is we'll get married soon. As far as I'm concerned, everything that is mine is yours. I haven't exaggerated when I've said that in the past."

"Don't you want a prenup?"

The look he gives me makes me want to disappear into the mattress. It's part insulted, part determined, and, I think, part is silently asking me if I'm stupid.

"*Malyshka*, I will never force you to stay with me. If you want a divorce, I will not contest it. I will try to convince you not to leave. I will do everything I can to make you happy, so you want a life with me. But you will give up so much to be with me. If it means fifty percent is yours after a divorce, then you deserve that and more. I don't need one to feel like my assets are protected. I wouldn't keep anything from you that you're entitled to. Do you want one?"

I shake my head. I never imagined he'd try to leave me destitute, and I have no real assets to shelter.

"I just wanted you to feel protected if you need it. I don't know what your brothers expect since you're a quarter owner in your business."

"None of them have prenups. Honestly, I don't know that it's ever come up. If it would make you feel better, then we can have one."

"No. Aleks, I'm not going anywhere. You are my soulmate. I know you wouldn't bring me into your family if you weren't certain this is for life. But if, for some reason, this doesn't work out, I know you'll be fair. It's not in your nature to be otherwise. Besides, there are seven other very large, very convincing men who would make sure you did the honorable thing."

I tickle his ribs, and he rolls me onto my back.

"I love you, *malyshka*. Not every day will be perfect. Some will be harder than anything you ever imagined. We won't always agree or want the same things. There might be times when we don't even like each other. But I want you by my side for the rest of my life."

"I want the same."

"Where do you want to go, baby girl?"

"Iceland."

After all the couples came back downstairs yesterday morning, and we had breakfast with the parents, we gathered at Maks and Laura's house. Galina and the other parents stayed at her place, and the men locked themselves away in the office Maks and Laura share. Christina needed some fresh air because of her queasiness, so she and I did a few laps around the garden. It was freezing, but the crisp air felt good. The others stayed inside and worked. When the men finally emerged, Aleks only said he and his brothers had an errand to run. Anton, Sergei, Misha, and Pasha remained at the house with us.

When they returned from wherever, Aleks suggested my family should have dinner with his. He feels it's time for everyone to meet each other. I'm not so certain, but I agreed. According to Aleks, everything with Danielle is on hold for right now, so we're flying out tomorrow morning. I think it'll be good for us to get away, so he isn't an accessible target. I haven't shared my reasoning with anyone.

"Are you ready, baby girl?"

"Yes, Daddy."

I slip on my shoes as I take a last look in the mirror. I can't wait for spring. The dress I'm wearing is thick, which is great for when I'm outside. But if wherever we're going has the heat turned up, I will swelter. I don't even know where we're headed. Aleks won't tell me.

"Let me help you with your coat."

He holds it out for me, and I slip into it. He's already wearing his. When we get to the lobby, I see Misha waiting for us. He raises his eyebrows at Aleks, who nods. What does that mean?

"Close your eyes, *malyshka*."

The car door has barely closed when that commanding voice shoots an arrow of arousal straight to my pussy. I obey, and he slips a blindfold over my eyes. He lifts me onto his lap, so my legs drape over the empty seat. His hand slides between my thighs until he gets to my pussy. I open my legs to his questing fingers. He's home, which means I don't bother with a thong. I won't lie. It thrills me that he wants to always have free access to my pussy.

"I'm going to edge you until we're almost there. Then I'm going to suck your clit until you come. If you get off before then, I will spank you and edge you. But I won't let you come again. I'll leave you aching and ready to beg for my dick by the time we get through the first course."

"I'd have to slip into the restroom and ease the need."

A shiver skids down my spine when he chuckles. It's dark. Super dark. His fingers play with my pussy lips and graze the inside of my thighs, creating a different type of shiver. I'm growing restless already.

"You wouldn't dare. I would follow you, fuck you until I come, pull out, and spank your ass red. You'd have my cum dripping down your thighs while you're even more desperate to get off."

I know he would, and it almost tempts me into disobeying him in the car and in the restaurant. If this were just a date and the two of us, I would. But the idea of needing to come while having his cum inside me at dinner with our entire family mortifies me. What if people figured it out? The men in his family are as horny as he is, and none of the women are any better than me. They'd guess in an instant.

"Let me work your pussy, baby girl. Relax against me."

"Yes, Daddy. Can I suck you off later?"

"When you ask so nicely, how could I say no? It would be rude."

I laugh, but it turns to a gasp when he hits my g spot. He rubs it until I can't stop squirming. With a come-hither motion, he works my pussy until I feel like I might pee. Holy shit. Am I going to squirt? I've never done that before. I breathe through it, waiting to see what happens as the sensation becomes so strong I almost fear it. Nothing comes out of me, but I have the most intense orgasm ever that didn't come from a dick in me.

"*Malyshka*, are you all right? Did I hurt you?"

"What?"

His questions disorient me. Of course, I'm all right. I just had one of the best orgasms of my life.

"You went completely still, and everything felt like it contracted. You didn't make a sound."

"Daddy, I came. I'm sorry."

"You came? You had an orgasm?"

"Yes. It was the most powerful one I've ever had from being fingered. I thought I might squirt."

"That wouldn't be good, considering we're here and about to have dinner with your family and mine. But we can explore this more when we get home."

"Yes, please, Daddy. You're not upset that I came?

"No, baby girl. I think that was well beyond your control."

"Where are we?"

"You'll see in a moment."

He places me back on my seat, cleans his fingers, then slides out when the driver opens the door. He helps me out. I practically choke him when my arms shoot out and wrap around his neck. I was unprepared for him to pick me up.

"There are too many steps along the way, baby girl. You're not breaking your neck."

There's no point in arguing, so I rest my head against his chest and enjoy being in his arms. The flooring under his feet changes because his shoes sound different, like we're on wood instead of concrete. He puts me down and guides me forward with his arm around my waist. When we stop, he takes off my coat. I sense someone else is nearby.

"Are you ready, *malyshka*?"

"Yes."

I nearly said Daddy since it feels like we're alone, even though I think we aren't. He eases the blindfold off, and I can't believe where I'm standing. My gaze sweeps over all the people gathered to the ropes and curtains before turning to the orchestra pit and balconies. We're in a Broadway theater. I turn back to Aleks, and my hands fly to my mouth. He's stealthy. I'm right next to him, but I didn't notice him going down on one knee.

"*Malyshka*, I love you. You know I never imagined I would have a chance to make a life with my soulmate. I never imagined finding you. But I've known since the very beginning that my future is with you. I want to share my life with you and build one together. Will you marry me?"

I nod, tears filling my eyes.

"I need to hear you, *malyshka*."

His voice is soft, but the command only heightens this moment. It's everything I need with him. Tenderness, dominance, affection, love. It's all here.

"Yes, Aleks. Yes."

He flips open a tiny box, and my eyes nearly fall out of my head. I have never seen something so exquisite, and I've seen the other women's engagement rings. This is spectacular. It's a huge, what must be flawless diamond set in rose gold with amethysts on each side. Pink and purple. A reminder of when we met. My hand trembles as he slides it on. I almost crush his suit coat as I tug, urging him to stand. He lifts me off my feet as we kiss. It's the cheers from our families that remind me we aren't alone. I'd forgotten for a moment. I whisper in his ear what I'd really wanted to say.

"Yes, Daddy. I want to be your *malyshka* for forever."

"You already are, baby girl. But now it's official."

We kiss again before he puts me back on my feet. I'm not ready to let go, so we embrace until we know we can't ignore everyone any longer. My parents hug me while Galina hugs Aleks, then we swap. My parents don't know Aleks beyond the dinner we had together, which makes me feel bad, considering how well I'm getting to know Galina.

"When you asked me yesterday if you could marry Heather, I didn't think it would be this unique."

I listen to my dad, but I'm looking at Aleks.

"You asked my dad?"

"Of course. If you haven't noticed, I'm a little old-world about some things."

I fight the urge to laugh, but it's a losing battle.

"Yes, some things."

I wink, and it's Aleks's turn to try not to laugh. I think he might even be blushing. We accept our families' congratulations and well wishes. Mike puts aside whatever issues he had, or has, with Aleks while they shake hands, and he hugs me. That, or he's confident something horrible is going to happen to Aleks, and he's silently enjoying knowing that. Why did I let myself imagine that?

There are so many people on the stage that I didn't notice the enormous table. It must be several put together. Aleks walks me to a seat in the middle and pulls out my chair. The men in his family do the same thing for their wives. Grigori sits between Alina and Galina, so he pulls out both. It's not for show. It's ingrained into their DNA. My dad and brothers-in-law aren't sure what to do since my mom and sisters have already pulled out their own chairs. A fleet of servers appears from the wings. I hear champagne open, and it's soon flowing. I notice bottles of sparkling cider appear for Christina and Laura, who's still nursing. The twins are asleep in a stroller behind her and Maks.

I look out to the seats and catch sight of shadows near the doors. Bodyguards. They are like ghosts, but they no longer surprise me. I turn to Aleks when he takes my hand. His thumb runs over the band before we lace our fingers together.

"This is so incredible. I never imagined having dinner on a Broadway stage. I never imagined being proposed to on a Broadway stage. I could never have fathomed before tonight having our entire family gathered together to see us get engaged, then share dinner with us, all while on a Broadway stage. No other proposal in the history of proposals has ever been this special. Thank you."

"You like it?"

I lift his hand and kiss the back of it. I see and hear his nervousness. He's letting me in again, even though other people —people outside his family—might see. I don't think he intends to shut me out anymore. I think when it happens, it's a force of habit and still fear that somehow it'll leave me unprotected.

"Aleks, you took something you know I love and gave it to me. An entire theater, even if it's only for tonight. You included our families. What you said melted my heart into a gooey puddle in my chest. This is so perfect."

The servers bring out the first course, but we continue to talk.

"You don't mind other people being here? It's become a family tradition among my brothers."

"I know. Laura, Christina, and Ana told me about how Maks, Bogdan, and Niko proposed. Laura told me about the good one and the bad one. Sumiko admitted she proposed to Pasha, but she didn't share any details. I think it must have been really private."

I suspect they were having sex, but I would never ask.

"Family is everything to us. Yours might not be as quick to welcome me into theirs, but I consider them part of mine."

"I love you."

We kiss, and people tap their wine glasses as though we're at a wedding. Except they don't need to. We happily kiss throughout the evening with no prompting. I know we're there for at least five hours, but it feels like five minutes. There's a copious amount of food, and the laughter doesn't stop. Our families swap stories about Aleks and me when we were little. His brothers and my sisters are happy to share some not-sodelightfully funny ones that leave us both shooting death stares at them.

By the time we're ready to leave, I can tell my family is far more at ease with Aleks and his. I suppose they seem more human to my family. All I know is that it's the most perfect night of my life. I hope our getaway proves to be the most perfect vacation ever.

Chapter Twenty-Five

Aleks

The errand my brothers and I ran the other day was to a jeweler in Manhattan. It's the same one my other brothers and Pasha used. Blessedly, the man's daughter wasn't there. She was a complete bitch flirting with—trying to flirt with—Maks when he went with Laura. She made the same mistake when we went with Bogdan, but without Christina. She'd learned by the time it was Niko's turn, and she practically kept out of sight when we went with Pasha.

I called her dad on the way. It was a courtesy, but it was also practical. I want to include her family and respect their relationship with Heather. I never want to come between them, but I probably will if things go to shit with Danielle and Mike, and Shannon and Steven. There's also the issue that her dad hasn't retired yet. He started the process, but it's not as quick as quitting. He and I talked the entire way from Queens to Manhattan. It was purposely vague, but we understood each other. He will support us as best he can, but he will put a bullet through my brain if this life jeopardizes Heather's. Fair enough.

"Are you ready to land, *malyshka*?"

"Yes. I'm so excited."

I know how excited my baby girl is. She showed me three times in the private cabin on our corporate jet. The moment it was safe to take off our seatbelts, she practically dragged me by the collar to the aft. We've been in here ever since. She assured me she'd gotten her birth control shot a week ago, so we're still in the clear to have as much sex as we want. I didn't expect the slight disappointment I felt. The right time will come, but I realized I want a family far sooner than I imagined.

"I can tell."

I waggle my eyebrows as I look at the bed, then the door. I'd barely closed it before she was pushing me against it. She'd offered to go down on me last night, and she made good on it today. Then it was a race to get naked.

"Daddy, are we going to have time to even explore? I might not let you out of the bedroom."

"We have ten days, baby girl."

"I know. But you've looked so relaxed and happy since the moment the wheels went up. I'm so grateful for this trip. I can barely keep my hands off you."

"Barely?"

I chuckle, and she shoots me a look that makes me laugh harder. We return to our seats to prepare for landing. I glance over at my cousins. They look utterly disinterested in us. They're used to our family's antics by now. Anton, Sergei, and Misha continue to chat. Niko and Pasha are asleep. I wanted Niko and Pasha to come, but I didn't ask. They offered, and I appreciate it. It's the first time either of them is traveling without their wife, and I know they aren't thrilled to leave them at home. But they understand the weight it takes off my shoulders to have more of my family with us to guard Heather. She believes they're along for both of us, but they all know who the priority is.

It was a five-and-a-half-hour flight from New York to Reykjavik, and we set off at dawn. We have all afternoon and tonight to enjoy ourselves. Cars are waiting for us on the tarmac, and Heather stares in amazement. It surprised her when we arrived at the private airfield and merely walked straight onto the plane. Officials will check with the pilot, but we're on our way to our first hotel.

"Do you need a nap, Daddy?"

"Afraid you wore me out?"

"Yes."

"Angel, truly, I'm all right. My back itches, but even with stitches still in it, I feel fine."

I won't tell her it felt like it was on fire the entire night while we were on the mission. It was painful while we had sex. And it aches now, along with itching. I consider myself fine because it's pain I'm used to, a level I learned to accept and carry on a long time ago. It would only upset her to know, and I won't ruin a moment of this trip.

We check into the Domes before we explore Reykjavik. By the time we return to our yurt, it's dark. The bed covered in sheepskins is inviting, and I look forward to climbing in. But not yet.

"*Malyshka*, I have something for you."

I hand her a gift-wrapped box and watch her lift the lid. She pushes aside the tissue paper and stares before she puts the box on the bed and lifts out two bikini tops.

"You have got to be kidding. I may as well be naked, Daddy."

"I'd prefer that, but you have to wear something between slipping off the robe and getting in the hot tub."

"You're fucking lucky it's pitch-black outside, or I wouldn't consider it. I am not wearing these in public, Aleks."

"And I wouldn't want you to. These are for our private time. I'm way too possessive to handle other men seeing you in these."

She laughs.

"You should have opened this gift to yourself. Which one tonight, Daddy? Blue and orange or pink and purple. I think I can guess."

She places the pink and purple string bikini top back in the box before I point to the blue and orange. I still tease her she should dye her hair that. I miss the pink and purple. She agreed to trying blue when we get home.

When she pulls out the bottoms, she shakes her head.

"No. Not even in the dark. This won't even cover my anything."

The top is basically two pasties on strings, and the bottoms are almost entirely string with a strip of material that'll cover her pussy from anyone looking at her from the front. As much I'd like to see her in them, I meant them in jest too.

When her gaze meets mine, she gets it. Her lips purse before she pulls her sweater off. I watch her strip off her shirt and bra, too. Then off come her jeans and the thermal leggings. I expect her to grab one of her own bathing suits from the suitcase next to the bed. Instead, she ties the neck straps and slips on the top.

"You're wearing it?"

"It would be rude to reject your gift, Daddy."

"You know I was only joking, right?"

I do not want anyone, even my family, to see my fiancée in that dental floss.

"Hmm. Challenge accepted."

"*Malyshka.*"

She ignores my demand and puts on the rest of her—threads. She sways her hips before she walks over to her suitcase and bends over, her ass to me. I march over and land a ringing slap across it. She wiggles her hips. I land two more that are even harder. She pushes her hips. I was already unfastening my pants. My arm goes around her as I yank my boxer briefs over my cock, which is possibly harder than it's ever been. That's hard to imagine considering I've been fucking hard most of every day ever since the fucking grocery store. From behind, there's nothing to move aside before I impale her.

"I think my *malyshka* needs a reminder of who's in charge. This cunt is mine, baby girl. It is not for any other man to see. Not for any other man to fantasize about being in. The only man coming from this pretty pink pussy is me. Maybe a good fucking and my cum will remind you of that."

"I think I forgot, *sudar'*. I definitely need that reminder. I think I need reminding a little harder."

I pull her upright, then press my teeth into the crook of her neck while my free hand pinches her nipple as hard as I dare.

"When do you get to come?"

"When you tell me I can, *sudar'*."

"Do you want me to fill this perfect little pussy?"

"Yes. With your fucking cock, then your cum."

I'm not into the idea of calling her a slut or a whore. I know that gets some people off, but I prefer our praise kink.

"Mmm. You and your dirty little mouth, *malyshka*. I can think of what to wash it out with."

"Fuck, fuck, fuckiddy, fuck, Daddy."

"I should edge you and make you blow me, but I'm not leaving your cunt until we both come. You feel too damn good."

"I know, *sudar'*. I thought you liked it."

"Cheeky, *malyshka*."

She wiggles her ass cheeks against my hips.

"That's it. Widen your legs."

She obeys immediately. I slap her pussy, then rub her clit.

"Fucking come. Take my cock and fucking come."

I'm growling my command as I continue to slap and rub. She reaches back and wraps her hands over my shoulders and turns her head. She tries to pull me down for a kiss, but I resist. I harden my gaze, and I feel her body relax against mine. A sigh escapes as her eyes drift closed. Then I kiss her. I pour every ounce of feeling into it. This is how we work. I am Daddy or *sudar'*, and she is my baby girl, my *malyshka*.

"*Sudar'*. I'm coming. I'm coming."

I revel in how her back arches against me, and she shudders her release. I'm right there with her. We stand together, both of my arms wrapped around her. Her arms slide beneath my upper arms and wrap over my forearms. We're content for a moment, but then she pulls away entirely too soon.

"I have something for you too, Daddy."

Her tone tells me I'm going to hate it as much as I love it. She reaches into her suitcase and pulls out a gift box. It's wrapped much like mine was. I rip through it, making her laugh. My expression must match hers because peals of laughter fill the yurt.

"No."

"Oh, yes, Daddy. If I'm wearing this, you are wearing that. One hundred percent."

I wrap an arm around her waist and fling us onto the bed. I tickle her, and she's merciless when she returns the favor. When we're breathless once again, we lie together, the goofiest grins on our face.

"You're still wearing it."

She pushes off the bed and darts to the door, grabbing her robe along the way. She slips it on and waits for me. She knows not to leave without me, even if the guys are nearby. They won't go to bed until they see the lights go off in our dome.

"It's a good thing I love you, *malyshka*."

"I know."

She giggles, and it's the sweetest sound. With a huff, I strip off my clothes and put on her gift. I don my robe, and we head to the hot tub. I close my eyes and press my lips together, shaking my head as the laughter in the dark fills the night air when I disrobe.

Fucking Speedo. She gave me a motherfucking Speedo.

"When in Rome, Daddy. Guys still wear them in Europe."

"I won't soon forget this."

"I know. The girls warned me that all of you have a penchant for buying the most ridiculous bathing suits. We get why you do, and we're flattered that you enjoy seeing us that much. But not a one of us likes these damn things. It's a good thing our men are overly confident for us. If I hadn't been fore-warned and able to gear up for this, I would have refused."

I shrug. It's no secret that each of us believes the woman we're with is the most beautiful in the world. It's no secret how much we desire our partners. We're all possessive and protective, but we're also all healthy men. If they can't get away with being totally naked, then these swimsuits are close enough.

We ease into the water, and she floats toward me to straddle my lap. She drapes her arms around my neck.

"Aleks, are you happy? Like truly happy. Like you can relax, even if it's only for a minute, without worrying something's going to happen."

"Yes. I'm vigilant, and I'm aware. I will never be able to stop that. It's in my blood and bones. But I'm not scanning every nook and cranny for a threat. I'm wholly here in the moment with you, Heather. You give me that. It's not like I never smiled or laughed before we got together, but I told you,

I've always been the most reserved. To where I'm called dour. You heard my brother call me Eeyore. I thought my sense of humor was irreparable years ago. What did I have to laugh about beyond something funny here or there? With you, I laugh all the time. I honestly finally feel my age. I'm thirty, not seventy."

"I'm glad I can do that for you. I'm happy, not because you spoil me—though I appreciate all of that."

I know she glances at her ring.

"It's not that I used to feel unsafe, but I feel so safe with you. I never realized how good that would feel until being with you. Everything feels so much easier now that I have a partner. I love sharing these high points. And I love knowing you are so damn reliable that I will always turn to you. I talked to Stephanie the other day, and I was trying to explain. It made me sad when I realized she doesn't have with her husband what I have with you. It's not that I think there's anything bad or wrong with her marriage. I just don't think she feels the same connection with him that I do with you. It's like—like a part of me lives outside my body, and that part is you. I feel on an elemental level like I know you as well as I know myself. I get there are parts of the past, present, and future that you will never tell me about. That makes me sad because I hate knowing you bear that weight alone. But that doesn't detract from how I feel bound to you from our very atomic core."

"I feel the same, and that's how I know we're soulmates. A part of my soul lives within yours, and I feel yours inside me. You truly fill the holes. I wasn't exaggerating when I told you that."

"When can we get married, Aleks? I don't want to wait."

"Neither do I. Baby girl, we need to talk about something because I never want you to think this is the reason I'm marrying you."

"That doesn't sound ominous or anything."

"In our world, there was a rule that was supposed to be utterly unbreakable. In the past year, the Italians, Irish, and Colombians have broken it. The Irish did from the top down. Salvatore and Enrique haven't condoned what their men have done, but it's clear they don't have the control they once did. Enrique only had one bad apple to deal with, and we took care of it for him. But Salvatore's trouble shares his blood. Right now, it ties his hands, and we get that. I also think they're near the edge of his good graces, and he will solve the problem permanently."

My arms loosely rest around her hips, but now my hands squeeze her waist and rest heavily there.

"Women and children used to be off limits. Specifically, wives and children, but everyone knew that meant mothers, sisters, nieces. Everyone but us has broken that rule. We will never fight our battles through those who don't have the means to fight back. When Sylvia told you to go to her if ever you can't get to us, that's why. It's bad enough that the matriarch of another syndicate offered you shelter. When we marry, I need you to really understand that you're not just marrying into my family. You're not just becoming a Kutsenko. You're marrying into the bratva. You will never be part of bratva business, but you are, by default, a member. That means the police and feds could target you. It means that you become more valuable to our enemies. But it also means that the entire bratva owes you their loyalty and their protection as the wife of an Elite Group member and the *pakhan's* sister."

"What does *pakhan* mean? I've heard it before."

"The literal translation is boss. But in the bratva, it means the leader. It's the same as being the don or the *jefe*. The Irish don't have the same formal structure that the rest of us do. What they have, when they use it, are positions similar to the

Navy. Their Godfather or leader is a captain or skipper. There are terms for other positions, but the hierarchy doesn't exist the same way as with us and the Italians in particular."

I haven't told her the inner workings of the bratva before, but I think it's time.

"You already know my brothers and I are Maks's senior advisors and make up the Elite Group. Sergei is the *sovietnik*, heading our security group. He gathers intelligence, but he also helps keep things running within the organization, and he is often a liaison with other syndicates, if the issue isn't serious enough for Maks or the Elite Group. Anton is the *obshchak*, heading the support group. He's our best strategist for our operations that aren't aboveboard. He's also our enforcer and makes sure those who owe us give us what they should."

"And I guess Pasha and Misha have specific jobs, too."

"Yes. Pasha is our *derzhatel obshchaka*. He works with Anton since he's our accountant. Sumiko handles our legal businesses, but Pasha handles what she doesn't. He lets Anton know who he needs to see. Misha and Pasha are both *avotoritets*, or brigadiers. They're like generals. The word means authority. They lead our foot soldiers, and they lead my brothers, Sergei, Anton, and me, during ops. Misha doesn't have an official title like my other cousins, but he's emerged as the strongest *avotoritets*. Pasha defers to him. We've all held that position and still can, but they've proven to be the best."

"Does it bother Misha that he doesn't have a specific title or role?"

"No. Everyone knows he's the brigadier-in-charge, even if there isn't a specific name. Because of Pasha's other responsibilities, Misha is the one who gives out assignments to our *boyeviks*, or foot soldiers. In other bratvas, they're also recruiters. When Vlad died, we stopped actively recruiting. Some men come to us, but most of it remains hereditary. When there's a specific operation or something has to be done, a brigadier is in charge of five or six men who're called *patsanov* or *brodyaga*. Sometimes they're called *bratok*. They have specific duties for our illegal activities."

"You said most come to you because it's hereditary. That means our children too, right?"

"None of us know yet, *malyshka*. All of us thought the bratva ties would die with us. It's not something Sergei and Anton worry about, though they would probably make the best fathers out of all of us. But now that all of us but Misha are in committed relationships, we're having to reconsider that. It would be sons, not daughters. Older members might push for arranged marriages for Mila and any of her girl cousins, but they wouldn't try too hard. They know we won't accept it at all. It's not even remotely something my brothers, cousins, and I will consider. The old Elite Group tried to push Maks into an arranged marriage. It was horrible. Maks could never do it to Mila, so he would never do it to someone else's daughter. He wouldn't do it to Konstantin either, so none of our sons. But I don't know what will happen when any of our sons are old enough to join."

"You told me Bogdan was eleven. Is that normal?"

I sigh. These are fair questions, and I opened the door. But I don't like any of the answers I have to give.

"*Shestyorka*, or six, are errand boys. They don't take part in any of the activities, but they can stand as lookouts. They bring us information. These can be adults despite the title, but usually tweens and teens in other bratvas. It's not unheard of to have *shestyorka* younger than that, but Maks doesn't allow it. He won't allow anyone younger than eighteen to join. Either they prove themselves and become full members or they're cast aside. There's a greater risk of them narcing with young adults than with kids, but it's a risk we take. We will steal no one's childhood. In the beginning, men still left over from Vlad's time tried to get us to accept their sons and grandsons as kids. Maks is no tyrant, but people knew when he was sworn in that he wouldn't be led by anyone."

"So our sons wouldn't have to join until they're adults."

The relief in her voice is palpable. I hate crushing it.

"Not exactly. We will keep them away from all of this for as long as we can. But it would be better if we explain some things before they guess or talk to the wrong person. Before we were old enough to go on missions, we used to help our uncles and other *brodyaga* prepare. We learned as much from that as we did from half of Vlad's training. If our sons must join, that's where they would start."

"How old?"

"Fifteen, sixteen."

"Do the other wives know all of this? Did Laura know before she got pregnant?"

"No, she didn't. They didn't plan to have children so soon, though I don't think Maks or Laura could imagine not having the twins. I don't know exactly what the other wives know, but I think they know all of this now. But I don't think any knew before they got married. It's not that my brothers or Pasha hid this from them. I have the benefit of seeing how things went for them and learning from them. It was hardest for Maks because he had no idea what was safe for Laura to know. It's gotten a bit easier with each relationship. But don't think this is simple for me. I believe you should know, but it terrifies me that you do."

"Do you think I would tell someone, even by accident?"

"No. I'm just not convinced letting you into any of this is safe for you. But the fear that it's more dangerous for you not to know is stronger."

"This is a lot to digest."

"I know. If you have questions, you know I'll do my best to

answer. But if I don't, it's because I don't think it's a good idea to tell you. There's one other thing we should talk about. You know about the warehouse. You know it's a controlled place for us. We don't always have that opportunity. Sometimes things go sideways. If I ever call you and tell you to go into your office or a guest bedroom and stay there, or if I tell you that when I get home, I need you to do it. I need you not to ask questions. It's not that I don't want to be with you. It's that I don't want you to be near me. It means I need to get cleaned up, and it means I need to calm down. I will never hurt you. Never. No matter what state of mind I am in, but I don't want you to see me like that."

She swallows before she nods.

"Does that happen often?"

"No. Next to never, but it's not impossible."

She moves her arms around my back, and I realize too late that I'm not supposed to have my stitches submerged. Fuck. Too fucking late now. I'll have to shower and check them before we go to bed. Her hold keeps tightening until I think she's squeezing me as hard as she can. She's holding onto me as though I might run away.

"*Malyshka?*"

"I'm all right, Daddy."

"I don't think you are. Are you angry?"

"Yes. But not at you."

"What do you mean?"

"I'm fucking furious. Livid. I'm angry because of what those men did to you, what they and this life have forced you to do. I'm angry that I can't fix this and take you away from all of this. I'm angry that you are ever scared about anything, especially about me and my safety. I'm angry about the life they stole from you. I really fucking hate that I can't do a fucking thing to protect you or erase your past. I love the man you are, and I know much of that is a product of what happened and how you've coped. But I fucking hate it."

"Baby girl—"

She leans back and shakes her head.

"No. I don't need you to soothe me or reassure me. Just the opposite. Aleks, no matter what happens outside our home, when you walk through that door, you are home. You are the man I love. The man I'm going to have a family with and grow old with. I cannot change a damn thing about any of this, but I will always welcome you into my arms. Whatever you can or can't tell me doesn't matter. I will be here for you however you need me. If it's listening or be a shoulder to lean on. If it's companionable silence. If it's a good hard fuck to get it out of your system, I stand with you. Or sometimes lie with you."

I chuckle when she tries to lighten what's become a pretty dark conversation.

"*Malyshka*, you've always been meant to be part of this family. The women have a heavy cross to bear, but they are fiercely loyal and protective. They don't show it the same way as the men, but they don't feel it any less. I think you're like that, too."

"I am. Aleks, I don't know the details, and I'm certain I don't want to, and no one will ever tell me. But I know some shit went sideways with Ana in Greece. I know Laura had to do some shit, too. It's not that I believe everyone has a propensity toward violence, but I know that there is no limit to what I would do to protect you and our family. That's not just any children. That's everyone on both sides. I hope it never comes to that, but I need you to understand that there's a part of me that is more like you than you want to know."

"*Mal—*"

"No. Don't placate me. I'm not exaggerating. Something happened to Mikayla that no one else knows about. Not

Danielle, not my parents. Her husband, Rick, might know—probably knows. But no one else. Do you remember Teddy Toscano? He was Maks's year."

"Yeah."

"Do you remember how everyone thought he was in a car accident, and that's how he got that huge gash on the side of his head and lost part of his left ear?"

"Yeah. It happened his senior year."

"There was no car accident. Mikayla's car broke down on the way home from a volleyball game. My mom was out of town, and my dad was at work. Danielle was out with her boyfriend. I went to get her. When I pulled up, there was a car behind hers. I recognized it. It was Teddy's. I heard my sister screaming before I even turned off the engine. I got out and could see him on top of her in the ditch by the road. Aleks, I did not think twice. I popped the trunk open, grabbed the tire iron, and slid down the embankment. I brought it down on his head and dragged it once it made contact. I didn't stop. I cracked six ribs on his right side and eight on his left. I cut his ear so badly, it couldn't be repaired."

I listen in shock as she tells me this story. I remember more now that I think about it, and I can picture Teddy with the stitches. He was out for a few days, then came back with the bandages, but I'd forgotten about his ribs. Shit. This story only gets worse.

"When he rolled off Mikayla, his dick was out. He'd been trying to get it in, but my sister fought too hard. The moment I saw that, I lost the little control I had left. I doubt he's ever told anyone at school, but I may as well have castrated him. I took the tire iron to his balls like I was playing golf—which I do. Not just putt-putt. I was a competitive golfer in high school, not just a theater nerd. Once I got Mikayla into the car, I went to hers and pulled out a towel I knew she had in her gym bag. I wrapped the tire iron in it because it was bloody. I put it in a plastic grocery bag I had in my car. I was actually driving my mom's. I got the tire iron from Mikayla's car and punctured the tube on each of Teddy's tires. As far as I was concerned, he could die out there, but he wasn't following us that night."

She's completely calm as she tells me this story where she nearly killed a guy when she was seventeen. She doesn't sound detached or remorseful. She may as well be telling me what we're having for breakfast.

"Do you remember Mikey Beneventi?"

"Yeah. His dad owned a trash collection company and a garage. Mikey used to drive a tow truck on the weekends."

"He was also the guy I was messing around with back then. We'd been friends since elementary school, and I know I can still trust him. I knew back then the shady shit his family was into. They probably worked for Salvatore and still do. It was a risk since I know Teddy's dad was tied to the *Cosa Nostra*, but that's why I called Mikey. He didn't ask questions. He came and towed Mikayla's car to his dad's garage. Mikey didn't know what happened because Mikayla was in the car, and I did all the talking. By the time he got there, I'd pulled Teddy's pants up, so his dick wasn't hanging out. Mikey took one look at Teddy, grinned, and hooked his truck up."

"Teddy never tried to retaliate?"

"To a cop's daughter? He didn't make the same mistake twice. He stayed the fuck away from my sisters and me. He's lucky I didn't kill him. The only reason I didn't was because I didn't want Mikayla to see that. If she hadn't been too scared for me to leave her alone at the house, I would have gone back and finished him. So when I tell you there is nothing I won't do to protect you and our family, do not fucking underestimate me, Aleks. I was seventeen then. I'm a fuck ton more jaded with life and the world than I was back then. I slept like a baby that night and every night after. I'll do the same now."

Damn. I get why neither Mikayla nor Heather wanted to call the police, since she's right that Teddy and Mikey's families are *Cosa Nostra*. I get why she wouldn't want the cops to know since her dad was one, too. But her dad could have had Teddy locked up. Not that, that would have made it better. He would have become Salvatore's target.

"I pray you are never in that situation again, *malyshka*. That story doesn't make me worry any less. But I didn't doubt you before you told me, and I don't doubt you now. That's why I know you belong in this family and will fit in. I told you, you're like the other wives with this. Salvatore is so fucking scared of Ana that he'll leave a room. Enrique has known Laura since she was two. He knew she was stubborn as a child. He knows her iron will as an adult. He has a healthy dose of fear for a woman he used to give piggyback rides to."

"And Christina and Sumiko?"

"Christina's dad is Scottish and was a British Royal Marine. She took Bogdan to the mat and kept him there. She can do more than swing a fist and run. I didn't know this until right before we ran into each other at the grocery store, but Sumiko's been training in Brazilian Jiu-Jitsu since she was a kid. She stopped for a few years, but she's back to it."

"Your mom and aunts?"

"Grew up in Russia."

She nods. She needs no more explanation than that. After Aunt Alina was taken, my dad and uncles made sure my mom and aunts can shoot, wield a knife, and grapple. They might all be in their fifties, but my money is on my mom and aunts. And God help the person who comes near any of their sons or nephews.

I remember when I was ten, a group of men approached my

brothers, cousins, and me in a park. They were Podolskaya bratva. They knew whose children we were, but our dads were in Chechnya. They didn't see our moms on a bench a few hundred yards away. They thought they could fuck with us. None of us knew our moms never left home without guns in their purses. Those men found out at the same time we did. My mom and aunts scared them off without hitting any of them. They couldn't risk that kind of retaliation. But those men knew our moms didn't miss by accident.

"I won't ask what you're remembering, Aleks. But I think I'm just twisted enough to fit in."

Chapter Twenty-Six

Heather

"I can't believe how fast ten days have gone, Daddy."

We're back in the same dome in Reykjavik as the night we arrived. It's been a whirlwind tour of an entire country. We've stayed somewhere different every night, and every single one has been the lap of luxury unless it was rustic. Even then, none has been a hardship. Even this yurt has a private bathroom, and the private hot tub.

"What's been your favorite place, *malyshka?*"

I run my hand over the sheepskin blanket as we lie in bed together.

"I don't know. I've loved all of it. The Glacier Lagoon in Jökulsarlón was spectacular, and so was seeing the Gullfoss. That waterfall is just beyond incredible. All of that area of the Golden Circle, and the South Coast, was so memorable. I completely get why they film so many movies here. The Snæfellsnes Peninsula was like seeing all of Iceland in one place. The volcanic beaches, the Kirkjufellsfoss waterfall. I mean, that should be one of the Seven Wonders of the World. The Northern Lights have been clear everywhere but seeing them at Kirkjufellsfoss was a bucket list item I didn't even know I had. And I loved Sænautasel. That turf house was like visiting the shire in *The Hobbit*. Oh, and swimming among the glaciers and lava in the hot springs at Hveravellir was just...I don't even know. This has been so far past anything I could have ever imagined, Daddy. Thank you."

"I will consider this a success then."

"Most definitely. I wish we could just stay here and spend all day hiking. You could probably spend a year and not take every trail."

"We can always come back."

"I'd love that."

I fight—unsuccessfully—the yawn that creeps up. I might need a vacation from our vacation. I snuggle closer to Aleks, and we're asleep almost immediately. It's way too soon when the sun comes in, and it's time for us to head to the airport. But as we fly back to New York, I sort through the thousand or so photos I took. I seriously think I took a hundred a day. Some are total duds, so I delete those. I put the other ones in folders on my cloud. I'll print singles of some and collages of others. The best ones of Aleks smiling are getting a wall to themselves in my office. He laughed so much. But each mile that takes us closer to New York makes him grow more serious. By the time we land, he's once more the reserved man everyone claims he is.

Two town cars greet us at the airport. Aleks and I get in the back of one, and Misha gets in the front. Pasha, Anton, Sergei, and Niko are in the second. They'll drop Pasha and Niko off at Pasha's place, where Sumiko and Ana are waiting. Then Anton and Sergei will go home to their places. At least, officially they will.

"Are you hungry, *malyshka?* Do you want to have lunch on the way home or just go straight to the penthouse?"

"I don't mind. I need to go grocery shopping. We don't have a ton left."

"We'll go together. I'll be traffic control while you push the cart."

"One time."

I jokingly roll my eyes and wave my index finger.

"That I saw. I think you do that pretty often with Cadence."

"Humph. Spoil sport."

Aleks drops the privacy glass and tells the driver something. I assume a restaurant because I've learned a few phrases, and I didn't hear home, house, or place. I rest against him and sigh. It's always nice to come home to the familiar and your own stuff, but it's also totally anticlimactic. Our bliss is over.

The car stops outside a sushi restaurant a few blocks from the penthouse. Even though we had a lot of fresh seafood in Iceland, sushi sounds awesome. Misha goes in first and takes up residence near the fire exit. Once he nods to Aleks, we follow the host to our table. I'm pretty predictable with sushi. I know what I like, and I stick with it. Aleks will try just about anything. The man has a cast iron stomach.

"There is no way I'm trying any of what you're ordering."

I grin as the waitress takes our menus. Aleks leans across the table to whisper.

"Good, because I'm a growing boy who needs all his sustenance."

I snort.

"I know what's growing. I'll feed you twenty-four-seven if I have to."

"I know."

"I have never met anyone who can eat as much as you,

Daddy. Seriously. Like you eat twice as much as all the other guys. And Sergei's the biggest of you and lifts weights the most. His plate is a child's serving compared to what I've seen you put away. How? Just how?"

"I don't know. I've always been that way. I enjoy food, but I've always just been the one who needs the most fuel, I guess. Sergei's only a little broader across the back and chest than the rest of us. We can still share clothes. Anton's bulkier than me and weighs the most of all of us. But he's the same size clothes as all of us. But I can still eat laps around them. The others gave up trying to keep up. We'd have eating contests when we were teenagers. I would win, and the others would puke."

"You just need to remember your mom and I cannot eat like you do. I swear, the servings you give us each could feed the two of us."

He's sat between Galina and me a couple times at meals. He piles food on, and we either have to swap plates with him, or push half onto his plate. I don't know if food was scarce when he was young, and so he equates food with security. I don't know if Galina cooked a lot when they were little, and he equates it with love. Or he could just have no idea what a normal person's serving is. But I know he serves his mom and me so much because he cares, not because he's careless.

"Heather, I know you've taken way more time off from your job than you should have. The time I was in the hospital, the few days after, and now we've been away for ten days. Are you going to get written up or something?"

"No. It's inconvenient for the office manager to find subs for that long, but my friend has been happy to have three full weeks of work. The kids like her, but I know it's not the same. Fortunately, a parent is a stage director at one of the prestigious Harlem theaters. He's stepped forward to help. I called in a favor since he was also one of my undergrad professors who now lives in New York too."

"We never talked about what you said before I left. You talked about making a permanent change."

"I want to leave my position, Aleks. I know Svetlana is an art teacher and has made it work for decades. But that's not the same as being responsible for stage productions that require not only coaching for the actors, but stage design, choreography in some cases, and music selection for a band or orchestra. I have to work with the art teacher, dance teacher, and music teachers. There's a lot more that goes into it than listening to the kids practice their lines. I can't be in and out every time you need me to stay indoors."

"I don't want you to give this up. You love teaching, and you love the theater. You're passionate about both, and they make you happy."

"I am, and they do. But I don't feel the same as I did three months ago. It's nowhere near as exciting, but I have written curriculum before. I would still work, but I could develop curriculum for theater programs anywhere in the country. I could work directly with districts, or I could work for a design company. That's more likely, but I can work from home for either. I have a friend who did it while she took an extended maternity leave. It kept money coming in, and it allowed her time with her baby."

"Are you concerned about having an income? Do you feel like I expect it? Or are you worried about not having your own money?"

"None of that. I'm not concerned, but I still want to contribute. I don't think you expect it, and you're hardly stingy. I don't feel like I need a rainy-day fund in case things don't work out."

"*Malyshka*, money will never be something to worry about.

There are very few people in this world who have as much as I do, and next to none of them are women. I will always be able to and be willing to provide for our family. I will never look for someone else because they have money. There doesn't have to be his and hers unless you want that. You could make a penny a year or a million a month. It doesn't matter to me. I just want you to be fulfilled by what you choose."

"I know."

We pause our conversation as the waitress delivers our rolls. I look at his with the insane amounts of Sriracha sauce and wasabi compared to my relatively bland choices. Rather him than me.

I continue to explain.

"I'm not worried about the money. I want to work because I need something to fill my days. I've already spent years giving away hours for free as a public school teacher. If I'm going to keep working and do it in the private sector, I sure as fuck am not working for free. That's all I meant."

"When do you want to make it happen?"

I bite my bottom lip as I look at my plate.

"Did you already resign?"

"No. Not officially. But I told my principal it was coming. I asked her not to take any official steps yet to get my replacement, but she should put our feelers."

"How did you explain that?"

"I didn't. I just said another opportunity was presenting itself."

"Do people know we're together?"

"Yes."

My brow furrows as Aleks sits back. There's a little perspiration beading along his forehead. The food must be spicier than I thought.

"As far they know, you're dating a rich Russian man. Some

might even guess we're mafia. They're going to think I'm some type of oligarch insisting my little woman knows her place, which is behind me and in the home."

"No, they won't."

His cocked eyebrow says it all.

"Fine. Maybe some will. What does it matter? Those aren't my friends or people who matter to me. My friends will see us together as a normal couple. I don't care about the other people's opinion. I care about our relationship and what works for us."

He takes a swig of water, and he looks uncomfortable.

"Aleks?"

"Hmm."

"Did you finally meet your match? Are these rolls too hot for you?"

"No. We need to go."

"Aleks?"

"Not now."

He pulls a wad of money from his wallet, and his hands are shaking. Something is wrong. I look at Misha and signal him over. He looks around before making his way to the table. Immediately, he knows something is off. He says something to Aleks in Russian, and I'm not sure even Misha can understand what Aleks mumbles back.

"Heather, stay here. I'm going to help Aleks to the restroom."

"No. She doesn't stay alone."

Aleks's words are slurred, like his tongue is too thick for his mouth. My eyes widen. He's having an allergic reaction, or someone's drugged him. I stand as Misha helps Aleks to his feet. He wobbles for a moment, but a few deep breaths steady him. We make it to the hallway with the restrooms. As soon as Aleks is certain no one can see him, he slumps against the wall.

Misha pushes open the restroom door and practically drags Aleks in as he speaks.

"You need to puke, Aleks. Now."

I don't know if it's too late. I don't know if I should go inside. I don't know if I'll be in the way or if I should stand watch. I'm about to follow Aleks and Misha in when I hear voices outside the back door that's propped open a couple inches. I slip down the hall, looking back at the restroom, but Misha is inside and focused on Aleks. I should be too, but I understand what these guys are saying.

"*¿Cuánto le pusiste a esos rollos?*" How much did you put on those rolls?

"*No pensé que fuera tanto. Solo lo suficiente para hacer el trabajo.*" I didn't think it was that much. Just enough to do the job.

"*Bueno, lo que sea que hayas hecho probablemente lo matará aquí. Se suponía que iba a llegar a casa. Se suponía que debía verse como si lo hubiera hecho.*" Well, whatever you did is probably going to kill him here. He was supposed to make it home. She was supposed to look like she did it.

She? What the hell? Do they mean me? Were they going to make me look like I drugged him? Wait. No, not drugged. They said kill. They fucking mean poisoned. Who the fuck are these guys?

"*Sé lo que se suponía que iba a pasar. No hace falta que me lo digas. Yo estaba allí cuando recibimos las instrucciones. ¿Quién diablos sabe? Tal vez es demasiado sensible a estas cosas o algo así. De cualquier manera, ahora estamos jodidamente atrapados aquí para asegurarnos de que funcione.*" I know what was supposed to happen. You don't need to fucking tell me. I was there when we got the instructions. Who the fuck knows? Maybe he's like overly sensitive to this stuff or something. Either way, now we're fucking stuck here to make sure it works.

How would they know if it worked at our place? Is the penthouse bugged or something? Would they wait for Aleks's family to storm in and leave with me in a black bag or rolled up in the rug? Would they wait for Aleks's funeral? Do Russian Orthodox do wakes?

"Voy a dar la vuelta al frente. Tu vuelve a entrar." I'll go around front. You go back in.

It's the first guy who spoke, and the voice is a little louder. I spin on my heel and bolt back to the restroom. I push the door open and find Aleks and Misha sitting on the floor. Aleks looks like shit. He's so damn pale, he could be a corpse. But his eyes are clear.

"We need to take him home."

I shake my head when Misha speaks. I put my finger to my lips and look back over my shoulder. I hear someone walk past. I cross the restroom and squat in front of Aleks and Misha. I whisper to them.

"I just heard two guys speaking Spanish outside. They intended to poison you. It wasn't supposed to work until we got home. I don't know how they knew to be here, but they tampered with your food. They wanted to pin the blame on me. If we go back to the penthouse, they'll follow, or somehow they'll know how you're doing. We need to go somewhere else. And you need a doctor."

Misha glances at the door.

"Where are they now?"

"One was supposed to stay out back, but I think he just walked past. The other is going around front. Aleks, are you okay? How do you feel?"

"Like shit. I can't remember the last time I puked that much. But my tongue doesn't feel swollen anymore. We'll go to my mom's. Misha, call Boris from the car. Help me up."

Misha's on his feet in one fluid motion. Aleks isn't so graceful, but he stands on his own. The guy is immortal, or the level of fucked-uppedness that exists in their lives is beyond my comprehension. If he can pretend to look this well when he almost died, then his training to hide his emotions was way more sadistic than I can wrap my head around. I already know it's the latter.

"*Malyshka*, I know what you're thinking like it's going through my own head. I have never felt worse than I do right now. But I cannot walk out of this restaurant looking ill. It's bad enough some people saw Misha have to help me in here. When we get in the car, all I want is to hold your hand and close my eyes. I don't want to talk."

"Whatever you need."

I want to hug him and hold him, but he just told me what he wants. What I want isn't what matters right now. I'll content myself with holding his hand. We head out of the restroom, and I look around. No one is near the hallway, and the backdoor is closed. As we turn the corner, I bump into Aleks's back because I'm not watching where I'm going.

"Aleks, go to the car and go to your mom's. Send someone for me or leave Mikhail here."

"What? No."

"Aleks, Danielle and Mike are having lunch with a couple who I strongly suspect are Shannon and Steven. The woman is staring at us. She looks smug. Like not just a regular resting bitch face. Like pleased by what she sees. Danielle's seen me too. I can't ignore my sister. Go to your mom's."

"Misha, stay with Heather. Mikhail and I will wait in the car. I'm not arguing, Heather."

"And neither am I. Go to your mother's and see a doctor, or you won't come near me for a month. You need to trust me right now, Aleks. And I need to trust you're going to have enough sense to keep yourself alive. Go."

I don't wait for either of them to say anything. I wave to my sister as I walk over.

"Hi."

Danielle stands up and gives me a hug.

"Is Aleks okay?"

"Yeah. We just discovered he has an allergy or something to one of the fish. He's fine now and headed home. Luckily, he only ate a little. How're you? What're you doing in Manhattan?"

I'm not fucking saying whose home in case Shannon is part of this.

"These are our friends, Shannon and Steven McGillis."

I shake hands with each of them and feign ignorance.

"It's nice to meet you. Do you guys live or work around here?"

"Yes."

It's Steven who answers. Maybe he's a good therapist because he prefers to listen than talk. I wish I hadn't thought that. Now I'm picturing him spanking my sister as he stands behind her. I stop the image before I see him fucking her.

"Where's Cadence?"

I shift my gaze from Steven to Danielle. She's a stay-at-home mom, so she's rarely without my nephew during the day. Then again, if she has weekly sessions with Steven and Shannon, then she must have someone babysitting him who I don't know about.

"He's with Mom."

"Fun. She spoils him even more than I do."

Shannon keeps glancing toward the front door that Aleks and Misha went through. I noticed her look down the hallway to the restrooms, then over at a table with two Latino men. They have menus, so they look like they just arrived. Are they the two I heard? Does Shannon know something?

Shannon's question shocks the shit out of me, but she's putting out feelers.

"Did Aleks recognize me? We've known each other since we were kids."

"Yes. I know your long family history with the Kutsenkos."

Did I just tip my hand too soon? A flash of uncertainty crosses her face before she smiles. She's a pretty woman, but there is no warmth. She feels utterly fake.

"Danielle mentioned you two just got engaged. Congratulations."

"Thank you. Did you know I've known Aleks and his family since I was in high school? So did Danielle."

"She mentioned that."

"Today?"

"When she told me you two were dating. Such a small world."

"So small sometimes it's like there are only four families in it."

Shannon's eyes narrow and dart to Steven. I can see his face, and he looks surprised. I move my gaze to my sister, who's watching Steven as though she's judging how to react by him. Is he her Dom even now? Mike's watching the Shannon the same way as Danielle's watching Steven.

"Too true."

Shannon looks back at me before she responds. There's a lull in the conversation as I watch Shannon, and she watches me. Silence makes Danielle uneasy, so I knew I could count on her saying something to fill the void.

"Do you need to check on Aleks?"

"No. Like I said, he's headed home. He knows I'm happy to see you, so we decided I'd go after I got to say hi."

"Aleks and Heather got back from Iceland this morning. How was the trip? Amazing?"

"Pictures don't do it justice. Not even seeing it on the big screen. It's awe inspiring. I'd go back in a heartbeat."

"I can't wait to see all the photos. We should all have dinner together at Mom and Dad's."

"We should. Talk to Mom about it when you pick up Cadence. Let me know what days work for everyone. I'm sure Aleks and I can make it, assuming nothing comes up at work again."

I look at Shannon, then Steven. I don't know any details, but I know that the night Aleks and the others were away, they dealt with the Irish and the Italians. I got the feeling he saw Shannon wherever he went before the warehouse.

"Oh, I didn't tell you."

My sister catches my attention. I lift my eyebrows.

"Yeah, Mike just got a motorcycle. He's going to learn to ride. Shannon and Steven have had one for years. They belong to a club, and they invited us to join."

"Oh? That sounds like fun. Which one?"

"The Iron Order. Isn't that name so cool?"

I look at Danielle as though she's lost her mind. She must have.

"Have you told Dad that?"

"No. Why?"

Okay. This is going too far too fast.

"Are either of you veterans or cops?"

I look at Steven, then Shannon. I already know the fucking answer to the second option. I don't wait for them to answer.

"No. Then why the Iron Order?"

Neither of them speaks up. It's Danielle who asks the next question.

"Why does that matter?"

"Because it's a motorcycle club with a dubious reputation, even though its members are supposedly the most law-abiding citizens. Dad warned us about them when we were in high school. That rookie he had was a member, and he tried flirting with you. He offered to take you for a ride on his bike and out to one of their events."

I look at Shannon and don't ask a question. It's a statement.

"You're members because you're an O'Rourke."

"No, she's not. She's a McGillis."

It's Mike's turn to speak up. I pierce him with my gaze, and for once, he keeps quiet.

"Before Shannon was a McGillis, she was an O'Rourke. Danielle, you know what that means."

"I do."

There's a frostiness to my sister's voice, but when I look at her, I realize it's directed to me.

"Shannon was not an O'Rourke. She was a McGinty. Her family owns that pub you go to."

"There are no McGintys, Danielle. The O'Rourkes own it. Finn O'Rourke, her cousin, served my drinks the last time I was there. I didn't know that they owned it when I walked in. Now I do."

Now we're eyeballs deep. I look behind me at the empty table and grab a chair. I invite myself to sit.

"You're wrong, Heather."

I noticed something when I walked over, but I wasn't going to say anything. Now I will.

"Move your watch band, Shannon."

"What?"

"Move it."

It's a command. Shannon moves her watch up her arm a little. There's a shamrock with a capital O in the center. I look at my sister.

"Who's lying now, Danielle?"

"But—but—that must be a coincidence."

"You are the daughter of a New York City police officer with a grandfather who was a cop with that same damn tattoo. You know exactly what the fuck that means. Are you telling me you've never noticed it before? Or did you ignore it?"

"I—"

"You are unreal, Danielle. If you don't tell Dad, I will." I turn to Mike. "You're even worse. You knew all along, even when you accused Aleks."

"I've never seen—"

"Shut up, Mike. I know you've seen a shit ton more of Shannon's skin than just her wrist."

"Heather!"

Danielle's mortified.

"You and I are going to talk alone. Then I am going home to my fiancé. You are going to talk to Dad." I lean forward until I am eye level with Shannon. "You are going to stay the fuck away from my family, or this shit will be between us. Fuck the O'Rourkes and fuck the Kutsenkos. I will come for you, and I will drag you. Nothing either of our families could do will match what I will if you continue this fucked up charade. I know, Shannon. I know all of it. Sleep with one motherfucking eye open."

I grab Danielle's wrist and drag her to the restroom. We wait until a woman leaves, then I lock the door.

"Shannon O'Rourke isn't just Mike's Domme. Her cousin, Dillan, is the leader of the Irish mob. Her older brother attacked Bogdan, and Aleks defended his little brother. A week later, her two younger brothers came after Aleks for what happened. The same thing happened to them as it did to her older brother. She blames Aleks and has for more than a decade. It might be a coincidence, how Steven became your Dom and Shannon became Mike's, but they have been feeding every fucking thing you've told them about Mike's work and now me and Aleks back to Dillan."

"No—"

"Danielle, I'm not lying. I shouldn't be telling you a damn thing about this. I may lose Aleks over it. My engagement might be over by tonight. But you are my sister, and you are messing with dangerous people. The Iron Order is filled with corrupt cops. Cops like Grandpa was. Most of them are on the mob's payroll. That's why Dad wanted us away from them." I close my eyes as I remember something. "Danielle, does Steven have the same shamrock tattoo on his chest?"

"Yes."

I look at her, and I'm filled with doubt. I can't look at her.

"Have you known this all along and kept seeing them once you knew about Aleks and me?"

"You're asking if I chose them over you. If you knew this shit about them, then why didn't you say something sooner? Was it more convenient to keep that secret to help your mafia boyfriend?"

"There is nothing fucking convenient about any of this. Not falling in love with a man with a life like Aleks's. Not finding out your sister and brother-in-law are being played by a family who'd love to see my future family dead. Shannon might not kill you, but I don't know that Dillan wouldn't. I said nothing because I wasn't sure—I'm still not fucking sure, but the cat's out of the damn bag—that it was safe for you to know. I feared what they might do if you ended your arrangement before they got everything they wanted from you. Danielle, Shannon talks to Dillan after every session she has with Mike. She shares Steven's notes with him."

I run my hand over my face.

"Danielle, a car bomb that exploded a few seconds after Aleks opened the door on my side nearly killed Aleks and me.

Someone detonated it with a remote. Someone watched us, knew Aleks wasn't alone. It happened a few days before we got engaged. There's a strong likelihood it was Dillan who ordered it. But there's also a good chance Shannon did. Either way, it happened after her family found out from her through you that Aleks and I are together."

"Or your mafia fiancé pissed off someone else, and they did it."

"You say that with such a superiority complex. I'm not the only one fucking a mobster, Danielle. You've been banging Steven for longer than I've been with Aleks. I told you, I know. I wish I didn't. There is nothing pleasant about this conversation, and it's one I didn't think I would have. I know you don't give a shit what happens to Aleks. You've made that clear. But I thought you might give a shit what happens to me. If Aleks hadn't protected me, I would have died. Maybe it was the O'Rourkes this time, maybe it wasn't. But some of the shady shit that's happened to Aleks's family came from information your husband dug up because he's pissed he nearly lost his job twice when Kutsenko Partners took over RK Group. He thought he was bitching to his therapist, his Domme. He was feeding intel to them. You did the same thing. You had to know who you were talking to, and you did it anyway. Take Aleks and me out of the equation. You still know this would upset Dad, and you did it anyway. I can't believe you."

I unlock the door and yank it open. I step out and turn toward the main area. A blaze of white-hot fire goes through the back of my shoulder, and Danielle screams. I stagger and slam into the wall. Misha is at my side before I take another step.

"Go!"

I point toward the backdoor. Misha pushes past Danielle and bolts. I hear it bang open, then bang shut. Danielle pulls me back into the bathroom. She pulls off her sweater and presses it against my shoulder.

"Heather?"

"I'm all right, Danny. It hurts."

I don't call my sister by that nickname very often, but I always did when I was sick or hurt. She was almost as good as my mom at taking care of me.

"I'm calling an ambulance."

"No! No. Danny, we wait for Misha. He'll know what to do, but we do not call an ambulance. A gunshot wound means calling the police and answering too many questions at the hospital. Two relatives of the Irish mob are out there, and you've figured out who Aleks is. None of us want the police here."

"Heather, I saw who it was."

I look back at her, and tears are pouring down her cheeks. There is pure anguish on her face, and my heart breaks.

"Steven?"

She nods.

"I'm so sorry, Heather."

"No. Aleks is going to go berserk over this, but he's going to be just as pissed when he finds out I confronted you. I caused this situation. I backed them into a corner when I was in way over my head."

"That doesn't mean anyone gets to shoot you."

"In this world it does."

"What have we done?"

Good fucking question.

Chapter Twenty-Seven

Aleks

"Aleksei! Aleksei!"

I glance at our family doctor as my mom runs to my room. Her expression has me throwing back the covers and pushing past Boris, our family doctor. I'm not dead, but from the way my mom looks, someone might be.

"Heather's here. Her brother-in-law's carrying her in. She's hurt."

I still feel like shit. Boris confirmed someone tried to poison me, but he doesn't know what with. I storm past my mom and Boris and run toward the stairs. Mike's walking through the door as I make it to the last four steps, which I jump down.

"What happened? Where's Misha? Who did—"

I'm firing off questions as I practically yank Heather from Mike's arms. She turns her head toward me as she whimpers. Her voice is a thready whisper.

"Shh, Daddy. Just hold me."

I look down at her before spinning around and taking the

steps two at a time. I barely notice Danielle standing next to Mike. The adrenaline coursing through me makes me feel like the Hulk Cadence called me. Hulk smash. That's what I want once I figure out what the hell happened. Until then, until I can kill who did this, I hurry back to my room.

"Boris!"

"*Da.* Put your lady on bed."

I've known Boris my entire life. His English is excellent, but he sounds more Russian than not. He served in the KGB with my dad and uncles, then he was Podolskaya bratva too. He used to take care of them when they were away, and he took care of my family when they were home. He's tended to every bullet wound I've had, so I recognized Heather's injury as soon as I spotted something bunched in the front and back of her sweater at her shoulder.

"I'm Boris. I'm Kutsenkos' doctor."

"Hello, Dr. Boris."

That's all Heather has the strength to say right now, but I can tell she wants to say more. I move to put her on the bed, but she grabs at my shirt.

"*Malyshka,* I have to put you down so Boris can take care of you."

"Don't let go."

She's been calm until this moment. Panic fills her gaze, and I can't bear to make it worse. I know I jostle her, but I climb onto the bed with her in my lap. Boris goes into the bathroom to scrub his hands. He'll wear gloves, but he's always been meticulous about hygiene given where he's sometimes had to operate.

"*Maly*—"

"I called Sergei. They took Misha."

"Who?"

Heather is fading, and her eyelids droop. My mom comes to help me take her sweater off, then leaves. It's bloody, but

I'm unprepared for how soaked her t-shirt and someone else's is as Boris peels them from the front and back of her shoulder. The bullet went straight through. I look up and spy Danielle and Mike standing inside the door. Blood covers Danielle's hands. My *malyshka's* blood. I breathe through the rage that threatens to erupt. This isn't the time. Every ounce of restraint branded into me struggles, but I remain—or at least appear —calm.

"What happened?"

I force myself to modulate my tone as I look at my future in-laws. Danielle walks to the end of the bed, tears pouring down her cheeks.

"After you left, she came to talk to us. It went from bad to worse. It was all right until I mentioned Mike and me joining the Iron Order, since Steven and Shannon suggested it. She told Shannon to move her watch band to show her tattoo. She knew what it was. I did too. She knew I knew whether Steven had the same one on his chest. My guess is whatever she knows about that, you know, too."

"Yes. She confronted Shannon?"

"That wasn't her plan. Like I said, it went from bad to worse. Once she knew about the motorcycle club, she insisted I tell Dad. He warned us away from them when we were in high school because his rookie joined and kept trying to ask me out. He was gross. She was very clear that Shannon and Steven should stay away from us. She and I went to the restroom to talk, and we argued. We'd barely stepped out when someone shot her from the backdoor. Misha was there in an instant and went after him. Heather told him to. I took her back into the restroom."

My head is spinning as Danielle recounts what happened. I look down at Heather, who passed out. It's just as well because Boris is cleaning her wound. He's gentle as a lamb with his patients, even if he's not as sympathetic with men as he's turned out to be with women.

"What happened to Misha?"

"We don't know. Mikhail came in through the backdoor. He said he heard shots as he pulled up. Steven was dead, and Misha was gone. He found us because he was checking the restrooms as he made his way into the restaurant. Mike heard the gunshot that hit Heather because he was coming to get me. He was already picking her up when Mikhail burst in. He nearly shot Mike before he recognized him."

"Where's Shannon?"

I look at Mike, loathing pouring into my words and my tone.

"She bolted the moment Heather and Danielle went to the restroom. I knew about the tattoos, but I didn't know their meaning until Danielle explained in the car."

Mike looks at his wife, and there's betrayal in his gaze. Maybe he didn't know Shannon's ties, but Danielle did. Maybe she thought Shannon and Steven were harmless, but they weren't. Danielle shakes her head.

"I asked her about it from the start. She said they were stupid college kids when they got them, thinking it was senti-mental to get Shannon's family crest or whatever. They were already engaged."

Heather's eyes fly open as Boris scrubs around her wound. Her back arches, and she howls in pain before passing out again. Every second of her agony only makes that rage boil dangerously close to the surface. I narrow my eyes at Danielle and Mike. She takes a step back, and Mike's arm comes around her shoulders. He might be pissed at her, but he'll still protect her. I suppose that's something.

"Danielle, you knew she had ties to the O'Rourkes before Heather started seeing me. You knew what Mike was telling

Shannon and what you were repeating to Steven. You kept doing it, and you let Mike keep doing it, despite knowing I'm going to become part of your family. Even if you didn't imagine Steven would resort to violence, you still knew you were hurting Heather. You did it anyway. Anything that damages or threatens Kutsenko Partners is a threat to this family. Mike, you still went after my brothers and me, despite knowing how serious Heather and I are. You knew what you were doing, and you didn't give a shit about your sister."

"Don't tell me how I feel about my sister."

Danielle snaps at me, but my expression mocks her.

"You did nothing to protect her. She would have taken your secrets to the grave to protect you."

"But she didn't, did she, if you know?"

Mike sneers at me.

"Are you that fucking stupid? Who do you think had to be there when she found out?"

"Had to? I bet you loved it."

I look down at Heather in my arms as Boris stitches her up. She's the only thing keeping me from lashing out at Mike.

"We had reason to suspect Shannon, so we looked into it. It wasn't hard to find out you were her patient and what arrangement you had. From there, it was one step to discover Danielle's connection to Steven. No one outside those who need to know in my family does. It scared Heather that Shannon and Steven might do something to you if you learned who they were and their ties. It embarrassed her to learn something so private, and she didn't want to hurt you by letting you know she found out. Like I said, she tried to protect you. You kept seeing them, telling them the information you found out about my business and my family, Danielle. You didn't warn Mike. You chose them over your sister."

"And I call bullshit. My sister chose you and your family

over ours. She didn't warn us you investigated our private lives."

"We didn't. You happened to be part of Shannon and Steven's. Let me guess. Mike, you knew Shannon was a therapist and what she was into because you dated in college. You went to her because of trouble at home. The moment you mentioned work, she started focusing on that as the reason you were having issues. You expressed what you thought would help, and Steven just happened to be available. From there, Danielle starts therapy with him, and you continue to see her. They probe you both about your work. Direct questions sometimes and sly ones at others."

Much like Boris usually does, he slips away to wash his hands in the bathroom, then packs up his supplies. He leaves medicine on the bedside table before he leaves.

Danielle's anger from a moment ago fades. I think she's remembering conversations she had with Steven and what she knows about Mike's sessions. She looks at me.

"How do you know?

"Because they infiltrated you and interrogated you. Shannon calls Dillan, her cousin, after every session. She reports to him what you tell her, Mike. She reports what Steven tells her. Since Steven shot Heather, it's looking like Shannon set up the car bomb that nearly killed Heather and me. She probably arranged for a guy to slip a tracker into Heather's bag while she was on campus. We're nearly certain it wasn't Dillan. He didn't know until after it happened."

Mike and Danielle stand, staring at me. It's finally sinking in. They aren't directly part of this world. Sure, they knew they were telling other people—people Danielle knew were linked to the Irish mob—about us. And sure, it started out about work, but I can bet a dollar for a penny that Mike—and, in turn, Danielle—complained about my relationship with Heather.

Mike speaks up while Danielle shifts her gaze to Heather.

"If Steven shot Heather, and Misha shot Steven, how far will Shannon go now? She knows we know about her connection to the Irish mob through her family and, presumably, the Iron Order. Heather was furious about that. Do we need to get Cadence and hide?"

"No. But your parents need to bring Cadence here. It's the safest place you can be right now. Your dad and I need to talk."

He pulls out his phone as I hear Anton calling to me.

"Aleks!"

"*V moyey komnate!*" In my room!

Anton rushes through the door and stops short, his eyes widening. He didn't know. He sticks to Russian.

"*Chto sluchilos? Khizer pozvonila Sergeyu i skazala, chto Mishi net. Ona ne skazala yemu, chto yeye zastrelili. Mikhail tozhe nichego ne skazal, kogda my yemu pozvonili.*" What happened? Heather called Sergei and said Misha was gone. She didn't tell him she was shot. Mikhail didn't say anything either when we called him.

"*On, navernoye, dumal, chto ona rasskazala Sergeyu. Eto byl Stiven. Chto vy uznali o Mishe?*" He probably thought she told Sergei. It was Steven. What have you found about Misha?

"*Nichego takogo. Il'ya byl ryadom, poetomu on zabotilsya o Stivene. Pasha i Bogdan poshli k Shennon, no tam nikogo ne bylo. Maks i Niko nablyudayut za Dillanom. Sergey pytayet'sya poymat' treker Mishi, no nichego ne pinguyet'sya.*" Nothing. Ilya was close, so he took care of Steven. Pasha and Bogdan went to Shannon's, but no one was there. Maks and Niko are watching Dillan. Sergei's trying to pick up on Misha's tracker, but nothing is pinging.

All of us have trackers inside our belt buckles. If Misha's isn't giving a location, then it's broken, or he's somewhere jamming the signal. That tells us this is a pro. They know to disable it. It reminds me I need to get Heather something that she can wear. The other ladies have jewelry that can't come off without a special key.

"*Ya ne mogu uyti.*" I can't leave.

"*My ne ozhidali, chto vy. Ya rasskazhu ostal'nym, chto sluchilos' s Khizer.*" We wouldn't expect you to. I'll tell the others what happened to Heather.

Anton leaves, and I'm stuck with Danielle and Mike. She sits at the foot of the bed and watches her sister while Mike sits in the chair by the window. I continue to hold my angel. I know from experience that she'll recover from this. It'll hurt for what feels like forever. Boris would have told me if he thought she would lose the use of her arm.

It's nearly an hour before Heather's parents arrive with Cadence. We hear them, and Danielle finally snaps to. She runs into the bathroom and scrubs her hands while Mike goes down to greet them. Her parents come up, but Mike stays downstairs with Cadence.

Her mom rushes forward. I try to put Heather on the bed, so it'll give her mom more space, but Heather's arms flail as she reaches for me. She cries out in pain again. I look at her mom. I haven't felt this helpless since the day I met Vlad.

"It's all right. She's where she needs to be."

"Mrs. Hampton, I..."

I don't know what to say. I'm sorry I got your daughter shot, even if I wasn't there. I'm sorry she won't let go so you can hug your own daughter.

"We told you at the first dinner you had with us, it's Maureen and John."

They won't try to break us up. At least a little weight lifts from my shoulders. John must see it.

"Aleks, the two of you belong together. She might not have fully understood what she was agreeing to with this life, but she'd accepted it. She knew the danger from the beginning and agreed to the bodyguards because of it."

"Dad?"

Danielle's voice is hoarse even though she hasn't spoken in nearly an hour.

"Yes, pumpkin."

"This is my fault. I did this to her. I may as well have pulled the trigger. It's too embarrassing to explain all the details, but Mike's been seeing Shannon McGillis as his therapist, and I'm seeing her husband, Steven, as mine. Mike told her things about work, and she started prompting him for more info about the Kutsenkos. Steven did the same. We didn't realize they were feeding it all back to the mob."

"McGillis?"

When John asks, I answer, my gaze locking with his.

"O'Rourke. Dillan's cousin. Patrick, Denny, and Harry's sister."

John realizes the gravity of the situation now. He turns back to Danielle, and his demeanor is completely different. He's hyper aware of everything Danielle tells him. He will remember every detail, and he'll infer what she doesn't say from her body language and her tone. He'll be a cop questioning his daughter.

"What sorts of things?"

"Mike's been digging around trying to find anything to prove Aleks and his family are mafia. He's shared how frustrated he gets because he can find nothing. The little scraps he finds, he tells me. I've been worried about Heather. I told Steven these things to explain my fears. We don't have a—typical—doctors-patients—arrangement."

That's certainly one way to put it. John's eyes narrow, and they dart to Maureen, who's watching Heather sleep.

"I know of Shannon McGillis's practice. I work with

someone who's also her patient. I assume her husband uses similar forms of therapy."

I feel bad for Danielle as she stares at her father. My family might not always be the most discreet with our affection or when we slip away with our partner. But we do not share the private details. Ever. We could probably guess what happens, since I'm fairly certain we all share the same dynamics with our women. Danielle's facing her father, and he's all but said his daughter is into BDSM.

She nods and can't look at him. She looks at Heather instead.

"Aleks and Heather had lunch at the same sushi place Mike and I were at with Shannon and Steve. Aleks wasn't feeling well, so they were leaving. Heather spotted us and came to our table while Aleks left. There was a lot of tension, but Shannon and Heather said outright nothing until I told Heather we're joining the Iron Order Motorcycle Club. She was pissed. She told me to tell you. Then she noticed Shannon's wrist tattoo. She told Shannon to move her watch. I already knew Shannon has a shamrock with an O in the center. Heather asked if Steven had the same one on his chest."

How the hell did Heather know about that?

"Dad, I knew what they meant, but Shannon said she and Steven were in college and thought it would be sentimental for her family. They were engaged, and Steven wanted to fit in. It made sense the way she said it. I didn't think it meant what you told us. She's a woman, so how could it mean the mob? Steven was marrying into the family, not the other way around. I figured he wasn't in either."

John listens attentively, and his expression is neutral. But the tension radiates from him. The waves are hitting me from across the length of the bed.

"You knew, just like Heather did, that I wouldn't approve

of this. You're not a child anymore, but you have a child. What the hell were you thinking? I told you over a decade ago to stay away from that club. It was bad enough that a twenty-year-old rookie was hitting on my seventeen-year-old daughter practically in front of me. Then he tries to get you to ride with him and the Iron Order. I told you half the police members are affiliated with the mob. What made you think that's changed? Or did you not care? For Christ's sake, Danielle. Neither you nor Mike are veterans or cops. What the hell did you think would happen if they let you in? Why would they recruit you?"

"If you know their type of therapy, then you can guess how convincing they are. Look at what they got us to divulge. I thought I would have something in common with them since I'm a cop's daughter. I thought some members might be kind of shady, but we would steer clear of them. It's not like we had to be super active with them."

"Do you hear yourself? Danielle, I never would have taken you for someone so foolish. If the club wouldn't matter that much, then why not just ride with Shannon and Steven on the weekends or something? Why join a club you know I disapprove of and understand why I do? There's no being not super active. You're in and pledged for life or you're out and have nothing to do with them. There are no shades of gray. What the hell do you think would happen when a bunch of dirty cops find out you're a clean cop's daughter? Or did you just not damn well think?"

"We hadn't said yes. They invited us, and we were thinking about it. What you've said is why we haven't committed."

That's a relief. John and I thought the worst. The same questions he spoke were the ones rattling around in my head.

"Dad?"

"Yeah?"

"We didn't call the police. Heather said we couldn't, and we couldn't call an ambulance."

They turn their heads, and Maureen looks up at me. John and Maureen know. They haven't questioned why we're here and not at a hospital. John hasn't even questioned me about my role or what I know. I meet Danielle's gaze.

"Don't ask questions you already know the answer to."

Chapter Twenty-Eight

Heather

The pain must be what woke me. Holy fuck. I've seen Aleks's scars. He's survived being shot more than once. How the hell has he done it? This is excruciating.

"Daddy?"

"Yes, honey."

Honey? That's my dad, not Aleks. Oh, shit. My eyes finally open, and my dad is looking down at me from where he's standing beside the bed. I recognize the room as Aleks's in Galina's house. I turn my head when I feel someone squeeze my hand. Relief. It's so powerful that some of the physical pain eases.

"*Malyshka*, how do you feel?"

"Like shit."

Aleks smiles before he looks across me and past my dad. I follow his gaze.

"Sorry, Mom. Sorry, Galina."

My mom hurries over to me and practically shoves my dad

aside to make room to sit on the edge of the bed. She takes my free hand and sighs. The relief must be immense for her too. Galina stands off to the side, and even she looks less haggard than a moment ago.

"Aleks, how did I get here? Misha never came for me."

"I know, *malyshka*. Mike found you, then Mikhail. They brought you here, along with Danielle. Someone took Misha."

"The Irish or the Cartel?"

"Cartel?"

I try to sit up, but searing pain shoots through my arm. Aleks and my dad help while my mom shoves pillows behind me.

"Yeah. When you went to throw up, I overheard two men speaking Spanish. They were the ones to poison you. They said it wasn't supposed to kick in until we got home. They would watch our place, and they thought it would look like I did it. I was going to tell you once we were in the car. Then I spotted Shannon and Steven. You were alive and walking on your own, so all I could think about was Danielle and Mike being with them. We exchanged words, and it went south. I think I said something to the effect of fuck the O'Rourkes and fuck the Kutsenkos. Leave my sister alone because you should be way more scared of me. Probably not my finest choice, considering I have a bullet wound. But I still mean it."

I look at my parents, then Galina, then Danielle. She's on the other side of the bed, and I didn't notice her at first. If she's still with me, then she must know some shit. I look back at Aleks.

"I know you won't touch Shannon because she's a woman. I have no such reservations. You can have Steven, and I have her. Everyone can talk until they're blue in the face. Her husband shot me, and she's trying to destroy my family. I don't need to go to *that* place. You know what I'm willing to do,

Aleks. I'm giving you a heads up. I am not asking your permission."

"Heather—"

My head swings around to my dad. I'm done. I'm in pain, and I'm not fucking arguing.

"Remember hearing about how that guy at my school who got jumped and left for dead? The one who everyone supposed was in the car accident." My dad nods. "I did that. He tried to hurt Mikayla. I left him for dead. If she hadn't been so upset, I would have gone back to make sure he was or finished what I started. I slept fine that night and every one after. I'm the fun one until someone touches my family."

I can tell I shock the shit out of my father. My mom and Danielle are confused. My dad and I lock gazes. I won't blink first. He puffs out a breath of air.

"*Malyshka*, I will lock you in the tallest tower or the deepest basement before that happens. I'm giving you a heads up. I'm not asking for permission."

It's Aleks's turn to lock eyes with me, and I won't blink first. Except, he's way better at this than I am. It's not that my dad's given in. With three daughters, he learned to take the path of least resistance, and he'll find some other way to stop me.

"*Malyshka*."

"*Sudar'*."

His gaze hardens as I rebel.

"You are *not* getting involved in this part of the bratva's business. And what did you hear those people say in Spanish? Why do you think they're Cartel?"

"Because it wasn't the Castilian I learned in school or the Mexican I've heard on vacation. But they were talking about killing you. Since it wasn't Mexican Spanish, my guess is a cartel from there isn't trying to kill you. That leaves the Colombian Cartel. Besides, it was Manhattan. Way less likelihood to hear Spanish behind a sushi restaurant than in other parts of the city. I hurried into the restroom when I heard one of them getting ready to come back inside. By the time I got to my sister's table, they were at a table nearby. I recognized their voices. When I got up to take my sister to the restroom to talk, I noticed they were already gone."

Aleks pulls out his phone and hits a couple buttons once it's unlocked. Whoever it is must answer on the first ring. He says something in Russian. When he hangs up, he presses a soft kiss to my lips.

"I have to go. They have Misha."

"What?"

"He took care of Steven, then someone grabbed him. We haven't been able to get a single hit on his tracker. Now we know who to target. Enrique broke the truce. Misha's most likely somewhere in Jackson Heights."

"I'm going with you."

Everyone looks at my dad. Aleks shakes his head.

"Yes, I am. Juan Diaz was my rookie. My father-in-law got paid a ton of money to get Juan into the academy, then I got stuck with the little shit even after I finished as his training officer. My father-in-law arranged for Juan to be my partner for nearly three years. Believe me, I know Enrique, Luis, and Pablo Diaz far too well. If they have your cousin, then it's the same as having my family. You and your brothers do not go in there, guns blazing. I negotiate. Only if that fails, do you do what you do. I'll be beside you."

My dad turns around and lifts his sweater. He has a gun at his lower back, like Aleks usually does. He pulls it out, keeping it pointed to the floor, but he holds it up for Aleks to see. I don't get why until Aleks lifts his chin, then nods.

"Heather, that is not your father's service weapon. That's a personally owned gun. The bullets won't have been issued to him either. He's not a cop right now. He's a dad, and that's far more dangerous. If the Diazes were smart, they'd be saying their rosaries right now."

Danielle speaks up for the first time.

"Dad?"

She's aghast, but it surprises neither my mom nor me. I recognize his expression, and it's one he's never turned on my sisters or me. It's his work face, the one I've seen when he's in cop mode. What the fuck did my sister tell him about Shannon and Steven?

"Even if Mike hadn't called to tattle that night Heather babysat Cadence, the moment I heard the Kutsenko name, I would have known. Mike cared because he's bitter. You cared because you're worried about Heather. But I've known their family for nearly twenty years. Your grandfather—Mom's dad— was my training officer. He was not a clean cop. He took money from Enrique to get his nephew onto the force. But he was also taking bratva money. Being his partner and son-in-law forced me to get involved. He was selling information about the Irish to the bratva's old leader. You knew Grandpa had the same tattoo as Shannon and Steven. Liam O'Rourke found out he was passing information and put a bullet through your grandfather's heart. He was four leaders ago. There's been a lot of— turnover—with the Irish leadership in the past year. But back when Liam was in charge... well, the moment your grandfather's casket was in the ground, I got a new partner."

That stuns me as much as it does Danielle. But it doesn't surprise my mom and Aleks.

"Heather, I wish our family had no ties to the underworld. I thought I'd severed them. But I know Aleks's uncles Grigori and Radomir. They're good men. I heard stories about Aleks's dad, Kirill. If Aleks, his brothers, and cousins are anything like their fathers, then there is no better man for you, mafia or not."

"My uncles never mentioned knowing you."

"It's been nearly twenty years. I was barely an acquaintance, but I saw them often and heard plenty about them. Honestly, I'm not sure they ever knew my name. If they did, it probably came from your *sovietnik* back then, but I never said it. My father-in-law was careful not to mention my name either. He didn't want anyone looking at Maureen."

I watch Aleks's reaction, but there is none. The wall is up, and he isn't letting anyone know his thoughts. He stares at my dad for a long time.

"Was your hair darker, and did you wear glasses back then?"

"Yes."

"Do you have a bulldog tattoo on your left arm?"

"Yes."

"I remember you. You were a Marine before you became a cop."

"Yes, for four years. Then I got out and went to the academy."

"You talked to my youngest brother once. It was summer, and you noticed he'd been beaten up. That was the day after everything started with Shannon O'Rourke. I met her brother in an alley after he jumped Bogdan. A week later, I had a similar encounter with her other brothers."

"Yeah. Larry kept bragging about how Vlad had this batch of new recruits. Four brothers and four cousins. Apparently, they had a lot of potential. That's when I first learned your family name. I didn't know until today the kid I was talking to was Bogdan Kutsenko. He refused to tell me his name. I should have known years later when I saw Niko in that play. You could be quadruplets. I should have figured out the kid with the dark hair and the most piercing blue eyes I'd ever seen was related to the teenager on stage with Heather. It wasn't long after that I got my transfer out of Queens and went to Brooklyn."

Aleks kisses me again.

"*Malyshka*, I still have to go. The others will be here, and I still need to get dressed."

I watch him ease off the bed, so he doesn't jostle me. Then he's grabbing stuff out of the closet and heading into the bathroom. I knew he kept some clothes here, but it looked like the stuff the guards here wear. My dad and mom are whispering, and Danielle is staring at me. All I can do is stare back. Tears start falling from her chin onto her thigh. I reach out my hand to her, and she moves toward the side where my parents are, but I pat the bed where Aleks just was.

Aleks is back out before I can organize my thoughts and talk to my sister. He waits for my dad to kiss me goodbye and my parents to kiss. He slides his hand into my hair but doesn't fist it, knowing Danielle can see. This kiss is one that no one else should see, but I don't give a shit. He whispers so softly I can barely hear him.

"Stay in this house. If you leave without it being under attack or on fire, the spanking I give you will be unlike anything you could imagine. There will be no pleasure for either of us. You are not dealing with Shannon. Do you understand me, *malyshka*?"

"Yes, *sudar'*."

"If I'm going to be gone more than three days, I will let you know. I promise someone will get a message to you. When this is done, you have a week to plan a wedding or plan an elopement. I'm not waiting a fucking minute longer."

"A week?"

I practically squeak.

"Maks gave Laura two days, and she negotiated three. Be

glad I'm giving you seven. I'd drag a priest back with me if I could."

"Do you know any? You could."

Aleks's smile makes my pussy clench. My response makes him happy, and I'm glad for it. I've been unconscious for hours without a thought about any of this. He's been worrying about me and Misha.

"Aleks!"

"That's Maks, baby girl. We have to go. I love you."

"I love you, Daddy."

One more quick, hard kiss, and he's gone. My dad goes with him. I can see Galina and Aleks in the hallway. He engulfs his mother in a hug and kisses her cheek. I can tell she tightens her arms and kisses his cheek in return. She says something, and Aleks nods before hurrying down the stairs. She comes into the bedroom. Another time when she's sending her four children into the unknown.

"All will be well, *pchelka*. Are you hungry? Did you know you've been asleep nearly ten hours?"

"Ten!"

I turn a horrified expression to my mom. No one told me that. That means Misha's been gone for nearly twelve. I look back at the door, and my good shoulder slumps. I swallow the lump in my throat and focus on Galina. She offers me a soft smile and a nod.

She's not just worried about her sons. She has four nephews too; one of whom is missing and the reason for the other seven to leave. Aleks's stoicism hits me with the force of a wrecking ball. He was calm and attentive to me since the moment I woke. It wasn't just with my dad that the wall was up. It was with me, too. He did it with my dad to be evasive. He did it with me to take care of me.

She asks me a second time, and her offer registers with me.

"Are you hungry, *pchelka?*"

"Yes. I just realized we didn't finish lunch. Galina, is Aleks really all right? Boris was already here to see him."

"Yes. Whatever it was, was strong enough to start working quickly. But Aleks purged his system immediately. Boris gave him something to help whatever it was he thought they gave Aleks. Once you were settled, he made himself throw up until there was nothing left, just to be sure. I'll make all of us something to eat."

"It's the middle of the night. Has no one had dinner?"

My mom is the one to answer.

"Galina has taken excellent care of us. We've had everything we need and then some. I'll help."

I think the moms know we sisters need to talk.

"Aleks was super quiet, but I have mom ears. They're better than a dog. I heard what he told you."

I suck in a sharp breath.

"Then you know I was never judging you and Mike for the type of therapy you used or what you do in your marriage. It shocked the shit out of me, and I immediately thought Mike was cheating on you until Sergei had the uncomfortable job of explaining everything. It was always about the who, not the what."

"I never imagined you and I would share a similar taste in this."

"Danny, he isn't my Dom, and I'm not his sub. That's not how we are. We're kinky, and I suppose you would call it some domestic discipline. But it is only when I put myself in danger or something really serious happens. Otherwise, it's purely for enjoyment. But I get it. It feels good to relinquish control and let him take care of me."

"It is. Mike's a good husband, and I love him. That's never been in doubt. Because of that, we entered our arrangement.

He has a demanding job, and it's not been good since the Kutsenkos merged, then acquired RK Group. He wants to relinquish that control when he gets home, and I'm just not the dominant one. He could be to an extent when we were dating and newly married. But when stress started affecting other stuff, he and I talked about therapy. We agreed together, Heather, what kind. It's not like he insisted or something. For him, it wasn't about having sex with Shannon. They didn't. For me, it started out as something for Mike, so we could go back to our own intimacy. It worked. But it didn't take long to figure out what I needed from Steven wasn't the same thing Mike needed from Shannon."

"But how did it go from doctor-patient to friends?"

Danielle puffs an exhale through her nose before taking a deep inhale.

"I guess you'd say they groomed us. It took months, but they started to suggest we try doing things away from their office to see how we felt as individuals and as a couple. We had fun together, and it became a friendship outside of the Dom/sub dynamics. I am not in love with Steven or anything close. I would have no interest in him if he weren't my Dom. Wasn't."

"How do you feel about knowing he's dead?"

"Strange. Like I said, I wasn't in love with him. I didn't want to have an affair or anything close to that. We were all friends, but I was closer to Shannon, and Mike was closer to Steven. I'm sad that I've lost my Dom, too. That's rather scary, actually. But I'm not devastated."

"Where is Mike?"

"He and Cadence are asleep next door."

"Danny, I'm so sorry this happened."

"Don't be. Sorry implies you did something wrong. I hate it when that word gets used that way. I get you mean sympathy, but because this shitstorm is the way it is, I don't want you to say that. I'm the one who is sorry. You're right. I picked them over you. I thought it was harmless, but I did it. Shannon convinced me she has nothing to do with her family. She said she cut ties when she left for college. She wanted nothing to do with the mob. That's why the invitation to the Iron Order surprised us. But it was more about the dirty cops. It surprised me that she wants to be near that because I figured the motorcycle club would remind her of her family. I didn't realize the MC was still linked to the mob. If she was a member and wanted nothing to do with her family, then how could it be? I'm humiliated, but way worse is how ashamed I am. Mike and I really thought we were discussing stressors in our lives with therapists who were helping us work through them."

"But Mike's still so angry. Didn't either of you question whether the therapy was working if he didn't gain any coping skills?"

"I pointed that out to Mike and mentioned it in a session. A couple weeks later is when they suggested we try stuff outside the office. I get now that they were trying to make sure we didn't stop seeing them. The whole MC thing is when I made the worst choice. We were leaning toward joining. Even if the club weren't tied to the mob, there are plenty of dirty cops who would happily fuck with my future in-laws. I knew that. I knew there was the possibility it's still a front for the mob. I would have chosen my friends—people I thought were my friends— and the mob over my sister and the bratva. I wouldn't have chosen blood."

"When I found out about this, I was scared I was choosing Aleks and the bratva over you. I wanted to warn you. It felt dishonest and like a betrayal not to. But then I understood it could have been more dangerous to tell you. If you confronted them or even stopped going to them, they might retaliate. If they thought the bratva or I had anything to do with it, they might have retaliated against Aleks's family."

"No one's said it, but did Aleks kill her brothers?"

I keep my expression neutral as I look at her. But I will not answer that. Ever. I will never say aloud anything Aleks or his family does that could wind any of them on death row.

"Her brother must have hurt Aleks's brother badly for Dad to talk to him."

I still don't respond.

"Heather, what you said earlier. That's how I feel about any threat to Cadence. I want to believe I could feel that protective of everyone else in our family, but I don't doubt it for a moment if it's protecting my child. If you're this fierce now, then you'll make an amazing mom one day. One who can handle this life. I don't want you to go near Shannon, but I can respect your feelings. Why didn't you or Mikayla ever tell me what happened?"

"If I hadn't reacted the way I did, we would have. It's bad enough Mikayla knows I nearly killed Teddy. We were scared what might happen if anyone found out. We didn't want anyone else involved. We all knew Teddy's family was *Costa Nostra*. There was no speculating like there was with the Kutsenkos. Teddy didn't hide it. Dad's a police officer. We didn't want them going after him or doing something to you or mom to get to him. We were barely more than kids. We didn't know how any of this works. I'm still learning. Danielle, you know shit now that you can never tell a living soul. You can't even think about confessing it to a dead one. It wouldn't just be about Aleks and the men in this family. It would be me. It would be my future sisters-in-law, my future aunts-in-law, my future mother-in-law, any nieces or nephews, *my children*. They have legit businesses that employ thousands of people and keep large parts of the poorer Russian communities afloat."

"I've fucked up enough, Heather. You could have died today. This shit is as real as shit gets. Not only did Mike and I almost tie ourselves to the mob, Dad just admitted he took bribes, and our grandfather apparently took massive ones. None of that needs to get out, either."

"What about Mike?"

Danielle hesitates.

"Danielle, you will be Aleks's sister-in-law in a week. He will do what he can to protect you and Cadence. But he will not choose Mike over his family, me, or the bratva. Mike needs to decide pretty fucking fast whether or not he wants to live. Aleks might not be the one, but he won't stop it. He can't. I won't ask him to."

"I know. He's smart enough not to tell anyone. But I know he thinks—wants them to think—he's unreliable. He'll try to blackmail them into keeping quiet."

"That's the worst fucking thing he can do. They are not men to be tested, Heather. They are not forgiving. If he wages his vendetta, he will lose. They might show him some mercy for my sake. I don't know. If they did, my guess is he'd have a shadow for the rest of his life. He'll never be without a reminder to keep his mouth shut. You've been a stay-at-home mom for five years. You don't have your own income. Savings will only go so far. He will leave you and Cadence unprotected financially. As long as he keeps his mouth shut, I think Aleks and the others will keep the Irish away from you. I can't guarantee any kind of protection if he doesn't. He'd leave you vulnerable that way, too."

"Do you think maybe they could give Mike a job somewhere? Things aren't stable at RK, so a job would go a long way. I mean, they'd have control over him."

"He's not Russian."

"Don't they employ any non-Russians?"

"Yes, of course. But he will never be bratva. He will never have their loyalty, so there's no reason beyond a favor to me for them to do that. I am not asking for it. At least, not yet."

"I get it. Wishful thinking. Can you forgive me?"

"Yes. You're my sister. Some of this was on purpose, but a lot of it was an accident. You're here right now, and I believe you're choosing me over Shannon."

"My gut reaction is to say always, but clearly, I haven't proven that. I will do better. I don't want to lose my sister because of me. I can't do that to Mom and Dad or Mikayla and Cadence. I wouldn't do it to Aleks, either. And I don't know that I could survive it."

Suddenly, I'm exhausted. I reach for the bottle on the bedside table. It's a pretty strong painkiller, but the way things feel now, this thing can't kick in fast enough. Danielle opens the bottle for me and pours out a pill into my hand. It's an awkward angle to get the waterglass, but I do. I shift the pillow around until I'm lying down, and they support my shoulder.

"Danny, will you stay with me until I fall asleep?"

"Of course."

God only knows what I'm going to wake up to.

Chapter Twenty-Nine

Aleks

Maks isn't thrilled to have another father-in-law, or future one, along on a mission. It's becoming a fucked-up family tradition. I'm in the SUV with Pasha, Maks, Niko, and Bogdan. Ilya's driving the second one with Anton, Sergei, Uncle Radomir, and Uncle Grigori. Sergei and Uncle Radomir...I can only shake my head. Sergei's a bit bigger than us because of how much he loves to lift weights. He got that from my uncle. They used to lift together all the time. He's the biggest of all of us, and it's not middle-aged dad bod bigger either. Anton and Uncle Grigori were ready to tear the place down when we went after Pasha. They're lambs compared to the wolves Sergei and Uncle Radomir are. They both have tempers they've tamed over the years. Unleashed... Fuck. Misha takes after my aunt Svetlana. She laughs and is much more lighthearted. She's not a woman to cross, but she doesn't have a temper, and neither does Misha.

"*Aleks, eto fuflo zakanchivayetsya privlecheniyem v bratvu postoronnikh.*" Aleks, this bullshit ends with bringing outsiders into the bratva.

"*Kak lyuboy iz nas mog znat' o nikh? On nuzhen nam pryamo seychas.*" How could any of us have known about them? We need him right now.

"*Net, ne znayem.*" No, we don't.

"*Yest' veroyatnost', chto nikto iz nas ne budet zastrelen. U moyey nevesty tol'ko chto pulya vyletela iz plecha, i ya, blyad', ne propushchu svoyu svad'bu na sleduyushchey nedele iz-za togo, chto ya mertv ili na pokhoronakh. My dogovarivayemsya, Maks. S nimi. Ya ne vedu s toboy peregovorov.*" There's a chance none of us will get shot. My fiancée just had a bullet taken out of her shoulder, and I'm not fucking missing my wedding next week because I'm dead or at a funeral. We negotiate, Maks. *With them.* I'm not negotiating with you.

Bogdan, of course, chimes in. God save me from little brothers.

"*Ty zhenish'sya na sleduyushchey nedele? Ty poteryal moye grebanoye priglasheniye?*" You're getting married next week? Did you lose my fucking invitation?

"*Ya skazal yey pered ot"yezdom, chto u neye yest' sem' dney. Po krayney mere, ya boleye sgovorchiv, chem Maks.*" I told her before I left that she has seven days. At least, I'm more accommodating than Maks.

"*Ot"yebis', bratishka.*" Fuck off, little brother.

"*Ey, ya skazal yey, chto v itoge ty dal Lore tri dnya vmesto dvukh, starik. Spasibo za to, chto zastavil menya khorosho vyglyadet'.*" Hey, I told her you ended up giving Laura three days instead of two, old man. Thanks for making me look good.

He'll always be "old man" to us, and we'll all be "little brother." Me included, and I'm only ten months younger than him. For two months out of the year, we're the same age. Misha and Sergei, and Pasha and Anton say the same things.

Everyone but Pasha turns to look at John. Pasha watches him for a moment through the rearview mirror. Maks understandably has questions.

"When do you retire?"

"I already am as of yesterday. The ceremony is supposed to be in three days. Finding out my daughter got shot wasn't how I planned to celebrate."

"You've handed over your badge and gun?"

"So to speak. The gun went back to the armory. The badge is a—souvenir."

He doesn't exactly sound thrilled about that. I thought he'd call it a keepsake or something.

"How well do you know Enrique?"

"Too well. I went to Sunday dinner with Juan several times when his parents hosted their neighbors. Enrique was often there."

"Then you probably know my wife."

Maks's tone hardens with that statement.

"Your wife?"

"Laura."

John's clearly shocked.

"You married Laura Doyle?"

"Laura Kutsenko, and yes."

He sighs and looks out the window.

"That's why no one's seen Juan in so long, and no one will tell me where he went."

"You still check up on him?"

"The little shit was quiet for too long. Made me nervous. I hated working with him. Once we weren't partners, I kept an eye on him to make sure he did nothing that could fall back on me. He is not someone worth losing a career and pension over."

"I agree."

Maks's gaze bores into John, but the man doesn't shrink from it.

"Anyway, Enrique thought he was going to have to bribe me like he did my father-in-law, Larry. I didn't take his money."

"But you took ours."

"If you know that, then you know why I couldn't reject that with Larry around. The money paid for all three of my daughters to go to college."

I cut in.

"We know. So you had dinner with the Diazes. That doesn't tell us what you know about Enrique."

"He'll blackmail before shooting any day of the week and twice on Holy Days. You must know that. He'll give Misha back for the right price. If you were willing to kill the *jefe*, you would have already. Same thing with Pablo. *El patron* is reasonable until he's not. Pablo's learned a lot about leading from his tío Enrique since his dad travels so much. Luis has been a guest in a few Colombian prisons, from what I've heard. What Pablo learned from his dad are skills none of them are stupid enough to have him use on the *pakhan's* cousin."

Shit. He does know a lot. Pablo is Enrique's heir and second-in-command. But everyone thought Enrique would eventually have a son—have kids. Pablo was meant to be the head enforcer, and that's what they trained him to be before it became obvious he'll be *jefe* one day. My family shares the duties when it comes to our guests at the warehouse. We don't know for sure, but from the way Pablo's changed since we were all kids, we think he's the only enforcer. He's way darker than any of us. There's something—menacing about him, whereas we're intimidating. We prefer it that way. I don't think Pablo can help it.

Maks disagrees with John, and when he points it out, I get it.

"Enrique sent guys to kill Aleks. Why would he only kidnap Misha? If he would do that to my brother, then why keep my cousin?"

"I don't know. But he hasn't claimed a kill, so Misha's still alive. He would have sent proof if Misha was dead."

That's true. Most likely a photo of Misha's dead body with a C carved into his chest. The Cartel's calling card.

I look out the window as we enter Jackson Heights, the hub of Colombian New York. None of Enrique's family lives here. Luis and his wife, Margherita, still live next door to Laura's parents in northern New Jersey. Pablo has a place in Manhattan. Enrique's got a condo in Manhattan, but he prefers his compound in Connecticut.

We're here because there's a bodega where he holds court once a week. People from the neighborhood can come and air their grievances. And he sits there like some medieval lord or king, passing down judgment from upon high. Once that's done, he usually stays and plays dice or cards. At this time of night, it should just be him and his men.

John double checks the wire he's wearing, and we can all hear him through our earpieces in both SUVs. We stop half a block from the store.

"Be careful. I'm not explaining to Heather why her dad didn't come home."

"I have a daughter to walk down the aisle. I'll put a bullet through his heart before he takes that away from me."

John's out the door before I can say anything else. We watch him walk through the door, then we have to rely on the wire to know what's happening.

"*Buenas noches señor.*" Good evening, sir.

"*Buenas noches.* I'm here to see the *jefe*. Tell him Hampton is here."

There's a long pause before we hear distorted voices in the background. Then it's clear John is walking down steps.

"John, what brings you here?"

It's Enrique.

"We're having a little family problem that you need to solve."

"Family problem I need to solve? *Que pasó?*" What happened?

"You tried to kill my son-in-law."

I recognize Enrique's laugh. The one with no humor.

"Which one?"

"The brand new one. The wedding's next week."

"So he's not your son-in-law yet."

"The moment he put an engagement ring on my daughter's finger, he became my son. You know how I feel about family, Enrique. It's why we get along. I'll give you the benefit of the doubt that maybe you didn't know Aleks and Heather are engaged. But now you have Misha, and the Kutsenkos aren't willing to turn the other cheek twice."

"Hold on, Hampton. I do not have Misha, and I did not try to kill Aleks."

"Enrique, we've always been as honest as we can be with each other. That's why I'm here. You're both still breathing, and the Kutsenkos haven't ended a dynasty."

Pablo must be there, too.

"I don't lie. I don't know what you're talking about. *Sobrino?*" Nephew.

"Mr. Hampton, we do not have Misha. Why would we? And why would we kill Aleks? We're barely holding onto a truce with the Kutsenkos. Shit happened between Laura and Juan that nearly destroyed us. Maks would light this place up without a second thought if he believed we had Misha or tried to kill Aleks."

"He did give it a second thought. That's why I'm here. What do you want in exchange for the *pakhan's* cousin? Killing Misha isn't worth it, *jefe*. You know that. I'll try to figure out why you went for Aleks later. What's the ransom?"

"Hampton, you are wearing out your welcome. I rarely repeat myself, and I already have."

"Then why did Heather hear Colombians talking about poisoning Aleks and blaming her?"

"How does she know they were Colombians?"

"Because it wasn't Castilian, and it wasn't Mexican Spanish. That rules out the Mexican Cartels. That leaves yours. In Manhattan, at a sushi restaurant, there's not a whole lot of likelihood to hear Spanish out back."

"Neither my *tío* nor I authorized this. She's mistaken."

"Your tone makes me think you're really calling her a liar, Pablo. I'm here to keep the peace. I'll go, then it's up to the Kutsenkos to decide what to do. You know they'll pay. Just give me your price."

Enrique sounds pissed when he responds.

"I've already told you we don't have the *huevón*." Asshole.

He should watch who he's calling names. Neither Enrique nor Pablo is stupid enough not to know we can hear everything. They haven't shot John, so they don't care that we're listening.

"Fine. I'll go. Give my regards to Margherita the next time you see her."

A chair skids backwards.

"Are you threatening my sister-in-law?"

"Why so defensive, Enrique? Luis and Margherita had me over for dinner many times. I was being polite. The Kutsenkos don't target women, and neither do I. Funny how Misha's gone, Aleks got poisoned, and someone tried to blow Heather and Aleks up. And the only language heard conspiring is Spanish. Just connecting the dots. Someone's not leaving women and children out of this, and that's not my son-in-law's family."

"You should leave. You're testing my patience, Hampton."

"Maybe, but I'm giving you every chance. Once I leave, there's no negotiating."

There's some background noise after John speaks, but it isn't clear.

"*Malparido*, there's no negotiating because we haven't done any fucking thing." Mothefucker.

"All right. I'll let them know."

I look at my brothers as I consider what we heard.

"Maks, I believe him. I'm going in. I think I know who did this. It wasn't Shannon and Steven who blew up the car. It was Steven who shot Heather, but it was someone Colombian who hit us at the restaurant. That means the bomb was likely the same person—people. I think Enrique has the same problem as Salvatore. His minions are rising against him."

"You are not going anywhere. Hampton comes out, then I call Enrique."

"No, Maks. A call gives Enrique time to warn them. This ends tonight."

I'm out of the SUV, and I know Pasha and my brothers are pissed. But they won't make a scene now that I'm outside. I go into the bodega and shoot the shopkeeper one look. He points to the back. I make my way downstairs. Unannounced visitors get a lot of guns pointed at them.

"I'm fucking Lazarus raised from the dead, Diaz. They didn't do such a good job with the bomb or the fish."

"What the hell do you want, Kutsenko?"

"*¿Donde estan los tres Js?*" Where are the three Js?

I think Enrique's ready to snarl at me since he's baring his teeth. But when I mention his other three nephews Javier, Jorge, and Joaquin, the air in the basement shifts. Enrique reaches out and catches his closest man by the front of the guy's shirt.

"*¿Dónde están mis sobrinos?*" Where are my nephews?

The guy looks ready to pee himself, and the other men are looking around. They all know what's going on.

"Looks like you have the same problem as Salvatore. Your *niños* think they're ready to walk alongside the grownups. You've lost control of your family, Enrique. First, Juan. Now, your batshit crazy nephews. Maybe you shouldn't have played favorites and spent so much time housebreaking Pablo because these little shits are pissing on the rug."

His nephews are a few years younger than me, so not the children I called them. But they are definitely in over their heads, thinking they can play grownup.

"You don't know—"

"Give me a photo of them. I can know in a minute."

"Why?"

"My fiancée saw them. She'll know. Give me the fucking photo, Enrique. My patience is wearing thin, and Sergei's and Uncle Radomir's is gone."

"Radomir's with you?"

"Your fucking family has his son. What the fuck do you think?"

"*Caremondas.*"

Pablo mutters a phrase I don't know. John leans toward me.

"It means penis face. Same thing as dickheads."

I look up at Pablo.

"Really? That's all you're going to call them."

"Not my cousins. These fuckers in here who knew and didn't tell us."

Pablo steps forward from where he'd stood behind Enrique's right shoulder. The men take a collective step back.

Ah. The art of the understatement. These men know they aren't going home.

"Here."

Enrique holds out his phone. I take a picture and send it to Heather.

> Do you recognize these guys?

I'm praying she's awake.

> This is Danielle. She just fell asleep.

> Wake her. I need her to look at the photo I just sent.

I have to wait what feels like an eternity, but it's less than a minute.

> Two of those guys were at the restaurant. Who are they?

> I'll explain when I get home. Rest, malyshka. I'll be back as soon as I can. Sorry I woke you. Sweet dreams.

> Be careful.

> I am.

"Heather recognized two of them from the restaurant. Find your fucking nephews, Enrique. Get to them first, and they might live. If we find them, then there will be no second chance like with Juan. They are ours until we're done."

"No. Same as with Carmine, Luca, and Gabriele. *Tres Js* are my family. I deal with it. If they were any of these dumb fucks who thought to keep secrets from me, I would let you have them. In fact, take any of the *carechimba*."

Enrique rolls his eyes when I show my confusion. John leans over again. The man has an interesting vocabulary.

"It's a short version of *cara de chimba*. It means face of a vagina."

"That one I will remember. But interesting phrases aside, I don't give a shit about any of these fuckers. Jorge, Joaquin, and Javier. Ours. Now."

"Not possible, and you know it. I already lost Juan. If you leave me with only Alejandro and Pablo, I'd be fucking happier than a puppy with two peters. But it upsets the balance. You don't need the Sinaloa getting any stronger here. Weaken my family, and then you have no one to blame but yourself for the shit that happens. Unless you want New York to turn into Tijuana or Chihuahua, then you want the Colombians running things. We keep our kills clean and quiet. They'll fucking behead people and leave them for the cops to find like they do in Mexico. That shit gets messy for all of us, not just my cartel."

"Find them first, and they live. If Misha's hurt or dead, or we get to them before you, then they're ours. Let's go, John."

I'm confident none of them will shoot me in the back. John leads us out to the cars. Maks glares at me. I'll hear about this later, but now we know. A town car pulls out from behind the building with the bodega. My brothers and I have four lions tattooed on our backs. One for each of us. In the bratva, they represent strength and as a pack, a thief's symbol. These big cats are about to chase a few mice. When it's time, we will pounce.

Chapter Thirty

Heather

"Who were those guys in the photo?"

I'm groggy since I fell back to sleep as soon as I stopped texting with Aleks. I barely remember any of it, and it doesn't feel like only two hours ago.

"Two of them were at the restaurant. They were sitting kinda close to your table. I heard them outside, then they left when you and I went to the restroom."

"Wait. Let me see that again."

Danielle's voice sounds urgent. I unlock my phone and hand it to her, thinking belatedly about if there are any private messages she might accidentally see.

"Heather, two of these guys were talking to Shannon and Steven when Mike and I arrived. They seemed to know each other really well. Shannon said they knew each other as kids. They were the same age as her younger brothers. Those must have been the ones you said got into it with Aleks."

I push myself up and brush my hair out of my face.

"What were they talking about? Did you hear any of it?"

"Not really. I only caught the tail end. Shannon said something about wishing she hadn't missed the fireworks. I assumed she meant New Year's Eve or something."

"Did she say anything else?"

"Something about needing to brush up on her Spanish if they were going to work together. I didn't have time to ask what type of work. I figured as a therapist, she couldn't tell me."

"Give me the phone back."

Answer. Answer. Answer.

"Aleks."

"*Malyshka*, what's the matter?"

"Shannon and those guys know each other. Danielle recognized them from the restaurant, too. Shannon was talking to them when she and Mike arrived. Shannon said something about being sad she missed the fireworks and that she needs to brush up on her Spanish if they're going to work together. The fireworks are the car bomb, right?"

"That's my guess."

"Who are those guys?"

"Not yet, *malyshka*. I'll tell you when I get home."

"I—"

An alarm goes off.

"*Malyshka!*"

"I don't know what's happening."

"That's not a smoke detector. Where's my mom?"

"She went to the kitchen with my mom."

"No. She went to her room. They came up with food, but you were asleep. That was hours ago. She showed Mom to one too."

"Aleks, did you hear that?"

"Yes. You—"

"Heather, Danielle, come now."

I look up as Galina runs past the door to the room where Mike and Cadence must be.

"*Malyshka*, was that my mom?"

"Yes. She just went to get Mike and Cadence. I'm getting out of bed. Danielle, where's Mom? Aleks, what's happening?"

"I don't know. Follow my mom to the panic room."

"Panic room?"

"Yes. Just go. I'm coming, baby girl. Hang on."

"No, there are guards here. Do you have Misha? Get him."

"We have him. I'm coming. Stay on the phone with me."

Danielle helps me since I'm wobbly on my feet when I stand. The pain meds keep knocking me out. When we go out in the hall, Mike is carrying Cadence, who's terrified. Galina has her arm around my mom. I don't know where she came from. Galina leads the way, but we go past the stairs down to the main floor. Instead, we go to what looks like a linen closet. She opens it, and I'm completely unprepared for what could be a bank vault. She punches in a code, and the door opens with a weird puff of air. It has some kind of sealing mechanism. There are stairs to what must be part of the attic. I follow Danielle, who follows Mike with Cadence. My mom is behind me. I look back and nearly fall over when I hear the door slam shut. Three beeps sound like an alarm being set. The house alarm is still going off.

"*Malyshka*, did my mom just set the alarm?"

"Yes. What's going on? Why do we have to come up here?"

"I don't know yet. Maks is on the phone trying to get any guard to answer. All of our phones went off when someone triggered the alarm."

"You all get notifications when the alarm goes off?"

"She's my mom. If any of our alarm systems are triggered, we all get notifications. They're sensitive but not unreliable. There are monitors up there. Is my mom turning them on?"

"Yeah. Shit. There are men driving through the gate, and I don't know if they're yours."

"They are. They came from Bogdan and Christina's. They're the closest. Maks can't get anyone from my mom's detail."

I step beside Galina and squint at the screen. Then I look up at her.

"Aleks, there are six bodies in the front drive. None look like they're moving."

"What else can you see?"

"I—Aleks, the power just went out."

"It's okay. The panic room has its own generator that's separate from the rest of the property."

"No, Aleks. The power went out in here."

He says something in Russian, and I hear an engine rev.

"*Malyshka*, can your mom, Mike, or Danielle shoot?"

"No. I used to go to the range with my dad. None of them were ever interested."

"Okay. Listen to me. Put me on speaker."

I hurry to do as he says.

"Mama?"

"*Da.*"

"Get the long guns out. Give Heather whatever she knows how to handle among the handguns. Get Cadence in the cubby. We're ten minutes out. Heather, if that door opens, and I haven't told you it's safe, shoot. Do not wait. Whoever it is, is not ours. Can you do that?"

"Yes."

My mom and Danielle shine their phone flashlights on an arsenal of weapons. My shoulder is screaming at me, and it threatens to steal my breath. I think about the pain Aleks must have been in when he insisted upon leaving the hospital. I think about the pain he endured when he went on that mission.

I am not fucking tapping out when people who mean more to me than my own life now depend on me.

"Galina, give me that rifle. I'll take the 9mm too. Can you load the shotgun? That's my last resort because of the kickback. But I can use it."

"Heather, there are night vision goggles in the bag at the bottom of the gun safe. My mom can show you how to use them."

Galina hands a pair to me and shows me how to turn them on and off before she hurries to get Cadence hidden somewhere. I don't turn to look.

"Heather?"

"I'm here, Aleks. I'm just waiting. I have the goggles on."

"Mama?"

"I'm here. Maureen and Danielle are next to Cadence. Mike is in the back right corner. We're ready."

Ready? Ready for what? How the hell did someone break in? Where are those guys we saw coming through the gate? I watch the door as I position myself on my belly at the top of the stairs. Galina gets into the same position. She and I are in matching poses. It's obvious someone taught her what to do. My dad taught me. I thought I wanted to be a police officer too when I was little. Then I fell in love with the theater. Can't get much more opposite, I suppose.

There's a noise at the bottom of the steps, then I hear the seal. I shove my phone under my hip to hide the screen's light. The goggles allow me to make out three guys. Galina takes the first and third one. I get the second. It's like riding a bike. It all comes back to me. I slow my breathing. I tighten my core. I make sure I'm locked on to my target, then I squeeze. Two more guys follow the first three. It's my bullets. Galina rolled away to check on Cadence, who's screaming. There's no pretending we aren't up here. If they get past me, then she'll protect him.

A bullet whizzes way too close. Someone has already shot me once in the last twenty-four hours. I'm not eager to have it happen again. Whoever this is, I can tell they don't have NVGs like Galina and me. They're shooting blind. Their aim assumes someone is standing or sitting.

"*Todos están ahí arriba.*" They're all up there.

I recognize that voice. It's a guy from the restaurant.

"*Entonces sube allí. ¿Qué estás esperando? Te pagué bien por esta mierda.*" Then go up there. What're you waiting for? I paid you well for this shit.

Shannon?

"*Cinco de mis muchachos están muertos. Me dijiste que no sabían disparar.*" Five of my guys are dead. You told me they didn't know how to shoot.

"*Probablemente es esa vieja puta rusa.*" It's probably that old Russian bitch.

There is nothing old or bitchy about Galina. She looks my age, not like a woman with four adult sons. She's the single most beautiful woman I have ever seen, in real life or on screen. So beautiful that it's almost hard to believe she's real. She's also got the kindest heart of anyone I know.

"It's me, Shannon."

I call down to them.

"*¿Quién eres tú?*" Who are you?

It's not the same guy. I don't recognize this guy's voice. It's easier for me to think in English, so I pick that.

"I'm Aleks's fiancée. The one you tried to blow up."

"Don't forget we tried to shoot you, too. You're stronger than you look, little girl."

They were in the car that raced up the ramp. I barely got the elevator doors closed in time. I can hear the bullets hitting the metal all over again.

"I'm also a damn good shot. You've got a do over. How about we see who's better?"

I grab the handgun and aim for the small crack where the door's open. I shoot. It's a warning. I'm not wasting any of the high-powered rifle bullets.

"The bitch shot me."

I didn't expect that. It's the first guy talking again.

"We're done! They're surrounding the place. Time's up. We gotta go!"

I recognize that voice too, but it's farther away. It was the second guy at the restaurant.

"We're not done until they are. We can't leave them alive."

The door opens wider, and Shannon sounds panicky.

"You're on your own."

I hear heavy footsteps running away from the stairs.

"Are you a good Catholic, Shannon?"

"Fuck you."

"That's not very Christian of you." I see her shape against the door. "Do you remember how to make the sign of the cross? I do."

I squeeze off five shots. Forehead, belly, left lung, right lung, heart.

There are voices yelling in Russian and the sound of several men approaching.

"Heather!"

"I'm all right, Aleks. Are you at the panic room door?"

"Yeah. It's me."

I move the rifle, handgun, and shotgun aside before struggling onto my knees. I don't notice Cadence is still screaming. I tuned him out, or he stopped for a while. I'm not sure. Aleks is halfway up the stairs when the lights come back on. I push up the NVGs. I can see around Aleks to the men on the ground, but only for a moment. Then Maks, Niko, and Bogdan are swarming in, pushing each other up the stairs.

"Move, old man."

Bogdan's trying to get past Maks.

"Age before beauty, little brother."

"Can both of you fat asses move? I want to see Mama."

Niko's pushing them both. Aleks barely scoops me out of the way before the tidal wave of men surges onto the landing. Galina rushes forward, her arms open. Then she disappears among her sons. I don't understand any of the Russian, but I don't care. Aleks is holding me.

"*Malyshka?*"

"I'm safe, Daddy. What about you?"

"I am now that I'm with you."

Our kiss blazes hotter than a thousand suns. His hand is fisting my hair as his other hand squeezes my ass. He moves his mouth to my ear.

"Am I hurting you?"

"I didn't say beets, Daddy."

"Baby girl, that is not the right answer."

"You're not hurting me, Daddy. I just want to be alone, so your hand is on my bare ass when you do that."

It disappoints me when he eases his grip. I fist the front of his shirt like he's still doing to my hair.

"Baby, you need rest. You must be tired, and it's going to be awhile before I can come to bed. But when I do, I'm holding you until our wedding."

"Promise, Daddy."

"Absolutely."

"Maks?"

We both look toward the stairs as Sergei calls up them. He's bending over the pile of bodies Maks, Niko, and Bogdan ignored. Shannon's blonde head is clearly on top, but she's face up now. She'd collapsed face down.

"Yeah."

"*Vam nuzhno eto uvidet? Tetya Galina, eto vy sdelali?*" You need to see this? Aunt Galina, did you do it?

Aleks whispers to me as he interprets.

"Sergei, I did it."

Aleks stares at me before looking at Shannon. Maks, Niko, and Bogdan have matching expressions. Completely unreadable. It's the same one Aleks is giving me again. When I talk all of them look down at Shannon.

"She was wearing a thick crucifix necklace at lunch. I could see her smaller necklace through the goggles, even though it wasn't super clear. I asked if she was a good Catholic. I thought I could convince her to spare Cadence seeing anything. When she told me to fuck off, I asked her if she remembered how to make the sign of the cross. Then I showed her."

Four identical faces turn to me, and Aleks is still looking at me. It's remarkable how much Sergei and Misha look like Aleks and his brothers, even with blond hair. At the same time, on the completely opposite side of the family, Anton and Pasha look exactly like them, expect with brown eyes. It's still disconcerting. It's like being in a house of mirrors.

Galina steps forward and talks to Sergei, who could be even more easily believed to be her son.

"Get the bodies out of here. We need to get Heather's family out too."

"Where's my dad, Aleks?"

Sergei and the others follow Galina's directions immediately, but I need to know.

"He's all right. He recognized a few guys and is questioning them. We won't call the police. He's as close as we get."

"Misha?"

"My uncles took him up to a room. He's all right. He's pretty beaten up. Boris is on his way. But nothing that'll kill him. He's too stubborn, and Sergei threatened to resurrect him just to kill him if he was ballsy enough to die."

"The men in your family are interesting."

Aleks laughs.

"Don't be fooled by their appearances. We get our merciless teasing from our mothers. I'll teach you Russian just so you can understand how they talk to each other. Do not tell a soul this because she will kill me if you do. When Laura was pregnant, she was over here with them. I walked in just as she came rushing out of the living room. Her hand was over—well, they made her laugh so hard she peed a little."

"Is Laura really that fluent?"

"Yes. Like a born and bred native. Her Russian's even better than Ana's."

That must say something, since Ana's father is Russian, and she grew up speaking it. As far as I know, no one in Laura's family does. She learned in college.

Aleks carries me downstairs after the bodies disappear. I hear the rest of my family following us, but I'm suddenly so exhausted. I sag against Aleks. We go all the way to the main floor. My mom runs to my dad, and it's sweet to see them together.

"Daddy, I'm exhausted. Can I go to bed now? I know you said you have stuff to do."

"Can you tell us a little more about what happened? My mom wasn't next to you."

"She went to check on Cadence because he was freaking out. His crying and screaming gave us away."

"No. They had infrared. They already knew you were up here."

I look around and realize Danielle, Mike, and Cadence

didn't come downstairs with us. I suppose they're calming him down. I know he saw nothing, but it surely still traumatized him. What therapist can they take him to who won't ask questions when Cadence tells them he was in a shootout?

As we pass the kitchen, I see Alina and Svetlana in there. They have food on plates and trays. There are glasses and mugs out too. Galina joins them, and they cling to each other. Alina nearly lost her closest friend, and Svetlana nearly lost her sister. They all almost lost their sons, and Alina and Svetlana could have lost their husbands. Can I be as brave as them?

Aleks sits on the sofa with me in his lap while the other men sit on the other sofas and armchairs. I open my eyes and look at Maks.

"I'll tell you everything I can as fast as I can. I'm sure you want to go home to your wives. Maks, I'm sure you want to see your babies. I was on the phone with Aleks when the alarms went off. I don't know what triggered them. I never had a chance to ask. We got to the panic room, and I saw more of your men coming through the gate. Before I could see them get close to the house, the power went out. Galina handed me the weapons and the NVGs. She and I shot the first three guys. Then she went to be closer to Cadence. I shot the next two. Then a guy from the restaurant was complaining to Shannon about not signing onto this, that we weren't supposed to be able to shoot. A guy, whose voice I didn't know, said they were done, and that they should go. I assume they did. But Shannon came through the door. I told you what I said before I shot her. It felt like a minute later, you were here. Did they get away?"

Maks takes a deep inhale before he nods.

"Yeah. They came over the wall. That's what triggered the alarm. There's a pressure sensor the run along the entire top. If anything heavier than a racoon touches it, it goes off. Someone killed a couple guards and got in through a basement window they broke. The same shooter killed the two men we had at the back gate. That's probably how Shannon got in, and it's how the *Tres Js* got out."

"*Tres Js?*"

I look back at Aleks.

"Javier, Jorge, Joaquin. They're Enrique's nephews through his younger sister. They are certifiable. Enrique and Pablo truly didn't know. When they left to deal with the *Tres Js*, we followed them. We're certain they knew we followed because they tried to lose us. Sergei slipped a tracker on their car while your dad and I were inside talking to them. When we got to the place, it only took a few minutes to realize the *Tres Js* weren't there, but we found Misha. Enrique and Pablo brought him out with a hood on and got him into a car. We got that call right away. We followed them to a neutral spot and got Misha."

"Is that it?"

Aleks looks at his family before he shakes his head.

"No. There's only one sniper who could have killed those guards from the angle the bullet came from. Robert Simms isn't done with us yet. We won't go after Enrique's nephews. It's not the right time. But the truce is beyond repair."

Maks mutters something before he speaks up.

"Heather, is there anything else? Anything that might seem unimportant now, but you might mention to Laura?"

"No. Why?"

Maks inhales, and I sense there's pride behind his next words, even though he doesn't want me to know.

"When she finds out who came into our mom's home and threatened her newest sister, she will be the one to call Enrique. She will declare war. God help them. She's relentless, and she's the smartest person I have ever met. And that's saying something considering Sergei and Anton are practically geniuses. She'll want to strategize with Anton, and he's smart enough to listen."

"Will she be one of your averatetits?"

"One of our what?"

"Brigadiers."

Niko and Bogdan react like it's the funniest shit they've ever heard. Sergei and Anton are choking on their laughter. Radomir and Grigori are grinning like idiots, and Aleks is crowing with laughter. He corrects my pronunciation. I was sorta close. He tells me the right word.

"*Avotoritet*. And no, Maks would never allow it."

"Because she's a woman?"

"Because he'd be deposed if the rest of the bratva realized she's the brains behind his brawn."

"I was *pakhan* for seven years before I met my wife, thank you very much."

Aleks shoots his older brother a smirk.

"*Malyshka*, she's like a secret weapon. Just like everyone underestimates Sergei and Anton because they look like body-builders more often than anything else, we're keeping her hidden. No one knows Sergei is a hacker, and no one knows for certain Anton is our strategist. No one can know Laura could step in and lead if anything happened to us."

"But for now, the most immediate threats are gone?"

"Yes, Shannon and Steven are. I doubt it'll take Sergei long to find proof that Shannon and Steven hired Jorge, Joaquin, and Javier. They want to prove themselves to Enrique. But they picked the worst way. Unlike Salvatore and his nephews, Enrique really will punish them."

Maks's phone rings, and he holds it up. Speak of the fucking devil.

"You're on speaker, Diaz. We're all here."

I glance around and realize my parents went upstairs. They're not privy to this family meeting, but I am.

"You better not be recording this because I never want to hear this played back. You were right."

It's finally Maks's turn to smile. I'd usually say he's the most intimidating of the four brothers, but when he smiles—he's almost as hot as Aleks.

"You'll have to be a bit more specific, or I'll assume you mean about everything."

"Those *culocagados* came running here. I'm surprised they weren't crying for their mama. Spoiled little turds."

Ass shits? Maybe that's Colombian slang. I get the feeling it's not literal. Like maybe something about annoying kids.

"And?"

Maks's smile is gone, and I can tell he's impatient.

"And Pablo is talking to them. Luis is making a run tomorrow, and he now has *tres putitas* to take with him." Three little bitches.

I look at Aleks, completely confused. He whispers to me.

"Luis goes to Colombia when there's a significant shipment coming up or when he has to deal with someone causing trouble in prison. My guess is he's going to drop them off and leave them. Then he'll make sure they end up in jail. They'll be there until Enrique decides they can come home. If they live, that is."

Seems pretty fucking Draconian to me, but what the fuck do I know yet about how the mafias deal with their own?

It's not long before everyone drifts to their homes, and Aleks carries me upstairs. We won't leave until my family does. I don't bother knocking on my parents' door. Aleks puts me down, and I knock on the one I know Mike and Cadence were in while I slept. Danielle eases the door open.

"How are you?"

We ask each other the same question. I look past her and raise my eyebrows.

"I think he'll be okay. He saw nothing. He said it was the noise, and us being upset that upset him. He doesn't know there was any danger."

"What about Mike?"

She glances back before she steps into the hallway.

"It's completely fucked up that our son could have died for him to admit finally what a mistake we made trusting Shannon and Steven. I didn't want to say anything earlier, but he stayed with Cadence because he still wanted to side with Shannon and Steven. I couldn't stand to look at him. We have some work to do on our marriage—alone—but he gets now that the Kutsenkos are not the bad guys he wanted to believe for so long. It was easier to blame your in-laws than admit he's been coasting for years, and he wasn't ready for anyone to call him out."

"I wish you weren't in the middle of this three-ring circus."

"I'll survive. What about you? You must be in so much pain."

I shoot her a stare, but it's too late. Aleks has me in his arms.

"I'm all right, Aleks. Yeah, it hurts. But nothing some pain meds and sleep won't improve."

"Goodnight, Danielle."

I guess Aleks is done with our conversation. Danielle smiles before slipping back into her room. When we get to our bed, Aleks is incredibly gentle as he helps me undress. He gets me more water, so I can take my meds. Then he tucks me in before he strips and climbs in next to me. Our kisses are heated, but we both accept that doing anything more wouldn't be wise now that I'm lying down again. He knows I'm in more pain than I want to admit. He holds me as the narcotic pain killers start to kick in. Between them and my exhaustion, I'm a little loopy.

"Daddy?"

"Yes, *malyshka*."

"Can I tell you a story until I fall asleep?"

"I'm not sure that's how it works."

"Humor me. Once upon a time, the Incredible Hulk is grocery shopping. He's minding his own business when Jem comes racing down the aisle with her Share Bear Care Bear instead of her Holograms."

"Going back way old school. I can't believe you remember those right now."

"Shh, Daddy. My story. Anyway, Jem almost smashes into the Hulk, which is funny because it's the Hulk who usually smashes. Share Bear thinks it's terrific, but Jem's too busy thinking about how badly she wants to know how Hulk tastes. He's the hottest man she's ever seen. Turns out, Hulk is a big guy, but he's secretly a gentle giant. He asks Jem out, and they have the best date she's ever been on. She's pretty sure she falls in love with him that night. Jem and Hulk seem like opposites to everyone in their families, but Hulk needs to laugh more, and Jem needs to feel appreciated. She didn't know that until Hulk takes care of her. It's not long before Jem discovers Hulk loves her as much as she loves him. Hulk has this castle that looks out over his kingdom. Did I tell you that when Jem kisses Hulk, he changes back into his real form? He's Prince Charming. There are bad guys who try to hurt Hulk and Jem. Foolish villains. Hulk smashes and keeps Princess Jem safe and happy. Hulk tries to make all the bad guys go away, and even with the Avengers to follow his lead, they can't get rid of all of them right away. But that's all right because Princess Jem knows their happily ever after is guaranteed. They're soulmates."

I yawn, and my story is only half making sense to me. I don't know if it makes any sense to Aleks.

"Did you know that story, Daddy?"

"Yes, *malyshka*. There's more to it. It's the power of Jem's love that allows Hulk to become Prince Charming. They placed a horrible curse on him when he was a child, and he thought he would always be the Hulk. He'd forgotten he was Prince Charming."

I can tell Aleks is trying not to laugh every time he says he's Prince Charming. He continues to play along as he tells more of the story.

"Just like there's Hulk and Prince Charming who are the same person, Jem also has Jerrica. Jerrica is the perfect complement, with her seriousness and thoughtfulness, to Jem's wild and artistic side. Prince Hulk loves them both. Lucky for him, Jem let him in on the secret, so he never has to choose. Things aren't always perfect, but Hulk and Jem are just as perfect together as Prince Charming and Jerrica. It is always them against the world, just like it's always us against the world, *malyshka*. Just like in your story, we get our happily ever after."

I yawn.

"Yes, but we have way more sex."

"I love you, *malyshka*.

"I love you, Prince Daddy Charming Hulk."

The last thing I hear is Aleks's laughter. If laughter is the best medicine, then I'll be the perfect patient and take every dose Aleks gives me. He promised me a happily ever after, and I know Aleks never makes a promise he won't keep.

Epilogue

Heather

"You're only supposed to carry me over the threshold, not around the entire house. And not every house we go into."

"If I want to hold my wife, I will. I'm rather big. Who's going to stop me?"

"I know exactly how big you are, Daddy."

"Sassy, *malyshka*."

"Seriously though, you can put me down."

"When we're old and dead."

I give up and lean against him. He carried me over the threshold to our suite on our wedding night. Then he carried me over the threshold of the cottage we rented in Iceland. He wasn't done and carried me over the threshold when we got home to our penthouse. We closed on our house this morning and just got the keys. I barely had the door unlocked before he swooped me up.

We're four blocks down from Sumiko and Pasha, and around the corner and up three blocks from Laura and Maks.

Bogdan and Christina are two blocks from us at the crow flies. Niko and Ana are across the street. Galina is sort of in the middle.

Before marrying into the Kutsenkos, I never could have imagined a family living so close to each other. It seemed crazy to picture. But now I wouldn't have it any other way. I love the idea that my in-laws are within walking distance. It means when all of us have kids, they can grow up as close as Aleks did with his brothers and cousins.

"What do you want to do first, Daddy?"

"Christen our room."

"There's not even a bed in there yet. The movers don't get here for another hour."

"When has a bed ever been a requirement?"

"Never."

He flips me over his shoulder and lands a ringing slap across my ass. Life has been blissful for the past three weeks while we were on our honeymoon. Sergei, Anton, and Misha came. He was still looking a little worse for wear by the time we left immediately after the wedding, but he insisted. There was some fallout from Shannon's death that forced us to wait ten days instead of seven to get married. I think Aleks might have kidnapped me if anything else delayed it. I'm pretty sure I would have done the same thing and taken us to the courthouse.

"There are more than enough walls to fuck me against," I say.

"And massive soaking tub, too."

"And a beautifully tiled walk-in shower."

"Mhmm. So many choices. But the most pressing questions is: where would my *malyshka* like her first spanking?"

"Spanking? What did I do?"

"You were entirely too enticing during the closing. I

386

couldn't stop thinking about tasting you. You were very naughty, being such a distraction."

"If that's the case, then I should get to spank you too. I kept thinking about using my pussy to squeeze the cum right out of your dick."

"Is that so?"

"Yes, *papochka*."

Aleks puts me down in the bathroom. I'm undressed and standing naked with him fully clothed behind me within minutes. His hands wrap around me. His right arm is over my hip, his fingers pressing into my pussy. His left arm drapes over my shoulder and across my throat as he kneads my tit. The weight of his arm on my throat is extra arousing. My wound isn't completely healed, so he's careful never to press on it or jar it.

"No coming yet, baby girl. You can't have your dessert before you eat your vegetables. Bend over."

"Daddy, do you remember who's cooking dinner tonight?"

"You said you would, *malyshka*."

"That's right. Unless you'd like to start with *lyubovnitsa*, followed by *botvinya*, then *borscht*, you'll let me have my dessert now."

I looked up recipes with beets just to tease him. *Lyubovnitsa* is a layered salad, and *botvinya* is a soup. And *borscht* is pretty much beets and broth.

"Lucky for you, baby girl, *lyubovnitsa* is supposedly an aphrodisiac. Maybe you'll get me to like them after all."

"What? An aphrodisiac? You do not need anything to make you last longer or get you going faster. You're getting some good ole processed chicken nuggets with canned corn and Jell-O."

"I can live with that since there's a particular pink little pussy that will be my appetizer. Now bend over, angel. Daddy's headed to the promised land."

Don't miss the next installment

Preorder and have it ready when you wake on Jan 24th.

I can't resist her. I don't want to…

She's tried to leave our life behind, but no one walks away from the bratva.

She can run, but she can't hide.

I'll be the one to catch her when she falls. And she will because she's walking a fine line.

I'll be there because she's mine.

I'll go to the ends of the Earth for her. She'll discover her limits and realize only I can please her.

She's my soulmate, and I'm hers. Heaven help anyone who gets in the way.

Preorder now for Jan 24th.

Thank you for reading Bratva Angel

Sabine Barclay, a nom de plume also writing Historical Romance as Celeste Barclay, lives near the Southern California coast with her husband and sons. Growing up in the Midwest, Celeste enjoyed spending as much time in and on the water as she could. Now she lives near the beach. She's an avid swimmer, a hopeful future surfer, and a former rower. When she's not writing, she's working or being a mom.

Subscribe to Sabine's bimonthly newsletter to receive exclusive insider perks.

www.sabinebarclay.com

Join the fun and get exclusive insider giveaways, sneak peeks, and new release announcements in
Sabine Barclay's Facebook Dubious Dames Group

Do you also enjoy steamy Historical Romance? Discover Sabine's books written as Celeste Barclay.

The Ivankov Brotherhood

Bratva Darling

BOOK ONE SNEAK PEEK

LAURA

As I sit across from the four Kutsenko brothers, I press my lips together to keep from drooling. No four men should be so strikingly handsome. Not all from the same family, anyway. I fight a valiant battle against letting my gaze drift toward the eldest, Maksim, whose ice-blue eyes bore into me. After years of negotiating billion-dollar investment contracts while facing countless ruthless businessmen, I've learned to keep my expression studiously blank. But it's a true struggle today. Instead, I focus my attention on the squirrelly lawyer sitting across the conference table. While he's disingenuous with each comment, he's a good negotiator. But I'm better. How cliché am I?

While I feel Maksim watching me, I focus on Dmitry Yakovitch as he continues to argue the merits of the venture capitalist company I represent, RK Capital Group, merging with Kutsenko Partners. What he means is the merits of Kutsenko Partners acquiring RK Capital Group, then stripping it and making it another money-laundering shell corporation. While most people in New York have little awareness of the Russian mafia, I do. The Kutsenko brothers' names appear on no titles or deeds anywhere in New York City, but it wasn't difficult to determine which shell companies likely belong to them. Their assumption that I'm unfamiliar with them is proving beneficial to me as they continue to whisper amongst themselves in Russian. I think they may even believe they're convincing me that they don't speak much English.

The senior partners of RK Capital Group know who I'm negotiating with, though they may not know I'm aware of these Russians' more nefarious operations. They've given me the go-ahead to agree to a merger with an eventual acquisition, but only for the right price. A price to the tune of twenty billion dollars. Considering an investment firm like Goldman Sachs is worth nearly one-hundred-and-twenty billion dollars, my clients' asking price appears reasonable.

"Mr. Yakovitch, I shall stop you now." I raise my left hand, pen caught between my index and middle fingers. When I have his attention, I lean back in my chair and casually twirl the pen over my index finger and thumb. "Fifty billion is my clients' asking price. You know that. Your clients know that. RK doesn't oppose the merger. What they oppose is the insulting offer you've made. It's nearly noon, and I'm hungry, Mr. Yakovitch. I have a delicious ham sandwich waiting for me. I even have three chocolate chip cookies waiting for me. If we aren't going to make any progress, I shall let you go, so I can move onto my eagerly anticipated lunch."

I cant my head just enough for me to appear as though my gaze rests solely on the opposing attorney's face, but I can see each Kutsenko brothers' reaction. My face battles yet again against showing my emotions as I fight not to smirk. Their muted but surprised expressions confirm what I already know.

"Please tell your clients to make a reasonable counteroffer, or I will conclude this meeting and enjoy my ham sandwich and cookies."

Dmitry glares at me before turning to Maksim and his three brothers. In rapid Russian, he doesn't interpret my suggestion. Oh no. There's no need for that. I can't catch every word because his voice is too low. But I catch something along the lines of "The bitch refuses to budge. What now? A fucking ham sandwich. More like a stick up her ass."

Maksim swivels his chair to look at his brothers. In Russian, he says, "Fifty billion is ridiculous. She's not so stupid or naïve not to know that. My guess is they'll settle for twenty billion. We offer fifteen."

"That's barely better than what we already offered," Aleksei, the second-oldest brother, argues. "She'll be eating the fucking sandwich and dipping her cookies in milk before we walk out the door. We need the buildings."

"We offer twenty, Maks," Bogdan, the youngest, insists.

As I watch the brothers discuss, their voices barely lowered, I pull my lunch sack from the black leather satchel by my feet and set it beside my laptop. It's a ridiculously pink floral bag with an embroidered monogram, the L and D overlapping. It's an empty prop, but they don't know that. I watch as five sets of eyes narrow. I offer a smile that would appear innocent in any setting other than this meeting. It's patronizing, and I know it.

Bratva Sweetheat

Bratva Treasure

Bratva Beauty

Bratva Angel

Bratva Jewel (Coming 1.24.23)